TOYMAKER

RETURN OF THE LOST TOYS

TONY BERTAUSKI

Copyright © 2022 by Tony Bertauski

All rights reserved.

No part of this book may be reproduced in any form or by any electronic or mechanical means, including information storage and retrieval systems, without written permission from the author, except for the use of brief quotations in a book review.

TOYMAKER

The 9th standalone novel in the Claus Universe.

It started with a present.

One Christmas morning, a mystery gift appeared under trees all around the world. These lucky recipients didn't know who gave it to them. It was the exact same gift, inscribed with the maker's initials in tiny letters: BT and Company. It was months before anyone knew exactly what the gift did.

Avery Tannenbaum's brother was one of the lucky few to receive one. It was on her birthday when the mysterious gifts came to life. A contest was announced. It was also on that very same day Avery's grandmother passed away.

An eccentric, wealthy woman, Nana Rai left detailed instructions on how to commemorate her passing, a celebration to be held on Christmas morning, which just so happened to be the same day the contest was set to end. Avery's family travels to a cold and snowy land to honor her grandmother's wishes. And it's here she uncovers the true purpose of the mystery gift and why the makers launched a global contest.

As Nana Rai's celebration nears, Avery follows clues her grandmother left behind. BT and Company are searching for the Toymaker. And Avery knows what they'll do when they find him. She becomes part of her grandmother's plan to stop them. The real mystery isn't where the Toymaker is hiding.

It's why he's hiding in the first place.

PROLOGUE

"What's this?" Mom said.

The gift was under a pile of wrapping paper. Mom reached for it, the sleeve of her brand-new robe sliding down her arm. Avery watched her examine the expert wrapping, the corners sharp and the folds precise. The dragons tussled on the back of her mom's brand-new robe. The robe Avery's dad had bought on a trip overseas, the white silk matching her mom's pale white skin.

"Who's it for?" Avery asked.

There wasn't a tag or a name scribbled on the paper. Mom slid the loose end of the ribbon between her fingers, where a name had been typed.

"Bradley," she said.

Avery's brother didn't answer. He was on the couch, his hands on his thighs. A certain sparkle made his eyes look like emeralds.

"Bradley?" Mom's pale cheeks were suddenly rosy. "Please tell me you are not working, son."

He was in deep. Didn't even blink when she said it. He thought gift-giving was over, activated a virtual connection. His lenses glittered with fractal images.

"Avery, please." Mom's lips drew thinner than pine needles.

Avery crawled to the couch and smacked his leg. "Hey!"

He started, then looked around. The optic glitter faded from his virtual lenses. "I thought we were done—"

Mom threw the gift on his lap. He struggled to catch it. Dad sipped his coffee and sighed. Avery smiled. He totally deserved it.

"Who's it from?" he said.

"Secret Santa," Mom said.

"I thought we weren't doing that anymore." He looked at Avery. "Are we doing that?"

They weren't doing Secret Santa anymore, but she wasn't going to help him out of the hole he'd dug. He knew the rules. And, if she was honest, she wanted to watch him squirm.

"Bradley." Mom tapped her temple. "How many times have I asked?"

The answer was five. It had been five years since he'd finished college. Five years he'd been caught working while they were opening presents or eating Christmas dinner. And five years Mom had tried to move him out of the house. If Dad had his way, Bradley would live with them forever.

"Be right back," Dad said. "Don't open without me."

Mom creased wrapping paper into neat piles while they waited. Her legs were folded beneath her, her posture perfect. She grew up in a wealthy family that, according to Avery's friends, was sort of like royalty. Avery knew where her mom grew up. It wasn't royalty. But it was hard to ignore her perfect manners and impeccable posture. She knew the proper etiquette at formal dinner parties, which fork to use. Things Avery didn't care about.

Avery counted her gifts. A dream journal was on top, the cover with white floating bubbles containing tiny figures. Nana Rai gave her one every year. *Never forget your dreams,* Nana would say.

She had been wanting a sensory jack kit since she was in grade school. Her friends all had looker kits. Avery would watch them go virtual while she waited for them to come out. She hoped this was the year she would join them.

This was not the year.

Instead, Santa brought her a high beam laptop with virtual projection and thought manipulation. The flat chrome plate with expandable multi-fold capability, magnetic keying and temple strobe linkage. Images could be pulled with three-dimensional scaling and holographic mining. It was first class. It was not a virtual looker kit.

"Do you like it?" Mom said.

Avery tried not to sound disappointed. Mom knew. Discussions had been had at the dinner table. It was unfair Bradley had had a blaze gamer kit with wraparound lens slicks when he was ten. *Blaze kits aren't immersive*, Mom would say. But they were. Just because they didn't transport, they were still immersive. And that was why he was the best virtual striker at Avocado, Inc. Why? Because he'd started gaming at ten.

Avery's phone buzzed. "I'm going to the bathroom. Don't let Bradley open it till I'm back."

"Hmm."

Iona sent a photo of her Christmas haul. Clothes and accessories and, of course, immersive add-ons because her parents didn't say no to first-rate technology. *Look what my mom got*, Iona added. It was a new virtual looker kit, of course, but not a brand Avery had ever seen. Maybe it was a fancy hiwire sensory jacker that co-opted *all* the senses. Lookers grabbed sight and sound and, sometimes, smell. Hiwires added touch and taste. They were things of rumor, the complete and total immersive experience that was always being promised to the general public.

Iona's mom's lookers were sleek black. Like polished obsidian. Feathered wraparounds to entwine around the head; convex eyeblades with a logo embossed between them.

"I know what you're doing." Bradley thumped on the bathroom door.

She flushed the toilet and ran the water in the sink. He was waiting. His eyes were muddy green without the lenses, the whites tinted yellow.

"You should take notes." She hid her phone in her waistband.

Dad was on the couch, running his finger along the sharp edge of the mystery gift. Mom had pressed all the Christmas paper flat.

"Who's it from?" Bradley picked up the gift. "Seriously."

Dad didn't know who half the gifts were from. "Only one way to find out," he said.

Avery assumed Mom really was playing Secret Santa, which gave Avery hope there was another present under those squashed piles of wrapping paper.

Bradley fell on the couch. Dad spilled his coffee. Add a touch of creamer and it would match her dad's complexion. They waited for him to clean up. Bradley examined the perfect wrapping. It was like a machine had sealed the seams. A work of art that deserved a pedestal. It would be a shame to tear it open. He found a tab at the bottom.

Dad came back with a brown robe with pockets in the front and the Avocado, Inc., logo above the right breast. Bradley didn't wait for him to sit down before pulling the tab. It was impressive what happened next. It unfolded like origami in reverse. The top flipped and the sides dropped. A clear plexi box was inside.

"Wow," Bradley said. "Thanks, Mom."

"It wasn't me, darling." They traded glances. Mom wasn't playing this time.

"Dad?"

He shook his head, his attention on the display box. The plexi sides fell like mechanical walls. Bradley picked up what was inside. Dad leaned in for a closer look. "Who is this?" Dad pointed at an inscription inside the wraparound band. The engraved letters were almost microscopic. "BT and Company?"

"A start-up?" Bradley said.

They were intrigued and concerned. It was flawless design. Avocado was the top-line company in virtual environments. Everyone copied their designs. But this... this was an original. And elegant.

"Iona's mom got one," Avery said. "Looks just like that."

"She did?" Mom said. "How do you know?"

"She texted when I was in the bathroom."

Bradley and Dad examined the sleek black finish, the seamless eyeblades, the integrated sensory pads. This was like driving a brand-new sports car into a car collector's living room. One no one had ever heard of.

"Who was it from?" Mom asked.

Avery shrugged. Later that afternoon, she would find out that Iona's family was just as perplexed as they were. A mystery gift that hadn't been there the night before. A tightly wrapped gift with Iona's mom's name stamped on red ribbon.

"Think it was Jerri?" Bradley said.

Dad grunted. The Avocado CEO was generous. She'd lavished the employees with gifts before, but always at the company party. Never delivering secret packages. *Besides, why didn't Mom and Dad get one?* Mom had been with the company for ten years. Dad had been there twenty, had gotten Bradley his internship. Bradley had only been full-time for two years, and Iona's mom had been with Avocado for three.

"What's that?" Mom said.

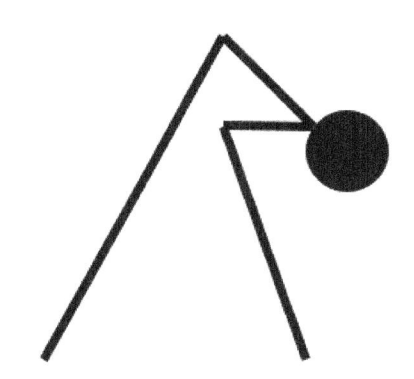

The logo between the eyeblades was etched in simple green lines. Bradley ran his fingers over the engraving. "Bird Time and Company?"

"Bird time?" Avery said.

"It looks like a bird eating a giant seed," he said. "Maybe Jerri sent out prototypes."

"I haven't heard anything." Dad would know. Products like this took ten years to design and trial. How could they produce this without him knowing? Besides, it said BT and Company.

Bradley and Dad discussed the possibilities. Maybe they should reach out to Iona's mom first, find out if anyone else in the company got one. It would turn out quite a few people did. And not just Avocado employees. People all over the world. Same box, same ribbon. Same black looker kit.

Avery picked it up. It was heavier than she expected. Like some sort of metal that was never at room temperature. The surface didn't smudge. Her fingerprints disappeared. There were no external controls, no override button or external power feed. She looked inside the eyeblades. They looked like black holes in a dark room. Dense. No reflection. It would have to be paired in order to find a line. She slid the bands over her ears, felt the feathered ends crawl through the tight curls along her scalp. Even though the material was heavy and solid, it flexed and molded around her head. The eyeblades cupped her eye sockets.

A deep hum gonged between her eyes. A mysterious distant bell that never faded. There were no images, just a strange sense of falling. Floating in nothingness. Bodiless. But she wasn't alone. Something was out there.

"Hey, no."

Bradley stripped the lookers off. It pulled small hairs from her head, brought sharp tears to her eyes. Avery teetered off a speeding merry-go-round. A slight wave of nausea quickly settled. Dad wasn't on the couch. He had gone to the kitchen. And Bradley was wearing a different shirt. *How long was I wearing them?*

"You can't just put these on," Bradley said. "We don't know what these are."

"They're immersives."

"Not what I mean, skunk. We don't know if these are neuronet enabled or just projectors. You can't just pair up. Think. What if these plant a bug in your brain?"

"*Please.*"

But he was right. She'd seen the movies where minds were hijacked by rogue immersives. They were movies, sure. But those things had happened. They didn't exactly make zombies, but she could end up with programmed thoughts that weren't hers.

Bradley took the looker kit down to the basement. Mom warned him not to work. It would be eight months to the day before anyone knew what the mystery gift did. The whole world would find out.

And the hunt would begin.

PART I

The wicker chair splintered and sagged.

An old woman set a heavy book on her knees. Her knobby fingers caressed the cool leather. Red and green lights flashed through the window. Soft shadows blinked on the child beneath them. Blanket to her chin. A fist to her lips and the rhythmic swick-swick-swick *of her thumb in her mouth.*

The child's eyes were dinner plates aimed at the ceiling, seeing dreams only a child could see. The old woman slowly pulled the cover open. There were dreams she wanted to share. And there was no audience in the world she would rather share them with than the one tucked tightly in bed.

"Once upon a time..."

1

"Avery, darling," Mom called, "will you retrieve the piece?"

Avery shuffled downstairs; the cuffs of her Melvin-Guneer designer pants dragged the bamboo flooring. A birthday present from Dad that was too long for her legs and too wide for her hips. His heart was bigger than his fashion sense. They were off-white with a burgundy strip down each leg, a hot item in whatever country he got them. He'd added a thin faux leather belt with tiny studs. The pants would end up on a hanger next to last year's birthday present. But today, she would wear them.

There was a small table next to the front door. It was a pedestal for car keys. It just so happened to be a display for a special carving. *The piece,* Mom called it, only came out on Christmas. It was August. Mom decided it should always be on display. It was that special.

Avery looked in the mirror next to the front door. Tight curls were cut close to her scalp, almost as short as her dad's hair. Her skin was somewhere between her dad's ebony complexion and her mom's ivory tone. Mocha, Dad called it. Her skin was smooth and unblemished, unlike most sixteen-year-olds. Not even the occasional zit. But she didn't like her face. It was round. Not chubby, just round. Josh Maynard had called her a ballface in third grade. Then Mary Hayden said Avery's eyes looked like green marbles shoved in clay. Mary's words didn't hurt. The way she said them did.

Avery smoothed the front of her chartreuse blouse with long lapels. The material was cool. A birthday present from Bradley, probably something he ordered online, clicked the first item on sale. It would go in the closet next to the pants she was wearing. At least it fit. It did make her arms look good. She could still beat Bradley in arm wrestling.

"Avery?" Mom called.

"Got it."

She picked up the piece with both hands. Dad was in the kitchen, singing along to a playlist. He didn't know the words, played percussion on countertops. It wasn't always charming. The dining table was polished and decorated with tree branches and palm fronds from the backyard, laced with strings of ribbon and shiny bows. Candles as thick as logs streamed dark wisps of smoke. The chairs were pulled back. Five of them had gunmetal cubes on the seat.

"Over there, darling." She pointed.

Avery carefully put the sculpture in the center. The family heirloom was displayed on the table only two days out of the year: Christmas and August twenty-fifth.

The piece was made from cedar. The base was wide and stable. It tapered almost eighteen inches like a roughhewn stump shaved with an ax. But on top, whittled with delicate tools and expert craftsmanship, was a stout figure. It was six inches tall with a generous belly. The curls on the beard were dug with exquisite detail. She could count the hair follicles.

It had been stained with natural dyes, her mom once told her. The cheeks rosy, the long coat forest green. The eyes had a magical gleam when candlelight hit them, deep set and green like the floppy hat he was wearing. Avery's family tree was rich with artists. Nana Rai molded glazed pottery. Avery had looked it up once, saw what a collector once paid for a Nana Rai original. It was enough to buy a house. A modest one, but still. A house.

Avery once finished a paint-by-numbers kit with her friend Ally

Brentwood. Nana Rai scowled when she saw a picture of it. She overheard her nana say, *There is no creativity in that.* Avery was seven.

"Turn it, please." Mom pointed in one direction. Avery turned the sculpture. Mom's Harleston heels clapped the floor. She dimmed the lights. Avery turned the sculpture two more times before she was happy.

"Make way."

Dad toted a glass tray with a simmering chicken beneath tinfoil. *It's All Good,* read his apron. He adjusted his chef's hat. *It's a toque,* he would remind them. The hat, they still called it, came out for special occasions. He set the stage: roasted baby potatoes with onions and garlic, seasoned steamed asparagus and kale salad picked from the garden.

"Something is not quite right," Mom said.

"The overlay will adjust," he said.

"We double imaged last Christmas."

"It'll be fine."

He took her hands. The ridge of her brow deepened. He spun her around. Avery liked the way they danced. Just so pretty together, even when Mom was caught in thoughts. It was like this every time the family projected in. Dad was singing, and Mom was like epoxy beginning to set.

"Can you scan the room again?" she asked.

"I did it three times already," he sang.

"Indulge me."

"Four it is, my queen." He was unshakable.

He removed the toque and crawled under the dining table. Tiny lights, red and green, flickered on a workstation. The cubes on the chairs, about the size of dice, changed from dull metal to rainbows of oil in water.

"Where is your brother?" Mom said. "Will you fetch him, please."

Avery grabbed her phone, but Mom's expression said otherwise. If Avery texted him, he'd promise to be right up and then wouldn't come. She went to get him. It was her birthday.

❄

THE BASEMENT DOOR was made of heavy wood, walnut her dad said, with paint peeling in sunken panels and a loose brassy knob. Her dad had come home with it strapped to his car, announced it was a real find. Mom didn't think so, but she let him win one every so often.

The stairwell was dark, the air cool and dry. With each creaky step, a guttural hum of machinery grew louder. Racks of boxes, made of two-by-fours, were along the walls. Plastic containers of Christmas decorations, baby clothes, forgotten crafts and spelling bee trophies. A dusty drum kit was stuffed in the corner. Next to it was a box of old toys.

The basement, once wide-open, gray and musty, was now sealed with a glossy coat and dehumidified. Avery could feel her lips dehydrate. She needed lip balm every time she came down. A laminated wall bisected the basement, leaving the bare minimum for basement things.

An LED light flashed above an aluminum door. A black lens, the size of a lady beetle, captured her approach. Company secrets were on the other side of the door. Mom wouldn't let Avery have a spy eye. No one wanted to steal homework. She wasn't supposed to knock. She did anyway. The surface rang like a steel plate. She kept knocking.

"What?" Bradley peeked out.

"What?" she repeated. "Are you serious?"

He looked back in his room and cursed. He had no idea what time it was. Avery caught the door with her toe. It swung open slowly. He was tossing clothes with a toothbrush in his mouth, smelling a shirt before stripping off his sweater.

"Don't wear that." Avery touched her chest, signaling the Avocado logo on the shirt he was about to put on. Mom didn't allow company wear at dinner.

He lived like a fifteen-year-old, the room lit with hardware and scrollers, glass cases and racks of A-40 cable. Gear was stashed at random, an organized chaos only he could decipher. The mystery gift from last Christmas was on a stack of paper. He called them surfers, but they didn't surf anything. Not the line, the web or public-access television. No one knew what they did. They didn't power on, didn't project or come with instructions. Eight months and they were basically an expensive paperweight.

He tucked a different shirt into beige trousers, both looked like they came out of a grocery bag, and rinsed his mouth in the corner sink. He had his own kitchenette. No wonder he didn't move out.

"She mad?" he said.

"Nuclear."

He looked in the mirror, ran his hand over his smooth scalp. He didn't care what he looked like. Appearances were an inconvenience. Therefore wrinkled pants and shaved head. Mom said he'd never find a girlfriend. She missed the bigger picture. He didn't want one.

"Anything new?" She pointed at the surfers.

He tried to smooth out the wrinkles. He looked around like there could possibly be an ironed pair waiting for him in the pile. He huffed into his palm, smelled his breath, then stuffed something in his pocket.

"Get out," he said.

"What'd you put in your pocket?"

"A canary. Come on, go."

It looked like a glove. Just one. "You going out tonight? Like dancing?"

A film of toothpaste dried on his lips. He pushed her toward the door. She crossed her arms. He hadn't said *happy birthday* to her, not once. Probably wouldn't even sing when they lit the candles. She'd be happy to let him go upstairs with toothpaste painted on his lips.

"What?" His eyes were shimmering.

Avery pointed at his face. It took a second. Then he rushed back into the bedroom to remove his virtual lenses. That would have been the end of the world.

"Bradley!" Mom shouted.

"Go, go," Bradley said. "You go first."

"My name's not Bradley," Avery said.

"Will you just go?"

"You're, like, twenty-five years old."

"You're, like, fifteen," he sneered. "So go."

"Are you serious?"

She blocked the doorway, wanted him to make him sweat for all the dumb birthday presents he'd given her: the broken walkie-talkies, a water filter, a company T-shirt he took from work, probably from the lost and found. He didn't even know how old she was.

"Hello!" Mom's distant voice was strained with false cheer. "Oh, it's so good to see you!"

Bradley took the stairs three steps at a time.

❄

The dinner table was full.

Mom was next to Aunt Mag, laughing in a way reserved only for her sister: a high register climb that ended with a snort. Uncle Sage had his elbows on the table, the sleeves of his navy-blue jacket with gold buttons hiked past his wrists, each arm with a copper bracelet that left blue marks on his skin. The cousins were across the table from their parents, sneaking peeks at their phones. A very old woman sat at the head of the table, staring with the focus of an enlightened monk.

"Hello, everyone!" Avery said. No one answered.

"They can't see us, ding dong," Bradley whispered.

"Hon," Dad said, "your presence." He gestured to the corner of the room.

Bradley was the first one on the dull, metal plate about the size of a Hula-Hoop. A blue line crawled up his wrinkled pant legs, leaving behind a netted matrix that faded when it reached the top of his head.

"There's the genius!" Uncle Sage smiled with his glossy white smile and a mustache so thin it looked drawn with a marker. His forehead was dotted with beads of perspiration. *He'd sweat naked in a snowstorm.*

"You shaved your head," Aunt Mag said.

Bradley presented a well-rehearsed smile. It was too bad he didn't smile more. It was magnetic when he made an effort. The cousins, Flinn and Meeho, ditched their phones. They didn't swoon, but they always said he was good looking. For a techno.

"Happy birthday, Nana Rai," he said.

Grandmother Raiya Noel nodded, her hands folded on her lap. Opal earrings the size of quarters, a silk watercolor scarf with red and green print around her neck that, most likely, she'd painted herself. *You're never too old to create,* Nana Rai would say. *Or too young.*

She had turned ninety on the day Avery was born. They had celebrated their birthday together ever since. In fact, Nana Rai had named her in the hospital. Avery was a day old, and Mom and Dad still hadn't picked a name. Dad wanted to name her Pearl. Nana Rai insisted on Avery. *Avery Neva Tannenbaum.*

"Where's Av?" Aunt Mag said.

"She's here." Mom spoke with the tension of a violin string.

Avery stepped onto the animating disk. The creep of the blue line felt like taut wire beneath her clothing, wrapping her flesh in thin electric fabric. When it reached her head, the digital cocoon dissolved.

"There she is," Uncle Sage announced. No *genius* for her.

"Happy birthday, young lady." Aunt Mag clapped. The cousins did, too. The wrinkled webbing of Nana Rai's cheeks moved slightly.

"You cut your hair," Aunt Mag said. Neither Avery nor Bradley had cut their hair any different since Christmas.

"Have a seat, have a seat," Uncle Sage said, rubbing his hands.

Avery sat between Flinn and Meeho: twins who looked the same, dressed the same, and spoke the same. Even their zits were identical. Today was blonde-white bangs pulled back with barrettes, sparkly black sweaters and a pimple on their chins.

There was a short bit of conversation—*How does it feel to be sixteen? Do you have a boyfriend?*—before Uncle Sage unfolded his napkin and announced the time.

"Everyone," Mom said.

She grasped Dad's hand. Uncle Sage and Aunt Mag held hands. The cousins' hands passed through Avery's hands. Avery could see the cubes on their chairs glimmer. Their touch was a cool shadow. Nana Rai, her voice a slight quiver, spoke.

"With gratitude, we share this moment."

Science brought them together. Somewhere across the planet, in a very cold land, Aunt Mag and her family were sitting at Nana Rai's table. Distance and time had been conquered. Nana Rai insisted magic didn't exist. Magic was only science that had not yet been understood. Avery believed science was still magical.

Food was passed around the table. It appeared from empty space on Uncle Sage's plate. Occasionally, wisps of double images wavered as the mapping reconciled conflicting actions. But once they began eating, it was easy to forget they weren't actually in the room.

Uncle Sage took big bites; his face turned pink when he laughed, laughter so loud it rattled silverware. Nana Rai cut tiny pieces, putting her knife down to chew her food completely. Her eyes cruised the room. She could only see vague figures. Conversation, sometimes, was difficult to follow, especially when Uncle Sage was in the room. Avery had a sense that Nana Rai saw more than she let on.

The cousins talked about boys. They talked about school and virtual modeling. They'd had looker kits since they could talk. Aunt Mag wanted them to be fluent in technology. They were burning lens like Bradley. Avery was still looking at a computer.

"A laptop?" Meeho said. "That's a dip."

"Language," Aunt Mag said.

"That's quite magnificent," Flinn said. "I mean, you can still link up. We're casting a raw dome—what? That's what it's called, Mom. It's not slang. It's actually called *casting a dome*."

"It is," Meeho said. "Casting a dome."

Avery explained her limitations. Her laptop, from last Christmas, was top shelf. But that was like taking a pony to the race when everyone else was driving monster trucks. It could be the fastest pony in the world. But it was still a pony.

Flinn whispered, "Ways around that."

Everyone was finished eating when Dad went to the kitchen. The cousins left the table, vanishing as the cubes no longer projected their images. Nana Rai was content, silverware on her plate, hands in her lap. Her eyes were closed, perhaps a short nap, but her posture still perfect. Moments later, the singing began.

"Happy birthday..." Dad started in deep vibrato. The rest of the room joined in.

He was carrying a chocolate cake nearly half as tall as his stovepipe hat, with white dollops of icing that were meant to be snowflakes. He did it every year, and every year the snowflakes got bigger, to remind everyone it had snowed on the day Avery was born. It didn't actually snow. Her middle name was snow. *Neva*.

The cousins sat down with a cookie sheet between them. Nana Rai quietly opened her eyes. Beneath one hundred and six candles was a thick layer of fudge over a slab of vanilla ice cream. Uncle Sage still had his napkin tucked into his collar.

"Happy birthday to Avery Neva and Nana Rai," they sang. "Happy birthday to yooooous."

It ended with applause and a countdown to blow out the candles. Avery waited for Nana Rai, who simply looked around the table. She held up her hands for quiet, then raised her glass.

"Happy birthday, Avery Neva."

Avery's heart warmed. "Happy birthday, Nana Rai."

Avery blew out her candles. The cousins did the work for Nana Rai, waving the smoke away. Dessert was served with smiles and reminiscences of the days they were born, ninety years apart.

Presents were brought out. Avery and Nana Rai took turns. Bradley had already given her the shirt she was wearing. He also gave her cash, which was better than a sweatshirt from the lost and found. The next one was a box from Mom and Dad: too small to be a looker kit. It was a silver bracelet with an iridescent snowflake that changed colors as it spun on a link. Avery knew that Nana Rai had made it, which made it extra special.

Nana Rai was given a quilt with family photos handstitched into the fabric: Bradley when he was five and shirtless at his drum set,

Avery at six covered in mud. Mom painting a still life as a little girl, pink tongue between her lips. Nana Rai was transported back in time, to each moment, as everyone remembered their picture.

"One more, darling." Mom slid a box to Avery. It was wrapped in pale blue wrapping with specks of snow. Small twigs were tucked under the bow with dry pressed flowers. Aunt Mag was looking at Mom. Avery had a strange feeling.

"It doesn't open itself." Uncle Sage licked his fork.

The gift was weighty. Solid. There was no name on it, but everyone knew who it was from. Only one person wrapped gifts like that. They were all watching as she tugged the bow. The loops came undone. The tape tore away. The box was generic without a label or logo. Avery opened the lid. Then looked at Mom.

"What is it, darling?"

"Nana Rai had them custom made," Aunt Mag said. "She designed the build and wrote the specs. She's been working on it since Christmas."

Mom's smile dimmed. "Specs?"

Avery reached in the box. It was dense, what she imagined solid gold must feel like. A coolness that would warm slowly in the sun. It was a silver band with sensory pads and retractable eyeblades. They were etched with symbols and flowing lines filled with burnt amber and toasted orange; a half dome slider was designed to nestle over her forehead, cradle the back of her head. It was beautiful. And for a second, she thought, perhaps, it was simply that: a work of art, not meant to transport, but merely to admire.

Hiwires was stenciled in fine print.

Mom's confusion transformed into hurt. The family knew how she felt. That was why Aunt Mag was nervous. But it was Nana Rai who gave them to Avery. She designed them. Maybe they didn't even work.

"I... I can't accept this," Avery said.

"Of course you can. They're a gift," Nana Rai said. "You need them."

Avery avoided looking at Mom. "Thank you," Avery said.

"Do you like them?" Nana Rai said.

"Of course. You made them."

A smile creased the old woman's lips. Then a slight nod. Tension stretched along the spine of silence that grew longer and thinner. Mom maintained an appropriate smile. They would talk later.

"Actually, there's one more gift," Bradley said. He pulled out the glove Avery had seen him put in his pocket. "Uncle Sage?"

Uncle Sage had an identical glove and a mischievous smile. Bradley asked Mom to hold out her hand. The glove was made of thick, stretchy rubber. It was much too big for Mom's slender hand. The cuff went past her delicate wrist, then began to shrink, like air leaking from an inner tube, until it was snug. There was a bit of musical chairs as people moved about, images vanishing and reappearing. When they were done, Mom was next to Nana Rai. They were both wearing a glove.

"Mom," Bradley said, "if you'd take Nana Rai's hand."

Mom shook her head. Nana Rai was a projected image. They could pretend to hold hands all they wanted, it would still be empty space and cold air. But Bradley, with his smile on high beam, kept nodding, and, hesitantly, Mom reached out. Nana Rai rolled her hand over, palm up, as if the glove were too heavy. Avery knew what would happen: their hands would pass through each other. But then Mom's hand suddenly stopped. The glove sort of creaked like rubber stretching.

"What's happening?" Aunt Mag said.

Mom looked stunned, like the moment the impossible happens. The wonderfully impossible. Like flying to the moon or printing a human organ or quantum computing. Or two people, thousands of miles apart, holding hands.

Like magic.

"It's a prototype," Bradley said. "Tactile transport through neural netting. We're still years away from any sort of public announcement, but the early results are promising. I mean, we're talking smell and taste, too. Full body transponding." Bradley talked fast when he shared exciting work. "It's theoretically possible we'll create a transference mode. Mom and Aunt Mag *could swap bodies through a neural network.* I'm talking like Mom actually being with Nana but in Aunt Mag's body."

No one heard that. It was ludicrous, trading bodies. Bradley was a dreamer. It was also what made him good: imagining the impossible. Mom had tears. She tried to grasp Nana Rai with her other hand, but only their gloves allowed them to feel each other. Nana Rai's expression changed more than Avery had ever remembered. It had been many, many years since they'd been to visit her.

"Genius," Uncle Sage said.

They passed the glove around, each of them taking Nana Rai's hand. When it was Avery's turn, she felt the glove squeeze. She held Nana Rai's hand like a trembling leaf. The wrinkles on the old woman's face creased yet again, her gray eyes smiling.

"What about your present?" Nana Rai said. "The one in the box."

Avery grabbed Nana Rai's birthday present with a twinge of guilt. Nana Rai shook her head.

"The black ones."

Avery was confused. Aunt Mag asked Nana Rai what she meant. She must be tired. It had been a long dinner, lots of gifts, one hundred and six candles and the tactile glove. Nana Rai never wavered. Beneath her gray and tired eyes, there was something blue and sharp, so sharp and burning cold. Ice crystals swimming in dark puddles.

"I believe they're in Bradley's room," Nana Rai said.

❄

Bradley returned with the mystery Christmas present. The surfers that had never turned on.

"These were given to Bradley, Mother. Not Avery," Mom said. "Did you send them?"

Of course she didn't. People all over the world had received one. Avery wondered, at first, how she knew they were in Bradley's room. But that would be obvious. Everything was in his room.

Nana Rai pointed. "Place them there, Bradley."

He hesitated. There was no harm in what she asked. Bradley returned with a roll of paper towels, put several layers down, then a piece of plastic wrap. Then he put the sleek, black surfers in front of Avery like they were made of fragile toothpicks. Mom explained they didn't know how the present got under the tree or who it was from.

"There are literally thousands of them," Flinn said. "Your country alone has four hundred twenty of them, each wrapped and delivered the exact same, all recipients working in neural networking or gaming."

"How do you know that?" Bradley said.

"Uh, the line?" Flinn and Meeho said. *Like, search the line, Bradley.* He assumed they weren't privy to information he had, but Flinn and Meeho explained it wasn't a secret. There was a website dedicated to the mystery gifts.

"So what do they do?" Aunt Mag said.

"The Hunt," Flinn said.

"The Hunt," Aunt Mag repeated. "The hunt for what?"

"They're all in clamp," Meeho said.

"Language," Aunt Mag said.

"They were designed to only work for the person who received them," Flinn said. "When the game's over, they won't work anymore."

"Game?" Bradley said. "What game?"

"The Hunt," the cousins said. *Like, search the line, Bradley.*

"The hunt for what?" he said.

"It hasn't started yet," Meeho said.

It didn't make sense. The surfers had been dormant for eight months. How did anyone know about a hunt? Why hadn't it started? The investment in that sophisticated gear was clearly steep. So just for one game, one time? The line was clogged with fake news. Flinn and Meeho were getting bad information.

"You haven't put them on?" Flinn said.

"Bradley is prudent," Mom said. "No one knows who gifted them or why. Someone took the time and, by the looks of it, spent quite a bit of money to craft an exquisite immersive. Certainly it's not simply for a game."

"Hear, hear," Uncle Sage chimed in.

"Darling," Nana Rai said to Avery, "could you..." She twirled her knobby finger.

Avery turned the surfers over. She could feel Bradley wince. Nana Rai glanced at the logo. A very definite, very secretive grin curled her lips.

"I don't know how they work yet," Bradley said. "The power source is internal with no recognizable charging system. I haven't sorted the connectivity source or if there even is one. Analysis suggests that it's self-contained."

"It's not," Meeho said. "It's networked."

"How do you know?" Bradley said.

"It's what the hunters say," Flinn added.

Bradley shook his head. "What hunters?"

"You," Flinn said. "And the ones who were gifted."

Avery was convinced they were eating gossip by the gallon. If anyone knew a single thing about the surfers, Bradley would be first.

"Rubbish." Uncle Sage threw his napkin on his plate. "The whole thing sounds trite. Just turn them on and have a look now, Bradley. Let's get on with it."

Bradley shrugged. "I don't know how."

"What do you mean you don't know how? Strap them on, lad. Easy as pie."

Bradley argued that, even if he knew how, it would be unwise. Mom and Dad agreed. They needed to be properly vetted before giving them neural permission to access his senses. Of course, there were others out there with a pair of surfers strapping on without a care. Aunt Mag nodded along, not quite understanding the risk. Neural networking was as foreign to her as quantum mechanics. The cousins, of course, were on Uncle Sage's side, although for different reasons. They wanted to see them work. He was hungry.

"Well," Uncle Sage said, shaking his finger, "what does that mean there?"

"It's a logo, Dad," Flinn said.

"I see that." His cheeks were as red as cherry pie. "Do a search; find a match. It can't be that hard. Nothing's a secret these days." He looked around the table. "Santa Claus, maybe. But nothing else."

The cousins nodded. They hadn't believed in Santa since Uncle Sage told them he wasn't real. That was first grade. They told Avery. After that, the tooth fairy, Easter bunny and all the childhood magic fell away like empty husks. It was too soon. Avery had wanted to believe just a little bit longer.

"It's a bird, I think," Bradley said.

"A bird?" Uncle Sage chortled.

Bradley explained the company name, BT and Company. There was no trace of them as a registered entity. It wasn't a legit company, just a made-up name. Uncle Sage suggested it looked more like a man on broken stilts, which was dumber than a bird eating a seed. The cousins had their guesses—a tumbling tower of chaos, a broken pyramid.

Nana Rai had disappeared in thought. Avery wondered if she was thinking at all. She was so present that time didn't exist for her. Just this moment. That was her secret to a long life, she once said.

There isn't here.

But she wasn't looking at nothing. Nana Rai was focused on the sculpture. The carving in the center of the table. The little fat man with the green, floppy hat and a grin so jolly his cheeks were as full and round as a chipmunk storing acorns. Nana Rai felt Avery watching her, because at that moment, she glanced at Avery. Avery looked at the sculpture. Looked at the logo. The bent lines. The circle at the end.

Then Avery muttered something.

A light, bright and white, flashed from the surfers and streaked through the room. Avery momentarily felt plunged into a frozen lake. Aunt Mag spilled her wine. Dad jumped up. Everyone jumped up. Everyone except Nana Rai.

"What happened?" Bradley said.

They watched him cradle the surfers, peer into the eyeblades, turn them over, hopeful they had suddenly turned on. Hopeful this moment was the moment the mystery would be revealed. Avery was still cold and quivering, unsure if anyone else had felt the icy plunge. Aunt Mag's voice quivered.

"Mother?"

There would be no stories to end this year's birthday celebration. No goodbyes or virtual hugs. No handshakes through networked gloves. This year they were painfully aware of just how far away they were from each other.

2

Tears tracked like hot coals on a frosted slope.

Avery didn't know cold could do that. She blinked her eyes, wiped the drip from her nose. She'd never been in the cold before. Not serious cold. Not since she was very little. She didn't remember her cheeks turning plastic.

Uncle Sage pulled their luggage from the trunk while Avery and her mother waited on the sidewalk. The grass shattered beneath their footsteps, leaving solid tracks on the frozen earth. A dusting of frost covered the front lawn. Mom was layered in sweaters beneath a long gray coat. Her boots were fuzzy with deep rubber treads. Avery's coat was shorter but thicker. She wished she'd put on sweaters, though. She didn't own winter gear.

"You'll get used to it." Uncle Sage wore a windbreaker and gym shoes. His cheeks were ruddy, but he was sweating with a suitcase in each hand. "Nice day, today, really. Early winter is good luck, you know. Watch your step."

There were clots of ice on the sidewalk. Mom was frozen to the concrete, looking at the house. A tear had fallen. It wasn't the cold. Her lower lip, painted red and smudged, was trembling. Three stories was steeply pitched in sheets of copper. The shutters were as red as

Mom's lipstick. There were candles in the dark windows and a wreath on the door.

Uncle Sage climbed wide steps. A wooden ramp sloped in front of the bushes. The balusters were carved in intricate detail by a craft master's hand. The ground was littered with flowers—long-stemmed yellow roses, bouquets of daisies, banded bundles of grasses—among cards and hand-painted signs.

Her mom dabbed her nose with a tissue. Avery tucked her hand in the crook of Mom's arm. She could feel her mom quaking beneath all those sweaters. She hadn't eaten much in a month. At dinner, she would push her food around. Even when Dad brought her breakfast in bed, she would take a bite and thank him. She was already long and thin. Now she was gaunt and as pale as bedsheets. The cold piled onto the pain she already felt.

They walked, side by side, up the steps. Mom paused on the old wooden boards, looking at the porch swing slightly swaying. Looking like she saw someone, remembering dangling her legs from it when she was a child.

Uncle Sage waited with his bare hand, no gloves for him, on the brassy handle. He wiped his blustery cheek on his sleeve and nodded to Avery's mom. When she was ready, he opened it. Warm air exhaled from the house.

"They're expecting you," he said.

Mom patted Avery's hand. "Help your uncle, darling."

Avery watched her carefully. Mom was a bit wobbly, the nostalgic weight heavy and uneven. The ceilings were high and the walls covered in art—paintings of still lifes and photos of snowy landscapes. Mom's footsteps echoed on the wood planks. How many times had she run down these halls barefoot in summer, dressed for school in winter? Avery had only been there one time. She was five years old and barely remembered how big the house was, how the rooms were endless and ceilings as high as the sky.

Uncle Sage threw logs into the fireplace. Embers showered the hearth. Black suspenders cut into his shoulders. The mantel held an assortment of pinecones and winding garland. Carvings stood like miniature sentinels among the greenery, the pale autumn light casting faded shadows over the intricate features. Little fat elves wearing different coats in different poses. All with a floppy hat. They numbered five across the mantel. But one was missing. That one, Avery was sure, was cradled in bubble wrap, packed safely in one of the suitcases.

"Uncle Sage?"

"Huh?" He jumped a little. Perhaps he forgot she was there.

"Where should I take these?" She lifted the luggage.

"Oh, you're a dear. Go say hi to the others. I'll tidy your belongings."

She had a thought to open her mom's bag, to dig out the elf in its bed of a plastic bubbles, and place it with the others. But that was for Mom to do.

"All right, then," he said. "I'll be with you shortly."

The furniture in the next room was antique, the sort that would be in a museum, with plush fabric and sweeping armrests, legs with wooden paws. Sculptures in marble were on the floor, abstract things that looked heavy, and glazed pots on pedestals. Glass and wire creatures hung from cast-iron posts that reached out with curving fingers. Soft light from recessed fixtures cast colors across the floor.

A small sculpture watched her from the corner. It was a fat man with a round face and small eyes. The arms were strangely short. It was carved from granite. The belly had been worn smooth for luck. Long locks of hair cascaded over the shoulders, the details finely chiseled.

Avery went back to the front door to shed her boots and hang her coat. The fire was more than enough to chase away the cold. The floor was firm but giving. She crossed rugs with frilled edges. Voices echoed down a hallway. She found them three doorways on the left in a barrel-shaped room with a domed ceiling. They sat at a round table. Beneath a landslide of oversized plans and stacks of noted papers, the surface was dark brown and shiny.

They sat in high-back chairs. All the men, except for one, had thick beards and eyebrows to match. The women were stout, most of them anyway, with tightly creased lips. Mom and Aunt Mag were hugging in front of a fireplace, gently swaying, whispering to each other. Aunt Mag turned to Avery.

"Look at you, dear. All grown up. So beautiful."

She embraced Avery. Unlike Mom, she was warm and doughy. Avery got those genes, but didn't think of herself as beautiful. The lack of boys' attention confirmed that. But when Aunt Mag said it, she believed it.

"I'm sorry I couldn't pick you up," Aunt Mag said.

"We had delays," Avery said. "Slept in the airport."

"You'll be sleeping in a bed tonight." Aunt Mag wiped her eyes. "Everyone, this is my lovely niece, Avery Neva. Named by the person we're preparing to honor." They introduced themselves, some warmer than others. But, overall, pleasant.

"The girls will be here tomorrow," Aunt Mag said.

A grandfather clock began to chime.

Uncle Sage came in with a bundle of logs, tossing them into the round room's fireplace. One of the suspenders dangled at his side. He tucked his T-shirt into the back of his pants with one hand, reached over a frail old man and snatched a sugar cookie from a plate.

"Right this way, lass," he said.

❄

THE STAIRCASE SPIRALED up to the third floor with a dull black post in the center. The treads creaked under Uncle Sage, the luggage banging the steps behind him. The bannister was slick and cool. The walls were cluttered with paintings and photos of winterscapes and barren stretches of snow. Avery's breath came in thin puffs that grew thicker.

"There's an elevator," Uncle Sage grumbled.

"Why didn't we take it?"

"Ask your aunt."

Avery felt a little vertigo near the top. It was impossible to fall over the railing, but there was so much space below. She wasn't good with heights. Once, in middle school, they went on the roof in astronomy class to spy on Venus. She had to sit down. She preferred her feet on the earth. And the earth to be flat.

At the top, the floor was slightly warped. The wheels on the luggage thumped in uneven rhythm. Uncle Sage leaned her bag against the wall and went to the right. Old candles were mounted on the walls; solid puddles dripped from their bases in waxy globs. Blackened curly wicks. Uncle Sage wiped his forehead with a handkerchief.

A door was at the dark end of the hall. The doorknob rattled in his hand. "Right."

"Is it locked?" Avery said.

"Tight as a fiddle."

He turned around and started the other way. She thought he was going to find a key, wondering if he would survive another trip down the stairs and back. But he grabbed her bag and kept going.

"It looks old, yeah," he said. "But it's quite modern. Bathroom is there. Towels, there."

He stopped at the opposite end of the hall and nudged the door.

"Here we are," he said. "The master suite. Nana Rai's favorite. Not that she made it up here in quite some time." He stepped aside and gestured. "You have the entire floor. Your mother will be in the room below. So no parties, right."

He chuckled, then coughed.

Avery stood at the entrance. It was indeed a master room. Almost as large as their family room. The bed was twice the size as hers and twice as thick. A four-poster with fabric draped over the top. A large desk by a circular window. A sitting area with a low table and a furry rug in the center. A bureau with enough drawers to hold all the clothes she'd ever owned.

"Why isn't my mom sleeping in here?" she said.

Uncle Sage shrugged. "You don't like it?"

"No, I just... it's big. That's all."

He lugged the suitcase onto the bed. A dusty cloud puffed from the bedspread. "She thought you'd be comfortable here."

"Mom did?"

"Nana. Always said she thought you'd feel at home in here."

"Me?"

"You are Avery Neva, right?"

A pang of guilt struck her just below the rib cage. She'd only been there once to visit. It wasn't like she didn't want to come. Several thousand miles away, she didn't have a choice. Now it felt like Nana Rai was disappointed.

"You, uh, you want some tea?" Uncle Sage said.

"No, thank you."

"I'll bring you up some. Might change your mind. Yes." He patted her shoulder. He smelled a bit sour. "They'll be at it down there for a bit longer. You can join them, I suppose."

"What are they doing?"

"Boring stuff. Trust me. Right, so I'll leave you to it. Call if you need anything."

"Call you?"

"Sure." He shrugged. "Or just call out. The house is wired to help."

"What do you mean?"

"Well, it's... your brother would understand. Too bad he couldn't make it."

He forced a smile, a strange one that looked clownish. The kind that was well-meaning. Not necessarily rude. The floor creaked under his retreat.

"Uncle Sage?"

"Mm-mmm."

"What were all the flowers for? You know, the ones in front of the house. For Nana Rai?"

"Of course."

"Who are they from?"

"She was quite loved in these parts. You don't live that long without making friends. You'll see."

Avery didn't know much about her grandmother. Avery was fond of her, but she always assumed it was a familial bond that stoked those feelings. People didn't usually fill a yard with tokens of affection like that. At least not where she grew up.

"You okay, then?" Uncle Sage said.

Avery was staring at her feet. A heavy feeling of sadness draped over her. It must've been apparent for him to ask. *Why didn't I visit sooner?*

"It wasn't your fault," he said. "These things happen. Sooner or later."

His words trailed off, as if he had nothing left to say. Then he gently and quietly pulled the door closed behind him. The hallway echoed beneath his feet. Then the spiral staircase creaked.

Avery collapsed at the desk. She hadn't been on her feet much, but she was exhausted. Through the circular window, dusk was falling. A gray landscape with patches of icy snow led into trees. And far beyond, in the distance, the snowy peaks of mountains. She wanted to go back downstairs, listen to what they were doing, talk to Aunt Mag. Instead, she lay next to her suitcase and fell asleep with an empty stomach and a question as heavy as her emotions.

Why would it be my fault?

❄

AVERY WAS SURROUNDED by skyscraper trees. Things hid behind the trunks, glassy eyes peeking through foliage. *Those aren't animals*, she thought. They were too fuzzy. Unnatural in color.

The click of a doorknob woke her.

Avery was buried in a feathery pillow, fully dressed between a thick comforter and a soft mattress. A circle of daylight knifed through the room, stretching a geometric pattern across the floor. Two figures—one in a long black coat, the other in white—were looking at her. Shiny blond hair flowed over their shoulders.

"Icicles," Flinn said.

Avery tossed the weighty covers off. The cousins ran in heavy-heeled boots. They hugged in the center of a round rug. It had been grade school when Avery last touched them. Projections were so realistic, but it couldn't beat the skin. They smelled like honey and felt wiry beneath their coats.

"You looked ragged," Meeho said.

"Thanks." She felt like a ragged bag of sand in wrinkled clothes.

They asked about her flight. She told them about the delay, sleeping on the floor in the airport, sitting on the tarmac, and the little kid who kicked her seat for six hours.

A cup of cold tea was on the desk. "What time is it?" Avery said.

"You missed breakfast," Flinn said, brushing a blonde strand from her eyes. "Your mom sent us up. We been parked forev."

Avery kept up with the slang. *I overslept, and they've been waiting forever.*

"It took you a month to get over here," Flinn said.

"Mom had things to do. Dad was trying to help," Avery said. "Your mom said not to be in a hurry. Guess that's why all the flowers are out front, then. Your dad said people put them there."

"The Nana love is nonstop. You here for a block?" Meeho asked.

"I, uh, you mean how long we staying?" Avery didn't know how long, if that was what she meant. Mom never said when they would go home. They were planning something for December. "A while."

"No school, then?" Flinn said.

"Yeah, school," Avery said. "I got these."

A box was tucked into the inside pocket of her suitcase. She pulled out the looker kit Nana Rai had given her. After all that had happened, Mom suddenly seemed okay with them. Even reminded her to bring them.

"Oh, then. Hiwires," Meeho said. "You're piping into school, yeah?"

Virtually going to school? "That's the plan."

"Nana Rai specced those just for you," Flinn said. "She never did that for us, but okay. We already got kits, that's probably why."

"Probably why," Meeho said.

"How did you—stop!" Flinn looked very serious. "What are you doing?"

Avery put the hiwires on the desk, her hand still hovering over them. "What?"

"Never, ever put them down like that." Flinn turned the hiwires over. "Lens down, Av. Always lens down."

"Lenses down? Why lenses down?"

"Peepers," Meeho said, "can hack through and watch you. Happens on the nightly."

That didn't seem likely, but okay. She didn't want anyone watching her get out of the shower. Bradley never did that, though. He always put them lenses up, to keep from scratching them. His bedroom might be a disaster, but his lookers were never scratched.

"How the hiwires working?" Flinn asked. "You got them anchored?"

"I haven't even used them yet."

"Hold," Meeho said. "You got hiwires a month ago and haven't even tried them?"

"No."

Flinn and Meeho grinned and said, "Stainless."

"What's that? What's stainless?"

"You're shiny new, Av," Flinn said. "You've never immersed."

"Bradley was supposed to teach me, but..." She shook her head.

"He coming?" Flinn applied lip gloss.

Bradley and Dad had stayed home. There was a bit of an argument about that, but Mom insisted they stay. It was better that way. Bradley would be a distraction. Dad, he wanted to come, but Mom said he should stay with Bradley. There would be plenty to do. When she was ready, Mom would call for them.

"He on the hunt, then?" Meeho said. "Bradley?"

"No."

"He's on the hunt," Flinn stated. "Trust me."

"I don't think he is."

The cousins looked at each other. "He's on the hunt, Av."

"Am I missing something?"

Flinn said something, and Meeho left. The spiral staircase

whined under her rapid descent. Flinn pushed the chair under the desk, the table over a few feet. "We got time," she said.

"Time for what?"

The staircase announced Meeho's return. The cousins pulled two lookers from backpacks. They were wraparound snapwear with platinum sensory pads and retractable eyeblades. The finish gleamed like polished steel in the morning sun. They consulted in cousin-speak, looking around the room, pointing out hot spots and terrain grid.

"Let's do this," Meeho said.

"Do what?" Avery said. "You mean, like, use the hiwires?"

"Nana Rai always said," Flinn said, *"now is here."*

Avery was hungry. The last thing she'd eaten was a bag of pretzels. The cousins were tossing pillows on the rug. *Now is here.*

They sat on the floor in a tight circle, knees touching. The cousins mounted their lookers, eyeblades still retracted. Their icy blue eyes watched her fuss with hiwires. Avery had tried them on but never used them. The leap, though, through the void—that bodiless trip to the virtual environment of the line—was intimidating. Mom didn't want her experimenting until Bradley walked her through it.

"You charged?" Flinn said. Avery didn't know if her hiwires had ever been charged. "We'll do a short sesh."

"Pair up, then," Meeho said.

"How?" Avery said.

"Close your eyes," Flinn said. "Empty your head. Feel your body and the space."

"That's it?" Avery said.

The cousins closed their eyes. Simultaneously, their eyeblades snapped down. Avery's distorted reflection looked back from convex bug eyes. She could hear them quietly humming.

"This helps," Flinn said. "Humming. Feel it in your head."

The hiwires were tight around Avery's head. It was smooth and cool, then quickly warmed. It started to undulate. It was a little frightening. Avery did what they said. Her model didn't have eyeblades. Bradley had explained, briefly, that Nana Rai had made them lensless. Some sort of retinal feed that she didn't understand and he didn't explain, other than *these aren't ordinary lookers, skunk; these are hiwires.* She closed her eyes. And started to hum.

"Imagine you're underwater," Flinn said. "And the water touches the floor and the walls. Circles your body."

Avery felt silly. She woke up in a strange bed, saw her cousins in the skin for the first time in ten years, and now she was humming in a cross-legged ceremony. It wasn't working. There were people who effortlessly leapt into the line. Their brains were just made for it. But not everyone could do it. Maybe Avery was one of those who couldn't. She was afraid of that.

Then she began to melt into the floor, seep into the walls. She felt the bumps and uneven boards, the grain in the wood and the creases between them. Then the odd shapes of the chairs and the solid plaster walls with specks of painted imperfections. The light bulbs in the fixtures. And her cousins in front of her. A strange tickle cascaded over her scalp and down her spine. Her eyes itched.

"Ready to shine?" Flinn's voice echoed.

Avery didn't feel her eyelids open. The room just slowly appeared. The details were off. The colors rich and vivid, the angles slightly askew. The cousins were right in front of her. Their eyes big and blue, almost glowing. Their hair flowed like streams of gold.

Avery had had a cavity filled last summer. The dentist had numbed her gums, and hours later, the side of her face was still dead. That was how she felt all over. Her blood had become syrup, like her body couldn't keep up with her brain.

This is it.

She'd seen the interface videos, the first-person recordings of people immersing on the line. But that was like seeing a photo of a mountain, not standing on top of it. Her hands were smooth and brown, her palms faintly creased. She was wearing vanilla clothes, some kind of generic gi her friend Maypop Belkin wore to karate lessons.

"Woo," Flinn said, her voice vaguely underwater.

"You clear?" Meeho said.

Avery nodded. Her head was floating off her shoulders. Then the floor was sinking.

"Steady." Flinn touched her knee. "Bit of a balance beam at first."

Avery kept her eyes open. *Are they really open?* This was a weird state. She'd lucid dreamed once. This wasn't much different.

"Good now," Meeho said. "Say something. Like a word. Think it, visualize it. Project it."

Avery tried to close her eyes, but her eyelids didn't work. The cousins stared ice blue. Like parents waiting for their baby's first words.

"W-w-w..." she started. Then, "Woooo."

"Yeah, right. Woo," Flinn said. "Woo on that, Av. Full flesh on the first ride."

"Nana Rai put some fuel in those hiwires," Meeho said.

They wore something like future warrior outfits that hugged curves their skin didn't have, their bodies morphed into something dangerous and rippling, long fingernails and sharp elbows. They looked sort of like themselves. In the line, you could look like anything. Avery looked the same, just sharper. Realer. Like high plasma definition.

"This is..." Avery wet her lips. She felt the tip of her tongue. "This is—"

"A trip. Yeah, first time is always a fall," Flinn said. "You're in sharp, Av. Nana Rai knows the way."

It was the hiwires. They were even higher grade than she thought. This was learning to drive in a space rocket. The cousins were *bleeding jelly*. Avery stood up.

"Woo-woo. Stay static." Flinn grabbed her. "This isn't skin, remember. Just a mock. You start walking around and you could eat a wall."

This looks like the room, but it's not the room. This wasn't a dream. If she started walking, she'd really be walking around the bedroom she wasn't seeing and run into a wall. It was better to sit the first ride.

"So how do I..." She looked around. "How do I, like, pipe into school?"

"Cake."

Meeho explained the call-ups, demoed gestures, accessed pipelines and code-ups. It wasn't much different than searching a website. Only thoughts not words. And no need for usernames and passwords. Identity was confirmed through brainwave and retinal function. Meeho drew a three-dimensional search engine off the floor.

"Before you peek school," Flinn said, "you gotta see the puppet."

"The puppet?"

Trading glances, their eyes spiraled white lines. "You ain't seen the Big Welcome?" Flinn said.

Avery thought it was more cousin-speak. They stared at each other, and Avery felt a ripple of tiny shock waves. They looked frozen. Avery began to panic, like what would happen if the line locked up and she was all alone? *How do I get out of here?*

Flinn raised her hand. "We're logging a port. It's backed up traffic. You'd think they'd have the bandwidth, being the most popular contest on the planet. Nana Rai's sys could be slowing us down. Meeho is switching to satellite. It'll take a tick."

The website is busy was all Avery got from that.

A holographic image transformed into a replica of Nana Rai's house. Flinn spun it around. The house was bigger than Avery thought. If that was really the house.

"What's the Big Welcome?" Avery said.

"You'll see," Flinn said. Meeho's eyes were still streaming. "How you feeling? You in the bones?"

"Yeah, good. Good," Avery said, not really sure what in the bones meant. But she did feel good. Almost too good. Already it felt like normal. She had to remind herself it wasn't real or normal. *The brain adapts.* They waited for Meeho to come back.

"Can I ask you something?" Avery said. "Your dad said it wasn't my fault. You know, when Nana Rai... when she—"

"He said that?"

"Yeah. I mean, like he meant it. Like he was really sorry for me. But, like, I don't understand why he would say it wasn't my fault."

The data stream paused in Meeho's saucer eyes. She'd heard.

Avery felt the ripple between her cousins. They were communicating on another line, somehow. "It was just," Flinn said, "when you lit the surfers, you know? That was when Nana Rai, you know, when she…"

Avery still didn't understand. The surfers lit at the birthday party. The Hunt officially started. *When Nana Rai died.*

"But I didn't do anything," Avery said.

"You solved the logo, Av," Meeho said. "Remember?"

She didn't solve anything. Bradley thought the logo was a bird eating seed. Uncle Sage thought it was a man on broken stilts. Avery was looking at the sculpture. She saw a resemblance between the elf and the logo. That was right before the surfers lit up and Nana Rai had closed her eyes for good.

It's a hat, Avery had said.

"You solved it," Flinn said, "and the Hunt began."

"Because I said it was a hat?"

Flinn's square shoulders lifted like platforms. "Either way, it wasn't your fault Nana Rai died."

"Yeah. I know. How could it be my fault?"

"I'm sorry, Av," Meeho said. "Dad was just being nice. He didn't mean it."

She wanted to argue it was impossible, what they were saying. All those surfers were dormant for eight months, and all it took for the Hunt to begin was someone saying the logo looked like a hat? It was a coincidence. Plain and simple. *And so was Nana Rai.*

"Got it now." Meeho's eyes were pools of rippling water.

Flinn grabbed Avery's hand. It was distant pressure, like weight pushing through layers of fabric. "This is your first leap, Av."

"Wait. This isn't it?" *Didn't we leap into this room?*

"This is just a homeroom. We're piping to a public domain. It'll feel like falling off the high dive." Avery felt her squeeze. "Ready?"

Avery wasn't nervous before she said that. Everyone did this. It wasn't a big deal. But maybe not the first time. Flinn's smile creased her face. She turned to Meeho.

"Stamp it."

There was a bell in the distance, then the percussion of shock waves. The rush of space. Everything dissolved into tiny symbols. Avery held onto the cousins' hands as it swirled around them, then, in an instant, expanded into infinite space. For a second, they hovered in a black void before dusty symbols returned, latching onto each other like insects. Colors bloomed; textures unfolded. A white blanket unfurled. Evergreen trees with weighty branches sprang toward a cloudless blue sky.

A puppet stood in front of them.

"Lock it," Flinn said.

Snowflakes froze in midflight. Their crystalline structures glittered. The puppet, it was maybe five feet tall, was still. Its mouth, a slit across the bottom of a smooth maplewood head, the color of their dining table, had started to open.

"You tight?" Flinn said, shaking Avery's hand.

Avery let go slowly, like releasing a bike the first time without training wheels. A trace of vertigo swirling in her head. She wasn't sure if it was the sudden change of scenery or the surreal puppet. This was a vivid environment, a psychedelic coloring book. The textures and angles had a dreamy quality. *This isn't real,* she reminded herself.

"What is that?" Avery said.

The puppet's eyes were big and round on a polished wooden face. A top hat tipped at an angle with a red bow above the rim. The cheeks were slightly rosy. It wasn't wearing clothes, just blocks of wood and jointed appendages. And a green scarf that dragged the ground.

"The Big Welcome," Meeho said.

"Everyone with surfers saw this when the contest started," Flinn said. "Then it posted public for everyone to see."

Avery had heard there was an announcement, but she was too busy, too distracted to care about a stupid game after her birthday. She didn't even see her friends before leaving. The snow began drifting again. Birdsong twittered. The puppet's mouth split open.

"Hello!" It waved a floppy arm. The voice was smooth and lovely, the resonance of a public figure. "And a big welcome to the greatest experience of all." He leaned toward them at the waist. She thought he might topple over. "Welcome, boys and girls, to the Hunt."

He splayed his jointed fingers over a ripe red heart painted on his chest. The head tipped back, and laughter, the kind that was infectiously jolly, bellowed into the sky.

"I am BT, your host, your guide, your adventure aficionado. You have questions, and I have clues."

The puppet chattered when he spoke, the two halves of his mouth clapping together.

"This, boys and girls, is an experience on another level. A world to explore, a world as real as real. This technology, I'm sure you wonder, has been around for a very, very, very long time. How, you wonder? You're about to discover how." He produced a cane from behind his back, like a magician grabbing a rabbit by the ears: a gnarly stick with a crooked handle. "This world, you will see, is just... like... yours."

He hooked the cane over the jointed elbow. A planet appeared between his hand, slowly rotating. Avery couldn't help but wonder what that meant. *Just like yours?* A stuffed rabbit, a toy rabbit, hopped toward him. The puppet bent over with the aid of the cane and stroked the bunny's ears. "You've been invited to play a game because you have the skills, the genetic predisposition, and, above all, the courage."

The genetic predisposition?

Other toys joined him. Teddy bears, ballerinas, plastic robots and fuzzy puppies, big-headed dolls and rubber balls.

"There will be winners." The puppet stood carefully, leaning on the cane. "If you are successful, you will keep your magnificent looking gear. Think of it. Your very own world in the palm of your hands. A place to escape, to explore, to be whatever you want. It'll be your personal world you never want to leave."

His mouth clapped together. Avery wondered if he was trying to smile.

"The rest of you, I wouldn't say losers, but for you the lookers will turn off. Forever. Never will you visit this world again. Perhaps that doesn't seem like incentive, but I think you'll understand. Once you begin the Hunt."

More toys were coming from the trees, gathering around the puppet, climbing onto each other. A toy Jeep rolled on lumpy wheels. A soldier limped through the snow.

"So the exciting stuff, then, shall we? How do you win? It's quite simple." He counted his fingers until there was one. "You find someone."

Avery was slightly relieved. This was called the Hunt. Inflicting pain on something to win made her ill. She didn't like seeing characters suffer, even if they weren't real. A dark figure appeared behind the puppet. It was a shadowy figure, as if the light couldn't touch it. A three-dimensional shadow that was as fat as it was tall.

"Where is this someone? That is the question, hunters. No one knows. Not even us. You will help us find him. If you have questions, we won't have answers. Only clues."

The puppet swung the cane around. Flinn and Meeho were looking at where the puppet was pointing. He unwrapped a present, cutting the shiny paper with the sharp edge of his wooden finger. The gift was under a Christmas tree heavy with ornaments and a bright star on top. The puppet peered inside. His eyes seemed to grow wider. He looked up, and the mouth opened with echoing laughter. He stumbled slightly, holding his belly, then wiped a nonexistent tear.

"It is August 25." It took Avery a moment to remember this had started a month ago, on her birthday. He pulled a pocket watch from behind his back. "You have four months."

The puppet held the watch by the chain, slowly swinging it back and forth. The snow began to fall harder, snowflakes sticking to his scarf, accumulating on his top hat, covering the toys around him.

"Four months to find the Toymaker."

3

Avery was rinsing a teapot.

People had come to the house at all hours in the last couple of weeks. She looked forward to warm soapy water after two weeks of homework and Uncle Sage's stories. There was always something to clean. Mom and Aunt Mag were always busy in the round room, debating details and proceedings, invitations and waivers. Avery sometimes listened. Adult stuff was tedious.

"Oh, thank you for coming so quickly." Aunt Mag's voice travelled across the house.

Avery dried her hands. She didn't hear whoever was at the door, just heavy footsteps stamping the porch.

"This is my sister, Grace." Avery's mom said hello. "Yes, well, she tried talking to her husband, they're from other parts of the world, but the monitor kept freezing. And Avery, my niece, can't, uh, she can't *pipe* into school." It sounded like a cuss word coming from Aunt Mag. "The girls say it's the network. I'm sure you know how to fix it."

Avery strained to hear someone answer. She got the feeling whoever it was didn't need any more information beyond *you know how to fix it*. Aunt Mag continued about the ceremony website and the volunteers and the committees, and she had a list for the mystery guest that was growing longer by the minute.

"Well, I shouldn't keep you. We're meeting with the mayor. You know your way around the house. Avery is here, if you need anything. Avery?"

"Yes!" Avery called.

There was muttering, another thank you, and then the door closed. Mom was pulling on slim leather gloves. She wore a silk scarf tucked into a black overcoat. Avery put the dishes in the cabinet.

"Darling, we're leaving. We'll be back in a couple of hours. Will you be all right by yourself?"

Avery laughed. "I think so, Mom."

"It's just... I apologize."

"It's okay, Mom. I'm fine. I've got homework to do."

Wrinkles had permanently furrowed her forehead, a look she'd worn since they'd arrived. It was only October. It wasn't just the planning, which Avery still didn't understand, but the indelible memories that popped up in every little thing. A box of Band-Aids had brought her to tears one morning.

Mom touched her cheek. "I love you, darling."

"Love you, too."

※

No one drank coffee. It was always tea. Aunt Mag, Uncle Sage, the cousins and every guest would sit at the round table, dipping a tea bag in conversation. Avery didn't mind it so much. It was hot. She made a cup while listening to the house settle. Every once in a while, heavy footsteps crossed the front porch.

She carried the cup and saucer to the next room.

The breakfast nook was an atrium at the back of the house with a dome of glass. Striped shadows lined the floor. A small table, with a laptop and notebooks and stacks of other things she'd collected, overlooked a spacious backyard hemmed in by stalwart evergreens. The frosty tips of mountains peered above them. A thin layer of powder hid the grass. Not enough to build a snowman, but the remnants of her first snow angel was still on the ground.

She thought of the atrium as her office. Her bedroom was such a climb, and the kitchen only a short walk. Besides, it was the best place in the house for the spotty Wi-Fi. Mom and Dad's video chat barely worked. She touched the laptop and waited for assignments to load. The teacher had posted, earlier that week, that students were prohibited from watching the Hunt during school. Apparently, that was a problem. Avery had watched the Big Welcome a dozen times on her laptop. She was embarrassed to admit that she was too nervous to try the hiwires alone.

She sipped the tea—she was fond of chamomile—and opened a big book. The binding creased. The leather cover had been shined. It was oversized with thick yellow pages and uneven margins. Photos were stuck beneath sheets of protective plastic. There were gaps where pictures were missing, where Mom or Aunt Mag had pulled them for the upcoming ceremony, to scan for a website or put on posterboard. Avery hadn't asked to take the photo album from the round room. There was so much clutter, it was doubtful they would know it was missing.

Some of the photos looked a hundred years old. Avery had heard the stories, that her grandmother had seen a good bit of the world. But she hadn't seen the places she'd gone. She'd taken trips to a lot of snowy regions, some with legit castles made of giant stones, hiking on mountaintops with rucksacks nearly as big as she was.

An inconspicuous photo of a cabin caught her attention. She carefully removed it from the page. There wasn't anything exciting about it: just a log cabin tucked beneath arching evergreens, smoke puffing from a cobbled chimney and a crooked window of yellow light. It seemed homey. The trees looked like the ones out back. She wondered if it was out there.

She lifted a pair of binoculars. They'd been sitting on a shelf the first day she came to the atrium. Avery wondered if Nana Rai had used them to glass the countryside, sitting in this very spot with a blanket over her lap and tea at her side. The trunks were dense, like a wall of timber. She scanned the trees, and there, just beyond a forgotten garden, was a small opening. She dialed the focus. It looked like someone was out there, just inside the shadows.

And then something moved.

Avery stood up. The chair almost tipped over. Someone walked across the backyard. More like wobbled. From this distance, it was hard to tell, he looked short and fat. *Not like the elf,* she thought, for some reason. *But sort of.*

He wore only a thick sweater, which was even less than Uncle Sage wore, and carried a stout tool bag in one hand. His gait was determined, shuffling straight for the trees. And not just the trees, but the gap she was watching. She dialed the binoculars and watched him disappear into the shadows. If someone was in there, like she thought, the man wasn't startled. She strained to see more and felt someone behind her.

The binoculars slipped from her hand. They hit the table and, the worst of all nightmares, tipped over the teacup. Tan liquid spread across the table, soaking her notes and, even worse, seeped beneath the photo album.

"Sorry, sorry, ma'am," said the boy.

Avery picked up the book, then ran to the kitchen for a towel, sopping up the tea dripping from the table. The boy, still standing there, staring through thick, square glasses, watched her.

"Ma'am?" she said.

He was her age. He adjusted his gray beanie, black curls escaping around his ears, and pointed at the man who crossed the field. "He is the, uh, he is fixing the network, ma'am."

"Thank you, sir." She went along with it. Maybe it was a cultural thing, although no one else talked like that. "Where's he going?"

"There is something out there. I help him sometimes." He showed her an instrument. It looked like a phone. "He is my, uh, my dad. So… I am sorry about scaring you. I did not know you were in here."

"It's okay. If you're helping him, why are you in here?"

"I am here to help." He showed her the blocky phone again. It didn't answer her question. "Do you live here, then?"

"No. No, this is Nana... my grandmother's house."

"Oh. Sorry." He poked the phone, his fingertips exposed in fingerless gloves. He pretended to look busy. "My dad, he worked for her. Do you know Hugo?"

She shook her head.

"He was pretty upset."

"Everyone is."

"You are part of the ceremony."

She didn't know anything about the ceremony, but he sounded pretty sure that was why she was here. Like he wasn't asking. Everyone was going to be there. The whole town, maybe, was coming. But part of it? No one said anything to her.

His shyness was adorable. He'd taken his shoes off. His big toe stuck through a hole in his sock. It looked like the toenail was painted silver. He didn't try to hide it. Maybe he wasn't shy. He shuffled toward the window.

"So how long are you staying here?" he asked.

"I'm not sure."

"You do not have school, then?"

She pointed at the laptop. That was school. Silence stretched like Silly Putty. He pretended to check readings again. Or maybe he was doing something. She didn't know what he was doing. She took the wet towel back to the kitchen and returned with her backpack, digging out the hiwires.

"I'm supposed to be using these," she said.

The cousins said there was a network issue, but Avery wasn't sure she could virtually connect with school if there weren't issues.

"Hugo made those." He took them from her. "My dad," he said, like he wanted to be clear. "Your nana was very specific about them and in a hurry. He worked late every night since Christmas. He was making them for you, then?"

"I suppose."

"How are they working?"

She shrugged. "I mean, my cousins... they showed me some stuff. Do you know them?"

"They are here?"

"No. Why?"

He kicked at the floor. "No reason."

They were pretty. Like, very. He fidgeted with the phone. Avery said, "They make you nervous?"

"No, no. Not like that. I mean..." He looked around like maybe someone would hear, whispered, "I cannot understand them."

"Oh, thank God." She smiled wider than she had in months. The boy stepped back, unsure what that smile meant. "I thought I was the only one. And then I thought everyone talked like them. You know, like, people our age."

He matched her smile. "No one talks like that."

It was such a relief to laugh, like laughter had been bottled under pressure. It popped out in big gulps. She tried to stop, afraid he thought she was laughing at him, wiping her eyes, holding up one hand and her stomach with the other. But he was still smiling.

"So what were you doing?" he said.

She sighed. "Homework."

"No, I mean with these." He set the hiwires on the table. "With your cousins."

Avery flipped them over so the lenses were facing down. "They showed me the Big Welcome."

"The Hunt?"

"Yeah. You follow?"

"Who doesn't?"

She'd watched the Big Welcome a dozen times on the website. There were progress videos of hunters opening clues under golden Christmas trees—giant snowmen popping out, a frozen-looking elf, an enormous reindeer. Things that didn't make much sense. The hunters collected items in virtual wallets. It looked like real people wandering around in a second life world. She didn't recognize any of them and wondered if that was what they looked like in the skin. None were Bradley. And none of them had names. Just numbers and letters.

"The entire contest," she said, "just to find an elf?"

"The Toymaker. And who said he was an elf?" His eyebrows rose above his glasses. *So he is into it.*

"Either way," she said. "Just find the Toymaker."

He shrugged. "Bad Toy likes to watch."

"Bad Toy?"

"BT."

Now she frowned. "The creepy puppet? That's his name?"

"That is what some call him. *Bad Toy is going to escape.*"

"Escape where?"

"Who knows? Everyone is too absorbed by the game to know what he really wants. The experience is very real. As real as this." He spread his arms. "Hunters stay in for days at a time. There have already been warnings about reality confusion. Do you know what reality confusion is?"

"My dad and brother work for Avocado."

He nodded, like that explained it. Everyone had heard of Avocado, Inc. So yeah, she knew people who spent too much time in virtual environments could get confused with where they were when they came out, confusing reality with virtual. They hallucinated, or worse. Like trying to fly off buildings. Bradley was routinely tested.

"I will bet that is why they made the game so short, only four months to find the Toymaker. Any longer and hunters will not know if they are in or out."

His phone beeped. He used it this time, tapping the glass and sliding his finger, looking out the window.

"The network will be good now. Your hiwires will work," he said.

"Oh. Great."

"Is there something wrong with them?"

"Nothing wrong." She didn't want to say she didn't really know how to use them. It was embarrassing. Like saying she didn't know how to brush her teeth. "I couldn't connect with class. Maybe it was the network. Here." She handed him the hiwires. "See if they work."

"Oh, no. I cannot."

"Why?"

"No, I mean not with these. These are imprinted for you. They are like the surfers. No one else can use them but you."

Surfers? Avery thought Bradley was the only one who called them that. Apparently, it was everyone. She wondered how BT and Company could make them that way? Wouldn't it require some personal information? And how did Nana Rai code the hiwires for her?

"I can show you with my lookers." He admired them once more. "But I do not have it here. Besides, Hugo is coming." His stocky father was wobbling across the backyard, tool bag at his side.

"Why do you call him Hugo?" she said.

"That is his name."

"How about *Dad*?"

"He likes it that way." He kicked the floor. "So, anyway. It was nice to meet you."

"Wait. You're leaving?"

"Not yet. Hugo, er, *Dad* is going to check the library before we leave. I need to pack up the van."

"There's a library?" No one said anything about a library. "Where is it?"

"Have you been on the elevator?" He rocked back on his heels, painted toe sticking out.

"Where is it?" This was like a quiz show.

"Unavailable. I am sorry about the, you know…" He nodded at the stains on her papers. "And your nana. Maybe I will see you at the ceremony."

He slid his feet on the way out. He seemed in a hurry. Avery looked out the window. Hugo was gone.

"Hey," she shouted.

She hesitated to follow him, wanting to ask when he would come back. The ceremony was months away. She didn't even know his name. The hallway was empty. Maybe, she thought, he went in a different direction, to help his dad in the library. She looked out the front window. Hugo was climbing into the driver's seat of a white van. He pulled away from the curb, smoke puffing from the tailpipe.

Guess he didn't need to go to the library.

4

Flames devoured the dry bark, sending embers crashing into the chain curtain.

Avery sank into the couch. It smelled like a resort for dust mites. The armrests were worn smooth. She wondered how many people had sat in it, propped their legs up and watched the fireplace. The heat drew sweat across her brow.

"Found it." Mom shook a tin can full of pebbles.

She was cocooned in a gray blanket, her feet tucked in fur-lined slippers. She put a teacup on a small table and snuggled into the couch, cinching the blanket around her neck.

"I can't believe she still has these." She turned the cannister around. An elaborate wintery scene wrapped around all four sides of snowy hills and sleds, children throwing snowballs. "Your nana would tell her stories this time of year. Well, maybe a bit closer to Christmas, but she always had a way of making every day feel special. We would build a fire in the backyard and sit around with hot cocoa and marshmallows. We would eat s'mores until our stomachs ached. And the stars, oh, the stars."

Mom looked at the ceiling.

"The sky is so big when you're young. Anything is possible and the world shiny and new."

She popped the lid off. A sulfuric smell puffed out. She poured granules into her glove and closed her eyes, the peculiar scent pulling memories from the past. She tossed them into the fire.

"We called these *magic flies*. Maggy and I would fight over who would throw them first."

The flames flickered blue, purple and green as potassium and copper burned, colorful sparks rising up the chimney.

"We pretended these were fairy seeds." She held out a handful. "The fire released them, and up, up they went into the cold night, little greens and blues and reds. Youth is so…" She shook her head. "So magical."

The memory deflated her mood like a sharp point. Then she began laughing, wiping her lower eyelid with her finger.

"What?" Avery said.

"Nana didn't believe in magic. She said magic was just phenomena we didn't understand. But the stories she told were just so, so magical."

"Like what?"

"Oooh, there's too many to remember. She had tales of reindeer whose bellies filled with helium, and they would fly across the moon."

She threw her arms out.

"And snowmen that were alive. But she didn't call them snowmen, it was abominables. And they didn't have snowball bodies, they were these massive torsos with this, this heart that generated gravitational fields. There were stories about toys that were alive and cookies that were best friends. And no matter how many questions Maggy and I asked, she always had an answer. She explained everything. It sounded like she made them up sometimes, but she always sounded so sure. We always believed."

The stories sounded familiar. Avery wanted them to sound familiar. Wanted to sit around a fire and hear them, too.

"Elves, too?" Avery said.

Mom looked at the sculptures on the mantel. The blank space was occupied with the one from home. Shadows danced along their sides.

"Her favorite," Mom said distantly.

She told how their feet were wide for trekking on snow, and the soles were scaly so they could slide on ice. Their bellies were round and generously insulated. Hairy and short, they were never without a smile.

"Nana made that for you," Mom said. "Do you remember?"

Avery was five years old when the elf sculpture had arrived. She remembered having more fun opening the Christmas present than what was inside. Her mom was quite taken by the gift, she remembered. She cried. It was very special, she told her. Avery didn't see it that way at the time. The sculpture wasn't something she could play with. It was just a decoration. And now it was a family heirloom.

"Do you miss living here?" Avery said.

"No. No, no. The cold was never for me." Her mom sipped her tea with both hands. Steam wafted over her cheeks. "I miss the memories. No matter how mighty you try, you never really understand how special those moments are when they're happening. And even when you do, you can't grasp them. They're like flowers. Enjoy them while they last."

She watched the colors in the fire. Like fragments of the Northern Lights.

"Your nana loved the cold, though," Mom said. "That's why she moved here."

Avery frowned. "I thought she grew up here."

"No, she grew up somewhere else. I don't know why she picked this town, other than it was cold. She came from a large family, all of them very talented. Artists. She went to school for it, you know. Yes." She nodded, sounding entertained by the sound of her own voice. "It was a special school for creative students. Her great-great-great-grandfather had been the headmaster at one time. Nana used to say he was rather famous for living so long, among other things."

"Like what?"

"She never really said." Mom leaned into her. "That's why she lived so long, though. Good genes. Maybe you'll be an artist as well."

Avery snorted. "Have you seen me draw?"

"It's not about that, darling. Beauty is something beyond pretty pictures. You ask anyone within a hundred miles, they'll tell you. Beauty flowed through Nana Rai's fingers. Everyone swore when they got a work from her, they felt better for seeing it. She had that effect."

"I've noticed."

Avery also noticed her mom was talking different. She always spoke so dignified, her enunciation sharp, grammar on point. Her words seemed so much more relaxed now. She was melting into the couch.

"Where was her studio?" Avery asked.

"She had one upstairs for a while. But then she moved it out back."

"There's not one in the library?"

"There is no library, darling."

"I thought the elevator went to it."

"Where'd you hear that?" Before Avery could answer, Mom said, "The elevator doesn't work."

"It doesn't? I thought the man who was here a few weeks ago used it."

"What man?"

"Hugo. He fixed the reception, went out back and then used the elevator to check on her library."

"You mean Nana Rai's assistant?"

"Is that what he is?"

"He's short and, you know, very round." Mom wouldn't dare say fat. It would sound too mean. "He's been here ever since I can remember. Did he tell you about the library, then?"

Avery nodded distantly. He didn't go to the library, like the boy said. But Mom's evasive answers confirmed there was one. She didn't know why she didn't tell her about the boy. It felt like she would get him in trouble. Or maybe she would get in trouble. *Why would I get in trouble?*

"So can I use the elevator?" Avery said.

"It's broken, darling." She smacked Avery's leg. "Why, are you tired of the stairwell?"

Mom took a deep breath, let it out slowly. Her eyes were heavy. She leaned her head on Avery's shoulder. It felt good to feel her mom so relaxed. The memories of this house were a thick comforter that smelled like home.

"Thank you," her mom said. "I know this is all boring, adult stuff and you'd rather be at home with your friends. The ceremony's just taking so much more planning than I thought. Nana had a lot of very specific requests. I'm just so grateful to have you here."

Funny thing was, Avery didn't mind being here. There wasn't much to do. But she didn't miss home.

"That's my phone." Mom scrambled in the pile of blankets. "Where's my phone?"

The ringtone echoed in another room. Avery took their mugs to the kitchen. Mom found it in the round room, her voice echoing throughout the house. It was Dad. Avery went up the winding staircase, the atmosphere cooler with each step, to her bedroom to change clothes. The fire had warmed her too much. She put on shorts and a T-shirt.

"Here's Avery." Mom pointed the phone when Avery returned. The blue light glowed in the hallway.

"There's my girl." Dad's smile was as bright as the screen.

Mom put another log on, insulating herself with another blanket. A twinge of homesickness stirred in Avery's stomach, seeing his smile, missing his good mornings and breakfast skillets. The way Mom looked when he kissed her.

"We'll be there soon," he said.

"You're coming?" Avery said. "Bradley, too?"

"Of course! If he's still alive."

"What does that mean, Dell?" Mom grabbed the phone. "Dell, that's not funny."

"He's fine, Grace. He's working a lot." His laughter was deep. "Here. Look."

The video swung around the room and down the steps. Mom felt like a frozen shell. Dad didn't always time his jokes right. Or pick the right ones. They watched him tread down to the basement and knock on the door. It took a minute for it to open. Mom held the phone with both hands.

"Hey, Mom." A patchwork of whiskers bristled on Bradley's chin.

"Bradley," Mom said, with tension in her voice, "you do not look well."

"I'm fine, Mom." He offered a smile. "Just getting ahead before we fly out."

Mom relaxed a bit. Their conversation was normal. Bradley was engaged. He seemed out of it at first. For a moment, Avery didn't recognize him. When it was Avery's turn, he threw her off a bit. "I miss you, skunk."

That wasn't something Bradley said. Dad was probably coaching him.

"Bradley," Mom said sharply. She didn't care for the nickname. One he'd branded her with when Avery farted once. The only time she ever farted in her life.

"You in the Hunt?" Avery asked.

"No. No, no. Just researching how the surfers work."

Mom talked to Dad about the ceremony, how much there was still left to do, what Nana Rai had requested. Avery sat back and watched the last of the colorful fairies dance in the fire. Wondering why she felt worried.

PART II

The wicker chair splintered. The old woman caressed the leather book.
   "Once upon a time, there was an elf who was colder than the coldest of any elf alive. An elf so cold his skin was as blue as the sky."

5

The house shook.

Avery's dream of a white tundra turned upside down. Toys tumbled into the sky. Toys of every color and every kind, disappearing into the sheet covering the world. She sat up, head swimming. Dust floated through an early morning sunbeam. A steady sharp warning was outside.

Beep. Beep. Beep.

She shuffled through papers on the bedspread, her laptop, and a plate of crumbs. She grabbed the hiwires before they slid off the bed. A shadow slowly moved into the sunbeam.

"Little more!" someone shouted.

The floor was cold on her feet. The window was frosty, the light soft and fuzzy, crystalline patterns sparkling on the glass, emitting tiny spectrums of light.

The house rattled again. A deep, resounding boom shook another layer of dust from the ceiling. The beeping continued. A long mechanical arm extended a box containing Hugo waving at the ground. An enormous spruce was tethered to a crane. He signaled an operator. The tip of the tree began to rise.

There were trucks in the backyard. People unloading boxes from pickups. A tractor rolled off a flatbed trailer, the exhaust pipe coughing black smoke. Mom looked elegant in a long mauve coat and a fluttering scarf next to Aunt Mag, drinking coffee, looking at a notebook. People from the committee were taking orders, but there were new people out there, people Avery hadn't seen before.

Hugo barked an order from the bucket. Mom and Aunt Mag pointed. The enormous spruce was nearly upright. A crew began hauling lumber beneath it. The boxes from the pickups were stacked around it. Ornaments dazzled in the morning light. It was November. *It's what Nana Rai wanted.*

The tractor travelled across the yard. Mechanical legs anchored on the ground. Its long arm began digging the frozen earth. People came with shovels and rakes, wheelbarrows with firewood, and benches. Uncle Sage drank coffee while they stacked the wood.

Nana Rai had been planning this day for quite a while, Mom had said. There were enough ornaments to lift spirits in a hundred-mile radius. Avery could feel it, too. This would be her first Christmas in the snow.

She grew up where carolers wore shorts and palm trees were wrapped in lights. There were no snowmen with twiggy arms and carrot noses, no hot chocolate or ruddy cheeks. No winter coats and ice-crusted scarves or stories told around a fire while marshmallows toasted on the end of sticks. Avery remembered how Mom said it felt when it snowed, how everything was soft and peaceful.

"Ahem."

Avery spun around. She caught the hiwires before they hit the floor. "What are you doing up here?" Avery said.

The boy stood in the open doorway. He was wearing the same clothes from the last time she'd seen him. The stocking cap, the rectangular glasses. A hole in one sock.

"The door was open," he said, backing up. "I heard you were up, and I just... should I leave? I should leave."

She hadn't heard him coming up the steps. "Shouldn't you be out there?"

"Hugo's not a patient man. Better out of his way than in it.

Besides, plenty of help out there. Your mom said to come wake you up. So… good morning!"

She looked out the window. "More like merry Christmas."

She'd stayed up late, wasting time on social media, seeing what her friends were doing at home. Iona said everything was boring, that her mom was in the Hunt, strapping on the surfers all day, every day. She didn't say exactly what her mom was doing. Her mom said she couldn't talk about it.

"Your nana was fond of Christmas." He stepped into the room. "Should I leave?" he said. "I'm sorry, it is rude of me to just… I will go."

"You're wearing the same socks."

"They all have holes."

She stared at the silver toenail.

"Oh. My sister." He wiggled his toes.

Sister. She thought he was lying. Hugo lowered the bucket to the ground. He waddled out to examine the height of the tree as it swayed from the crane. He was so much shorter than the people around him.

"You know, you don't look much like your dad," Avery said.

"I am adopted. Sort of."

"Sort of?"

"It is a long story."

It would be rude to ask him to explain. Ruder even than walking into someone's bedroom after they just woke up. "Since you keep sneaking up on me, you can at least tell me your name."

"I have many names," he said.

"Okay. One will do."

"Jenks. Sandy. Wirenut," he said. "The last one Hugo calls me."

Avery laughed. It wasn't funny. But it sort of was.

"So how is everything working?" he said.

"Oh, yeah." She held up the hiwires. "Great. I mean, they're so… sooo good. You know, just—"

"You have not used them."

"Yeah, no. I haven't." She'd been putting them on like the cousins showed her, sat in bed and stared at the virtual environment. But even that had become boring. She didn't know how to leap.

"You really should be using them," he said.

"I know, I know."

"Your cousins did not help?"

"They're busy. With all the planning and school and whatever."

"I know those do not come with a tutorial. They were made special." He reached in his pocket. "But I can show you."

It was a sleek looker kit, curved and black. Similar to the surfers, but these were boxy with side clip projectors that rested on the nose.

"You just woke up." He raised his hands, fending off her hesitancy. "You have not had breakfast. I barged in here—"

"No, it's fine. Just let me... hang on."

He stepped out of the way. Avery went to the bathroom. She splashed cold water on her face. The tractor roared in the backyard. Everyone had gathered around the boxes, unloading ornaments to be loaded into the bucket, the crane still holding the tree upright.

Jenks seemed nice. (She decided to call him Jenks. Wirenut was a close second.) He sounded like he knew what he was doing. And the cousins weren't around much. And he was right, the hiwires didn't come with a tutorial. She soaked her face again and dried it with a towel, decided to let him show her how to use the hiwires somewhere besides her bedroom.

He wasn't in her bedroom, though. He was at the far end of the hallway.

"Your room is too small. This room will work much better." He pointed at the door. The room Uncle Sage had made sure was locked. "Do you have the hiwires?"

She was holding them.

The light fixtures on the walls flickered. The floor creaked on her approach. It was warmer at this end of the hall. It didn't smell like antique furniture. The door had three inset panels with intricate molding, the paint peeling in yellow strips, curling at the edges. The knob was dimpled and surprisingly warm. Jenks stood aside.

The latch gently popped open.

A breath of humid air exhaled thick and grassy, mixed with a rich scent of acrylics and cloth. Excitement knotted her stomach. It was difficult to determine how large the room was. She couldn't see the other side. It was cluttered with tables and easels, chairs and boxes, cloth draped over objects. Stacks of unfinished canvases splattered with paint. Statues half chiseled.

And a tree in the center. A living tree.

Its branches were knobby and coarse, the bark flaking off like old paint. Glossy oblong fruit, striped green and yellow, hung from the tips. There were no windows that she could see. Green-yellow light filtered through an opaque glass ceiling speckled with leaves and layers of algae.

"Your nana spent a lot of time here."

Avery was afraid to touch anything. There was no order to it, just a collection of a life's work in progress. Carefully, she walked past a copper cannister of gnarly canes made from tree branches, stepped over cups of crusted paintbrushes, down a wandering aisle of teetering boxes. A large chair was in a corner —more of a throne—with stuffed animals watching with glassy eyes.

A round table was beneath the tree, its surface littered with brittle leaves. There were dusty sketches of intricately designed orbs, like hieroglyphic ornaments, and mounds of half-molded clay. A wooden bowl, it looked hand-carved, was filled with green cubes, the kind you'd feed a horse.

"This was her studio," Avery wondered.

"Her special room."

A crumbling house made of toasted walls surrounded by cookie crumbs was in the center of the table. Gingerbread men leaned against it. Avery picked one up. The icing was cracked and broken.

"You seem to know a lot about her," Avery said.

"Hugo has worked with her all his life. He talks when he is in the mood, which is every leap year. But when she, you know, when she was gone... he talked a lot more. He sat in front of the fire and went on about when she first moved here, how she loved to travel, hiked in the hills, spent weeks camping. He said she was more special than the world knew."

He ducked under a limb. Leaves had collected on a large book.

"She told a lot of stories," he said.

Avery gently brushed leaves off the leather book. Lying next to it was a long white feather. The tip blackened and flat. A dried inkwell next to it. She wanted to open it, to see what Nana Rai had written, to imagine the stories she told around the fire when Mom was young.

"Over here," he said.

A wide path led to a faux wood panel door. It looked like it led to the exterior of the house. Colorful tracks of paint streaked the floor. Nana Rai had taken her wheelchair through here. The door folded open.

"I don't think that works," she said.

He stepped inside the elevator. "How do you think I got up here?"

This felt like trouble. She wanted to go back and look out the window, make sure her mom was still out there. The sounds of the tractor and crane, the shouting sounded like they were still very busy. There were two buttons on the wall.

"Are you sure about this?" she said.

"Hugo takes it all the time," he said. She was leaning in but hadn't put her foot inside. "We do not have to take the elevator. We can go somewhere else."

"Where does it go?"

He smiled. "The library, of course."

She ran her hand over her head. No one told her she couldn't go, just that the elevator didn't work. According to Jenks, it worked just fine. That was how he got up there. And the door was unlocked. There was no harm in looking.

She stepped inside. Jenks pointed. "That one."

She put her finger on the bottom button. The door folded closed. The elevator shuddered, and she imagined the cable snapping. She let out a small sound and reflexively reached out. Jenks stepped back before she could grab him. The elevator began a slow, steady descent.

Her breath began to fog. Goosebumps rose on her arms. She clutched the hiwires with both hands.

The door unfolded.

※

THE FLOOR WAS smooth and polished, with a bluish tinge—the color of ice—with two large circles in the middle. The walls were midnight black and depthless. They curved to form a seamless dome. Tiny specks were near the top, one brighter than all the rest. The room had the illusion of an endless horizon, a plate of ice that expanded outward.

"This isn't a library," she said.

"It was, once upon a time," Jenks said. "Before I was born, Hugo said. There were books all the way to the ceiling and sliding ladders and catwalks. She would come here to read, to imagine. There were birds, too. They would fly around and perch on shelves, eat seeds from feeders. They were not great for a library, very messy, but she always said nothing should be forever." He stepped without slipping or sliding, looking up at the stars. "Even books."

"What happened to the books?"

"She donated them. Hugo built this for her. She had a plan."

He went to one of the circles on the floor. They were ten feet in diameter, a darker shade of blue. Slightly raised with a rough texture. He held up his boxy looker kit.

"Should we be here?" she asked.

"Did anyone tell you not to be?"

"I wasn't supposed to use the elevator, I know that." She couldn't see a door leading to the house. The walls were so smooth.

"Hugo said the cousins were not allowed in here when they were little. This room was made for this." He held the lookers up again. "We will be here just long enough for me to show you how to use your hiwires."

She tested the floor. It was solid, not slippery. She stepped on one of the circles, the surface spongy, slightly bouncy.

"It is a treadway," he said. "Once you launch, it will track any direction. You can walk or run in place."

"Nana used this?"

"No. Not really."

"Then why did she build it?"

"She had a plan." He slid the boxy lookers onto his nose, peered over the top.

This place felt like a different world. The house was so old, but this room hi-tech. It was beyond anything she'd ever seen. Jenks was right. No one said not to come here. And the elevator was working. And she wasn't doing anything but using the hiwires, which her mom wanted her to learn.

"I don't know if these are charged," she said.

"It will not matter."

That was a strange thing to say. But there wasn't time to go back upstairs and charge them. If she was going to do this, it had to be now. "Okay," she said, more to herself than Jenks.

The hiwires fit snugly. There was the sound of something stacking in the claustrophobic dark, boards clicking together, metal wheels rolling on a hard surface. It echoed and grew louder like an approaching train. Details exploded from the void. She crouched like a frightened cat caught in the train's headlight. Walls circled her, rising higher and higher. Shelves rose into misty fog, light refracting bits of snow. Brass ladders shot from the floor.

It smelled like old paper.

Jenks was in front of her. He wasn't animated, like the cousins had been. He looked exactly the same, and so did she. Only one small detail was different. His toe poking through the hole. The toenail wasn't painted silver anymore.

"That was seamless," he said. "You are a natural."

She looked at her hands. Her skin brown and smooth, nails shiny. The veins on the back of her hands, the wrinkles so real. Even the small mole on her pinky finger. This was beyond what she'd experienced with the cousins. *This is too real.*

"Where are we?" she said.

"Your nana's library. It looked like this before she changed it. Well, sort of. It was not like that."

There wasn't a ceiling. If there was, she couldn't see it. The atmosphere was dense where the circular walls vanished. "She had that many books?"

"Well, no. Some of these are digital versions. Most of them are something else."

"What?"

"They are her stories."

Avery walked toward the wall, her footsteps echoing off polished marble. Despite the illusion of a solid surface, she felt the treadway's sponginess beneath her. The illusion made her quickly forget that in reality, her skin, she was walking in place.

"Choose one," he said.

"Which one?"

"The library will know."

The books were real enough. Hardbacks of different colors. Some as thick as encyclopedias, frayed at the edges, others as thin as a dishwasher manual. Most of them did not have titles. One caught her eye. It was a familiar color. She couldn't say why. It was bound in leather with white letters. She tipped her head to read the title.

Tales Beyond the Veil.

She tugged at the binding. It wouldn't budge, like it was glued in place. "It won't move."

"Then the book is not ready."

"What does that mean?"

"The library knows when it is time to see one, when it is not. Try another."

"Which one?"

"Not that one." He smiled.

Frustrated, she chose one without a title. It tipped off the shelf. The pages were as thin as newspaper, the edges painted silver. As the binding cracked, the walls began to swirl. She dropped the book. It vanished in a cloud of mist. Snow crept across the room. Trees sprouted through the floor.

They were in a forest.

Someone appeared in the room. A heavy backpack strapped over a thick coat. Foggy breath exhaled from a deep hood lined with snow-crusted fur. The stranger's footsteps crunched on the ground. The sound was soft and muffled, like Mom said it was when the snow came so thick you could barely see across the street. The stranger spiked climbing sticks into the ground and threw back the hood. Her curly hair was pulled back in a tight bun, cheeks rosy.

"Nana," Avery said.

She was so young. And beautiful. All alone on a rough trail. Avery could reach out and touch her, imagined the smell of the leather pack she peeled off her shoulders. Nana leaned against a narrow boulder—it was rectangular, shoulder height, like a monument marking a trail—and sipped water from a pouch. She looked up at the gray sky, snowflakes collecting on her cheeks.

"How am I seeing this?" Avery circled around. Nana Rai dug a notebook from the pack. "I mean, wouldn't she have to be filming this?"

"Mental interface. Her presentation is an amalgam of memories, since she cannot see herself. This is what she remembered this moment to be."

It seemed like such an ordinary event to have made such a vivid impression. Nana Rai stripped off a glove and scribbled on a blank page. Avery peered over her shoulder. A date, how far she'd come, the trees she had seen. But she looked so happy. As peaceful as the moment felt.

"Aren't memories flawed?" Avery said.

She remembered that from psychology class. The brain filtered sensory input. *It is impossible to experience a moment truly as it is*, Mrs. Bach had said. *The brain is built to survive, not see the truth.*

"The mind knows everything," Jenks said. "You just have to find it."

Nana Rai looked like a doe hearing a twig snap. She put the journal away. Avery heard a thump. It sounded like a neighbor chopping wood. Avery and Jenks followed her.

Nana Rai pushed between trees and stepped over logs. Avery felt pressure when she passed through a tree trunk, but it didn't stop her. The sound grew louder. A small clearing was up ahead. Nana Rai dropped her pack to retrieve a camera. She squatted behind a large pine.

The trees faded. The wall of books returned. Avery and Jenks were standing, once again, on a marble floor. The last vestiges of the story floated around them like fairy dust. She'd seen what Nana Rai was shooting with her camera. The picture from the photo album. Avery had peeled it from the protective cover when she'd spilled the tea.

The cabin.

❋

"That was... that was incredible," she said. "So real. All of this is so real."

"Yeah, well, it is just a start. This is just your nana's library. I should probably show you how to use your hiwires for school."

School was the last thing she wanted to do: make school more real. "How about something else?" she said.

"Like what?"

She shrugged, looking up the wall of books. "Something fun."

"Right." He dug into his pocket. "First, though, if we are going to venture out, you need an anchor."

"A what?"

"Something to remind you of where you are. If you stay inside too long, you can forget where you are. You need something like this." His toe poked through the hole in the sock. "Whenever I am unsure, I look at my toe."

"It's not silver."

"It is never silver when I am here. Always silver when I am not. So what do you have? It can be anything, like, uh, like the color of a tattoo or a ring. Something you do not have in the skin."

She held up her hand. The bracelet she got for her birthday, the one Nana Rai had made, jingled. The snowflake spun on its link.

"You wear that already," he said.

She never took it off. "Can I change the color?"

"Okay," he said, nodding. "Yes. Change the color."

"How do I…"

"Clear your mind until there is no thought. Only see the bracelet. It helps if you count your breath. Hold it up like this. Good." He picked up her arm. His touch was strange. It was more like pressure, something she could push through like the trees in Nana Rai's memory. Like he was there but not really.

"Breathe through it, now," he said. "One, two, three. On ten, fill your head with a color."

She did what he said, stared at the dangling snowflake until nothing else was around her, drawing deep breaths. It started to glow. When she lost concentration, it dimmed. It took three attempts before it turned white hot. And then she imagined a color.

The snowflake turned red.

"First lesson complete. The rest is easy-peasy." He pulled a marble from his pocket and tossed it a few times. It landed heavily in his hand. Suddenly, the marble stopped.

It hovered between them.

The air began to twist around it. *It's not air,* she thought, looking at the red snowflake. *This isn't real.* The edges began to soften, iridescent particles floating away from the marble. Something moved inside it. Little images began to form. The marble began to look more like a hole in space. And then it expanded to the size of a basketball, a scene inside a hovering globe.

"How'd you do that?" she said.

"It is an imagination engine. Sort of like a search engine, only you do not type. You imagine, like your bracelet. You do not need these." He had a pocketful of marbles. "They are just something to help me focus. Your hiwires are synced to do the same. We can use it to transport to your classroom—"

"No. No, that's all right. I just… where's that?"

She poked the membrane around a floating image. Her finger disappeared. It was strange, like a well of gravity inside a bubble.

"Glad you asked." He rubbed his hands deliciously. "Do you want to go?"

Do I want to go? She shook the red snowflake. What if the bracelet fell off? She should have tattooed her arm. Or made a green thumbnail. But Jenks was with her. She nodded.

The snow globe began to swell. Or were they leaning in? Everything twisted and warped. Her body began to melt like a snowman in July. She began to change her mind, her hesitancy causing a ripple. A subsonic boom disintegrated the library. The bubble exploded. Her stomach dropped.

They were on a razor ridge that serpentined the back of a snowy mountain, the sides steep and white, the sky blue and cloudless. There was barely enough room to stand. One step in either direction and she would be snowballing a hundred miles an hour.

His laughter vanished in the thin air. "Remember, you are standing in a room."

Her foot slipped off the edge, snow cascading down the face of the mountain. It didn't feel like a room. She wanted to grab him, grab something, to feel safe, reassured she wasn't about to fall off the edge of the world. He took her hand, gripped it with soft pressure, and held it up. The red snowflake rotated in the wind.

"Remember?" he said.

She imagined the treadway beneath her, felt the spongy give on the balls of her feet. She wouldn't fall. She opened her eyes without wavering. The wind whipped the curls around Jenks's cap. His rectangular glasses fogged. He smiled a row of crooked teeth.

"What now?" she shouted above the wind, wondering if she was shouting in the room, if someone would hear her in the house.

He held out his hands. Two long boards, one green and the other red, appeared. "How about this?"

She shook her head vigorously. *Are my cheeks cold?* She'd never been on a ski slope. She wasn't snowboarding down suicide hill. Real or not.

"We cannot waste a good illusion."

He tossed them down. They slid like bullets, leaving sleek trails and powdery wakes before cartwheeling over a tenuous, trembling drift. The view stirred vertigo in her head and legs. He rubbed his hands together, then pulled them apart like taffy stuck to his fingers. Shimmery red strands expanded like rising dough. He tossed the gelatinous goo in the snow. Sharp corners boxed the back end. The front billowed into graceful curves. Gold rails popped from the bottom.

Fully baked, a sleigh teetered on the ridge.

"How did you…" she said.

He climbed inside but didn't sit down. There was plenty of room to stand. The back was big enough to hold a refrigerator. It tipped back, then forward. Impossibly balanced. Like a polar bear standing on the edge of a nickel.

"No. No, I don't think—"

"This is your ride." He held up two fingers. He smiled like it was a promise. This was just an illusion. She could hang on. And if it got too scary, she'd just wake up in the library. It would be terrifying. And exhilarating.

She grasped the bar above the dashboard with dials and gauges, handles and buttons. A monitor in the center. It looked more like a spaceship. He stopped her from sitting.

"You cannot do that just yet. You will fall on the floor," he said. "Once you are proficient, you can do anything."

He brushed the red snowflake. She was standing in the room. Not a futuristic death sled. *When I am proficient?* She didn't understand the mechanics of how that would work, but then again, she didn't understand how any of this worked.

"Do not close your eyes," he said.

"Why?"

"You do not want to miss this."

❄

Tears flooded her eyes. The sleigh rocked to one side as Jenks bellowed. Every tissue in her body ached. Every muscle as rigid as winter steel, knees iron locked. Jenks's complete and senseless joy had somehow pried her eyelids open. Through frozen slits, she saw the snowy ledge ahead and just as quickly disappear below them.

They were soaring.

The wind screamed in her ears. Jenks laughed, and he let go of the bar and somehow didn't go flying. Avery couldn't unlock her fingers. The gauges bounced back and forth, lights turning red and green. The sleigh wasn't touching the slope. Her stomach was a mixed bag of fear and excitement. She closed her eyes before impact.

Snow exploded over the front, the sleigh rocking back and almost tossing her. Ice showered her cheeks. She felt it in her nostrils. And Jenks, cheering them on, whooped like a rodeo clown with nothing to lose. She thought, for a moment, of reaching up, clawing away the hiwires.

You do not want to miss this.

The slope was no longer a vertical drop. They cruised through virgin snow, a white rooster tail behind them, toward tightly packed trees. The titan trunks were as thick as water towers. They aimed for a narrow opening, like a bulldozer had cleared a path.

Into the shade of the forest, heavy branches zipped past, brushing the tops of their heads, tree trunks making *woop-woop-woop* sounds, serenading their slushing descent that kept going and going. When the ride eased to a gentle stop, there was only the sound of raspy breathing dampened by snow-laden trees. And Jenks's laughter.

Tears streamed down their cheeks. She didn't understand, couldn't comprehend, how all these sensations could be so real. Was she really just wearing hiwires? Her lips were numb, her legs frozen. Jenks bent over, gasping. She didn't know what to say. What words could she use to describe what she was feeling? Terrified. Shocked. And happy she had opened her eyes.

The snow began to melt, at warp speed, like the changing of seasons in time-lapse photography, revealing a black shiny floor. The trees thinned into book bindings. Avery and Jenks were bent over, hands on knees, gasping with smiles. The red snowflake jangled on her wrist.

Jenks said he should go, he'd been gone too long. Being out of Hugo's way was one thing. Disappearing made him grumpy. Avery was still searching for words.

"You can call out to end the session," he said. "Or swipe off."

He dragged his fingers over his eyes. His image vanished. She imagined he was back in the empty room, the looker kit in hand. She reached up, but saw something. A book had fallen off the shelf. It lay on the floor a few steps away. It was a big book, perhaps the biggest in the room, the binding nearly six inches thick. The cover was scuffed. She picked it up with both hands, traced her fingers across the title that sent shivers through her.

The Hunt.

6

There were potatoes to peel and carrots to slice. Bags of sugar were on the table, yams in a box, and a turkey in the refrigerator. All that was needed was a cook.

Avery was at the toaster. Smoke snaked from the orange coils. She looked at a black-and-white photo. That was what she'd seen in the library, Nana Rai's memory of finding the cabin. This was the picture she took. After a suicide ride down a vertical wall of snow, all she could think about was the cabin. She thought about something Jenks had said when she tried to choose a book. The library would know which one to show her.

It wanted me to see the cabin.

English muffins popped out. She melted pats of butter and plied a slab of marmalade over each one, the crusty bits crunching under the knife. She took a small dish through the hallway. The dining room table was set.

It was the exact same table at home. This was the table where Nana Rai and the family would sit, and Avery's family at home, connecting virtually with all those miles in between, would project from little cubes on chairs. Avery's family projected the exact same way. The table wasn't decorated. Except for the sculpture. It was in the middle, the elf watching Avery pass. It was still there from when they blew out birthday candles almost three months ago.

What about your present? Nana Rai had asked Avery. *The one in the box.*

She had asked Bradley to get it. Told him to give it to Avery. And what did Avery do? She guessed the logo was a hat. The Hunt began. Nana Rai closed her eyes.

It's not your fault.

On the far wall of the dining room was a strange door. Everything was a little strange: there was a chandelier with melted candles, an abstract painting, a wood carving of a spruce with feathered limbs. The arching door was heavy oak, the surface soaked with some blackish weather sealant, with a crusted iron ring in the center. Rounded rivets had been hammered into the hinges, which were anchored into rough-hewn stones. It looked like something from the Middle Ages.

An L-shaped handle, made of solid brass, was big enough for two hands. The lock, however, was modern. No skeleton key. Avery put the plate on the table. She put her ear to the door, just in case, and grabbed the latch. She leaned on it with all her weight, felt it give an inch before stopping. Even if it was unlocked, the door looked too heavy to open.

The back door of the house slammed. Someone was whistling, and heavy footsteps stamped through the house. She picked up her plate and walked quietly down a dark hall. Uncle Sage was stacking firewood on the hearth. A log in one hand, half a powdered donut in the other. Shirt crawling halfway up the small of his back. He plunked the logs down one at a time, humming with his mouth full. He slid the iron curtain open.

"Oh, sweet Christmas!" Uncle Sage caught his heel on a log and went down on his backside. "My lord, child," he said, "you walk like a cat."

"Expecting a ghost?" Avery said.

"Expecting no one." He took her offered hand and came up easily for a man his size. He brushed his pants, eyes shifting back and forth. "Have you seen one?"

"A ghost? No."

"Good. Good."

If ghosts were real, this house would be a resort. He retrieved the donut. A patch of powder and a splash of jelly remained on the brick face. He brushed the soot off one side and licked his finger.

"Perhaps you can help," he said, powder puffing from his lips. "Maggy wants a blazing fire when they get back from the airport. If you get this mess cleaned up, I'll do this over here."

She stacked the logs. It was the least she could do. She assumed Uncle Sage would get the fireplace prepped for lighting, but apparently, *doing this over here* meant eating the rest of the donut.

"Uncle Sage?"

"Hmm." He stood back. "Another load will do. There's more out back, if you wouldn't mind."

"Why is there a castle door?"

"A what?"

"A castle door in the dining room."

He scratched his ruddy cheek, squinting. "Your nana collected many strange things. Be more specific."

"The dining room, where you eat? There's a big heavy door on the wall with iron rings."

"Oh, that castle door," he finally said. "It's locked."

"But why a castle door?"

"Why did your nana do half the things she did?"

He had a point. "Why is it locked?"

"She locked it a few years back. Maybe it was ten years." He looked at the ceiling. "Or was it eight?"

"Is the elevator in there?"

"Well, that's part of it. The girls rode it constantly. Easier to lock it up than tell them no, which your nana did no less than a hundred times."

"Is it, uh, is the elevator still working?" She played it coy.

He shrugged, then knelt on the hearth with a groan and began scooping ashes with a small shovel. "Maggy called a locksmith to open the door. He hasn't come yet."

"What's in there?" Avery said.

He looked over his shoulder. Rolls bunched on the back of his neck. "You getting bored, is that it, lass? You came too early, you and your mum, seeing as the ceremony is a month away. Not much to do here except stay warm."

"Was it a library?" Avery said.

"Was?"

"Yeah, well, I just heard someone say it was a library. But not anymore." She didn't want to call out Jenks. That would lead to more questions.

"It was." Uncle Sage leaned his pudgy hands on the ash scoop. "It very well could be storage, for all we know. Nana Rai never threw anything away."

"So you don't know what's in there?"

"Nope."

He sneezed into a handkerchief. It sounded like a clown car. He stuffed a wad of newspaper under the rack and lit it, rubbing his hands together. He didn't seem to know anything about that room. The room she saw would have been a major renovation. Avery picked up her plate.

"So," he said, "more wood, then?"

"Right."

"And, um, any more of those?"

Avery offered the plate. He plucked off the half-eaten muffin.

❄

THE CHRISTMAS TREE was anchored in an elaborately engineered stand hidden beneath a velvet cover. Silver chimes and countless ornaments hung from the branches, making for a pleasant song when the wind blew. Sometimes Avery heard it at night, in her dreams, like the tree was singing. A star was on top and, mercifully, had not lit up. It was outside her bedroom window.

Fresh snow had fallen; frozen tracks from the trucks and tractors. A stage was halfway complete, boards stacked on sawhorses, boxes nestled under a blanket of snow. A firepit had been dug out, the dirt still in a pile. A ring of boulders was around the perimeter. Sections of a pine tree, the bark coarse and chunky, were placed for seating. In addition to the benches, the firepit would accommodate sixty people or more.

She started loading a cart with firewood. An ax was buried in a stump. There were fresh footsteps, wide and heavy, that led to the woods. Avery followed with a log in hand. The chimney on the house was puffing a thin stream of gray smoke. Uncle Sage already had the fire going.

She stepped into the shade of the trees, the temperature dropping a few degrees. The path was a soft bed of branches and needles; frosty layers accumulated where snow found a way through the trees. Her breath grew dense, and she had nearly turned around. A mossy roof caught her eye.

It was a shed. Not the cabin from the picture, but similar. Square-cut trunks dovetailed at the corners, the seams packed with mud. Cedar shingles were clumped with moss and algae, icicles clinging to the eaves. There were no windows.

Chairs, fashioned from saplings and vines, were outside the door overlooking a small stream, water trickling beneath the ice. A tiny figure made of sticks and twine was on a wrought-iron table between the chairs, the legs stuck between iron gaps, arms held out for a hug.

The ground was soft with needles. She imagined sleeping on it in the summer, tucked into a sleeping bag with the sound of the stream nearby. Getting up as the sun filtered through the limbs, dappling the ground, sitting in one of the chairs with coffee. She could see Nana Rai doing such a thing.

Voices were inside the shed.

They were muffled. Indecipherable. One was gruff, like sandpaper on a chalkboard. Footsteps wandered around, pacing from one end to the other. The person would pause and listen. She held her breath to hear someone answer. They weren't arguing, but the conversation was tense. She moved closer, pressed her ear to the door. The step creaked.

The voices went silent.

Avery swallowed her breath, fighting the urge to run. The door opened before she could turn around. It was dark inside. A short, bearded man peeked out. Small hazel eyes set deep in pudgy cheeks stared from beneath furrowed eyebrows.

"Sorry," Avery said. "I was just, I was looking for firewood and heard voices—"

Hugo stepped out. He turned on the top step. The door, unusually thick, snapped closed with a metallic click. Keys jangled out of his pocket. He turned not one but two locks, checking the doorknob before stepping to the ground, kicking up brown needles as he shuffled, twigs snapping under his wide boots.

He went back to the house. Without a word.

Avery's heart was in her throat. She didn't want to follow him. Just let him get back into his van and leave. She went to the shed and listened. Maybe she imagined there was another voice. She rapped on the door. It rang like a slab of iron. No one answered.

❄

"Happy Thanksgiving!"

Dad dropped his suitcase. Avery ran to the front porch, her bare feet on the frozen boards, and threw her arms around him. It had been two months since she'd seen him. It felt like two years. He was still thick in the middle, shoulders sharp like clothes hangers. And still smelled like Dad.

"Or should I say merry Christmas?" He looked at the lights hanging from the eaves.

Bradley lugged the rest of the bags, gawking at the house like Avery had done. His coat was too thin for the weather. Aunt Mag elbowed Uncle Sage when Bradley slipped on the frozen concrete. Uncle Sage had remembered the fireplace but not salting the sidewalk. Bradley took the steps one at a time, put one arm around Avery.

"Hey, skunk." It wasn't the nicest thing he could say, but she was glad to hear it. She could feel his ribs through the coat.

Mom stood at the car, dressed in her finest. Watching her kids hug was the only thing she wanted for Christmas. All it took was two months apart.

"Inside, ya warmbloods," Uncle Sage announced. "Before your snot freezes."

They stomped their shoes, then gathered around the fireplace. Mom hooked her arm around Dad's elbow, head on his shoulder. The cousins brought out trays of hot tea and coffee. Dad and Bradley had their hands at the fire, Bradley still with a bag slung over his shoulder, holding it to his chest.

"Thought you weren't coming till the ceremony," Uncle Sage said.

"Bradley insisted," Dad said. "Besides, I hear there's an opening for a cook."

He pulled up two sweatshirts. His apron was tucked into his pants. Uncle Sage bellowed laughter, then clapped like a little boy on Christmas morning.

"And we thought you could use some help," Dad said. "An extra pair of hands couldn't hurt."

"Well, you missed the heavy lifting out back," Uncle Sage said.

"So did someone else," Aunt Mag said.

"Without supervision," Uncle Sage said, "it's chaos."

They talked about the flight, the man who slept next to Dad with his mouth open, the snowstorm on their connection, and the turbulence that made Bradley sick. He hadn't eaten since they left. When the cousins offered a plate of cookies, he refused.

"Girls," Mom said, "why don't you show Bradley to his room."

The cousins tried to take his bags. "I've got it," he said.

They took the spiral staircase, the treads creaking under the weight. The cousins, wearing striped yoga pants and furry boots, gave him the grand tour Avery didn't get, the works of art on the walls, how they helped Nana Rai frame them, when the walls were a different color. Bradley was panting when they reached the third floor, dropping his bag but not the one over his shoulder.

"Two sleepers," Meeho said, pointing at the bedrooms. "Peepers on the back with connective ports in the baseboards."

Avery had no idea what that meant. Bradley was still taking in the sights and smells, history oozing from the walls like musty spirits. His breath came out in thin wisps; perhaps he was wishing he'd stayed by the fire a bit longer.

"The hole up." Meeho pointed at the room at the end of the hall.

"Hole up?" Bradley said.

"Nana Rai's room," Flinn said. "Locked and chocked for a clip."

Bradley looked at Avery. She knew what Flinn meant—*it's been locked for a while*—but didn't tell him. It didn't seem like the smart thing to say it wasn't locked a week ago.

Meeho opened the bedroom next to Avery's room. It was smaller. Bradley dropped a bag on the bed, looked out the window recessed in a slanted ceiling, holding the other bag against his chest. He took a deep breath, staring at the distant mountain.

"On the Hunt, B?" Flinn said.

He was startled by the question, deep in thought. Or maybe he was already running a lens. "No. Just researching," he said, without turning. "Need to be careful."

"BT posting a leaderboard now," Meeho said. "What's your serial?"

Bradley looked at Avery for translation again. Avery didn't know that one.

"Serial number scripted inside your surfers," Flinn said. "Tiny letter-numbers. Hello?"

"Oh, the identifier." He shook his head. "I don't know."

"You're a bit foggy?" Meeho said.

"No, I just don't know it. It's a long sequence."

"You toting?" Flinn gestured to the bag over his shoulder. He acted like a Secret Service agent guarding nuclear codes.

"I'm not hunting," he said.

"Just fine," Meeho said. "The Hunt's getting a bit slow. Some of the hunters aren't even trying to find the elf. I get it, though. Try to find an elf in the world like looking for a rock in the ocean. Scratch that."

"Toymaker." Bradley turned. "They're looking for the Toymaker."

The cousins looked at each other, then Avery. "'K then," Meeho said. "Ring-a-ding."

They left him at the window. Avery wanted to stay and talk, but it was better to get the cousins out of his room. He had a lot on his mind besides translating cousin-speak. They went down to Avery's room.

"*Research*." Meeho pulled purple gum between her teeth. "He's long hauling."

"What'd you mean?" Avery said.

"Some of the hunters aren't logging off," Flinn whispered. "They're just staying in the Hunt for, like, days and days. He's big eyed, Av. Just like long haulers."

He did look hyper alert. He'd also just travelled for twenty-four hours.

"You know about the body parlors?" Meeho said. "Sleep-ins where hunters go all in with catheters and feeder tubes. Like total commitment. Max obsession." Meeho made circles around her eyes. "Big eyes, Av."

Bradley is lying, they're saying. He's in the Hunt. He looks exhausted because he's long hauling. But if that's true, why would he insist on coming early?

The cousins speculated about Bradley's play. Avery couldn't understand them without her full attention. She figured they wanted to find him in the highlights that were posted public. They had their lookers tucked into the front pockets of their pink hoodies.

"Have you been inside Nana's room?" Avery asked. "The one at the end of the hall?"

"Been a clip," Meeho said.

"Like how long ago?"

Meeho and Flinn discussed it, adding numbers, deciding it was on their birthday when Nana Rai had locked it for good.

"Ten years?" Avery said.

"Point," Meeho said.

"What did you do in there before she locked it?" Avery said.

"Nana Rai told stories, did arts." Meeho looked at the ceiling like she was remembering. "Hearts, that room."

"Hearts," Flinn added.

"So what's it look like?" Avery said, pretending.

They shrugged, said there were books, boxes and things. They didn't seem impressed. *I mean, there's a glass ceiling and a gnarly tree. How could they not remember?*

"Why'd she lock it?" Avery asked.

"Elevator," they both said. Then, in cousin-speak, talked about riding up and down, jumping to make their stomachs flip, and doing that all day. Uncle Sage was right.

"So you went down to the library?" Avery asked.

"Library?" Flinn said. "You mean tearoom."

"It was a library, Flinn." Meeho stuck her gum on a piece of paper and left it on the desk. "Remember? Books on the shelves."

"Twenty books does not make a library, Mee," Flinn said.

"Oh, it was way more than twenty, Flee."

Flinn said it was a tearoom with books. Meeho said it was a library with tea. Then they argued about how many books were in there. Flinn finally admitted it was more like a thousand. Meeho said it was more than that.

"So the library is behind the castle door?" Avery said.

"Point," Meeho said. "Nana Rai locked that, too. Mom was more unhappy about that than we were. She said someone convinced Nana to do it."

"Who?" Avery said.

"Hugo," they said.

She went to the desk, wadded up the paper with Meeho's gum. "Who exactly is Hugo?" Avery asked.

"He's a helper," Flinn said. "*My helper* Nana Rai called him."

"Sir Grumpalot," Meeho said.

Flinn snorted. "Captain Bigfoot."

Uncle Sage was in the backyard, showing Dad the stage. They

craned their necks to look at the three-story Christmas tree, oblivious to the footsteps leading into the woods.

"I found a shed in the woods," Avery said.

"The playhouse," Flinn said. "She locked that, too."

"You've been inside it?" Avery asked.

They shook their heads. In the summer, they'd go play in the stream when they were little. They called it a playhouse because it looked like a playhouse. But it was always locked. And no one ever went inside.

"Hugo was in there," Avery said. "He was talking to someone. Then he heard me, I think, and came out."

"Probably talking to his self," Flinn said.

"It sounded like he was talking to his son." Avery paced around the rug. "And locked him in there."

"Grumpalot's got a son?" Meeho said.

"Is he cute?" Flinn asked.

Avery described him. Rectangular glasses, dark curly hair. Sort of skinny. She didn't think he was cute at first. But that had changed.

"Paints his toenail?" Meeho said.

"It's his anchor," Avery said.

They frowned, shook their heads. They didn't understand her, for once. Avery explained the anchor, like Jenks had taught her. She held up her hand, the silver snowflake dangling on her wrist.

"I bet he just paints his toenails," Meeho said. "Big hearts."

They touched fingertips. Avery had no idea what that meant. Maybe it had something to do with gum since they unwrapped a new piece, tore it in half and put it in each other's mouths.

Aunt Mag called up the staircase to come down. Bradley's bedroom was closed. The cousins had their phones out, fuzzy boots sliding across the floor. Meeho looked down the hall. As if reading Avery's mind, she went to Nana's room and turned the knob. She peeled a bubble off her lips.

It was locked.

7

Bluish moonlight passed through the window. The Christmas tree sang its song in a soft breeze. Avery turned the hiwires over in her hands, watching the branches sway, when she heard a door close.

Her dad's snores could be heard from the second floor. A tryptophan coma had overtaken him after dessert. Mom had pulled him up the steps. Avery stood outside her bedroom. The bathroom door opened. Bradley went back to his room. He'd been sullen at Thanksgiving, had gone upstairs before Dad passed out in front of the fireplace.

She crept down the hall, then, with one finger, lightly knocked. When he didn't answer, she did it again. He answered the third time. Fully dressed, a collared shirt buttoned all the way, wrinkled khakis and bare feet.

"Can't sleep?" she said.

"Jet lag."

"Right." She peered at his bed. Moonlight highlighted the surfers. "Can we talk?"

"It's midnight. Why not."

"Dad said you wanted to come early."

"This is keeping you awake?"

"I want to know why."

He ran his hand over his head. His hair, the longest it had been in years, combed between his fingers. "Family time, Av. Why else?"

"Family." She looked around, then whispered, "You know you rub your head when you lie. You know that, right?"

"What do you want me to say?"

She pushed past him. The chimes were louder in his room. The blankets were thrown back, the pillow dented. The surfers were on the mattress, so black they looked like an absence of space on a white sheet.

"Don't touch," he snapped. She jumped a little. Then he said, softer, "They're not for you."

"How much are you doing this? All day?"

"It's work, Av."

"Are you long hauling?"

"Long hauling?"

"Flinn and Meeho said people are hooking up to feeding tubes so they don't have to come out."

"Yeah, well, I eat like a normal person."

"You're not eating much."

He sat on the bed, putting the surfers in the bag, the one he'd refused to take off when he arrived. There was another looker kit inside. The normal kind. The kind for work. There was a stack of journals, folders and notebooks on the dresser to prove he was working, the Avocado logo on the covers. A shiny notebook was labelled *Project Apricot*.

She was tempted to pry it open, to see what he was doing, but he'd already snapped at her once.

"What's it like?" she said. "The Hunt."

He nodded, thinking. Debating whether to give a standard Bradley answer to end a conversation. Then he looked up, his eyes tired, green irises swimming in yellowish pools. "It's real in there, Av. So real that this, right now, feels like a dream."

Her heart skipped. "That... that sounds like reality confusion."

"I got a grip." He started reaching for his head. Stopped. "It's just work. It's what I do."

She believed him. At least, she wanted to. This was all he ever did, but the surfers were different. He was twitchy, the way his fingers crawled on his thigh, itching to get back to the surfers. But, if she was honest, she understood what he meant. It was like a whole new universe in there, waiting to be discovered. Like looking for that one piece of the puzzle, and when you got it, you wanted to find the next one. And the next.

"Do you have an anchor?" she said.

"How do you know about anchors?"

"It's 101 stuff. What is it?"

He pulled up his sleeve. The Hunt logo, the size of a quarter, was tattooed on the inside of his wrist, black lines slightly darker than his brown skin.

"Wow," she said dully. "You really did that."

"It turns white when I'm inside."

"Mom know you did that?"

"I'm a grown man, Av. Don't get any ideas."

"I'm not telling her."

"No, I mean don't stick yourself."

"I've already got an anchor." She shook her bracelet.

"What for?"

She opened his bedroom door and listened. Avery tugged on the bag that contained his looker kit and the surfers, held up her hiwires and whispered, "I'll show you."

She walked slowly, easing her weight into each step, half tiptoeing to time her creaking footsteps with Dad's snores. She didn't know if Bradley would follow. If he didn't, she would go without him.

A line of dim, bluish light was at the bottom of Nana's room door. She heard Bradley follow, the bag at his side. She didn't even know if this was going to work. If it didn't, she'd have to explain what was in there. It had been a week since she went with Jenks.

The latch popped.

The hinges groaned. Bradley groaned with curiosity. The room was steeped in moonlight. The tree reached out, softly lit from above, shadows scattered across the clutter, transforming objects into mysterious apparitions. Like things sleeping. The moon was partially obscured through the murky ceiling, the stars blurred points of light.

Bradley wandered in, mouth open, touching dusty items, looking up at the dangling fruit. She followed him to the table. The bag at his side knocked over a tin can.

"Careful," she whispered.

Everything on the table was exactly where it had been when Jenks had brought her. A small clay bowl, something Nana Rai would have made, was full of dried tubes of paint. Bradley picked one up.

"Come on," she whispered.

She was careful not to bump anything that would send a priceless tower of Nana Rai's memorabilia to the floor. She couldn't hear her dad anymore, hoping he'd just rolled over. The Christmas tree chimes, though, were singing louder. It was dark inside the elevator. She lit her phone to see the buttons.

"How'd you find this?" he said.

"A friend."

The elevator wobbled slightly when he stepped inside. The doors rumbled closed. Her phone illuminated the panel. She held her breath and pressed the bottom button. There was a sudden drop, like before. Bradley put his hand out. Avery tensed, hoping the sound of the elevator wouldn't wake their parents.

Slowly, smoothly, it descended. Her breath grew denser, whiter. The floor turned cold, chilling the soles of her feet. Her skin tightened. She'd forgotten about the temperature drop. Bradley was wearing a long-sleeved shirt. So was she, but he was a daisy, wilting at first frost. They should go back for warmer clothes.

The door slid open.

The frigid air stole her breath. The expanse contained an endless silence. Then she realized she couldn't hear the chimes anymore. Bradley wandered out, craning his neck to see the curved ceiling. It was dark, but light oozed from the walls, reflected off the polished floor. The matte treadways were dull and rough.

"What is this?" he said, his voice bouncing off the walls.

"I don't think anyone knows this is here. Nana Rai locked it up, like, ten years ago. Aunt Mag said the elevators weren't working; the cousins said it was because they rode the elevators too much."

He ran his fingers over the wall. Tracks momentarily glowed. He leaned in, watched them fade. "This is state of the art," he said, more to himself. "Hyper-conductive overlay with meshworking." He turned to her, amazement in his wide eyes. "How'd she do this?"

"Hugo did it."

He didn't know who Hugo was. Didn't seem to care. "How could no one not know she built this?"

"Maybe they do and just don't want anyone in here."

"So how did you find it?"

She explained who Jenks was, what Hugo did for Nana Rai. Bradley half-listened, ending up in the center of the room, bag in hand. The floor was as hard as ice and nearly as cold. It was painful on her feet. At least Bradley was wearing socks.

"These are integrated treadways." He bounced on the circular pad.

Avery stood on the other treadway, the warm texture bringing relief. "Wanna see the library?"

"No. No, not now. I want to see what this place does."

"That's what I mean." She held up her hiwires.

"You learned how to use them?"

"No thanks to you."

He smiled a guiltless smile, then dug the looker kit out of the bag. He put them on first, and she watched him look around, hands slowly lowering. She followed him in, the room transforming into the shelves and brassy ladders, mist rolling overhead, obscuring the endless heights.

"This..." he said, words trailing. "What is this?"

"It's her stories. She collected them, recorded them somehow. Put them in here. But I think it's more than that. He showed me one. It was totally immersive, and it didn't feel like a story."

"What was it?"

She told him about Nana Rai hiking, how young she looked. Happy. "I think they're memories."

He dragged his fingers over the bindings like she'd done the first time. Dust billowed from the jackets. He hooked his finger over the spine of a thick hardback, tipped it out. It opened in his hands. The pages fluttered, exhaled a blast of wind, letters tumbling off the pages like debris in a storm. They swirled around, clicking together like small keys finding slotted keyholes. A fire ignited. And then whoosh.

They were in a small room.

The walls were horizontal logs, roughhewn and pasted with plaster or mud, flickering with orange light from a roaring fireplace. Two stockings hung from the mantel, bulky with gifts. A small Christmas tree was in the corner with presents wrapped in brown paper, bows tied with coarse twine, sprigs of dried flowers tucked beneath. A stuffed toy beneath the branches, resembling a panda bear.

"She's beautiful," Bradley said.

He'd seen pictures of Nana Rai when she was younger, but standing in front of her was different. She was rocking in a chair, humming. The sound of a sharp edge on wood, shavings dropping into a bucket between her feet. The smell of fresh cedar.

"What was she using to record the experience?" he said. "This is all external. I mean, she could gloss the details from a memory download, but not what she looked like."

Jenks had explained it before, but she couldn't remember what he said. It made sense at the time, but now, listening to Bradley, it didn't. How could she have a vivid memory of what she looked like?

This was the cabin, the one Nana Rai had photographed. A small bed was in the corner. A table and two chairs, both carved from saplings, flecks of bark still attached to the legs. There was nothing remarkable about it. Just Nana Rai carving.

Something thunked outside. The hollow clatter of wood splitting, pieces falling into a pile. The window was an intricate pattern of frost, crusted with snow. The door was short. Bradley would have to duck to get through it. He was staring at pegs hammered into the wall.

Avery recognized the coat and hat that Nana Rai had been wearing in the first memory. The furry boots below them in a puddle of melted snow.

Next to it was a forest green coat. It was worn at the elbows, the tail ragged. Bradley studied it from both sides. Then he tried the door. It wouldn't move. The handle didn't budge, like it was chiseled from granite. He ran to the window.

"Where is this?" he said.

"Where's what?"

"The cabin!" He rubbed the window. It didn't make a sound, the frost obscuring his view. "Where's this cabin?"

"I don't know."

He went back to the door and desperately leaned into it. He was pushed back, rejected from going through the illusion, as if the door forbade it. Or there just wasn't anything out there. Just the sound of chopping.

"It's somewhere in the woods," was all Avery knew to say. "She was hiking—"

Bradley dragged his fingers across his eyes, stripping the looker kit off. His image dissolved. Avery was alone, wondering what just happened. Nana Rai's chair creaked. She had put the carving on the mantel above the stockings. It was taking shape. A plump little figure still unfinished. It didn't look like an elf yet. She reached into a big bag, retrieved a ball of yarn. Knitting needles clacked in one hand.

Avery reached up to pull the hiwires off just as a melody rose. Nana Rai began singing.

"Christmas is coming."

❋

THE LOOKER KIT was on the floor. Bradley wore the surfers now.

He was on the treadway, shivering, reaching to rearrange things she couldn't see, like invisible pegs on a pegboard. Sliding them, turning them, pulling something down to study. He moved slowly, the cold working deep inside him. He appeared to pack items on his hip. And then he was running, arms pumping, treadway sliding under his feet.

He's in the Hunt.

Something in the cabin had set him off. She could log onto the public domain that followed the Hunt, but she didn't know how to find it or if it was even live. Even if it was, she wouldn't know how to find him, not without the identifier stamped on his surfers, not without taking them off his face.

She put the hiwires back on. The library reappeared. She scanned the lower shelves, many of the spines lacking titles. It was a thick book she was looking for, gold lettering embossed on the cover. It had been on the floor when she last saw it. There were so many books. She'd never find it with a random search. But there, two shelves off the floor, sticking out an inch or two like it hadn't been fully shelved, was the one she was looking for. Like the library knew what she needed.

The Hunt.

She opened it. The pages shredded into bits of data. Snow-laden evergreens appeared in the haze. A blanket of snow spread under a clear blue sky, tiny flecks of drifting snowflakes reflecting the sunlight. There was a hum in the distance, like a gravity booster in a video game. Something glided over the flat land, weaving between trees. White waves tossed in its wake. It was a snowmobile, but, at least from a distance, it appeared to hover above the snow.

It veered away, turning toward the horizon. A white rooster tail tossed behind it, rainbows twinkling in the sunlight. The hum faded. The trees all looked the same, stalwarts in a frozen landscape. All except one.

It was dipped in gold and covered with ornaments. A glowing star on top. And presents beneath its sagging limbs. Someone was reaching for a gold-wrapped gift, the silver ribbon flecked with glitter. He wore black coveralls, snug and studded. A bag attached to a wide belt. And his head was shaved.

She started toward him, the snow nearly up to her knees. She trudged through it like a shallow pond, but the snow didn't move.

There were no tracks behind her. The person looked like Bradley: the cropped hair, hazel eyes. The ridge of his brow pinched in concentration.

"Bradley," she wheezed.

Undistracted, he pulled the silvery ribbon. The gift popped. Specks of confetti showered the snow. No jack-in-the-box sprang out. A glowing white orb floated out and hovered before him. Light swirled inside it, pulsing yellow sunbeams in all directions.

Avery couldn't look directly at it. She held up her hand, watched Bradley reach for it. The fiery ball swallowed his hand, turning his arm iridescent. The sleeve on his coveralls flipped colors—blacks turning white, whites turning black. He was pale, almost ghostly, when he opened the pouch on his hip. The hovering globe sucked inside like a vacuum pulling a dust bunny from the couch. The pouch bulged momentarily. And then it was gone. Just bits of confetti and the silver ribbon left in the snow.

"Assistance," he said.

An object fell from the sky. Thin translucent strands attached to wooden appendages, the life-sized puppet dropped like a superhero. The top hat tipped forward on a blocky head. He pushed it back with a shiny finger. The painted eyes peered up.

"Hello there, hunter." The puppet pulled a pocket watch from his hip. "How may I assist?"

"Give me a list of all the cabins in the world," Bradley said.

"Cabins?" BT placed his hand over the red heart. "Could you be just a tiny bit more specific?"

"One-room cabins made of logs. And a fireplace."

"Hmmm. A little vague."

"Remotely located where there's snow."

He wagged his finger. "Not much to go on, dear hunter."

"That's all I've got."

BT stood taller, the wonky joints clacking. The puppet sank the tip of its gnarly cane into the snow and gestured with an open palm. "There you have it."

Bright little bits floated from his hand like tiny embers. Bradley swept them up. They coalesced into lines. Bradley scrolled through the holographic code, muttering things to narrow his search. The list was quickly culled down to several lines.

He had only seen the inside of the cabin. Avery hadn't showed him the first memory when Nana Rai had discovered it, or the picture from the photo album. It might help him. But he couldn't hear her and clearly didn't see her standing next to him. And, for some reason, even if he could, she wasn't sure she wanted to tell him.

BT, with both hands over the end of the cane, teetered forward. Leaning at an impossible angle. The thin strands had vanished.

"A cabin, a cabin," he said. "Want to share what you know?"

Bradley continued working the list, talking to himself in the heat of discovery. BT peered at the data. Bradley ignored him.

The puppet's mouth fell open. "All the toys and little boys," he sang, off-tune and wavering, the mouth clapping open and closed, "the twirls and little girls, give what they need, to get what they want."

"Thass ahl." Bradley waved at the puppet, frustrated.

BT tipped the hat and bowed at the jointed waist. "Merry, merry then, dear hunter."

He held out his arms. The translucent strings reappeared to yank him into the blue sky. He launched like a rocket, a tiny speck that grew smaller and smaller. Then, bip, vanished. Bradley reached into the pouch. A slew of items fluttered out. They organized into icons and symbols, details bulleted beneath them. It was an inventory of things he'd collected. Where he'd stuffed the glowing orb that popped out of the gift.

He's playing the game.

He scrolled through it, each item ticking. His hands shook. The inventory contained brief flashes of elven with long coats and reindeer soaring across a full moon. Snowmen in blizzards and big red sleighs. Green floppy hats and intricately etched orbs. He found what he was looking for and threw it on the ground. A global map surrounded him. He pulled more items from the inventory. Little dots lit up. Lines crisscrossed and intersected, some glowing, others fading. He muttered gibberish, words blending together.

"Bradley?" she said. He looked through her, his teeth violently chattering. *Why can't he see me?*

He flipped through the inventory again. This time a giant machine fell on the snow, like the one she'd seen in the distance, a snowmobile thing without treads or skis. A big display inside a curved windshield. He checked the last few items of inventory, his fingers barely moving, his movements jerky and unsure. He was starting and stopping, like an overheated processor.

He's freezing.

Avery reached up to swipe off her hiwires; then, just as he mounted the vehicle, she grabbed his inventory before it sucked back into his pouch. It felt like particles of sand, the weight of it trickling up her arm.

She pulled the hiwires off. Bradley was on the treadway, bent at the knees. His body quaking. His lips an unnatural blue.

"Bradley!" she shouted, not caring if their parents heard her. "Bradley!"

She grabbed his hands, as cold as the Arctic. She shook his shoulders, screamed again. She was about to strip the surfers off, unsure if that would shock him, when he lifted his hand. Slowly, he pushed the surfers up. Eyes wide and white, he tried to say something, but the words swelled on his numb tongue.

8

"He's awake," Mom said.

"Did you tuck him in?" Dad said, his hands in soapy dishwater.

"Excuse me?"

"He's twenty-five, dear. It's just a cold."

Mom put her gloves on, leaning against the counter. "I'm concerned he's ill, Dell."

"Sorry." He pulled his hands out of the sink, suds dripping off pale green rubber gloves. "Of course, you're right."

She stared a moment longer. "Could you make him some tea?" she asked. "And something to eat. He looks like he hasn't eaten in days. Make something warm. And no sugar." She nodded firmly. "Please."

"At your service," he said.

"Avery," she said, "please dress appropriately. I do not need both of my children catching cold."

Avery, finishing her dad's omelet, had hoped Mom wouldn't notice her bare feet.

"When your father is done making his son breakfast," Mom said, wrapping a scarf around her neck, "please take it up to him."

"Yes, ma'am."

"I've got a meeting after lunch. I'll be home before dinner. I'm sure your father can manage while I'm gone." She stopped at the back door. "And I want Bradley outside when he's feeling well. He has spent too much time inside. He needs fresh air and exercise. There's plenty of that in the backyard."

Dad dried his hands, then buttoned the top button of her wool coat and tugged the knitted cap over her ears. Earrings swung on her earlobes.

"You look darling, darling." He kissed her nose. She thawed a bit, still not smiling, and slammed the back door on her way out. She wasn't mad, the door was sticky, but it was hard to tell.

Dad looked out the window, watching her cross the yard. He put the kettle on the stove, then heated a pan. He propped his phone on the windowsill, playing something festive, going to the refrigerator for eggs, alfalfa sprouts, and other things Mom would approve of.

Avery took out her phone. She'd been thinking about that folder on Bradley's dresser. Her search resulted in mostly dessert recipes and salads. She went directly to the Avocado, Inc., website. *The Future Is Now*, it said in bold font. Not very original. She searched the website, this time found something unrelated to food.

Project Apricot.

It was a page of current projects. Not much information, just fancy photos and current technology. A picture of Bradley leaning over technicians in white coats, who looked older than him.

"Dad?"

"Hmm."

"What's Project Apricot?"

He looked over his shoulder. "Why?"

"Bradley mentioned it." She shrugged. "Sounded interesting."

"Huh." He diced a green pepper. Bradley didn't talk about work. Not to Avery. "What'd he say?"

"Not much. Just that it's some sort of reality splitter. Like a mirrored alternate reality with the potential for experimentation without consequences, circumventing the need for immense resources through innovation."

The chopping stopped. "He said all that?"

"Well, that's what this says." She read it straight from the website. No company secrets revealed. Just enough to whet investor appetite.

"Ah," he said. "It's something the company's been developing for a while. A vivid virtual reality environment that's, I guess you could say, indistinguishable from reality." He knocked the counter, as if that meant something. *This right here is real.* Then he sliced an onion.

"Does it have anything to do with the Hunt?" she said.

"The Hunt?"

"Dad." She blinked heavily. He was playing dumb.

"Let's just say there's concern someone leaked company secrets."

Avery scrolled through the page, not finding any more information. If Project Apricot was searching to stabilize a mirrored reality, BT and Company had beat them to it. An ex-employee, maybe. Dad was tight-lipped about these things. Even with Mom.

"I thought the company was pursuing transference technology," she said.

"The what?" He wanted this conversation to end.

"Dad, that's not a secret. Bradley had the glove at my birthday; we all put it on. Nana Rai had one, remember? Bradley said you were working on body swapping through neural networking."

He chuckled. "Bradley's a bit optimistic."

Avery took her plate to the sink. The water was hot. She put the gloves on and cleaned her plate. Outside, the stage construction was in progress. Mom was with Aunt Maggy, leaning against each other for warmth, each holding one end of a fluttering paper. Someone was on a ladder, swinging a hammer.

"Have you been following it?" She turned and clarified, "The Hunt."

"Ah, well, it's a nice game. An elaborate environment." He said it sort of funny, half-jokey. The sort of response to a silly question.

"Is that all it is, a game?"

"We don't know yet. Still a lot of questions."

"What do you think it is?"

He shrugged. "Data collection, most likely."

"That's it?"

He cracked eggs in a bowl. "Hmm-mm."

He didn't want to talk about it. Okay. There was concern about what the game really was. Maybe his concern was more about Avocado company secrets. BT and Company did the mirrored reality first, which would mean Avocado research and development was lagging. Which could mean losing money. Lots of it.

A beam fell off a post outside, splintered a deck board. Hugo waved his arms. Mom and Aunt Mag checked on the volunteer to make sure he wasn't hurt. Avery stirred the onions and green peppers, watched Hugo assess the damage.

"How well did you know Nana Rai?" she asked.

"Nana Rai," Dad repeated cheerfully. Happy to change the subject. "We came here once after you were born. It was, as you can imagine, quite a show."

"Once?"

"Nana was always busy. Your mother felt we were a distraction. Besides, we were busy, too. Once virtual meetup was developed, it was so much easier to see her that way. Less stress on your mother. And Nana."

"Did Nana Rai ever visit us?" Avery asked.

"For a time, when you were little. You probably don't remember." He laughed as he poured tea. "She came to our wedding."

"What so funny?"

"It was an outdoor wedding in January. A bit chilly back home. Nothing like this, but frosty. Honestly, I think your mother wanted it that way so Nana would come. Nana wasn't fond of our summers. She sat in the front row, wearing this long green gown that looked sort of like sod. It wasn't actually grass. I'm not sure what it was, but there were little lights in it, tiny ones, flashing red and green and blue. It was so distracting. I remember reading our vows, thinking someone forgot to unplug the Christmas tree."

He laughed again, shaking his head.

"She had sticks in her hair."

"Sticks?" Avery said.

"Sticks. Random sticks with lichen and leaves and berries. It was... something. I'm not sure what people thought, but your nana wasn't much to care what people thought. She was who she was. That's why everyone loved her."

He pointed at the pan. Avery sprinkled the cheese. "She loved Christmas," Avery said.

"That she did. And that's why she stayed here, I think. The cold, the snow and ice. We always said the only way your nana would move is if they built a town on the North Pole."

"So why did Mom move away?"

"Well, for one, your mother doesn't like the cold. She hasn't an ounce of fat and shivers when she opens a refrigerator. And your nana insisted she leave."

"She kicked her out?"

"No, not that. She wanted her to see the world, to travel. Get far away from the nest. Then there was school and a career. Then there was me. And then there was Bradley."

He shoveled the omelet and gently slid it on a plate, sprinkled it with chives. He dumped some leftover potatoes in the pan to reheat and prepared a tray with a napkin and silverware. He sang along with the next song, banging a spoon on the counter. The hammering of nails seemed to fall in tune.

"Do you know where this is?" Avery pulled the photo of the cabin out of her pocket.

He held it with one hand and squinted. "Where'd you get this?" He grimaced honestly. "It could be anywhere, hon. Nana travelled all over the world. Speaking of which."

He peeked out the window. Hugo was pulling up the broken deck boards while volunteers hoisted the beam again.

"I'm not looking forward to the ceremony," he whispered.

"You're not?"

"The hike," he whispered. "Do you know how cold that's going to be? Your mother, oh, your mother. She won't thaw out till July."

"What hike?"

"It's all on your nana's wish list. But that... that should be fun." He nodded at the backyard. "I don't know why your nana wanted it so elaborate. Not that many people live around here. But your mother and aunt shall honor the list," he sang.

Dad scooped out the potatoes and handed the tray to Avery, wiping his hands on his apron. With a little salute, he bid her good luck on her journey up the steps.

"And your mom's right," he said. "Put some socks on."

❄

THE TEA SPILLED over the sides. A steaming pool crept across the tray. Avery couldn't stop it, climbing the awkward spiral, nursing resentment for having to tote food to her twenty-five-year-old brother.

She was halfway up when she heard footsteps. She got to the third floor. The hammering continued outside. The construction sounded like a symphony of blunt instruments, sometimes falling in synchrony. Mom and Aunt Mag conducting.

She knocked with her foot. Knocked again when Bradley didn't answer. He opened the door, wearing the same clothes from the night before, frumpy and wrinkled. His cheek was creased from folds in the pillowcase.

"I'm not hungry," he said.

"That's okay." She pushed past him. "I'm not getting paid to bring you food."

He still hadn't unpacked. A laptop was on his bed, the surfers put away so Mom wouldn't see them when she came to check on him. She dropped the tray on the desk, the tea sloshing onto the plate. Project Apricot and the other notebooks were gone. Bradley scooted across the bed, leaning against the wall. She peeled a piece off the omelet, stared at him while chewing. Blue light from the laptop in his eyes.

"Does the furnace work?" he said.

"Clothes are free heat." Dad had said that when Bradley

complained about the thermostat being too low. "Mom wants you outside, by the way," Avery said. "After you eat."

"Not. Hungry."

"Not. An option."

Avery tore off another piece and stared while he tapped the laptop keys. She chewed loudly. He was playing the Hunt. That was obvious. He hadn't admitted it when she'd asked him after he almost froze to death in the library. He wouldn't say anything. So she just stared and chewed, waiting him out. Finally, he closed the laptop and calmly looked up with tired eyes. Jaws grinding. He got up and looked out the window.

"How did you get the door to open?" he said.

"What door?" she said, playing dumb.

"Nana's room is locked."

"Not for me."

"Why?"

She shrugged. It was strange how it opened for her. Although, she thought, maybe it was just the way she turned the knob. He looked over his shoulder.

"I'm not opening it right now," she said.

"Then I'll tell Mom you took the elevator, that you've been going down there."

"Fine." She reached past him, tore off a big strip of omelet. "Then you won't go back, either."

He rubbed his head. He wasn't lying this time. Just bluffing. Honestly, she didn't want him to tell Mom. It would only upset her.

"Is this about Project Apricot?" she said. "I read the website, saw a photo of you giving orders. Dad said you were running it. Know what I think? I think BT beat you to it, and now Avocado is losing money."

"Something like that."

His voice trembled. Not from the cold. Her stomach sank like the soft spot on a rotten apple. She didn't want to act like that, make him feel like that. He reached under the bed, pulled the surfers out. Turned them over like a magic lantern that wouldn't give up a secret.

"Don't know how they did it," he said. "The Hunt is light-years ahead of us. We managed to create a small environment—it took an extraordinary number of resources to do it. We'd projected ten years to develop a virtual room not much bigger than this. But this." He shook the surfers. "They duplicated the entire world, Av. I've been through it; it's all there. It's some sort of-of-of... I don't know, quantum absorption of our world. It's seamless."

"It's a game."

"You don't understand," he said, then whispered, "Every detail mirrors our waking reality."

"Except flying puppets."

He didn't catch what she said, didn't realize that she had been there, with him, in the Hunt. She had been with him at the tree when BT dropped from the sky. Or maybe he thought she'd seen it on the Hunt's public website. Or maybe he didn't even hear her, staring with such fascination at the black object in his hand.

"Who is the Bad Toy?" Avery said.

"Who?"

"BT. Bad Toy."

He frowned, thinking. As if he hadn't heard that before. Avery had to think where she'd heard it, then remembered Jenks had told her.

"It's a company," he said. As if that answered the question. BT was just the face of some mystery company that did everything Bradley was trying to do. BT wasn't someone. He wasn't a bad toy.

"Dad thinks they're collecting data," she said.

"I think it's more than that."

"What, then?"

"I need to find the Toymaker."

"That's why you're playing the game."

"I'm not playing the game," he hissed. "There's a reason why the virtual world mirrors our reality. I think they're looking for someone here. Not there. And there's some secret, some really big secret behind it all."

Eloquent, she thought. *Really big secret.* He'd been reduced to a fourth-grade mystery novel. But he felt so vulnerable.

"Wait," she said, "is that why you came here early? To find the Toymaker, like, here?"

"I don't know."

"He's in there, Bradley." She pointed at the surfers. "In the game."

He put the laptop on the desk, opened a file. It was a recording of the August birthday party. Nana Rai looking across the table, disappearing in thought. Avery looking back at her, wondering if Nana Rai was thinking of anything at all. Nana Rai was staring at the elf perched atop the sculpture.

That was when Avery had recognized the elf's hat. Matched it with the logo on the surfers. Bradley stopped the video just before the flash of light, before the Hunt officially began. Just as Avery muttered the words.

"I've watched this fifty times." He zoomed in on Nana Rai's expression. The nearly imperceptible curl of a smile. "She knew, Av."

"Knew what?"

He wouldn't say it. Avery thought he was talking about what happened next, the flash. The panic. But he was talking about something else. Nana had carved that elf in a cabin. A cabin with a long green coat on a hook and someone chopping wood.

"The Toymaker?" Avery said. "You think she knew the Toymaker?"

Avery didn't know what to laugh at. Bradley suggesting the Toymaker was real, like real in this world and not in a video game, or that Nana Rai personally knew him. Wherever the laughter was coming from, it was quickly snuffed out with concern. Bradley wasn't looking for the Toymaker in the Hunt. *He's looking for him here.*

"Bradley—"

"We've got to find that cabin."

"We?"

"The library," he whispered, peeking out the window. "Nana Rai made that library for us. No one else has access to it."

"No. No, Bradley, that's not what's happening."

"Why else is it there?"

She shook her head. Nana Rai was an artist, a creative genius. The library was the pinnacle of her life, a collection of her stories. It wasn't a treasure chest of clues. *It's not for us.*

"Let's go," he said. "Now."

"No." She ran her hand over her head, fingers snagging in tight curls, realizing that was what Bradley did when he was bluffing. Or lying. She wasn't doing either. It was just something to put him at ease, put him off. "Mom's expecting you outside, and Dad's downstairs. You got to go out there, Bradley. Be part of the family. You've got to act normal." She grabbed his shoulders. They felt like sharp corners. "I'm worried about you."

He knew she was right. His jittery desperation bunched in the corners of his eyes. It was hard for him to pull back, so close to an imaginary secret. She didn't know if she was worried more about the way he looked or the things he was saying.

"Fine," he said.

She resisted plucking another bite off the omelet, regretting she'd already taken food off his plate and spilled the tea. Even considered going back to the kitchen to ask Dad to make more. *He's really hungry, Dad.*

"Hey, Bradley?" He was staring out the window, listening to the symphony of hammers and nails. "Did you open any presents?" she said. "The ones in the Hunt, under the golden trees?"

He turned slowly.

She avoided running her hand over her head, pretending not to know. "They don't post anything about what's in them on the website."

"Can't tell you," he said flatly.

"Why not?"

"It wouldn't make sense."

"Give me a hint?"

"They're just stories. They're not much help."

"Can you show me?"

"You can only see them through surfers. And you're not keyed to use them."

Avery went back downstairs. Dad made another omelet. When

she got back to his room, he was softly snoring. The food still there. She put the second omelet next to the first one. It would be cold when he woke up. Then she went back to her room.

There were a few things that kept her from telling Mom and Dad everything. The library, for one. She wanted to go back because, as crazy as everything was, she'd gone to the Hunt somehow. The library was special. She couldn't explain it any other way. Bradley's story, though, as mad as it sounded, was curious.

She ignited the hiwires, fitting them over her eyes, and wondered if that was how conspiracy theories took hold. First it was just a string or two, a knot tying coincidences together, before it was a blanket that covered everything with suspicion. She'd once heard someone deliver a compelling argument that the world was flat. But the world wasn't flat.

She was tempted to wander a little further down Bradley's story. See what was around the bend. And what he'd pulled from those presents beneath the tree. She'd taken the clues from his bag when she was in the Hunt. They were just stories, he said.

She wanted to hear them.

PART III

The wicker chair sagged. The old woman leaned forward.

"Once upon a time, there once was a reindeer. His antlers so mighty, they dwarfed a small car. He stood on the mountain and led the sleigh, a wary eye kept at night continued watch through the day."

9

Avery cleared her room, piled clothes on the bed, threw socks in the corner. Put two pillows on the rug. She peeked out the window, one last time, to see Mom and Aunt Mag poring over a document. Dad was with them now, shoulders hunched. She checked the lock on her bedroom door again.

A circle of sunlight, beaming through the window, was warm on her back. It calmed the flutter in her stomach. She wasn't nervous about getting caught—maybe a little—but more nervous about what she would see. What Bradley was saying was absurd. She was nervous, just a little, when she slid the hiwires on.

The sound of construction stopped. Dust particles evaporated. The walls took on a strange vividness, the colors slightly brighter. The edges of furniture sharper. Seamlessly, she slid into the artificial realm and lifted her arm.

The red snowflake dangled.

She swiped in front of her. An array of three-dimensional icons floated in space, laid out in arching rows: the navigation desktop the cousins had helped her build to organize files and folders for school and destination portals. She grabbed the downloads folder. Files expanded in hovering columns.

Dates, she thought.

The files reorganized by date. A tiny gift wrapped box was on top. The paper red, the bow green. It didn't have a file name. It contained copies of Bradley's inventory from the Hunt she'd swiped just before logging off. She didn't know if it would work, had no idea, really, if they would download into her hiwires. She spread her finger and thumb to expand the package. It contained shiny objects. She touched the first one. It popped like a bubble.

They're just stories.

Colors fractured and cascaded like tiny puzzle pieces, losing brilliance. Bleaching white. Then swirled around her. Wind howled in her ears. Figures formed in the churning haze, dull fuzzy lumps. The ceiling transformed into an endless gray sky. Color bled into the figures huddled near the ground.

She was surrounded by coats of green and red, purple and orange. Specks of snow clung to the fabric that whipped in the wind. Snowdrifts had built around them like toys left outside. They were shoulder to shoulder, swaying like penguins enduring a long winter. A sound rose above the howl. It was light, cheerful.

Elves were singing.

Crouched low, ice coating bushy eyebrows and thick beards, icicles clinging to chubby noses, they protected boxes between their legs and under their coats. The wrapping paper dulled with frost and spattered with ice. Some had long braided hair, others with floppy hats tightly fit.

There were no trees. No hills or valleys. Just an expanse of whiteness in the relentless flurry. Just beyond the gathering, where the last of the elves endured the bitter chill, large creatures roamed. Their antlers looked like tree limbs. The largest of them raised his head. A mournful howl shattered the wind and song, and Avery, for a second, felt a flutter of fear. She thought, for a moment, it was a warning she was there.

The elves stood in unison. At their fullest height, they were still shorter than her sitting down. They shuffled on wide feet. Whispers began, the chatter of rumors passed around. They moved closer, tightened the space around her. Claustrophobia held her uncomfortably. She considered swiping off the hiwires or climbing out of the circle.

Suddenly, there was a hole.

The snow caved in, falling into blue darkness. She leaned away from the edge crumbling near her. She heard something deep inside it. It echoed a tinny tune. A little bell.

A light floated out of the dark. It was a small orb, like a helium-filled paper ornament. It adjusted for the wind, swaying just above the opening, hovering like a lantern. An elf crawled out. As short and round as the ones around her, eyebrows like wooly caterpillars clenching in the gale, specks of snow catching in his reddish beard.

The gathering grew closer.

The red-bearded elf nodded once, steely eyes peering through slits. He stepped aside, hand extended, to help another elf climb out. Her hair as white as the snow. A long, thick braid thrown over her shoulder. Cheeks written with wrinkles of wisdom. A bundle of blankets, forest green, with silver bells sewn along the edges, rang with each step.

A collective gasp escaped the gathering.

She turned slowly, meeting their expectant gazes, a hint of a smile in her eyes. Then she began to unfold the bundle, exposing one large foot, then another. It was an infant. Doughy folds of flesh on his belly and a toothless yawn preceded a piercing cry. She held the child up, naked to the world, exposed to the elements, kicking wide feet. The wind tossed a thicket of hair on the infant's head.

The reindeer rose on hind legs. The elven cheered.

The red-bearded elf pulled a floppy green hat from his coat. He held it up for all to see. The elven began chanting as he pulled it over the child's mop of hair, the bell on the floppy end ringing in the wind. One by one, the elven approached with gifts in hand and laid them beneath the child with a short bow, tickling his paddle feet, pinching his cherub cheeks, poking his belly rolls. The child, with wide blue eyes, watched them curiously. At home in the cold.

The wind picked up as the congregation built their castle of gifts that grew so high it toppled over. Snow began rising off the ice. Avery covered her eyes, hearing the little bell ring on the end of the hat. Then she heard hammering.

She began to stand, fearing someone in the backyard had heard her. But it wasn't the sound of a hammer on nails. It was a mallet on blocks of wood. She bumped her head on the ceiling, slick and icy, and had to stoop without straightening her legs.

Tables were lined up in rows, long slabs of wood. Elves were on benches, shoulder to shoulder, humming a song, some in tune, others whistling. Their jolly bellies against tables, bare feet on the floor. Some with beards tucked into tunics or baggy sweatshirts, others smooth and wrinkly in button-up sweaters or fuzzy skirts. Braids over shoulders or down their backs or pinned in buns or balled in stacks. They were swinging mallets and turning screws, pulling wires two by two.

The tables littered with things to be played with, some in pieces, some on two legs, others sitting on their bottom. The elves pulled them from baskets and buckets, jars and boxes, plugging things in or welding them solid. A smorgasbord of toys waiting to be packed and sorted.

A young elf, by the look of her smooth girlish face, carried a gift in two hands. It was a delicate thing balanced on one toe, a ballerina with hands held high and a pointy nose. She pushed with one foot, her toenails alternating green and red, and slid past Avery like a runaway train. She turned her foot and stopped at a table on a platform, unpainted and plain.

There he was, an elf younger than the others, a green hat tightly flopped over the side of his head. His boyish face showed the faint shadow of stubble. He was bent over, tools in hands, steam rising from a round iron shell. He looked up for an instant, saw the elf waiting. Then he touched the tiny dancer and watched it turn about. She smiled with glee and carried it back.

He etched deeper his project, poking with wires. His carvings were intricate, designs complex. They looked more like circuitry than simple decoration. Something with purpose. He appeared to finish, his eyes somewhat tired, when he clapped the pieces together, turned and twisted. The seam between the iron shells vanished in a flash. Liquid luminescence flooded the elaborate channels.

He held it up. The singing stopped. The hammering and screwing, steaming and poking came to a halt. Avery was holding her breath. She didn't know what was next. He let go of the weighty orb.

It hung in space.

Gravity did not cling or pull it to the table. It defied the laws of physics. Avery was well aware this was just a story, that this simply wasn't real. There were no laws in virtual. Still, it seemed quite significant. The elves, however, did not seem impressed. But they waited and waited for what came next.

The orb began turning, slowly at first. Like a tiny planet with valleys and curves. But not an ooh or an aah or a clap of their hands. The elves kept waiting for something more grand. Even when space around it began to wrinkle, warping and bending like heat on a shingle, they waited and watched.

Avery was transfixed. Her eyes burned as she waited.

Buckets on the floor, packed with snow, began to rattle. The elves beside them took notice, but none looked away from the thing floating over the table. The first hint began with a snowflake that drifted off a pail's edge, floating up as if the ceiling were the floor and the floor the ceiling. Drifting a butterfly course toward the orb, and then, by some magic, it began to take orbit. Around and around, like a delicate satellite, it was joined by another and more. A line of white specks circling the orb.

The elves stood on benches and began to peer. The first sounds of amazement leaked from their lips, nudging each other and poking their hips. When all the snow had been emptied from the buckets, the oohs and aahs let loose. There was no longer an orbit of small little flakes. They encased the orb and began to take shape. Short arms and stout legs and a barrel-shaped chest. A head like a turret as it fell to the desk.

Thuds and squeals, the elves erupted.

A squat little snowman looked back at them all. It looked more like an abominable than three snowballs and sticks. Sort of menacing and friendly at the same time. The elf with the green hat stood back with a smile. The elven began to chant. But that wasn't all. The dwarf abominable took flight, soaring in the room, as if gravity had no claim to it or what it would do. They followed it, chased it and grabbed in vain. Snow and ice pulled from the table and curling green shoes, making it taller and wider and louder, it zoomed.

Avery didn't know what was happening, had nearly forgotten where she was. She found herself smiling as wide as the others. It was magic she watched, real or not. The abominable had swelled to great size, knocking over benches and tools and little playthings. Then the snow it had gathered exploded with a bang. Their cheers faded in a whiteout that was dense and steady.

Avery was alone in a storm of confetti.

She wondered if it was over. If that was all the clues from Bradley's inventory. She didn't know how many there were, when they started or ended. The snow settled, and she was back again. The tables were gone. The clutter was back, on shelves and on benches, the floor and strange tables. Things that were broken or half put together. No cheering or song, just the elf and his green hat.

He was on a short stool, three legs that looked crooked. His beard had grown long and was braided in two strands, where he scratched his chin that was hidden. Somewhere above the low icy ceiling, she heard the stomping of feet, distant singing and splashing. The pop and sizzle of things that exploded, a celebration in full throttle.

But the elf with the hat was fixated with trouble. Something in his hand knitted busy eyebrows together. It was deep in his palm, hidden from sight. She waited to see it move or wiggle or something. Hoping, deep inside, it would be more magic. But he didn't poke it or turn it or shine it on his sleeve. Just looked at it like there was something inside it to see. Finally, she moved, stepped over an old trunk, the kind for the storage of sweaters and stuff.

"What do you see?" A voice came from behind her.

It was an old elf she recognized, the one from the beginning. The elder dressed in white who carried the infant in the storm. A network of wrinkles deep in her cheeks, a small light in her eyes that twinkled. A long braid tied from the back of her head. She waited and waited until finally he said, "I'm not certain."

"'Tis the season," she said. "There's time tomorrow to see ahead."

He grunted and nodded, unsatisfied and troubled. He turned to the desk made of ice that was polished. Something dull and heavy rang in a bowl. Then he shoved on one foot, expertly carved between clutter, and followed her out. Moments later, there was a great roar. More explosions and cheers.

Avery waited for it to end.

With no transition this time, she felt the cold. It was time to escape and get back to her skin. Too long in the hiwires, the cousins had said, and you forget where you're going or where you've been. But one glance as she reached up, the red snowflake twirling on her wrist, to swipe off her gear, she saw on the desk in a strange bowl something familiar. It was nothing special, no carvings or shine. Just a dull metal marble, alone in the bottom.

Avery opened her eyes back in her room.

Sunlight had climbed the wall. She saw her breath in a fog and put on a sweater. Then noticed the sculpture on the desk where she'd put it. The one Nana Rai had carved all those years ago, the special piece they kept in their house. It was clear to her now. All the doubts she had about Bradley and what he had said. Now she wondered the same things. The veil between this place and that had never felt so thin. But she knew one thing more than ever, as if there was never a doubt.

She whispered out loud, to make sure she wasn't dreaming, the things she just saw. The elf with the hat, the one who seemed special, the infant, the boy and the bearded one troubled. That was him perched atop the carving of cedar. The name the elven had chanted when the infant was raised on the ice.

"Toymaker."

10

The wind nipped her nose. It wasn't like the air back home, muggy and humid that clung to her skin. She opened her coat, let it in. She took a long breath, let it cleanse her lungs, renew her mind, like blowing off thoughts of worry and doubt. Her legs felt fragile. The snow crunched under her boots, breaking through a thin crust in a satisfying way. Like there was goodness beneath a hard shell.

"Lost?" Flinn said.

The cousins surprised her. They were waiting on the back steps in long orange coats with oversized hoods that bunched behind bundles of blond hair. Meeho was snapping bright green gum, watching a crowd of strangers clopping around the stage.

"What are they doing?" Avery said.

Meeho said something about human piping and beating. Avery was too tired to translate.

Mom was passing papers out to the men and women on the new stage, each of them taking one, studying it like homework. Aunt Mag directed them where to stand. Bradley was just past the giant Christmas tree, with Dad and a group of people. Every day there were new faces and names. She'd started hiding inside under the guise of homework. She just wanted to stop shaking hands. But she didn't have the patience to talk to the cousins.

"There she is." Dad put his arm out, then buttoned her coat. "Have you met Earl Shiabow? He teaches art and worked with your nana Rai."

Mr. Shiabow had thin fingers that wrapped around Avery's hand. They were very smooth, lotioned but not soft. Clammy in a way she wanted to wipe her hand on her pants. There was also Clarice Cainhoi, head librarian, and John Faber, attorney-at-law, and Perry Shaffer, local business owner. And three more people whose names scrambled like eggs. They nodded, said hi. Merry Christmas, they said.

Bradley watched the introductions, shoulders hunched beneath a coat two sizes too big. An Uncle Sage hand-me-down.

"Your father was just saying you've been practicing hiwires," Gregory Popavich said. Streaks of gray in his trimmed beard matched the color of his stocking cap. He was stout with a chest like an exercise ball and meaty hands that were dry and callused.

"Kids today," Gregory said to the others with a lopsided grin. "More interested in thoughts than the world around them."

Gregory laughed like a sea lion.

"Mr. Popavich is leading the hike," Dad said.

"That's great," Avery said, feigning excitement.

"Your nana knew these mountains like the nose on her face," Gregory said. "In her day, the woman made her own trails. Didn't need a map, just the stars and the smell of the trees. Couldn't keep up with her, even in my youth."

"Where are we going?"

The others chuckled. Avery didn't get the joke.

Gregory pointed with the edge of his hand like a karate chop. "We'll start on the south fork and follow the creek. After that, it's up Scaly Pass over to Cedar Grove. A little cut through Chainey Briar will take us to Mountain Mixer. On a good day, we could do it in five, six hours."

"On a bad day?" Avery said.

The others laughed again.

Gregory told a story about the time Nana Rai made it to the peak. She was in her eighties. *Eighty-six, to be exact. Insisted on rucking her sack and beat us to the top!* Gregory had a booming voice. Avery snuck around her dad. Bradley was searching the crowd.

"You all right?" she said. He nodded absently.

"He's flakking," Flinn said.

Meeho added, "Hard."

Avery wished there was an app to decipher cousin-talk or for Aunt Mag to come offstage where she was moving people like pawns and get them to talk straight English. Avery felt like a cranky old woman.

Bradley let Flinn take his hand. She flexed his fingers. "On the crawl?" Flinn asked. "Closing the little man?"

"The Hunt," Avery said when he shook his head. "She wants to know if you found the Toymaker." He shook his head again, more vigorously. She could hear his brain hurting.

"Not dropping out, then?" Flinn said. "Like all the rest?"

"What's that mean?" Avery said.

"Hunters quitting," Meeho said. "Just the last two weeks, all were hot for the Hunt, and now they're breaking sticks like it was yesterday's quest. Just like that."

"Quitting the Hunt?" Avery said. "Is that true?" Bradley didn't answer or even look at her. "Why would they quit?" Avery said.

"Beats," Flinn said. "But the hunters still in the game are clustering up. They're coming here." She stomped her foot. "All them this way."

Bradley knew what they were saying. That hunters were migrating toward this location, where Nana Rai lived. Not actually here, in the skin, but in the virtual Hunt that mirrored reality. Bradley did them one better. He was actually here.

"You know about this, Bradley?" Avery said. "Hunters suddenly dropping out?"

He squinted like something far away was coming. She didn't know why that would make her shiver. She pulled her phone out and texted Iona. Wanted to find out what her mom was doing. If she was still in the Hunt.

"Shh-shh-shh." Mom came over.

People onstage were humming and swaying, a loosely gathered choir huddled in coats and stocking caps, papers in hands, reading the words Nana Rai had written. Conversation faded; the choir began to harmonize. Mom buttoned the top button on Avery's coat, then hooked an arm around her two children. A heavyset woman stepped forward.

"When the cold winds blow," she began to sing, "and bring the snow."

"Briiiiiing theeeeee snooooow," the choir sang.

It was stunning. Really. Avery didn't like that kind of music, but the resonance, the harmony filled her with helium; she closed her eyes, let the words lift her higher.

"Quite good, yes?" Clarice Cainhoi, the librarian, said quietly.

"Very," Avery said.

"One of my favorites." Clarice looked down the sharp edge of her nose. "It's a family song."

Family song? Who has a family song? Avery could say, with one hundred percent certainty, her family never sang that song.

"Every Christmas Eve, Nana Rai would lead carolers outside town hall. The residents would come from miles to listen. I was just a little girl then. Nana Rai's voice was beautiful. They would sing all the favorites, and then, just before midnight, they would sing 'Christmas is Coming.'"

"The year may be long," the choir sang, "but we can sing this song."

"Your nana only sang it then," Clarice said, hands poised in prayer. "That's what made it special, just as the town clock struck midnight, and we'd all look to the sky. I would imagine a sleigh streaking past the moon, my father would sometimes say he could hear someone barking commands to reindeer, and we would rush to climb in bed."

Her lips moved silently to the words. The choir sang the song a second time. Mom consulted with Aunt Mag. They prepared for a third rendition. Clarice sighed with a wide, tight smile that seemed to reach her ears.

"Your nana stopped singing as she got older. Her voice wasn't quite the same, and I think it was too difficult. She still came to listen. The last ten years, though, she couldn't make it to town hall. The carolers would come to her house. She'd watch from the window. Oh, this just brings back memories."

"Christmas is Coming" started again. For the third time, Avery felt transported. The arrangement was slightly different, but the words the same.

"Did she write the song?" she said.

Clarice, eyes closed and swaying, said, "She heard it in a dream."

A truck arrived. It was backing up along the house, the *beep-beep-beep* blaring. Exhaust huffed from the tailpipe, dusting the snow with soot. Hugo waved his arms for it to stop. Mom and Aunt Mag called those who were listening to gather.

Avery checked her phone. Iona hadn't answered her text.

"It was nice chatting," Clarice said. "I will see you later today."

A burly man with a walrus mustache rolled up the door on the back of the truck. It was full of brightly wrapped gifts. Aunt Mag organized everyone into a line. Hugo pulled himself inside the truck and handed the first one to waiting hands.

"Under the tree," Aunt Mag called. "No particular order for now."

Avery got in line. They handed the gifts off, one person to another, forming an exchange all the way to the giant Christmas tree. Boxes of glittering green and sparkly red wrappings, some with snowflake print, others with jolly faces and wide yellow bands or narrow silver strands or gold curly ribbons. No names on them. Just lightweight boxes beneath the branches.

"Bradley!" Dad waved.

Bradley was wandering behind the stage. He came over with his hands in his pockets to join a huddle of people with clipboards. Unwrapped boxes were stacked on the stage. Dad and Uncle Sage were pointing at the house, then at the firepit. They were consulting with Bradley. Avery couldn't step out of the line without being noticed. The truck was still half full, Hugo handing out gift after gift to be piled around the tree.

A frigid breeze blew through the backyard, stiff enough to ruffle scarves, ribbons fluttering on boxes. The papers the choir had been holding escaped the weight of a heavy book and scattered across the snow. Avery jumped out of line. Others joined her to chase down the litter. Bradley was examining boxes of cameras and cables, clamps and lights.

"Avery, darling!" Mom pointed. Papers tumbled into the trees.

Avery chased them down, clutching them one by one, moving into the shade, away from the wind. The trees buffered the voices and shuffle of boxes. The last page settled against the trunk of a spruce. She picked it up, looked back. Then kept going.

❄

THE GROUND SLOPED DOWN to a frozen stream, the ice dusted with snow, with bubbles trapped beneath. She could hear the water gurgling. There was a small clearing with logs rolled into place for someone to sit. She stepped on the edge of the stream, the ice breaking, the toe of her boot wet. She knelt down to scoop water into the palm of her hand. She splashed her face, feeling her cheeks go numb. It felt good. Cleared her head.

She picked up a stick, broke it into pieces and tossed them at the stream, watched them skitter over the ice and spin in circles. She hadn't realized just how much she'd been inside the house. The trees, the water, the snow stuck to her pants, the chill on her nose was exactly what she needed.

She grabbed another stick. This one was stuck in the snow where it leaned against a log. It was bound to another stick. It looked like arms and legs. A circle fashioned from a thin vine. It was a little stick person.

A door slammed behind her. The mossy roof of the shed was visible through the limbs. She worked her way toward it. Old tracks were in the snow, lightly covered with the previous night's flurry. The door was cracked open.

Avery hesitated. An engine rumbled through the trees. The delivery truck fired up. Despite the shiver down her back, she turned to the windowless shed. The step creaked under her. She peeked inside, the light yellow and bright. Several pairs of small eyes, close together, looked back. She held her breath, waiting for them to blink. They looked like raccoons caught raiding a dumpster.

With a slight nudge, the stiff hinges swung open. Warm air escaped, slightly musty. Nothing moved or scuffled. A bare bulb hung from the rafters, the coil inside glowing hot, casting sharp shadows across workbenches. Stuffed toys looked back. The light reflected in their glassy eyes. They were slumped and dusty, arms and legs stiff. Heads tilted. They were grouped in the corner, a cadre of animals with hopeful grins, some with button eyes, others with stripes, purple fur or plastic heads. A wooden soldier was standing guard.

There were jars of paint with crusty lids, wood shavings, metal rivets, googly eyes, tubes of glue and spools of ribbon. Tools hung on a pegboard. She stepped closer; the wood planks creaked with a hollow thump. She picked up an animal with arms long and purple. A broad smile on a worn face.

"That is a special one."

Avery spun around. She should be used to it by now. Jenks was in the corner. Wool cap, rectangular glasses.

"You've got to stop doing that," she said, squeezing the toy.

"I did not know who was coming inside. And then I waited too long to say something, and then I... I am sorry."

"What are you doing in here?"

He shrugged. Hiding, of course. A pattern was emerging. He wasn't trying to stay out of Hugo's way. He wiggled his toes in holey socks.

"Where are your shoes?" she said.

He pointed to a crumpled pair of boots under a bench. They looked too big. "I do not like them," he said. "They hurt my feet. Why are you here?"

"I heard a noise."

She squeezed the stuffed animal, propped it up where she'd found it. It smiled back. Stuffed animals had that way about them. Always looking. Always smiling.

"I heard voices in here the other day," she said, telling him how Hugo had locked the door. "I thought it sounded like you in here."

"Hugo talks to himself. He has a lot on his mind." He nodded at the stuffed animal. "You picked that Monkeybrain."

"What?"

"That is its name—I mean, *his* name," he said, then looked at the animal, and said, "Sorry, his name is Monkeybrain."

"What is this place?"

"What does it look like?"

She ran her finger over the workbench, left a trail in the dust. "From outside, a dungeon. No windows, two locks on the door. It's a little creepy, out here in the woods."

There were containers under the workbenches. Little red and green lights in the shadows where the single bulb couldn't reach. They were computers, which was strange. Because the benches were filled with crafty things—drills and hammers, scrolls of drawings, leather journals, and scribbled notes. A glass cookie jar of shiny things.

"I've seen these."

She reached inside the jar. It was a metal marble, heavy and cold in her palm. She told him where she'd seen them before, how she'd watched the clues in her room, had seen the Toymaker holding a metal marble, looking pensive. Worried.

"How did you get clues from the Hunt?" he asked.

"My brother. I took him to the library and then followed him."

Jenks nodded with a surprised frown. She told him about the book that was on the shelf, how it was there after he took her to the library. Somehow, the book had taken her to the Hunt.

"He didn't know I was there," she said. "I mean, it was like I was there, but no one could see me." She held up the metal marble. "What are these doing here?"

"Your nana's," he said. "She told stories with them, stories that weaved together, little ones that became big ones, like threads in a magnificent tapestry."

"She ever tell a story about the Toymaker?" she said.

Jenks smiled. "Of course."

She checked herself. *Of course, it's just a story.* "I don't like it."

"You do not like the story?"

"The game, the Hunt. Like they're *hunting* him."

She put the marble back. It thudded against the others with a dense clank. She didn't like it because the Toymaker seemed nice. Good. He was troubled by something he saw. Was that why they were hunting him? She looked at her wrist, checked the silver snowflake. A habit that was becoming more frequent.

"That is good," Jenks said.

"What?"

"Checking in like that. It feels real over there, does it not?"

"What does that mean, *over there*?"

He stepped back. The shadow from the door ran through the middle of his face. "Over there, they believe here is there, there is here, too. It does not matter, really, which is which. As long as you know where you are."

He sounded too much like a soothsayer. Talking in riddles. *Here is there, too?*

"What does that—what are you doing?"

He put his finger to his lips and crawled under the workbench, pulling his knees up to his chest, hiding behind a crate of yarn, knitting needles sticking out like thick quills.

"Avery?" Mom said, her expression troubled. "What are you doing in there?"

Hugo was behind her. His eyelids heavy. A frown hiding in his whiskers.

"I was just looking. The door was open."

"Who were you talking to?" Mom said.

Avery looked at Hugo. "Myself."

Wrinkles bunched between Mom's eyes when she saw the stuffed animals. She stepped inside, staring at them, but not touching them. "We're going to the library," she said.

"We are?" Avery said, a little surprised and a bit too excited. They were going to take the elevator, finally. They would all see what was in there. She wouldn't have to keep a secret anymore.

"Yes." Mom shook her head. "Your dad is warming up the car. Please dress a little warmer."

Avery realized there were other libraries than the one in Nana Rai's house, was relieved she hadn't said more. Mom stood there a moment longer, then ushered Avery out. She left the door open. They went back to the house to meet Dad.

Hugo stayed at the shed.

11

Important people were eating thin slices of important cheese. They held them on crackers, taking tiny bites, catching crumbs on napkins. Mayor Faber, a stout woman with bright blue eye shadow, nibbled a square of Swiss without a cracker, listening to a man with a blue blazer buttoned tightly over his stomach. He worked for the mayor. The other two with them, a man and woman, were of equal importance. Something to do with donors and architecture.

There were people with cameras. Others mingled in the lobby, their small talk muted and polite. A small radio played Christmas music behind a counter where a young man with a dull haircut pecked at a keyboard.

Avery forgot their names except for the mayor. And Clarice Cainhoi, the librarian, her lipstick as cheery as her mood. A ribbon hung across double doors, as wide as a pageantry sash, as red as Clarice's lipstick. *I'll see you later,* she had said after the choir was done singing.

Avery held a clear plastic cup of soda. The ice cube had melted. The sides sweated into a wet napkin. A man with glasses that slid down the oil slope of his nose had seen the Avocado logo on Bradley's sweater. They were discussing artificial intelligence. Bradley looked bored.

Avery's pocket buzzed. Iona was calling.

"Avery. Bradley." Mom waved them toward the skirted table of cheeses. "We're starting in a few minutes. I'd like you to stand with me."

"I have to go to the bathroom," Avery said.

Mom looked at her watch. "Hurry, darling."

Mayor Faber had skewered a green olive with a toothpick. Others were still arriving, brushing snow from their coats and scarves. The bathrooms were near the virtual cubicles. A little girl with yellow ribbons on swinging pigtails skipped from the playroom, holding her mom's hand. Avery picked up her pace, but not in time to beat them to the bathroom.

The bookshelves were short. She could see her mom and Aunt Mag greet the newcomers shedding coats. She fell on a sofa, just out of sight.

Hey, she texted. *Sorry, at a thing. Can't talk.*

A minute passed. Then, *Can't believe yur still there. When you coming home? Miss u.*

Nana ceremony on Christmas. So prolly new year.

Whole fam there now?

Bradley and dad here. We're all big and happy. How are things?

Just me and dad. He cant cook so we ship in every nite.

The little girl and her mom came out of the bathroom. Avery didn't notice. *Where's Mom?*

Work thing.

Where she go?

Dunno. Work yno.

Avery typed and deleted two responses. She felt slightly panicked, but not sure why. Avocado sent employees on assignment all the time, usually to collaborate on design or conferences. Avery didn't want to sound suspicious, but there wasn't time to be delicate.

She still in the Hunt?

The seconds ticked away. Avery peeked over the bookshelf. The important people were starting to gather at the double doors. Avery's leg was shaking. She started to text again when Iona replied.

She left her surfers. Said it was over.

The Hunt?

For her it is.

Avery didn't know what that meant. She needed to talk to Iona, hear her voice. Was she upset? Worried? Or was it just another day, another trip?

Find out where your mom went, Avery texted. Of all the things to say, she didn't know why she asked that.

Why?

Curious. She say why she quit?

Avery squeezed her phone. Three dots came up, disappeared. Came up again.

"What are you doing, young lady?" Mom, in power stance, towered over her, her face chiseled from concrete.

"Oh, sorry." She jumped up. "Iona texted, you know, boy problems. I'm sorry."

Mom held out her hand. Avery turned the phone over. Mom stared at it. Usually, it went right in her pocket and, depending on the crime, didn't come back for days. Sometimes weeks. This time she gave it back, her expression soft and feathery.

"I know why you're sneaking off to the bathroom or that shed." Hand on Avery's shoulder. "You're homesick."

"What?"

She waited. Maybe it was Avery's surprise that gave her mom pause. A hint that that wasn't what she was doing in the shed. "I've been asking quite a bit from you because this means so much to me. You've been great, darling. Really, I couldn't do this without you. Just be with me a little longer. Okay?"

Avery promised. *A little longer.*

❅

AVERY STOOD where she was told to stand. Smiled for pictures. Shook hands and laughed. Dad was there, too, mixing with new people, making friends, like he did. Bradley was in perfect work form. The cousins were in swag purple coats draped off their shoulders with sticks in their hair, in honor of Nana Rai, and talking to friends from school, who had no problem understanding them.

The show started with tearful gratitude. First from Aunt Mag. Next Mom. Dabbing her eyes, squeezing Avery's hand. How honored she was to be there, to see all these people, friends she hadn't seen since childhood. The mayor said a few words. Nana Rai's stories had become legends. And now they would never be forgotten. People nodded. A couple of hear-hears.

"It gives me great pleasure," the mayor said, taking scissors, "to open these doors."

With a snip, the ribbon fell. Cameras snapped. People applauded as a cover fell from above the doors, revealing a plaque. *The Nana Raiya Wing.*

It was a brand-new part of the building she had funded. More importantly, she'd filled its shelves. *That's where her books went.*

It smelled like fresh paint. The tables were shined, the walls splashed with murals of flying reindeer and shooting stars, elves throwing snowballs, gingerbread men and gingerbread women running through technicolor forests and psychedelic snowflakes. Strange things like snowmen made of sand, six-legged creatures, a hoity old man with a top hat, a red-robed woman and a Santa man in furs. Sculptures hung from the ceiling of stranger things abstract and odd—icy creatures and things made of logs, balls of string.

And not one single computer.

No looker kits, no monitors or keyboards or tablets to swipe. A sign at the entrance read *no electronic devices allowed.* It was just books and books, hardcover and soft, lining the shelves along the walls and down the aisles. Soft chairs to recline, couches to lie down and, oddly enough, food and drink were allowed.

There was a refreshment station inside the doors. No library Avery had visited allowed such things. But this was Nana Rai's wing. Posted above an array of ceramic mugs sculpted into ugly faces was a framed sign written in, if Avery was not mistaken, Nana Rai's handwriting.

Tea makes books better.

The crowd meandered inside, basking in the smell of old paper and binding glue, but not before obeying the cardinal rule: placing phones on the circulation desk. Avery dug into her pocket, checking it before handing it over. Iona hadn't replied. Avery went back to their conversation to remember what she'd last texted before her mom found her.

She say why she quit?

Iona's response was cryptic. But it was enough to connect a few dots. She hastily gave up her phone to search for a book. It had been in the library at the house when Jenks had taken her. A book she couldn't pull off the shelf. *It is not ready to see,* Jenks had said.

Let's see if it comes off the shelf now.

The books were in alphabetical order. She went to the end of the room. Past the Q and S and stopped at the T. The book was quite large compared to the others, as weighty as an encyclopedia. The corners of the cover bent. Bound in leather with white lettering.

Tales Beyond the Veil.

She slid her hands over the cover, a network of fine wrinkles on a cool, bumpy surface. The binding crackled. The print fine, the pages thin. There was no author listed. As if the stories belonged to no one. The dedication, if that was what it was, was on the first page.

To my little elf. Without understanding, we call it magic. Yet no less wondrous.

It was a collection of stories. Judging by the thickness, they weren't short. The table of contents was concise. Tales of snowmen and reindeer and the North Pole. There were several stories about elves, names that seemed vaguely familiar: Jocah, Janak, Tinsel, and Nog. And others, apparently not elves, but, still, names she had heard before: Eb, Wallace, and Heather. But where and when she'd heard them was not clear.

These are the stories you've heard round the fire, drinking hot chocolate and toasting marshmallows. Stories whispered while tucked into bed. Stories you believed as a child and wished were real. Stories that are real... somewhere, sometime. They're here when we're there, separated only by the thin fabric of imagination.

The fabric of the veil.

There, below the last sentence, was a little design. She felt the floor sink. She clutched the chair, then touched the page, to feel what she was reading was real. She read it again.

"Time to go." Bradley startled her, hands in his pockets, boredom in his eyes.

"She knew." Avery put her finger on the design. "Nana knew."

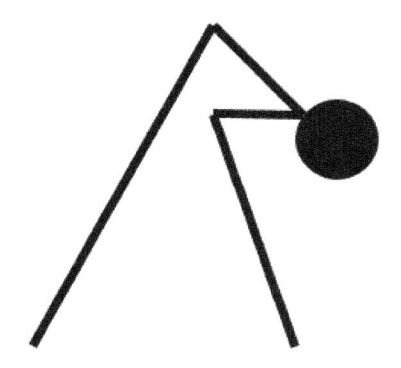

It was the logo engraved on the surfers. The same logo in a book that was older than Avery. Bradley took the book, flipped the pages, searched the cover. Nana Rai's name wasn't on it. But Avery knew it was her.

"What aren't you telling me about the Hunt?" she said.

He didn't answer, reading the introduction slowly, one word at a time, with that look in his eyes. There was something he wasn't seeing. Something right in front of him.

"The marbles," she said, "the ones from the clues. The Toymaker was looking at one, remember? I found those exact same marbles in Nana's shed, Bradley. A whole jar of them."

"Clues? How'd you see clues?"

"They leaked online," she lied. "It was them, I swear."

He shook his head, studying more pages.

"Are you going to tell me what's going on?" she said. "You might be playing the game, but—"

"I'm not playing the game."

"Then what are you doing?"

He took the book to the shelf. "We have to go."

"I want to check that out."

"You can't."

"Why?"

"It's the rules. Nana's rules, nothing leaves the library. Let's go."

"What's the veil?" she said. "It has something to do with the Hunt. Bradley, if you don't tell me, I'll just go back to the library at the house. That book is in there, too. I saw it."

He was at the end of the aisle. He wasn't stopping.

"I followed you to the Hunt," she blurted. That stopped him. "When we were down there, in the library, I followed you."

She told him about the book she found, what she saw when he opened it. She'd seen what he did, how he stopped at a tree, collected a clue, and BT fell out of the sky. She'd watched him chart a course. He listened, then slowly turned around. Like he was seeing her for the first time.

He whispered, "You can't go back there."

"I was just watching."

He looked around, thinking. Calculating. More pieces thrown into the puzzle. Pieces that didn't fit.

"I think Nana gave the hiwires to me for a reason," she said.

"No. No, she didn't." But he didn't believe what he was saying. "Promise me, Av, you won't go back."

"Why?"

"Just promise."

"If you tell me what you're doing, I'll promise."

He frowned, then nodded. He didn't mean it. Because when he walked away, he rubbed his head without knowing it. He'd tell her some things, but she didn't want to know *some* things. She wanted to know everything. Nana Rai had given her the hiwires for a reason. He knew it, too. But he'd tell her something because he wanted to go back to the library.

And she was the only one who could take him.

12

Hugo carried two twenty-foot ladders, one on each shoulder, to the white van. Icy tracks led to the curb. Mom held Dad's arm as they navigated the frozen path to an economy car. There were several cars parked out front, people taking baby steps, stopping to chat, breath puffing. Hugo kept his eyes on the ground, marching back around the house.

Avery stood in the front room, remembering Christmas when the virtual dinner wasn't a thing; it was just a short video call where everyone sat awkwardly in front of the laptop. The cousins looking bored. Bradley and Avery answering the same questions about school. It was just Avery's family then. Just the four of them.

Dad had this old-fashioned hockey game. The two-dimensional players slid down slots on a slick metal surface, swatting at a big plastic disc. It was always Mom and Bradley versus Dad and Avery. Mom was an animal. She broke the stick that controlled the hockey players one year. Avery remembered laughing so hard her ribs hurt the next morning. Mom and Bradley had come up with a victory dance that involved a lot of kicking. Avery couldn't even remember what presents she opened that year.

"They gone?"

Bradley was in front of the fireplace, bundled in a coat. Uncle Sage's turtleneck sweater was bunched under his chin like a pedestal for his head. The cars pulled away, Hugo the last one to leave. Avery heard the spiral staircase creak. She followed him upstairs. He waited at the far end of the hall, a bulge in his coat pocket. He rattled the door handle. It opened for Avery.

"Do it again," Bradley said.

She did it again.

It was an old handle, brassy and worn. No touch sensors that would know it was her. Still, Bradley didn't seem surprised. He walked inside, the air humid and green, and went straight for the elevator. His hand in his coat pocket, he waited for it to open.

"Tell me about the veil," Avery said. "What is it?"

"I'll tell you in the library." He was looking for a button.

"It won't work for you," she said.

She didn't know if that was true. That didn't stop him from searching. Avery meandered past the round table with the leather book and other clutter, deeper down a narrow aisle. Shelves of crusty paintbrushes and dusty canvases. A collection of things from faraway places: a bamboo bird cage, a rack of feathered spears, wooden skis, a pile of plaster masks, a box of paper lamps. She sat on a rocking horse and pulled a heavy shoebox from a cabinet missing drawers. It was filled with rocks, round and smooth.

"What are you doing?" Bradley said.

"Looking for answers."

She wanted to go to the library, just not with him. The book with the veil stories was there. Maybe the library would let her see them now, but she wanted him to talk first. He wasn't going to say much when he was down there. And, if she was honest, there was something about him disappearing into the Hunt that made her nervous.

He went around the other side of the striped-fruit tree, something heavy falling. He picked it up; then she saw him, not too far away, clear clutter from a large chair. He looked like a fatigued prince on a tired throne, slumped on the studded armrest. Avery counted the rocks. There were twenty-seven. She started stacking them.

He leaned on his knees. Sighed.

"When I was seven, I wanted a drum set. It was all I could think about. I watched videos of the world's greatest drummers, listened to them in bed, played an imaginary beat. I had no idea what I was doing or even how to play the drums. But when I closed my eyes, I was there. I could feel the percussion."

He put his hand over his heart, closed his eyes.

"The crowd was like an ocean, pumping their fists, roaring so loud I could barely hear the music. Sweat pouring like it did in the videos, soaking my shirt, splashing off the snare. And then the stage would unfold."

He was looking at Avery, but he wasn't seeing her.

"I imagined how a platform would lift me up and start spinning. And I would keep playing. It was so powerful that I felt like I disintegrated. It was just the spinning sticks and banging foot pedals. And sometimes, Av, when I opened my eyes, I was sweaty and exhausted, heart pounding. I could feel it, you know. Like I was there."

He looked through the opaque ceiling, the light diffuse and greenish. Head bumping to an imaginary beat, fingers drumming the armrests.

"You... want to play drums *now*?" Avery said.

He leaned on his knees again. "Dreams, Av, they're not nothing. Not when you're in them. When you see them and feel them. They become... *something*. Thoughts are the paint, our minds the canvas. Dreams create worlds, Av. Somewhere, sometime."

Somewhere, sometime.

He found a red balloon. He blew air in it, pinched it between his fingers.

"Dreams are out there, inside a membrane. Like a bubble, sometimes it pops, the membrane too thin, not fully realized, like a fleeting daydream." The balloon whistled. Deflated. "But when it's fully realized, when there's enough people wishing and hoping, believing the same thing, the dream becomes something. It becomes real."

The rocks Avery was stacking tipped over and scattered on the floor.

"What time of the year does everyone in the world wish for something, Av? When are we lying in bed, dreaming of something magical?"

"Christmas," Avery muttered.

He inflated the balloon, big and red, tied a knot. It floated toward her, twirling end over end.

"Not everyone wishes for a drum set, Bradley."

"When you're lying in bed, aren't you listening for the bells? Didn't we put milk and cookies out, throw carrots on the sidewalk?"

"Santa Claus," she deadpanned. "You're saying Santa Claus is real?" The balloon bumped toward the floor. "Bradley—"

"Maybe it doesn't take everyone to wish for the same thing. Maybe just one person. Someone very special, very creative. Maybe Nana figured it out. She made it all come true. It's the veil that holds dreams together. That's what she was talking about. The veil is the membrane that contains dreams. And dreams become an entire universe."

Avery scooped the rocks into the box, put it back onto the shelf. This wasn't what she expected. Bradley hadn't rubbed his head once. *He believes it.* He paced down the narrow aisle. Picked up the balloon, looking inside it. It squeaked in his hand.

"The Hunt isn't a game, Av. I think it's real."

"What does that mean?"

"I'm saying it's real. Like here, only there."

"Bradley." She chuckled. "Think about what you're saying. How is that even possible?"

"I don't know. Where is this? Where's our world, our universe? Where is space? Whoever is over there, in the Hunt, they don't want to be there. They want to be here. In our world."

Avery took his hand. She slid the sleeve of the coat past his wrist. The tattoo was there, the size of a quarter. Her bracelet was silver.

"Bradley," she said softly, "you need to stop. All right? Listen to me. I think you're in reality confusion."

"That's why they're looking for the Toymaker, Av. He's the one who can bring them here. That's why he's hiding from them."

"Bradley—"

"The game is a parallel universe of ours. They're using it to find him here."

"Okay. All right." She played along. Keep him safe until she could tell her parents, get him the help he needed. He was the smartest person she knew. But intelligence was no good when it was warped in reality confusion. "Let's say everything is true. What's the big deal? They, whoever they are, want to come to our world. Just let them, okay?"

He picked up the balloon. "There's a veil around our universe. And a veil around theirs. The veil contains our universes, just like the air. If they find the Toymaker—" The balloon popped. Avery yelped, then punched Bradley in the chest, heart racing. "Everything can go away."

"Nothing's going away, Bradley. It's. A. Game."

"I've got to find the Toymaker first. He's somewhere around here. Nana Rai knew it, too."

"Will you listen to yourself? The Toymaker is living here? An elf who will bring, what, *toys* from another universe into our world? You really believe that?"

"It doesn't matter what I believe."

Mom called from downstairs. Luckily they weren't in the library. Bradley believed it with every cell in his body. *The game made him believe the Toymaker is here.*

She took his hand. "Promise me you won't go in the Hunt. At least for a little while," she said. "The world will still be here if you stay here. Okay?"

He nodded. But he didn't mean it. He didn't need to rub his head for her to know he wasn't going to listen. He needed help.

"Tell Mom I've got a headache," he said.

Avery didn't want to tell their parents Bradley was reality confused, full throttle. Not with the celebration coming. Mom would worry. If Bradley could hold it together, she'd tell them after Christmas. It was just a game. He was safe. By Christmas, the Hunt would be over. Then, when the world didn't end and toys weren't walking down the street, the reality confusion might resolve. Bradley would know the veil wasn't real. Neither was the Toymaker.

Or Santa Claus.

PART IV

The wicker chair creaked. The old woman set a heavy book on her knees.

"Once upon a time, there was a woman who lived on an island whose spirit burned hot. A sandman kept her company, untangling shiny ribbons that had become quite a knot."

13

The presents were buried in snow.

Uncle Sage had draped a plastic sheet, at the direction of Aunt Mag, over them. Avery had watched him unfold it, the wind catching it like a sail, watched him trundle after it, falling in the snow, using logs to hold it down. He came back to the house like he'd been rolled in sugar.

He grumbled for days about it. *Why did we put the presents out so early?* Then a gust of wind would snatch the plastic from one of the logs, and outside he went, losing a little Christmas spirit each time.

A week before Christmas, it was a calm day. Uncle Sage was in good spirits that afternoon, toting an oversized mug of tea. The stage was finished. Garland hung from the pergola; lights twined around the posts. No more hammering. Logs were carried to the firepit to replace what Uncle Sage had used to hold down the plastic.

Bradley was working the electronics behind the stage. He was back to normal. Not once, since they'd been to Nana's room, had he asked her to go back. He was just normal Bradley, as if they'd never talked about drum sets or giant bubbles in the sky. Avery, sometimes, would walk through the woods and look up, squinting through the clouds, imagining a soapy membrane containing flying reindeer and singing elves. She liked the idea, silly as it was. But the more normal Bradley acted, the less she thought about that.

He was eating dinner with the family, joining conversation, cheerfully answering Uncle Sage's questions about Avocado inventions, joking about company secrets. *I'll tell you this,* Bradley would say, winking, *since we're family, but you can't tell anyone.* Uncle Sage would lean in, and Bradley would make something up about replicated babies made from human organ printers. Or consciousness transference. *Like body swapping?* Uncle Sage would say. Bradley would laugh, then wink.

Bradley joined them at the fireplace in the evening, listening to stories about Nana Rai. He even volunteered one of his own, about the time she'd sent him a present a month before his birthday. It was drumsticks. Avery wondered if it was just another story, waiting for him to glance at her and wink. Like Nana Rai knew he'd lain in bed at night dreaming about the big stage, sweat soaking his shirt as the stage unfolded. But he told it earnestly.

"She wrote me a letter," he had said. "Keep dreaming was all it said."

He was making that up, Avery had decided. Even if he didn't rub his head.

But now, rubbing his eyes, concentrating on fine wires between his cold fingers, he looked tired. He couldn't fool her. He wasn't sleeping. After all those stories in front of the fire, the laughs and normal talk, he was going up to his bedroom and closing the door. He would come out in the morning like a man who'd spent the night breaking rocks.

She knew what he was doing.

"Is your brother okay?" Mom snuck up behind Avery, blowing into her fuzzy gloves. "He seems distracted."

"Probably thinking of work."

"Is that all?"

Avery was careful not to hesitate too long. She'd decided not to tell her parents about the Hunt or that brief episode of reality confusion. It could wait till they got home. He was safe here, among family.

"Far as I know," Avery said. "You'll have to ask him."

Mom laughed. Bradley didn't talk about feelings. It would be like asking a tree if it was cold.

"So the plan is to televise the ceremony?" Avery asked.

"Your nana's wishes. She was preparing this for quite some time. She loved this community. This is something special. She wanted everyone to enjoy it."

"So livestreaming, then?"

"That is the plan."

"Even the hike?"

"All of it."

The cousins stood behind Bradley, wearing puffy pink coats trimmed with fake fur. Their sunglasses were like black tea saucers. Bradley was talking to them. He nodded, laughed. Avery knew he couldn't understand them. It was a good show, though.

"Is he still in the Hunt?" Mom asked.

Avery flinched. "I don't know. Why?"

"Your cousins said it was almost over. The people playing it were *dudding out*." Mom snorted and covered her mouth. "I think that means quitting."

Bradley stopped what he was doing, pointing. Avery felt a pang of guilt. That was the kind of brother she wanted, and now, watching him laugh, she felt irritated.

"Is it?" Mom turned to Avery.

"Is what?"

"Is it over, the Hunt?"

Suddenly, Avery felt the heat of Mom's X-ray vision. She'd disguised it as casual conversation. But she was looking for more. Did she know that Avery had gone down to the library? Had searched through Nana's room? *Are you done sneaking around, Avery?*

A bell rang. Aunt Mag stood on the back steps leading up to the house, swinging a handbell that clanged much louder than its size. It tickled Avery's ears.

"Food is ready!"

One by one, the volunteers stopped what they were doing, meandering toward the back porch. Huffing into their hands, helping each other navigate the frozen snow. They huddled near the steps. Aunt Mag waited till they were all there.

"I want to thank you for all your hard work. Nana Rai would be so proud to see her final wishes come true. And it wouldn't have been possible without your efforts. You all meant so much to her." Her eyes glittered. "I don't want to cry again, so come on, everyone, inside. Get some warm food and drink."

They stomped the snow off their boots, shucking them as they entered.

"Merry Christmas," Aunt Mag said to each and every one of them, hugging and shaking hands. "Merry Christmas."

"Where's Hugo?" Avery asked.

"He's off getting supplies," Mom said. "He'll be back this evening."

"Can I ask you something? Do you think Jenks is all right?" Avery hadn't seen him since the shed and hadn't told Mom he was hiding in there.

"Jenks?"

"Hugo's son. He comes every so often to help. Well, he does more hiding than helping."

Mom shook her head. "I didn't know he had a son. Come, let's get warm."

Uncle Sage, rushing the stairs, was held in check by Aunt Mag. He was sort of marching in place like a toddler needing the bathroom.

"I think I'll wait," Avery said. "I'm not hungry."

"Don't stay out here too long." Mom took her scarf off and wrapped it around Avery's neck. "I don't want you becoming sick."

The cousins walked inside, one on each side of Bradley, both talking at the same time. His attention was starting to wilt, whittled down by strange words and enthusiasm. Bradley didn't look back. Avery waited until the last of them entered and the door was closed. She could hear the celebration inside the house, the merry laughter and Christmas wishes. Then, with no one looking out the window, she wandered toward the woods.

❄

Snow had drifted against the shed.

There were no tracks. Just lumps of things beneath ghostly piles —the forgotten chair made of saplings, a small table for a cup of coffee. Avery approached slowly, her boots crunching, the sound muffled in the trees. She blew out a cloud, looked up at the blue sky. There was an occasional burble on water down the way, bubbles skating beneath the ice.

She tried the shed door. Apparently, her magic touch didn't extend outdoors. She went around the building, searching for a sign someone had been there, but the walls were all the same—frosted slats of cedar, icicles hanging from looping strands of Christmas lights as forgotten as the chair. She thought she'd go deeper into the woods, make a long afternoon of it, get lost for a while, when she came around the front.

The door was cracked opened.

Not a footprint but her own was there. She felt a shiver in her spine. Perhaps the door had loosened when she tried it earlier. The light was off.

"Hello?"

She didn't want Jenks springing out and apologizing. She nudged it open. Dark forms looked back. She stepped inside, the air musty as before. The smell of acrylics was stronger than she remembered, and a hint of wood, like fresh-cut lumber. She closed the door, lit the room with her phone, shadows stretching across the bench.

There was a strange energy. Maybe it was the creepiness of the shadows or the smell of glue, but she felt it tingle along her scalp; haunted by a ghost of creativity: an urge to make something, build it and paint it, make something that had never been made before. That was what Nana Rai had always said. *Create something the world has never seen.*

The jar of marbles was there. She put one in her pocket. She would show it to Bradley. But then that didn't seem like such a good idea. It would just stoke the embers of reality confusion that were still warm. The purple monkey was there, but the other toys had been moved. They were spread out on the bench. Looking at her.

There were cobwebs on the ceiling and wood shavings swept into a neat pile. Avery pulled open little drawers that contained rivets and staples, twine and tape; strange stuff like gumdrops and tubes of icing and what she thought was cinnamon. There were old tools on a pegboard and a bag for cake frosting.

The marble was warm. She held it in her pocket, felt the weight in her palm. She shined the light on it, staring at her warped reflection looking rounder than ever. Looking at it like the Toymaker had done, searching for something other than her reflection. *What did he see?*

Then she laughed and snorted, catching herself thinking something so absurd, as if the clue from the game was real and there was an elf somewhere worried about a marble. She needed to follow her own advice.

Something scuffled beneath the bench.

She spun around, expecting to see Jenks huddled in the corner. Or worse, a mouse. And those were its wood shavings gathered for a nest. The beam of light flashed past a pair of haggard lumps near the door. She brought it back, stepped closer.

Jenks's boots.

The leather tongues were folded out and the shoelaces frayed. A spiderweb was strung in the opening of one of them. He'd left them. They hadn't even moved. He'd been hiding next to them the last time she saw him, hunched over with his finger to his lips. Now there was an old crate made with wooden slats where he'd been. A wool blanket was tucked inside, folded over like it was keeping a loaf of bread warm. She pulled it open.

There were dusty blocks of wood inside. Small eyebolts were screwed into them. She took them out, set them on the floor. A short stick, crooked and polished, was hooked on the end. She connected the smaller blocks onto the largest one: a red blob peeling from the middle of it. She knew what it was, but her mind wouldn't let her see it. Her heart couldn't hide it. It was thumping in her throat.

It was the last piece, at the bottom of the blanket, she couldn't ignore. It had a line across it. She reconfigured the pieces, hooked the last piece on top, then, with her thumb, rubbed the dust from the large block. The red blob of paint was shaped like a heart.

❄

THE HOUSE HAD GROANED all night.

Avery was unsure when, or if, she ever fell asleep. Drifts had grown across the backyard. The plastic sheet snapped beneath the Christmas tree like a stiff flag. The logs holding it in place had doubled, protecting the presents beneath it. Some of the ornaments had fallen from the branches. Holes pitted the snow where they'd disappeared.

Hugo labored through it all. Waddling the way he did. His sweater tight across his back, a bag in one hand. Working his way toward the woods.

"It smells delightful in here, darling," Avery heard her mother say.

Avery stood in the kitchen doorway, watching Hugo through the window above the sink. A lump in her stomach rose in her throat, the way it did when she'd done something wrong. Like the time she'd cheated on a test, waiting outside the principal's office for Mom, just wanting it to be over.

Mom had her arms around Dad while he flipped bacon in a skillet, the kitchen steamy with grease. He was laughing, and Mom was swaying, the wool scarf swinging at her side.

"Bradley needs to stop," Avery blurted.

Dad dropped the spatula. Mom jumped back, hand to her chest. They turned and laughed. Avery must have looked too serious, the way their laughter faded.

"Stop what?" Dad said.

"The Hunt is doing something to him. To everyone playing it. Did you know Iona's mom left home? She took a leave from work and then went somewhere, just like that. Iona doesn't even know where. And she was playing the game. Like Bradley."

She couldn't stop the words. They heaved out of her, purging the guilt of stockpiled secrets. She had to get them out before she got sick.

"Darling," Mom said, "come. Sit down."

"They're hunting an elf, Mom," Avery said. "That's what the game is. Something's not right."

"Okay. All right." Dad wiped his hands on his apron. She had their full attention. "I didn't know you felt this way, Av. But listen, it's just a game. Come, like your mother said, sit. Get something to eat and—"

"Bradley is obsessed. Not like usual. It's different. You've seen it, the way he's tired, the way he's always looking around, hiding in his room. He's not sick." She clutched her backpack like a teddy bear. "You know why he wanted to come here early, Dad? He believes the Toymaker is real. He thinks he's here."

"Where is this coming from?" Mom said.

"There's a room upstairs. It's always locked except sometimes it's not." The words were slowing down. She didn't tell them it only opened for her. "Do you know what's in there?"

"What room?" Mom said.

"Down the hall from our bedrooms. Flinn and Meeho call it Nana's room. There's a tree in there with strange fruits and a-a-a glass ceiling and things from the Hunt in there, clues that are in the game. They're up there—"

"Slow down, darling." Mom held up a hand, her brows pinched. "Take a breath."

"There is a room full of things in Nana Rai's room," Avery said slowly, "that are also in the Hunt."

"Like what?" Mom said.

Avery couldn't remember what, exactly. She didn't know why she was even telling them about the room. She just needed to tell them everything, confess to it all. So she just started naming things, like a leather book and a gingerbread house and feathered quills and a box of rocks. None of those things, she realized, was in the Hunt. But she kept naming things, hoping something would make sense. Avoiding what was in the backpack.

"Hon," Dad said, "your nana travelled the world."

"Your father's right. She has storage rooms all over the house; some are so full you can barely open the door. What does this have to do with Bradley?"

Avery was laboring. Her head was going to float off her body. The bacon was burning. Or maybe it was her brain.

"Everything all right?" Aunt Mag entered, tying her hair back.

Avery took a deep breath. "I took the elevator down to the—"

"What?" Mom said.

"There's nothing wrong with it," Avery said. "Jenks said Nana only locked the room because Flinn and Meeho played in the elevator too much."

Mom looked worried and slightly embarrassed. "Avery—"

"You don't get it! Nana Rai has—"

"Avery." Dad turned on his dad voice. *Watch your tone.*

Avery paced to get blood pumping through her legs, to stay ahead of the fluttering in her stomach. "I know I shouldn't have, but it was open, and I just... it goes down to a big room, the one behind that weird castle door. She used to have a library in there; that's where all the books came from. She donated them to that new wing so she could build a virtual studio with integrated treadways. Bradley said he's never seen anything like it. The walls are, like, hyper-conductive with some sort of—"

"Bradley went with you?" Mom said.

"I took him there. I followed him into the Hunt. He was pulling clues from—"

"Wait, wait," Dad said. "You followed him? But you don't have—"

"It was the hiwires Nana Rai gave me," she said. "They're special."

"Did you know about this?" Mom asked.

Aunt Mag shook her head. "You sure about this, Av? The rooms are locked. We'll need a locksmith to open them. And I don't know anything about a-a virtual studio. How did you open the door?"

"I wasn't dreaming. I can take you."

"No," Aunt Mag said. "I don't want you on the elevator anymore. Whatever's down there can wait until after the ceremony. We don't need any more distractions. How did you even get to it?"

Avery swallowed. "Jenks showed me."

"Jenks?" Mom said.

"Hugo's son."

"Hon." Aunt Mag shook her head. "Hugo doesn't have a son."

"He's adopted. He's about my age, wears glasses, always has a stocking cap. Always dresses the same, takes his shoes off in the house."

"He's been in the house?" Aunt Mag said.

"He comes to help Hugo, but most of the time he's hiding. I don't think Hugo treats him well, so he stays out of his way. I was talking to him that one day in the shed, Mom. He was hiding. I didn't want to get him in trouble."

"The shed?" Aunt Mag said. Mom hadn't told her about that.

"The one in the woods, near the stream."

"How did you get in there?"

"It was open, I swear. There were just crafty things in there, like a workshop. A bunch of stuffed toys and this." She held the marble out. It was warm. It was always warm.

Mom and Dad were confused. She was holding a shiny metal ball like evidence. It was just a marble. Avery dropped it in Aunt Mag's hand. Aunt Mag seemed to weigh it, looking into her palm. A smile softened the hard wrinkles around her eyes.

"Where'd you find these?"

"They were on the bench," Avery said. "In a jar."

She worked the marble around her palm. "She would use these to warm her hands, said it eased her arthritis. She'd roll two of them in one hand, I think they're called Baoding balls, and rock in a chair. I haven't seen these in a long time. I thought they were lost."

"The jar was full," Avery said.

Aunt Mag nodded. Avery felt relief. She wasn't in trouble after all, maybe. But there was still one more thing. She reached into her backpack. The wood blocks knocked against each other. She latched the eyebolts together, held it by the head. A line was drawn for a mouth. A line that, in the Hunt, she'd seen open and close when it talked.

"Huh." Dad took it from her, the appendages swinging loosely. He rubbed his thumb where the red heart had been painted. "Where'd you find this?"

"It was in the shed."

"What is it?" Mom said.

"It's the guide in the Hunt." He held the puppet by the head. "It goes by BT."

"Bad Toy," Avery said.

"I hadn't heard that one," Dad said. "What was it doing in the shed?"

"Hugo," Aunt Mag said. "He still goes back there, something to do with Nana's network. He was sort of Nana's surrogate the last several years, doing things she just couldn't do anymore."

"But the puppet is old," Avery said. "I cleaned the dust off. It had been there a long time. Way before the Hunt."

"That is odd," Dad said.

"I think..." She searched for words. "Bradley told me about these veils, in the game. Nana Rai wrote about them, too. One of her books had all these stories in it, stories she said are really true, like they exist beyond the veil. Bradley thinks they're real, too."

"What kind of stories?" Mom said, her brow digging in again.

"Elves and reindeer. Santa Claus." She looked at her dad. "I think Bradley's in reality confusion, Dad. I know Avocado has a protocol for this, that you have to be tested when you work with virtual realities. And this Hunt, I've been there. It's so real, Dad. He's got to stop playing. He needs help."

Mom and Dad shared concern with unspoken glances.

"Look, he stays in his room all night," Avery said, "in the Hunt. That's why he's so tired. He believes these fantasies are true, that dreams can come true. He told me about his-his-his drum set, how he dreamed about it when he was little; then Nana sent him one for Christmas." Avery looked around the room. Frowns deepened and aimed at her. "He believes Santa Claus is—"

"Good morning, family!"

Bradley startled everyone. He entered with his arms raised, wearing a smile reserved for morning talk shows and beauty pageant contestants. His shirt, without wrinkles, was tucked into pressed khakis with a thin belt. He inhaled deeply.

"Do I smell bacon?" Oblivious to the puzzled looks, he went to the stove and peeked under a grease-soaked paper towel. A strip of bacon crunched between his teeth. He moaned. Actually moaned. "Why is everyone so glum? It's a beautiful day."

It was overcast and windy.

"Your sister is worried about you," Mom said.

"Why is that?"

"She's afraid you may be suffering from reality confusion."

He looked at Avery and snapped his teeth. It wasn't threatening or even intentional. More of a reflex.

"Dad," he said, "you want to administer a test? I'd be happy to take it. If it comes up positive, I'll submit to reality therapy right now."

"How about starting with no more engagement," Dad said, "in the Hunt."

Bradley nodded, chewing. He left the kitchen without a word. The spiral staircase creaked loudly. Avery's parents and Aunt Mag muttered to each other. Bradley returned with the surfers in hand. He put them on the counter, lenses up.

"Done," he said.

They stared at the sleek gear like, at any moment, they would hop up and dance.

"Done?" Dad said.

"It was a waste of time, Dad. All that research a total waste. I've prepared a report. I'll submit it after you and Mom have a chance to look it over. In a nutshell, the Hunt was what you suspected: data harvesting. But I believe its primary directive was distraction. I think whoever it is wanted to slow down our projects, send us down a dead-end street." He snuck another slice of bacon.

"Is that it?" Mom said.

"I've got some ideas on how we can mirror the technology, integrate it into the Apricot project."

He smiled brightly again, dark flecks stuck between his teeth. He peeked out the window and inhaled deeply.

Mom turned on her X-ray vision. "Are you feeling all right?"

He looked around, seeing the worry bunching on their brows. "Honestly, everyone, I feel great. I think it was just jet lag. And, you know, when I get tangled in a project, it weighs on me." He nodded at the surfers. "I decided last night there wasn't anything there. It feels like a lead blanket has been lifted. I'm good now. And ready to eat."

"Your sister told us about the elevator," Mom said, "and Nana Rai's library."

Bradley nodded thoughtfully. Looked at Avery with a hint of sorrow and admiration. "It was impressive, wasn't it? Nana had some real skills. You need to look at it, Dad."

"Not now," Aunt Mag insisted. "Whatever's down there can wait."

"Agree," Bradley said with a smile. "But wait till you see it, Dad. It's on a level with Avocado's lab. I can see why she was hiding it. A rig like that and everyone would want a piece." He pointed his last bite of bacon. "Nana was probably a little reality confused herself."

"You think she was in the Hunt?" Mom said.

"No." Bradley laughed. It was piercing and loud. "Wait. Are you serious?"

"What about this?" Dad held up the puppet. The limbs knocked together.

Bradley snapped his teeth. He took it from him carefully. Like a child holding a puppy. "Where did you find this?" he said.

"It was in the shed," Dad said. "Out back."

"Huh." That was all he had to say. He had answers for everything else. He shined the painted heart with his thumb.

"You think he's real," Avery said.

He held the puppet up. "Him?"

"The Toymaker. You told me so. You believe he's here. That's why you talked Dad into coming early, to find him. You didn't want to win the game, you wanted to find the Toymaker. You said that, Bradley. Don't lie."

Bradley listened patiently. He laid the puppet on the counter, gently, and put his hands on his hips. Stared out the window. He was touching his fingertips together, like they felt funny.

"I'm sorry," he said. Fear spread through Avery's stomach. She didn't know what he was about to admit. But then he said, "I was caught up in the game. I think, for a moment there, I wanted a reason to keep doing it. But, I swear, I never believed it was real, Av. It's just a game."

"And the veil?"

"Stories." He turned. "That's all."

She waited for him to rub his head, anything to give away his bluff. But he looked so genuine, soulful. Almost guilty. For what, she didn't know. Misleading her? Was he just messing with her, and now that she'd told their parents, he had to pretend it was something else? They'd be beyond worried if he admitted what he'd told her.

"Give me the test, Dad. I'll do whatever it says. I feel fine, but I know reality confusion can do that, too. I just want to be *here*. Honest."

Avery wanted to believe him.

"Let's all just let the day play out." Mom picked up the surfers. "I'll hang onto these."

"Absolutely," Bradley said. "Lock them up. We'll turn them over to Avocado when we get back."

Mom pointed at both of them. "No more elevator or opening locked doors until after the ceremony. Agree?"

Bradley held up three fingers, as if he were ever a Boy Scout. He hugged Mom, then Dad. Aunt Mag, too. Then he hugged Avery. Arms at her sides, she felt strange.

"Is that bacon?" Uncle Sage entered the kitchen, rubbing his hands. "Please tell me it's ready."

Aunt Mag ushered him to the side till the hugs were finished.

Then they grabbed plates. Dad began serving mounds of scrambled eggs, hash browns and piles of bacon. Uncle Sage wasn't surprised when he heard about the library being turned into a virtual lab. Nothing Nana did was surprising, he said.

"Mom, I wanted to talk to you and Aunt Mag," Bradley said with his mouth full. "I have an idea about the hike."

14

The doorbell played a merry tune. Avery was halfway up the spiral staircase, debating whether to answer it. The celebration committee was in the round room. Certainly, they'd heard it. There had been more laughter that afternoon than the past three months.

Avery stared at a painting. It was a white landscape beneath a white sky, the horizon delineated by the promise of morning light that would never arrive in the Arctic winter. Tracks dotted the landscape, leading to a lone figure in a barren world.

"Hello, welcome." Bradley answered the door, the wind whistling into the house. There was polite conversation. He introduced himself. "My sister's around here somewhere."

She was as still as a mouse. Not a single creak from the steps. Listening to the guests shedding their coats, the casual banter and soft footsteps in stocking feet. The smell of Dad's award-winning three-bean chili. There was a rise in voices and greetings of friends. All mourning seemed to have passed. Christmas was nearly here. *Exactly what Nana wanted,* her mom had said.

Avery climbed the stairs unnoticed.

She slid across the third floor, muting much of the popping

sounds the boards would make, and opened Bradley's room. The bed was made. The shirts folded in drawers; laptop stored in its case. She resisted snooping through his briefcase.

She went back to her room. She'd kept her promise. It had been two days since she told her parents. Not once did she use the hiwires or even try to open Nana's room. They'd been on the desk for two days, same spot. Never moving. She stared at them. Something was wrong.

The lenses are up.

She slid them on and entered a neutral virtual space, pulled down a menu and searched the history. No one had logged on since she used them. She was certain, mostly, that no one else could use them anyway. They were keyed for her eyes only. But if anyone could find a workaround, her brother could. And he would erase the log if he did.

The history was intact: where she'd gone, what she'd done. The last time she used them was with Bradley. She watched the recording of that day: standing at the tree, a clue springing from the gift. Bradley opened a map. The terrain highlighted possible treks to a cabin. *The cabin.*

"Avery?" Dad's voice echoed in the empty space.

She stripped off the hiwires. She wasn't doing anything wrong. The stairs were creaking. Quickly, she lay on her bed. Her dad knocked softly.

"Hey." He peeked in. "Lunch is ready."

"Okay."

He nudged the door. "You all right?"

"Fine. Just tired." She sighed. "It doesn't feel like Christmas."

He didn't disagree. This was a traditional Christmas with snow and cold. Just like home. Temperate holidays and blinking palm trees were all she knew. "Why don't you come down, get something to eat. Everyone's in the spirit."

"Maybe later."

"You feeling sick?"

"No. I just need a nap, that's all. I'll be all right."

He wasn't buying it. The edge of the bed sank under his weight.

He felt her forehead like she was a child pretending to be sick from school.

"Bradley seems fine, trust me. I'll insist he get tested, but he's not showing any symptoms."

"That's great." She tried to smile.

"Don't worry, Av." He kissed her forehead. "Christmas is coming."

She felt a chill. He used to do that when she was little, kiss her on the forehead on Christmas Eve, when she was snuggled up and excited. His whiskers sharp, his smell comforting. But he never said that. *Christmas is coming.*

She listened to his footsteps fade, the stairs creak until there was only the distant sound of merry laughter and the wind outside. She waited a bit longer, then grabbed the hiwires. She slid down the hall, pausing at the steps. Nana's room opened like always; the green smell of the strange tree and old things wafted out. She quickly closed it behind her, let the strangeness wash over her. Gray light tossed filtered shadows, turned objects into lurking ghosts. The elevator was open. It hadn't been open all the other times.

Round, black rocks were on the floor.

The last time she was there, she'd put them back in the box and set them on a small wicker table next to a pail of paintbrushes and feathers. Someone had knocked it over. *Am I imagining that?* She wanted to find proof something was wrong. What did her psychology teacher call that? *Desirability bias.*

It occurred to her that Mom might come up, especially if Dad said Avery wasn't feeling well. Avery rushed down the hall, put pillows under the blanket, then stuffed one in a stocking cap to make it look like she was nestled in. It could work if Mom only peeked into the room. Still, she'd better hurry.

When she returned to Nana's room, the door rattled in place. It was locked. She tried again, then stepped back and approached slower, not sure what it was she'd done to make it open. It was still locked. *What's different?* Her hands were empty.

The hiwires.

They were back in the room. She'd put them down when she

stuffed pillows in the bed. *Bring your hiwires,* Jenks had told her the first time. She went back for them, pausing at the steps. Conversation had grown louder. Plates clattered on tables. She approached the door, gripping the hiwires in one hand.

This time, the door opened.

So that's it. Nana Rai had given her the key. *And Bradley used it.*

He'd figured it out before she did, putting them back in her room. *Lenses up.* She stepped on the elevator, felt her stomach drop into cold silence. The black space of the library was like stepping into a void. She'd hoped, briefly, that a clue would be on the floor, a note on a scrap of paper that she could grab and go back upstairs before anyone came looking for her. The sound of her footsteps bounced around the domed ceiling. She put on the hiwires. The library appeared.

"What were you doing in here, Bradley?" she said to the library.

The room did not answer. No hint of what he might've done. She searched the shelf where she'd found the book that got her into the Hunt. Without it, she didn't know how to get in. There were too many books.

"Where's the Hunt?" she said.

Nothing stirred. A book did not fall; pages did not flutter. Only the sound of her voice echoed. Even if she found it, then what? Talk to the puppet? *Hey, you seen my brother? Skinny, shaved head. Handsome, I guess, in a sort of immature way.*

The puppet wouldn't answer her. He hadn't seen her the last time. *This is pointless.*

"What do you want, Nana Rai? Why did you build all this?" Her voice brought comfort, fending off the stifling silence that amplified her thoughts. "What do you want me to see?"

Something moved. It was the dry sound of a hardback sliding on wood. A thick spine stuck out, a bump in the long circular row of books. The cloth cover was forest green and frayed at the edges. The title was written in silver letters that shined like little metal bells.

The Book of Hugo.

The book was quite thick, too much to hold with one hand. She slid it halfway off the shelf and hesitated. The pages were thin and dense. She wasn't going to read it. She just needed to see it. The weight of the thing surprised her. It pulled off the shelf quite easily, but when it reached the tipping point, it fell like a boulder.

A white cloud engulfed the library. It stung her cheeks with tiny pellets; her ears ached. Cold scoured her cheeks, strafing away sensation. Frigid air numbed her throat.

Someone cried out.

Blurry trees were all around. A dim square of yellow light hovered in the dark. There was movement off to the side. A figure moved with a lantern, a long coat flailing behind him. Avery hunkered down. Snow up to her knees. Tears streaming. The wind ebbed near a small building.

The cabin!

She found refuge against the wall, rough-cut timbers stacked and coated. The window set deep, strands of garland and twigs framed the outside, scratching the glass. She rubbed her face. This was different than the first time she'd been there. It hadn't felt like this.

The door was short and wide. She tried the handle, but it didn't budge. Not even a little. She cupped her hands over the window. The fireplace blazed. Stockings hung from the mantel. Someone was on the floor.

Walnut brown hair pulled back, complexion pasty in the yellow light, Nana Rai was propped in a sitting position with pillows all around. A pile of blankets across her lap. Someone was with her, his back to the window. The long coat forest green, the fringes frozen. Avery couldn't hear what Nana Rai was saying. Avery tried to rub frost from the window, but it was no use.

A gust of wind assailed the cabin. The latch came undone, the door slamming against the wall. Snow trailed over the wood floor, pinecones danced with it, candles fell over. Avery ducked through the low doorway before anyone could close it.

Nana Rai groaned, pulling her legs up beneath the blankets. The roof shook, bits of snow finding ways through the shingles. The cabin was smoky and warm. Avery wiped her eyes. Nana Rai looked ill. She squirmed to escape discomfort, wiping her forehead with a damp cloth, looking up at the small tree decorated with ribbons and berries. A clock was next to a calendar, the days crossed off.

It was eleven o'clock. Christmas Eve.

"You should go," Nana Rai said. Her voice trembled. Avery was unsure if she was talking to her. Then Nana Rai said, "He'll be here soon."

The man answered, "I'll not be leaving, love."

And Avery knew who it was before he turned. His voice was deep. He waddled with a bucket in one hand, towels over his arm, and a mug in the other hand. Short and round. The long, green coat sweeping behind him. Bare toes, knobby with tufts of reddish hair, shuffled over the floor.

"He'll be here soon enough," the Toymaker said.

Avery was motionless next to the fireplace, her legs warm but unmoving, watching him place the bucket on the floor and wring a washcloth, dabbing Nana Rai's forehead and cheeks. Nana Rai smiled weakly, rubbing her stomach.

"There's still time," he said.

He dipped a wooden spoon into the mug, held a scoop of snow to her lips. She took it, staring at the ceiling. He pulled the blanket down. Beneath a cotton nightgown, her belly was almost as round as his.

"You must go," she said.

The Toymaker's eyebrows, wild and bushy, knitted tightly. His eyes sank deeper into wrinkled pockets. She took his hand from her belly, pressed it to her lips. Avery could smell the perspiration, the tang of anxiety. Nana Rai grimaced, squeezing his hand. She pulled him down when he tried to stand, her lips to his ear, and murmured.

"Hide the gift."

He did not go to the scrawny tree where gifts were wrapped, or the stockings hung from the mantel. He tossed a log on the fire, embers drifting toward the flue. His eyes glittered. The same troubled look, she recognized, when he had stared into the metal ball. Avery heard him grunt, a slight nod. He put his hand on her belly. She covered it with hers, clenching the rug with her other hand. The Toymaker began to shimmer.

The air warped, then congealed into a silky mist. It flowed from his chest, like a spring had been tapped, curled over his shoulders like morning fog, seeping through his beard and down his arm. Their fingers, laced, disappeared in the fog. The essence swirled and flowed over her belly.

Avery had seen that mist once before, when the Toymaker was an infant, brought up to the ice, raised up to the winter wind, elven cheering and chanting. Now that same essence flooded over Nana Rai. She quaked with another contraction. The Toymaker looked deflated, weak. Holding onto Nana Rai as she grasped the blankets and cried out.

When the clock struck midnight, a child was born.

Swaddled in warm blankets, pressed against his mother's bosom, they wept. The infant cried, then stared with big, round eyes. He was pudgy and squat. His feet were large. The Toymaker held them both. Nana Rai, as gray as the wool blanket, began to hum to the newborn.

Avery wiped her eyes. She was weeping, too. It was everything. The love, the birth, the song. The sense of heartbreak that hung as thick as smoke. Out there, somewhere high above, bells began to ring. Tiny bells chimed in rhythm to a steady gallop.

The Toymaker kissed Nana Rai's hand, then pressed his lips to her forehead. He kissed the infant on top of the head. Nana held him tightly; then, with tears puddling in her eyes, she nodded.

"Go," she whispered.

The cabin seemed to shrink. The Toymaker paused at the door, gripping the handle. He didn't look back, only stood for a moment. Then the cold swept inside. Avery looked through a clear patch in the window, where frost stretched crystallized fingers, to see his dark form trundle toward a herd of animals standing in a line, two by two. Snow snapped at his coat. The air twisted, then warped like a watery curtain. And then he was gone. The animals disappeared as if they were never there.

The fire crackled along with the suckling sounds of a child on his mother's breast. Nana Rai hummed, soothing the infant. Words came as she began to sing. "When the cold winds blow…"

Mom never mentioned a brother, Avery thought.

Avery stood like an invisible stranger. She wiped her nose, wishing she could dab Nana Rai's forehead, put her arms around her. *Why did he leave?*

The popping embers sounded like pages in a book. The colors of the room pixelated, smudging reds and greens. The walls fractured like blinds in a window. She was no longer in the cabin.

Trees were all around.

It was calm and brisk. A thin layer of frost sparkled in sunlight. Fallen leaves crunched on the forest floor. Nana Rai hiked past her with a large stick stripped of bark. A boy followed with his own stick and a backpack over his shoulders. He was short and stout, shuffling to keep up. Stopping to examine moss and lichen, putting shiny rocks in his pockets, running to catch up when Nana Rai called.

Space folded again.

They were on a hill overlooking a valley. A foundation had been built in a clearing. Skeletal walls were in place. Nana Rai was bundled in a thick coat, bracing against the wind. Strands of gray in her hair, new wrinkles at the corners of her eyes. A young man stood next to her, hefty and shorter than his mother. Despite the cold, he appeared quite comfortable in a T-shirt. A short beard covered his face, the whiskers coppery in the sunlight.

They walked towards the construction, what would be, Avery recognized, the house where Nana Rai would live the rest of her life. She watched them walk patiently, occasionally stopping to observe something on the ground—an interesting twig or lost beetle. The air turned dense and calm. The figures slowly faded. Avery's hands felt heavy.

The Book of Hugo was in her hands.

She was back in the library, still wearing the hiwires. A snowstorm of thoughts swirled in her head. She dropped the book. The veil between stories and reality felt thin. Nothing seemed impossible anymore. *Is this what Bradley feels like?*

She tried to pick up *The Book of Hugo*, to go back to the story. Her thoughts and suspicions wanted to see it all again. If they were right, there was only one conclusion. This was *The Book of Hugo*. And that could mean only one thing.

The book was immovable. Even the cover wouldn't budge. The space on the shelf, where she'd found it, was no longer empty. Another book had taken its place. This one narrow, the cover glossy and new. She tilted her head to read the title. The floor suddenly soft and unsteady.

The Book of Avery.

She reached in slow motion, the atmosphere as thick as freezing water. She pushed harder, grasped the slick cover. It was fixed on the shelf, as immobile as *The Book of Hugo*. She grunted, clawing at it with both hands, picking up her foot to gain leverage against the shelf.

"Avery!"

The voice frightened her. It was Jenks. But he wasn't in the library. He was calling from outside. She stripped off the hiwires, stood alone on the treadway. Her fingers and toes were numb. She was chattering. *How long have I been here?*

Panic gripped her. Mom and Dad, maybe everyone, could be looking for her. She ran for the elevator, the pounding of the floor sending painful waves through her feet. She held the hiwires tightly, eyes wide as the elevator ascended, anticipating they'd be waiting for her when the door opened. There was only one person in Nana's room. He stood beneath the contorted branches of the strange tree.

Jenks put his finger to his lips.

15

He was dressed the same. The glasses, the stocking cap. No smile this time. There were so many things she wanted to say, but he kept her quiet with his finger to his lips. And then she heard it.

The stairs creaked.

She slid across the room, careful not to bump anything along the way. Jenks was still under the tree, watching, as she quietly left the room. She made it to the top of the spiral staircase as someone made the last turn.

Bradley paused. Then smiled.

"Dad said you were napping." He climbed the remaining steps, glanced at the closed door, then at the hiwires. "Have you been reading books?"

"What does that mean?"

"You promised, Av. You promised you wouldn't go down there."

"You figured out how to open the door." She shook the hiwires at him. "What books did *you* read? Did you find the Toymaker?"

"Av, we talked about this." He reached for her. She pulled away. "The Toymaker's not real."

"I know where he is."

She shouldn't have said that. It just spilled out, like an animal escaping its cage. *At least,* she thought, *I didn't say who he is.*

His smile faded. He looked around, thinking. She felt a little uneasy, being alone with him. She didn't know why. He was her brother. He just didn't feel like her brother. She wanted her grumpy brother to call her skunk. Jenks was in Nana's room, though. Suspicion hopped through her like a timid bunny as Bradley stepped closer.

"You know where the Toymaker is?" he said.

"I figured out the clues."

"What clues?"

Doesn't he know where I got the clues? "When you were seven, what did you dream of getting for Christmas?"

"Is this a test?"

"It's a question. What did you want for Christmas more than anything else?"

He climbed the last step, brushed past. Staring at the closed door. She heard his teeth tap in an unsettling way. He stood completely still for several seconds. Nervousness drilled through Avery and shook her. She was about to call his name when he turned around and smiled.

"Drums," he said. "I wanted a drum kit. Did I pass?"

She nearly wilted with relief. She didn't know why she asked that question or what she would've done if he couldn't remember. "Are you okay?"

"I'm perfectly fine."

"You seem... different."

"Different?" What was she going to say? He was nicer? Happier? "Can I see those?" He held out his hand. "I'll give them back."

Reluctantly, she gave him the hiwires. He turned them over, like seeing them for the first time. He took them to the door, opened it. Looked inside. Avery held her breath. She was trying not to shiver. The feeling still hadn't returned to her fingers and toes. He closed it, turning the hiwires over again.

"You're right." He handed them back. "They do open the door."

"You already knew that."

"Listen, I think it'd be best if you kept your promise. Don't go in Nana's room. You'll ruin things if you do."

"I'll keep my promise if you do."

He held up his hands, surrendering. "Deal. So are you coming downstairs to join us? Or do you want me to tell Mom you're doing something else?"

"I'm tired, Bradley. I went to the bathroom, heard you coming up the stairs, and was waiting for you. You can tell her that."

"You went to the bathroom with the hiwires?"

"I don't trust them alone," she said. "Not anymore."

He nodded, then smiled, said, with a short wave, okay. He started down the steps, sliding his hand along the squeaky rail.

"Bradley?"

He went three more steps. "Yes?"

"If I don't keep my promise, what will I ruin?"

He smiled in a broad, strange way. Snapped his teeth. "Christmas. What else?"

Avery waited till he got to the bottom, until she heard his laughter with the others, the clatter of dishes in the kitchen, the call to return to the round room to plan whatever they were planning.

And then she immediately broke her promise.

Jenks wasn't in Nana's room. She walked around the tree, whispering his name. The elevator was closed. Perhaps he went to the library to hide. She wanted to go down there to see him, or try to open *The Book of Avery*. But there was no guarantee Bradley wouldn't tell Mom what she was doing.

When she got to her bedroom, Jenks was waiting for her.

❄

AVERY'S LEGS were columns of ice. Jenks stared back at her with equal paralysis. He was in Nana's room. Now he was in this room. No doors in between. Avery's mouth was suddenly dry. She placed the hiwires gently on the desk and leaned on it, scraped frost from the window. It peeled in thin white layers, melting on her fingertip. Someone was working on the stage.

"I feel the cold on this window," she said, the frost dripping from her finger. "I smell the dust in this room. Hear the wind blowing, see the ornaments on the tree. When I went down to the library, I smelled the musty cabin, felt the heat of a fire." Her voice trembled. Hugo was in the backyard. "I saw my grandmother give birth." *To Hugo,* she thought. "Bradley is reality confused. But maybe I am, too."

"You are not confused, Avery."

"Who are you?" she said. "You were in *that* room, Jenks. *And now you're here.*" She pointed at the floor. "Hugo *doesn't* have a son."

"I am his son. Just... not like you think."

"Not like I think?"

He pushed his glasses up. "Let me show you who I am."

He kept his hand out, like the answer was scrawled on his palm. His fingernails were dirty, knuckles scuffed. Maybe he knew a way through the walls, had crawled through secret tunnels to get from one end of the hallway to the other. *Maybe he's been living here.*

She opened the bedroom door and considered leaving. But there were more questions out there. He stood there, offering her an answer, without smiling. Expressionless. She went back inside, stood in front of him. He wanted to show her something. Fine. If it was another way to the library, even better. She reached out, bracing for something unexpected: a button to spring a trapdoor or hidden elevator. What happened stole her breath. There was no sensation in his grip. None at all.

Her hand passed through him.

Her legs thawed. She stumbled backwards. The air was suddenly stale and hot. She pulled short breaths in search of oxygen and collapsed in the chair.

"Slowly, Avery. Breathe slowly. Long exhales, let it out slowly. There you go."

She closed her eyes, trembling. It felt like she was breathing through a straw. The room was a carnival ride, centrifugal force holding her in the chair. The slow breathing helped. Her heart slowed to a trot. Jenks kneeled in front of her, counting her breaths.

I've never touched him.

He always stood near her. He'd had her push the button the first time they went down to the library, had stepped away when the elevator jolted. She never saw him leave the house, never talked to him outdoors. *Those weren't his boots in the shed.*

"What are you?" she said.

"I am part of the plan." He stood up. "To hide the gift."

"No. No, no, no... don't... what are you!"

He nodded. Like he understood. Her hand had just passed through him. He paced, feet thumping on the floor, sweatshirt rustling. Her head was in a spin cycle. *A ghost doesn't make sounds.*

"Hugo built this house," he said. "It was a networked system before computers were even invented. He's good with technology. It's in his nature."

He looked at the corners of the ceiling. Avery couldn't look away from him until he pointed. She didn't see what he was looking at, not at first. There was dust on the walls, a few cobwebs. And then she saw a black bead nestled in the plaster. There was one in each corner. She'd seen those before, at home, in the dining room. They would project the images of Aunt Mag, Uncle Sage and the cousins at the table for Christmas dinner and birthdays.

"I have been many things," he said. "This is home."

She pushed out of the chair, steadied like a newborn foal testing her legs. Arms at his sides, he didn't offer assistance. She stepped closer to examine him, trying to understand what exactly he was saying. The answer was in front of her. She tried to put her hand on his chest. There was no heartbeat. There wasn't anything.

"You're not here."

"I do not need a body to be real."

"You're a projection. That means you're somewhere. Where are you, Jenks?"

"I am here." A slight smile, arms out.

"What does that mean, *I am here?*"

"This is me, Avery."

She examined the beady black eyes. Looked back at him. *Just ask the house,* Jenks had once told her. *It will hear you.* "What are you saying? You're, like, some sort of... what, computer AI?"

"I am—"

"Don't say it, Jenks. Don't say you are here; just answer the question. Are you human, yes or no?"

He shook his head.

"You're *not* human."

She had to sit down again. This was all coming too fast. She tried to put it together, but the pieces were raining hard. He wasn't human. Which meant he was something else. He was a projection. She'd seen projections in school that were holographic representations of a computer interface.

"You're a computer."

"I am more than a computer."

"If you're not a computer, then what are you—and don't say *I am here*. That doesn't mean anything. Are you being projected by the home network, an artificial intelligence that Nana Rai or Hugo built?"

"Artificial is not entirely accurate. It is more like—"

"Hugo's your father," she blurted.

That was it. Hugo was his father, but not exactly. *Not like you think,* he had said. He talked differently. Formally. Enunciated his words perfectly. *He called me ma'am the first time we met.* He wasn't human; he existed only in this house.

"Why didn't you tell me? All the lies, the pretending to be Hugo's son." Her voice was rising. "You're a computer, admit it. You're smart. Aren't you smart? Did you think, or-or compute, I wasn't going to find out?"

"I have been called Dum-Dum before."

"That's not funny."

"I did not tell you who I really am because you were not ready."

"Like I'm ready now?"

"You needed time to grow. To discover."

"Discover what? I'm lost, Jenks, if you really have a name. Do you have another name?" He'd said there were other names, when they first met. Sandy and something else. "Forget it. I don't need to *discover* anything else. I don't know what Nana was doing here or why there's a computer projecting you to walk around and pretend to be real. There's already too much happening and now this."

He remained quiet. A first.

"Are you talking to anyone else? Forget it." She waved her hand. Obviously, he wasn't talking to them. They'd never heard of him. *Hugo doesn't have a son.* "I can't take any more surprises."

"I am here to guide you."

"Guide me where?"

"To know yourself."

"Great. That's great. A therapy ghost." She looked at the beads in the corners. What was the point of looking at him? That wasn't really him standing there. He wasn't anywhere. "There's a book in the library with my name on it. Is that what you mean?"

"You are not ready to see—"

"No, Jenks. Guide me. Tell me what to do. No more hints. What's in the book?"

"It does not work that way."

"You're a computer. An algorithm tells you what to do. You have instructions. Just do the same for me. Tell me where you're guiding me besides crazytown."

"You are human. It is not the same thing." He pointed at the silver snowflake. "You are exactly where you need to be."

"That's not what I mean and you know it. If you could just—"

He disappeared. No indention in the rug where he was standing. Just gone.

"Avery?" Mom pushed the door open. "Everything all right?"

Avery looked around, searching for words to explain. "Yeah. I, uh, yeah. Why?"

"You're pale, darling."

Avery's forehead was damp. "I had a bad dream. It's-it's nothing, Mom."

"I heard shouting. Who were you talking to?"

"Iona. I called her when I woke up." Her phone was on the bed. "We had an argument."

Mom wasn't buying it. But there was no evidence of anyone in the room. Not even footprints. "What were you arguing about?"

Avery played with the silver snowflake. "A boy."

PART V

The old woman set a heavy book on her knees. Knobby fingers caressed cool leather.

"Once upon a time, there was a greedy old man whose heart was too small, surrounded by money or nothing at all. But change was upon him, real change indeed. It's on Christmas he will be given not what he wants, but what he needs."

16

She stared at the corner. Right where the walls met the ceiling, where a black BB was concealed in the shadows. She'd stood on a chair, before nightfall, with the light of her phone to inspect it, to make sure she didn't imagine it. They were in every room of the house.

The blanket was up to her chin. She was hot despite the cold, but felt watched. *He's not a boy.* She'd decided at dinner she'd tell her parents about Jenks in the morning. Dad would know what the little black eyes did. Now she lay there, almost sweating, thinking about a book. *The Book of Avery*, she was certain, would tell her everything she wanted to know. It had appeared for a reason, even if she couldn't get it off the shelf. *You will know when it is time,* Jenks had said. But she wanted to know now.

The grandfather clock chimed twice.

In the dark, she got dressed. She was already warm, but it would be much different in the library. And, if all went well, she'd be down there for a while. Outside, the snow glittered on the Christmas tree. A storm had passed; the sky was clear, the moon nearly full. She tucked the hiwires in her pocket.

Dad was snoring. She timed her steps, sliding her fuzzy boots along the floor. She passed Bradley's door, paused to listen. She was barely a step past it when it opened. She squeaked like a mouse.

"I'm going to the bathroom," she blurted.

Bradley stepped out with a half-cocked smile. "You sure?"

"Yeah, I'm sure I'm going to the bathroom. Do I need a key?" He wore silk pajamas bunched around his ankles. "When'd you start wearing pajamas?"

He swiped the sleeve. "I like the way they feel."

"Were you awake? Or just watching me, too?" *Too?* At least she didn't say Jenks.

"Someone needs to."

A candle flickered in his room. He looked like a shadow reaching for her, tapping the lump in her pocket. She turned away, as if he might snatch the hiwires.

"I told you," she said, "I don't leave them in my room anymore."

"Mom won't be happy with a midnight trip. You don't want to upset her, do you? Christmas a few days away and everything."

"I'm going. To the bathroom."

"You know, you've been disconnected lately. A bit... *obsessed*." He tapped his chin, then pointed. "I'm worried."

"Well, don't be. I've gone to the bathroom before."

"These are symptoms of reality confusion."

She laughed. "Are you serious?"

"Seeing you like this, out of control. Doing things you shouldn't. Watch it, or you'll be on the naughty list. You know what the fat man gives naughty children?"

"Are you talking about Santa?"

"It's not coal. Maybe it was at one time, one lump in the stocking, but that was just a warning. Stay on the list, and it gets much worse." He loomed like a ghost, the candlelight casting a glow around the silk PJs. "He abandons you."

"Did you eat too much sugar?"

"Do you think I'm making it up?"

Do I think? "I think *you* think you're on the nice list."

"Isn't that what you always wanted?"

Yes. She wanted a brother on the nice list, someone to talk to. Someone who would check in on her. Someone who stood up for her. Protect her from bullies, listen to her, make her laugh, and smile when she told a joke even when the joke wasn't funny. Now, for reasons she couldn't explain, she wanted the brother who was hyperfocused and happy to see how far the rules would bend. The brother who didn't monitor the hallway.

"What are you doing with that?" she said.

The family heirloom was on his desk, shadows starkly dancing over the elf's features. "I'm keeping it safe," he said. "I'm following the rules. You should do the same."

He was creepier by the second. She went to the bathroom and felt him watching. When she came out, he was still there.

"Get some sleep," he said. "The sugarplums are warming up."

"You're so weird," she said.

She closed her door and locked it. The room with the little black eyes was much more comfortable than out there. Tomorrow night she'd see if there was another bedroom on the second floor. That would put her farther away from the elevator, but she'd sleep better knowing Bradley in silk pajamas wasn't patrolling the bathroom breaks.

She wanted to call Jenks. Just to see if he'd appear. But Bradley would hear her talking, and she couldn't take another conversation with him. There was one thing she could explore without her brother knowing. She propped pillows on the rug and folded her legs. Slipping the hiwires on, she opened a folder where files were hidden.

❄

SHE WAS ON A ROUND STAGE. The platform bluish and slick. The ceiling inches from her head.

Around her was a crowd of elven. Icy pillars supported the low ceiling. The elven couldn't sit still. They were up and down, dancing in aisles, tossing gifts like beach balls. Their beards were thick and bushy, some braided and long. Others round-faced and cherub and red as berries. They chattered and laughed, sang and hollered.

But not the elven on the stage.

Two of them, a merry couple in coats, the buttons straining across their bellies, slid around barefoot: feet as wide as snowboards. They cruised the edge of the stage, stopping to chat, to shake hands, to share a laugh. The one elf, his moppish hair brown and curly, did a magic trick for a group of teenaged elven, pulling a snowshoe hare from a coffee mug. The other elf, a long braid along her back, picked up an infant and sang a song, tickling the baby's doughy chin.

The other two elven were quite different.

They sat center stage. One wore a red coat, his beard bushy and round. Avery recognized the other elf wearing a coat as white as her hair. She had brought the infant Toymaker to the ice. An aura of something quite serious possessed the two of them. They were still and calm. Hands on their laps, the stage slowly turning, they were untouched by the merriment.

Somewhere a bell rang.

The vibrations shook the floor. Icy bits floated from the ceiling. The elven began shuffling to their places. The bell rang eleven more times. As the last one faded, silence settled. All the round and smiling faces watched the elven couple skating on bare feet.

"Nog," the elf with the braid said, "if you would bring the meeting to order."

Nog, the brown-mopped elf, bowed slightly. "It would be my pleasure, Merry."

Nog? The name was familiar. She'd seen it in a book. *Tales Beyond the Veil?*

He reached into his pocket for a scroll as thick as a pencil. It stretched between his hands, then with a quick flip, it unspooled to the stage. There was laughter as he cleared his throat and raised a finger.

"'Twas the night before Christmas…" he started.

The refrain was similar to the holiday poem. At least, it started out that way. She wasn't familiar with the rest of it, but the elven listened intently, clutching gifts in their laps, holding children still, as if it was the first time they'd heard such a beautiful refrain. When he finished, they bowed their heads.

"Merry Christmas!" Merry said.

The celebration was back. Clapping hands, stomping feet. Elven hugging with arms that couldn't reach past their bellies, bouncing off each other like rubber balls. When Merry and Nog settled them, announcements followed. They called names, and infants were raised. They praised accomplishments, and elven stood, things like sustainable energy storage and efficient timestopping generators.

With each announcement, the elf in the red coat would reach into a small, velvet bag and retrieve a gift that was far too large to fit inside. He passed it to Nog; then it went to Merry and out to the recipient with a cheer. The red-coated elf smiled with his eyes. The white-braided elf next to him applauded gently.

The celebration went on for half an hour or more. It was Merry who announced it was time for Jocah to speak. The elf in the white coat leaned forward. Then stopped. She peered across the room where elven had begun to gather. Murmurs spread across the room. Then, all at once, the crowd erupted. And he appeared. His long, green coat dragging the ice behind him. A green hat flopped on his head.

"Toymaker!"

His entrance was quite slow. The aisle was mobbed with elven reaching out, shaking his hand, touching his coat, handing him gifts that he politely accepted, then handed back, the lucky elven overjoyed with his or her brush with celebrity.

"Clear the way," Nog announced.

It hardly did any good. But eventually, the Toymaker reached the stage. Avery didn't know if she was caught up in the hysteria or if she really felt his presence. It emanated in cool waves, sank through her like a love song. A smile grew inside her. She resisted reaching for him as he slid past, watching him stop near the seated elven. Jocah leaned over as he whispered.

"Seated, please!" Merry's voice was amplified.

Several minutes passed before order was restored, the elven wiggling in their seats like children waiting to open presents on Christmas morning. Nog and Merry spoke with Jocah. This, it seemed, was unexpected. Nog pulled chairs from his little bag of magic, one for Merry and him. They sat next to Jocah and the elf in the red coat, four in a row. And then, almost imperceptibly, Jocah nodded.

The Toymaker stood still, gazing into his hands. Avery could see the object he was holding. Small and cold. Silver. His mood swept through the crowd, bringing complete silence. He looked up with a glimmer, a smile that took effort.

"Frosty Snowdrift." He pointed at an elf in the front row. "I remember when you were born. Twenty-two pounds on the eve of the Christmas blizzard. And Sleet Whiteout, you were born on the morning of summer solstice in a shallow pool of melt."

His hairy toes clutched the ice, and he drifted around the stage, pointing, remembering little details of elven who clutched the ones next to each other and beamed in the spotlight—elven who went polar-bearing for the first time, who rode the sky on full moons or led the procession of New Year. He circled the stage, his attention spreading warmth and good cheer.

"We are family," he said. "All these centuries, we have called the ice home."

He slid pensively. Coming to a stop, staring at the marble.

"We have witnessed the birth of humanity, watched them grow and evolve. Shared their joys and sorrows. And all this time, we have remained hidden in the place we call home. And why do we hide?"

There was grumbling. Confusion. This wasn't the celebratory speech they expected.

"Is it fear of rejection? That we will disrupt humanity's growth?

We watch them, care for them, love them as extended family, but we remain separate because of what we know. We know true magic."

Nog shook his head disapprovingly. *Magic,* Nana Rai would say, *is phenomena we don't understand.*

"I know," the Toymaker said, "more than anyone what true magic can do."

He spread his fingers. A swirl of white mist—the same white mist Avery had seen around him when he was carried to the ice as an infant, the swirl he had placed on Nana Rai's belly—emanated from his hand. Butterflies fluttered from his palm. They were yellow and white, some striped like zebras, others mottled orange and black, pitter-pattering over the crowd. Butterflies that dissolved in puffs of snow when elven touched them. Elven oohing and ahhing.

"It has been my honor to bear the gift. To share it with you and the world. Therefore, it is my duty to tell you what I have seen."

When the last butterfly melted on an elf's tongue, silence returned. And the pensive mood possessed the Toymaker once again. Rolling the marble between his fingers, he looked up and out, meeting expectant gazes.

"A man will come to us one day."

The unsettled crowd was filled with excitement and anxiety. The elven seated on the stage looked at each other. Jocah, however, was unperturbed.

"He will journey to the top of the world, the first human to venture into our home. And we will accept him as one of our own." There were audible gasps, clutching of sleeves. "He will be the first of his kind to discover us. This will be the beginning. Many like him will follow. We cannot stop what will come."

The elf in the red coat leaned over. Jocah raised her hand to stop whatever he was saying. Nog and Merry stood up to restore order, as gossip, good and bad, was already spreading.

"We have seen humanity grow," the Toymaker said. "I have seen what they will accomplish. There will be great feats. Soon they will communicate with devices that reach around the world. They will launch stars into space to watch Earth. They will fly in vehicles, soar through clouds. Build homes that pierce the sky."

While some elven gasped, many more burst into laughter. Avery imagined hearing such predictions at a time when humanity travelled by horse and wagon, plowed fields with oxen and built homes with logs. An airplane was impossible.

"Humanity will create their own magic." He slid around the perimeter. "Their technology will forge dreams into artificial realities. Without the wisdom to govern and protect such a gift, they will be capable of beginnings. And endings."

Bubbles streamed from his hands, each containing miniature scenes—people and castles, reindeer and snowmen. It delighted the youth, too young to understand the weight of the Toymaker's words.

"These endings will not be the endings of dreams. But of something much more."

The bubbles burst in unison, showering the young ones reaching for them with glittering fairies fading into ashes.

"They won't realize their dreams will become much more than dreams."

"Become what?" The elf in the red coat spoke, his voice amplified.

The Toymaker stopped. He shook his head, as if he didn't know. Avery suspected he didn't want to share with the colony. "I am the keeper of the gift. One day, it will be taken from me."

There was a collective gasp. Even the youth felt the gravity of his pronouncement. They stood and shuffled, called out and shouted. *Who would do this? Why?*

Jocah raised her hand. "What do you propose, Toymaker?"

He looked at the marble, the silky white magic hovering in his hands. "I must hide the gift."

"Okay, all right." The elf in the red coat stood up, his voice booming. Guttural laughter erupted from his belly with remarkable effect, spreading palpable joy. *Ho-ho-ho.* It soothed their concern, stirred the celebratory mood. "The council will take this into consideration. In the meantime, we celebrate this time of year as we have for centuries. Brothers and sisters, to the ice!"

He raised his hand. The crowd cheered, hesitant at first. *Ho-ho-ho!* They comforted each other, forgot about what would come someday, sliding into the aisles, gifts in hands. Nog and Merry joined them. A song spontaneously rose, harmonizing. Avery felt it in her chest, the goodness it possessed. The pure joy of the moment.

The elf in the red coat nodded at Jocah, then turned to the Toymaker. "This was not the time or place," he said grimly.

The room shimmered and disappeared. The ceiling was engulfed by swirling bands of green and red mist. The backdrop of a night sky dusted with stars. A lunar spotlight turned the snowy landscape bluish white. Something crossed the face of the full moon, pedaling four legs.

The Toymaker watched it recede.

On the ice, far away, elven were picking up remnants of a celebration. Giants were among them, massive snowy things with thick arms and legs: abominable snowmen swept up bits of wrapping paper. The elven appeared to fall through the snow, disappearing into the ice. They helped each other, arm in arm, swaying as they sang. The song faded as they fell, one by one.

The Toymaker walked in the opposite direction. Avery followed until he stopped and turned, one last glance. Then the snow caved in below them.

Avery tumbled into darkness. An icy slide slung her with greater momentum, spun her on her back like a disc, arms and legs flung wide. She came to a stop, staring at a low-hung ceiling, bluish and smooth.

It was a cluttered room. Shelves and boxes, crates and bags. Parts and pieces, shiny and dull. Plastic legs and fuzzy smiles. Blinking lights and things she'd never seen. The Toymaker was next to her. His coat hung at the end of a workbench. A single gray braid, as thick as mooring rope, lay across his back and touched the floor. He smelled like cinnamon. A green floppy hat on his head, the little bell ringing as he looked down at her.

She held still, feeling like this time he would see her, that this wasn't a virtual environment and, somehow, she wasn't in her bedroom anymore. He reached under the bench, tossing a blanket aside, and heaved out a box from hiding. Clearing space, little items tinkling onto the floor, he put the box on the bench.

She scrambled onto hands and knees, the ceiling far too low for her to stand, and watched him hold the marble between finger and thumb. He put it to his eye like a looking glass. His head was heavy as he reached into the box.

One at a time, he placed toys on the bench.

A little doll with a red coat and a white beard. He sat it down, legs out, and poked the doll's stuffed belly. The arms were open for a hug. Next was another doll, this one about half the size of the first one, made of some sort of hard yet moldable plastic. It looked like an elf, but bald. Not a single hair on head or chin. And, more strikingly, he was blue. Third was a Christmas ornament. It was a heavy orb with strange patterns etched around it. It was bigger than the marble. He set it next to the blue elf.

The Toymaker consulted the marble.

Fourth was something from a science fiction movie: a slender android with flexible arms, its skin dull gray and featureless. Only the bump of a nose hinted at a face. He bent the arms as if it beckoned to help.

Fifth was a tiny box from a jeweler, but made of fire-red cardboard. He positioned it next to the android and stood back, then pressed it like a doorbell. A blue flame ignited from the top. Avery expected the box to catch fire. There was no wick, no candle wax. Perhaps it contained oil, but the flame seemed to hover above it.

Next was a plastic toy that required both hands to lift. Its antlers spread like daggered shields. The eyes were angry. The Toymaker bent the reindeer's head slightly as if it were protecting the others. Lastly, a stuffed panda with emerald eyes that captured the flickering flame.

The Toymaker stood back, stubby fingers buried in his beard. He nudged the toys this way and that, looking for a specific pattern. Like a child setting up a tea party, the guests had to be just right. He stared into the marble once more and, after one final adjustment, placed a skinny holder in front of them. Delicately, he placed the marble where a candle would go.

He slid away.

It looked like something a child would do with their toys after Christmas. They were a strange lot, none of them looking like they had anything to do with the other. The first one he put down, the red coat and white beard, was unmistakable. It was the first Avery had seen of the jolly fat man. Santa hadn't been mentioned in any of the clues.

A man will come to us one day.

Santa hadn't arrived at the North Pole yet. No one had travelled to the top of the world yet, which meant this took place long before 1800.

"This isn't real," she muttered.

The Toymaker, standing at another bench, didn't hear her speak. He had a rolling pin with an assortment of containers, spices and such, humming as he cut a shape from dough, his mood elevated. He said a few things, as one would talk to oneself. Then he sprinkled what looked like cinnamon and flowed like pixie dust.

As strange as everything was, this was, for some reason, the strangest. The cookie peeled itself off the bench and stood up. It had a white icing bow tie and a white icing smile. It blinked round eyes. The Toymaker stood back.

"Off ye go."

The cookie sprang up like a wild animal, shooting around the room, tumbling through piles of ribbon and tearing through sheets of wrapping paper. And then *voooom* up an icy ramp. It was gone.

The Toymaker appeared pleased. He paused, looked around and, for a moment, looked directly at Avery. A chill took hold of her, as if she'd been caught. She thought maybe he winked, then straightened his green floppy hat. The little bell rang. He took careful steps, slowly inching his way up the slope, the soles of his disproportionate feet grabbing the ice.

Avery followed, grabbing at the walls, slipping her way to the surface. The Toymaker was waiting at the top. The sky was streaked with color. The abominable snowmen were gone. Far away, one elven remained on the ice, her coat as white as snow. She watched the Toymaker begin walking in the opposite direction.

At some point, he took the green hat off, carried it by his side. And just before the clue ended, she saw it slip from his hand. And bury in the snow.

17

They came wearing puffy coats and winter caps with earflaps. Boots and snow pants, the kind that made plastic noise when they walked. Some with snowsuits that zipped up the front. Fat gloves, long scarves, backpacks with bottles inside pockets, and ski poles dangling from hooks. They greeted each other with hugs and handshakes, drank coffee from mugs and talked about the beautiful morning. They studied maps, which they all seemed to have. None of them, though, not that Avery could see, were short and fat.

Avery opened her bedroom door. Bradley's door was open. His bed made without a wrinkle. The pajamas folded and stacked. There were more people downstairs, the clatter of dishes and the murmur of conversation. She went back to her room and paced around the rug. The little black eyes watched her from the corners. Time was speeding like a sleigh down the side of a mountain. She checked her bracelet, pinched her arm.

"Jenks," she said.

He appeared, just like that. A boy with a hole in his sock. Standing like a butler awaiting instructions. He was a multidirectional projection beaming from the corners of the room. She waved her hand through him, just to confirm she wasn't dreaming about the other day. She pinched herself again.

"He doesn't want the Toymaker," she said. "BT wants the gift."

Jenks didn't nod. She didn't expect him to. He just listened to her explain what she'd seen in the clues. The way the silky magic had seeped from Toymaker's hands. She looked out the window. The sun was still hours from breaching the mountains. There, among the growing crowd, a short, bearded man waddled through the powder snow, wearing a turtleneck sweater.

"Hugo was born in the cabin," she said. "I saw what the Toymaker did: he passed the gift to him just before he was born." Jenks listened patiently. "But you already knew that."

"BT wants to use the gift," he said.

"For what?"

He thought for a moment. She wondered if he was thinking or just calculating. "BT wants what everyone wants," he said. "To wake up."

Wake up? She didn't expect that answer. "You mean, like, cross the veil?"

That's what Bradley was saying before he turned nice. Something about finding the Toymaker before BT broke the veil.

"The veil," she said, "Bradley said it was like a membrane. And if it gets damaged, like if something crosses over, then it just... it'll pop."

He didn't answer. Either he didn't know, or there was something he wasn't telling her. And, given how things had already gone, it was the latter.

"What happened to Bradley?" she said. "He's different."

"Would you recognize your brother if he was lost?"

"Can you just answer a question?" Her frustration bubbled over. She paced the room. She couldn't see Mom or Dad, but there were so many people trampling the snow with big hats and oversized glasses.

"I saw the last clue." She picked up the hiwires. "The Toymaker was in this ice cave, but it was more like a workshop. Then he left for good. But before that, he, uh." She struggled to remember, like a fading dream. "He lined up these toys, little figurines from a box. He was planning something. The gingerbread cookie… it ran away. It's all connected, isn't it? The Toymaker, Nana, the toys. Am I right?"

"It has been a long time in the making."

"Because it wasn't enough for the Toymaker to hide the gift. He saw something in that marble. He couldn't tell the elven what he was going to do. Not even Santa."

She felt the floor bending, like reality tilting. She just said Santa like it really happened. Santa had found the Toymaker at the cabin when Hugo was born. He came for Toymaker, but the Toymaker had already hidden the gift.

If Avery believed there really was a gift, if she believed elven lived on the North Pole, then she had to believe Santa Claus did, too. She had to believe in flying reindeer.

"And the plan," she said, "it all leads up to now. This Christmas. What's going to happen?"

"I do not know." He answered that time. Which meant he knew everything she'd said so far.

"So what are you supposed to do? I mean, Nana or Hugo made you, right? You said you're part of the plan. What are you supposed to do, exactly?"

"There have been many parts to play and places to be before this day. Centuries in the making. The Toymaker put all the pieces on the table. We had to make it happen."

"Make what happen?"

"This day."

"Where is he, then? Where is the Toymaker?"

"The Toymaker is here."

"I saw Santa take him from the cabin. He took him to the North Pole. But his hat was missing. I-I-I saw him drop it in the snow when he left the North Pole. Hugo is still here, that means I'm right. Santa doesn't know Hugo is the Toymaker." She shook her head, hearing the things she was saying. She was all in. Santa, reindeer, everything. And now she was asking a computer to, like, call the North Pole on a secret Santa phone to report the missing Toymaker. *Dear Santa, Hugo is the Toymaker. Come get him so he's safe.*

Someone shouted instructions from the stage. It was Aunt Mag under all that winter gear. Mom and Dad must be in the crowd. Avery clutched her hiwires. If any of this was real, then there was a way to let them know. Bradley came here early because he believed the Toymaker was in the area. So he knew. That meant other people in the Hunt might know, too. *But do they know what is going to happen?*

She knew where the answers were.

"Can you watch the stairs?" she said. "I'm going to the library. I need to see the Hunt."

"You can—"

"It's my only chance! We'll be hiking and camping, and something's going to happen out there."

"You can see the Hunt right here." He reached for her hands, as if he could hold them. "You are the book."

"The book is in the library, Jenks."

"The entrance to that world is right here, Avery." He tapped his head.

The hiwires are special, she thought. He'd taken her to the library the first time, and she'd followed Bradley there the second time. She thought it was the book, the one titled *The Hunt,* that was the entrance. But it was the hiwires that took her to the Hunt.

"Quickly," he said. "There is not much time."

She didn't know where her phone was to check the time. The hike was starting soon. She locked the door. The hiwires fell on the rug. She rushed to open them.

"How do I do it?" she said.

"Just imagine," he said. "Feel where it is."

She didn't know what that meant, but she closed her eyes. The snow and trees, the way the sky felt, the crisp air on her nose. The magic that tasted wintergreen and sparkly when she inhaled. Her cheeks tightened. Her legs tingled. The wind passed through her hair. When she slid the hiwires on, she entered the white space.

Massive tree trunks appeared. A blanket of snow covered the undergrowth, branches and twigs poking out. Pinecones dangled like frosted ornaments. She raised her arm, her fingers already stiffening. The snowflake on her wrist was red.

"Just like that." Jenks was next to her, snow halfway up his shins.

"It feels different."

She didn't think it was possible, to feel realer than it had before. But she felt everything down to her bones. The wind and cold, the smell of the trees. Everything was alive, even the air she breathed. *It's real in there, Av*, Bradley had said. *So real that this, right now, feels like a dream.*

"The veil is thinning," he said.

The snow around her feet was crawling. Green things poked through the surface. She stooped down, tried to brush the snow away, but it wouldn't move. It wasn't ants marching below the surface. It was plastic army men.

There was a long line of them. They hauled each other over logs, locked arms to pull those who fell too deep, forming a chain of little plastic toys with little plastic weapons. Branches snapped behind her. A teddy bear was caught in a tangle of wiry vines. Thorns snagged the matted fur as it slowly tried to pull away, pushing with the blunt end of a muddy arm to escape, only to dig itself deeper. Stuffing puffed from a torn seam.

Avery tried to help, but, like everything in this world, she couldn't free the little bear. Like Jenks, she could only watch. There were other toys. They migrated from deep in the woods. A small plastic doll without clothing, face scuffed and smudged with bright colors from thick markers. A big-wheeled truck missing a back tire. A blue octopus with fabric legs and big round eyes and a joyless smile.

They helped each other through the woodsy maze, pushing rubber vehicles out of holes, tossing gremlins over obstacles. The blue octopus held the vines while a plastic baby doll shoved the teddy bear out of the barbed vine.

"Where are they going?" she said.

Jenks wasn't next to her. There were no tracks in the snow. When she lifted her foot, it didn't leave a hole. She thought, for a moment, he'd vanished. Then she saw him up ahead where the toys were, walking alongside the undulating snow where the plastic army men were tunneling. She worked around the dense trees, searched for openings till the forest opened up.

Jenks stood at the edge of a clearing.

The snow was much deeper. The army men disappeared, digging somewhere closer to the ground. The sky was clear blue with strange constellations too bright for daylight. The sun was peeking over distant mountains. At the bottom of the long slope, near a frozen crater lake, more toys were trekking toward them: a bizarre pilgrimage of misfit playthings. Heads hanging, limbs missing.

Jenks followed a robot with a square head and burn marks on a boxy chest. Frustrated, she hurried after him. Demanding answers didn't work with Jenks. Before she could ask him where they were going and where they were coming from, a stream of smoke appeared just beyond the crest. The peak of a roof and a cobblestone chimney. Toys crowded around a small building.

"The cabin," she said.

There were hundreds of them. And more were coming. Dolls without hair, cars without doors, clowns without clothing. As if they'd been plucked from a trash heap. Outdated. They were standing, some sitting, staring at the short door on the cabin. Avery's heart thumped. She had the urge to pick them up, hug them, fix them.

"They are waiting," Jenks said.

Waiting. Avery remembered something Bradley had said. Santa didn't leave a lump of coal for the naughty list. He had said it with such pain. *They were abandoned.*

One by one, the migration filled empty spaces. Toys helped each other stand or sit, quietly watching and waiting. They turned when a noise rumbled in the distance. A snowy rooster tail flared beyond the crest. A snowmobile came roaring toward them. It hovered a foot off the ground, the tail end carving ripples, the nose bearing down on a group of stumbling bunnies, plowing through them like bowling pins. A puff of white stuffing spit out the back. A wave of snow buried a fire engine and three plastic giraffes.

The rider yanked mirrored goggles off. Smiling big white pearls and chapped lips. She consulted a map hovering above the console, then leaped off, plodding straight for the cabin. A family of Tinkertoys barely escaped her knee-high boots with jingling buckles. She paused at the door, peeling off a leather cap, red spiky hair like flames. She turned around, looking at the sky, ignoring the toys creeping toward her. Her cheeks wet, she was weeping with a toothy smile.

"Is that one of them?" Avery said. "A hunter?"

The woman kicked the door open. She ducked to enter and hesitated. Second thoughts, momentarily, held her back. Then she rushed inside.

"Did she… did she just win?" Avery asked.

"She found what she was looking for," Jenks said flatly.

The motley crew of stuffed outcasts began limping and rolling, hopping and crawling closer to the cabin. Leaning against one another, waiting for something. Tension wrinkled the air. It squeezed Avery with a metallic grip. She tasted desperation.

The door opened. This time on its own.

Collectively, the toys moved toward it. A dog, the color of mud, its tail worn thin, the white tag frayed on the seam on its back leg, hobbled out of the mix. It went inside. The door closed. A wave of disappointment rippled through the toys, like air leaking from a balloon.

"What's happening?" she asked for the third time. "Jenks, tell me what's happening. What's going on with the-the-these toys and…" She wagged her finger. "What's in there?"

The answer was right in front of her. As always, just like Jenks, never to tell her, the answer was for her to discover. She was careful not to crush anything, stepping over a plastic duck with a crooked yellow bill and a fabric doll with coffee stains on a threaded smile. The door didn't respond to her touch. She expected that. Avery went to the frosted window. Nana Rai wasn't on the floor. There were people inside, though. Figures vague through the foggy glass. They were crowded together, standing like the toys. Waiting. Not talking.

Avery pressed closer. Someone was on the couch, arm hung limply over the side. Her hair spikey red. Like flames.

"What happened to her?" Avery turned around.

She wanted to grab Jenks. She just wanted to see who was in there, talk to them, find out what this meant. This was the Hunt. They were looking for the Toymaker. This was the cabin where he had been hiding, but she couldn't see who was in there. *Why are they still in there?*

"Is this a trap?" she said. "Is that what the whole thing is? Get them here for... for what?" She banged on the window. It didn't make a sound. "Bradley? Are you in there?"

She silently whaled on the glass hard. It should have shattered. The frost didn't even flake away. There, sitting against the wall, next to a sad Christmas tree, someone looked up. She couldn't see who it was or if he even heard her. Maybe he was looking at someone else. His head, though, was shaved.

She struck the window again. This time she heard it. It sounded like the ground shuddered beneath her. She screamed his name, using both fists. Each time she struck the window, the world grew brighter. Until, finally, everything was white. The knocking continued.

"Avery?" her mom called. "Avery, darling, wake up."

❄

"It was a bad dream," Avery said.

Her parents were dressed in snow gear. Dad was confused. Mom stiff behind a mask of irritated concern.

"You've been having a lot of those lately," Mom said.

"Yeah, I was up late." She squeezed the hiwires. "Sorry."

"Who were you talking to?" Mom said.

"It was just a dream, Mom."

"Avery."

There were too many thoughts. She needed to sort them out. Was Bradley in there? Was that part of the game? *Why doesn't Jenks just tell me?*

"Where's Bradley?" Avery said.

"Who were you talking to?" Dad used Dad-voice. It was powerful, bone-shaking, and demanded an answer.

"I was talking to Iona," she said.

Mom held out her hand. "Phone."

She didn't even know where her phone was. And if she did, Mom would see that she hadn't talked to Iona. She considered digging in deeper. She was talking to her in the hiwires, or video chatting on the laptop. But they already smelled the lie.

Avery sat on her bed. She fiddled with the hiwires, opening and closing them. She didn't want to weave the lie anymore. It was already so tight. They sat next to her, one parent on each side, the bed sinking under their weight. The nylon fabric of their snow gear rubbed together like slick plastic. They were patient, waiting for her to speak. She didn't know where to begin.

"I think it was too soon for these." Dad took the hiwires.

"I'm fine, Dad. I swear. I was just... those aren't the problem."

He opened them up. "Hon, these aren't charged."

"What?"

"Did you think they were working?" Dad glanced at Mom.

"They just died."

Truth was, she hadn't charged them since she got there. They just always worked when she put them on. She resisted lying some more. *I was talking to myself.* But the truth wasn't any better. *I went inside the Hunt. And I think Bradley is trapped.*

"Who were you talking to, Avery?" Mom said it gently.

Avery shook her head. Sighed. The truth came out.

"There's projectors in all the rooms." She pointed at the corners. "Nana Rai networked the entire house. And she's got her own AI system. Its name is Jenks."

Dad stood up. Hands on his hips, the snowsuit puffing out, his boots clopped across the rug. He stared into the corners. They had them in their house, too. It was what they used to hold virtual dinners on birthdays and holidays. But they didn't have them in all the rooms. *And our system doesn't have a hole in his sock.*

"You talk to Jenks?" Mom said. "Is he here now?"

"No."

"Jenks?" Dad said. "Show yourself."

Nothing happened. Avery wished he would appear. Partly to ease her parents' worry. But then they'd ask him all sorts of questions. Maybe he would answer them. But he didn't appear. Again, Mom and Dad looked at each other. Avery didn't like where this was going.

"What do you talk about?" Mom said.

"I didn't want you to worry, Mom. With all the things going on and Nana."

"What does he look like?" Dad said. "Jenks."

"He's just a... a boy. Like my age."

Another glance. "Didn't you say Jenks was Hugo's son?" Mom said.

"He is. Sort of." She sighed, using the truth to evade parental X-ray vision. "Hugo helped Nana build the network. At first, I didn't know Jenks was a projection. I thought he was real, but I know that now, Dad." Her voice rose an octave, heading off the next glance and what that meant. "I know he's not real."

She felt a twinge of guilt. She'd told Jenks he wasn't real. It didn't feel that way.

"I'm going to keep these in a safe place." Dad held up the hiwires. "When we get home, we'll do it right, get you training. And get you tested."

"Tested?" Avery said.

"We shouldn't have rushed this," Mom said. "Not here, not without—"

"You think I'm reality confused?"

"Bradley said you were trying to use the elevator last night. And he heard you talking to yourself, or Jenks. He's just worried about you, darling."

"Where is he?"

"He's outside with all the rest. We're waiting on you," Mom said.

Avery looked out the window. There were too many people to find him. She felt relieved. If he was down there, that meant he wasn't in the cabin. *He's not trapped.*

"The hike begins in an hour," Mom said. "I'd like you to come with us. Get outside, breathe fresh air. Get out of virtual reality. It's the best thing for you right now. It's what Nana Rai wanted. Can you be ready?"

Avery couldn't help but wonder what it was Nana Rai wanted. The Hunt was ending tonight. They'd be on the mountain when it did. At least they'd be isolated. No Wi-Fi, no computers, no network to get in the way. Maybe that was exactly what Nana Rai wanted. To get away from everything when it was over. Hugo would be safe.

All Avery had to do was keep a secret.

18

The sky was watercolor blue. Flawless. It had that endless feeling, like nothing was up there. No ceiling. Nothing holding them on the ground. If gravity stopped, they would float forever. *Like bubbles.* She didn't know why she was thinking those thoughts. Perhaps it was the crisp air clearing cobwebs in her head.

There were so many people. She could feel them looking at her. Their stares lingering from small pods with their insulated cups of coffee and stuffed packs. The hike was running late because of her. They were familiar, most of them. But some of these people she'd never seen. They wore bright colors—candy apple red stripes, lime green polka dots or tangerine zigzags. They were overcaffeinated, hopping in place or clapping their hands. Big smiles and loud laughter, too loud, looking up at the blue, blue sky, scooping up snow and tasting it. They were huddled in a large group. And Bradley was in the middle of them.

Hugo was near the stage. Everyone had fat backpacks loaded with sleeping bags and tents, hiking sticks and gas stoves to heat their morning coffee. Hugo, though, had nothing. Not even a water bottle.

"How are you feeling?" Mom was snug in a thick coat, her eyes hidden behind sunglasses. Avery's reflection was as round as a snowball. "Avery, darling?"

"I'm ready, Mom."

She zipped Avery's coat, then waved at Aunt Mag on the stage with Uncle Sage. The cousins were huddled near them like penguins in black and white snow gear. Aunt Mag called for everyone to gather. Uncle Sage walloped his hands like walrus paddles, letting loose a foghorn call.

Everyone lugged their packs onto their shoulders. A few of the ones around Bradley broke away. He was assigning gear for them to carry. Their packs were boxy and big, much bigger than anyone had packed. Like troops embarking on a crusade across the North Pole. Bradley was talking to a woman with a furry white coat. She tipped her head back when she laughed. The hood slipped off her head, the fuzzy trim bunching around her shoulders, contrasting with her dark complexion. It didn't look like Bradley had said anything funny. He looked very serious.

"Do you need help with your gear?" Mom said. "Here, I can—Avery?"

Avery bumped into someone without apologizing, watching the woman pull the hood over her head, wipe her nose before reaching for a box.

"Mrs. Baker?" Avery said.

The woman in the white coat looked at Bradley. A knot tightened between her brows. Then a smile stretched wide.

"Avery!" She threw her arms around her. "Oh my, oh my, oh me, oh my."

Iona's mom locked her arms around her, swinging back and forth. Squeezing the breath out of her. Bradley watched with a satisfied grin, then patted the woman on the shoulder. "Remember." He chuckled. "She has to breathe."

"Oh yes, yes, yes. Ha!" Iona's mom smoothed the wrinkles from Avery's coat, touched her cheek with a padded glove. "Look how you've changed. It feels like years."

Avery looked at Bradley. *What is she doing here?*

"Shaylene?" Mom said.

"Grace!" She applied another vise-gripping hug. "Oh, it's so wonderful to be *here*. The air is so clean. And the snow is so crunchy."

"What are you doing here?" Mom said.

"Didn't Bradley tell you? I got here last week. I'm so sorry about your mother. I just want to be part of this. I know I should've called, but I've been so busy, and you've been so busy." She hopped up and down. Three little jumps like a child about to open a present. "It's a long, long story, Grace. It's a project we've been working on—"

"I invited her, Mom," Bradley said.

Mom shook her head, looking back and forth. "Why?"

"It's complicated."

"Uncomplicate it, son."

"I'm…" Iona's mom hopped once. "I'm sorry, Grace. I know this is strange. There's so much to explain, and everything's happened so fast. The ceremony, it's so very special. I'm just happy to be part of it."

"Iona doesn't know where you are," Avery said.

"Ha!" Iona's mom covered her mouth. "Of course she does. Don't be silly. She knows about the project."

"The Hunt?" Avery said.

"We've been collaborating, your brother and me. Bradley told me what you were doing, and I was in the region. I didn't want to spend Christmas Eve alone and, you know. I hope you don't mind me being here. I really should've called. We've been so busy and—"

Mom held up her hand. "What's in the boxes?"

"Oh. Supplies."

"That's a lot of supplies," Mom said.

"Is it? I've never been camping in the cold. Bradley and the others said we can't be overprepared, so here we are." A laugh and a hop.

"Bradley?" Mom said. "What's this all about?"

"It's research, Mom."

"Research?"

"I didn't want this to get complicated or involve anyone else. Just a few things to record the event."

"What event?"

"The Hunt," Avery said.

Bradley smiled. "I was going to say the ceremony."

"I thought you were done with the Hunt?" Mom said.

"It's sort of the same thing," Iona's mom said. "We're just—"

Bradley touched her arm. "We're collecting data, Mom. That's all. I'll explain everything when we get there. I promise. We'll carry it all; no one will be burdened. Please don't worry."

He put his arm around her. Cracks of suspicion dug across her forehead. Research was what they did at Avocado, but this was unusual. Dad didn't say anything about it.

A bell rang.

One of the cousins held up a silver triangle while the other one banged a metal rod inside it. The crowd drew closer to the stage.

"Time to go." Bradley lifted a box. "I'll explain more tonight."

Avery and her mom watched them load their weighty bags and boxes, strapping them over their shoulders, hunched over to balance the weight. Others would have to lug the larger items between them. They looked like they wouldn't make it across the yard let alone up the mountain.

Dad handed Mom a travel mug, steam seeping from the vent. "Is that Shaylene?"

"Did you know she was here?" Mom said.

Dad didn't know. And wasn't aware of any research.

❋

AUNT MAG DELIVERED instructions from a scroll of parchment. There was laughter and cheers. Aunt Mag wiped her eyes as she passed it to Mom.

Hugo was alone.

He still didn't have a backpack. No sleeping bag. Just a bottle of water. He was kneeling, his worn boot buried in the snow. A small, ragged towel laid out. He smelled like he'd just come from the kitchen. Baking cookies. The smell of cloves.

"I know what's in the shed." She glanced around. Mom and Aunt

Mag were hugging, Uncle Sage and Dad comforting them. "I saw the puppet."

He hesitated, just for a moment, then rolled the bottle and a pouch of tools in the towel. It fit into a velvet bag with a gold drawstring. He stood slowly. The snow fell away from his boots. There was a hole in the right one, just above the big toe. She wondered if there was a hole in the sock as well.

"You were born in the cabin," she whispered. "You've barely aged. My mom doesn't know it, or Aunt Mag or anyone else. No one knows who you are."

There was a creaky sound and laughter. Aunt Mag held a conch shell to her lips. She tried again, then handed it to Mom, who barely made it whistle. Uncle Sage took it and, with cheeks ballooning, played it like a bassoon.

"Did you see all the gear Bradley and the others have?" she said. "They're going to do something up there. I don't think you should go. They're looking for *you*."

"Everybody wants something," he said, his voice deep and raspy. "It's what Christmas has become, child. Your nana knew this. Wanting something we don't possess is the reason I must go."

"But you're..." She saw Bradley marching for the trees, his band of brightly clad friends lugging their stuff. "You're the Toymaker," she whispered.

"There is only one Toymaker, child."

"But Jenks said—"

His laughter was a deep, jolly bellow. More than a few people turned around. The ones on the stage—Aunt Mag, Uncle Sage and the cousins—looked shocked. The timing for such a jolly laugh was impeccable, perhaps written on the parchment. Or, perhaps, it was the first time they'd ever heard Hugo laugh.

"Did that ruddy boy give you any answers, did he?" He secured the velvet bag to his belt.

"The Toymaker did a long time ago. He made a plan, and-and-and Nana helped him. Don't act like you don't know. That's why you're here." She leaned closer, hand on his shoulder, and said, barely above a whisper, "You're hiding the gift."

"Let's walk up the mountain. It would be a shame to miss out on what your nana wanted." He patted her hand. "It's almost Christmas."

He marched off without another word and barely a worry. Just a sweater and baggy pants. And a hole in his boot. He hurried around the line, heading to the front to lead them past the shed and toward the trailhead. He wasn't surprised by what she said. *He knows.*

"Is everything all right?" Mom asked.

Avery nodded as she watched the line disappear into the trees. Aunt Mag and Uncle Sage tidied a few things and, strapping on their packs, met her and her mom in front of the stage.

"I don't think I've heard Hugo laugh like that," Aunt Mag said.

"I've never heard him laugh," Uncle Sage said.

❄

AVERY PEELED OFF HER SOCKS. Her feet were swollen. The heel on her right foot was as red as a peppermint. She dropped a rock on the ice —it shattered like glass—and dunked her feet.

Hikers wandered through the forest, breaking sticks and cutting vines. This was another extended break, as outlined in Nana Rai's instructions. *Create something with nature.* So they were stacking rocks, hanging bundles of pinecones. Poking sticks into the snow. It was a ten-mile hike, but these stops would make it last all day.

"You are busted," Meeho said. She and her sister squatted next to Avery. "You get hypertherm doing that."

Flinn snorted. "It's hypotherm."

They argued about the word. Avery wasn't certain either one of them knew it was hypothermia, not hypotherm. Her feet were good and numb. She dried them with an extra T-shirt.

"How's the tail end?" Meeho asked. Avery had been at the end of the line for most of the day.

"Thought you were lagging to sneak a look at the Hunt," Flinn said.

"Out here?" Avery said.

"Looker kits." Meeho aimed a crooked stick behind them. "Sat wire for anylink."

She was pointing at Bradley and his bunch. They were sitting on their boxes like geese on nests, twisting pine needles into little knots.

"They have satellite gear?" Avery said. "How do you know that?"

"Peeked at the labels, the pokes and nodes," Flinn said. "We have remote gear like that at school. Connect anywhere in the world."

"You sure?" Avery said.

"The Hunt, cousin," Flinn said. "Today's the day."

He said they were doing research. It sounded extravagant and contradictory to what they were doing—slogging through the snow, breathing fresh air and becoming one with nature. And all so they could camp on the mountain to watch the Hunt? They could've done that in the backyard.

"Nana Rai request," Flinn said. "Mom doing everything on the list, word for word. Nana Rai wants us to watch the Hunt. We watch the Hunt."

Nana requested it? There were two arguments to be made. The pro-Hunt: Avery found the puppet in the shed, Nana had the marbles, and Nana made the hiwires. It didn't take a conspirator to connect those dots. Nana Rai definitely wanted them to see the Hunt. The anti-Hunt argument: the Hunt began on her birthday, so how did Nana know when it was going to end? Unless she knew about the Hunt before the birthday. *But why go to the mountain to watch the end?*

"Too bad your wires got snatched," Meeho said.

They knew Avery's parents had taken her hiwires. But if that box was filled with lookers, it wouldn't matter. She didn't want to watch the end. She wanted to keep an eye on Hugo. He was standing near the frozen stream, looking at the sky. Aunt Mag was talking to him, making sure he knew where he was going. The trail, sometimes, was quite rough. She showed him the map. He glanced at it, but he already knew this area. This was his backyard. *He was born here.*

"You don't believe, do you?" Meeho said.

"Believe what?" Avery said.

Meeho and Flinn glanced at each other. "Elves and that," Flinn said.

"Your mom said you're a little dusty, buying the game frag for real," Meeho said. "Like real-real. Like Santa Claus is coming to town real."

"Like checking his list real," Flinn said. "Living that North Pole life real."

They kept it up, not really talking to Avery anymore. So rumors were going around that Avery had a touch of reality confusion. She didn't believe in elves and Santa Claus. She did believe in the Toymaker, though. He was standing at the stream, talking to Aunt Mag, which presented a conundrum. *If the Toymaker is real, then elves are real. And if elves are real, then...* Avery put her boots on, the laces coated with ice. She couldn't decide on Santa Claus without her head spinning. That would open doors that definitely led to reality confusion. *Real-real.*

"Do you think it's just a game, then?" Avery said. "All these new people with Bradley, they're from the Hunt, you know. Players that dropped out of the game and flew all the way here for Nana Rai's celebration. They don't even know her, and they just show up on the day of the hike with boxes of satellite gear. You think that's a coincidence?"

The cousins watched Bradley and Friends, squinting like they might recognize them from the Hunt. Avery didn't know if they were all from the Hunt. But Iona's mom was. And that was weird enough.

"If it's just a game," Avery said, standing up, "what are they doing here?"

"Pilgrimage," Flinn said.

"Pilgrimage?" Avery repeated.

"Pilgrimage," Meeho said.

"What's that mean?" Avery said.

"Some mirror world alt-games are like that," Flinn said. "Players travel for the end game, see who wins."

"They go worldwide, Av." Meeho sounded bored, like everyone knew this. "Pilgrimage."

Avery translated. Some virtual contests were alternate realities that mirrored reality: the same cities, the same streets, even the same people. Just virtual. Bradley had even said as much: *the world of the Hunt is just like our world.* They were using it to find the Toymaker. That was why he'd talked Dad into coming out early. His friends were just players who actually flew to where the game was ending. And brought looker kits to watch.

The Hunt was ending here. Hugo knew it. Jenks knew it. It was all part of the plan.

Avery didn't know whether to say anything. The cousins were stacking pebbles, too relaxed about it, like no big deal. *Like, yeah, we're hiking up a mountain to watch the end.* Did they think Nana Rai was a gamer?

"Do you think he'll be up there?" Avery said.

"Who?" Meeho said.

"The Toymaker. That's how the Hunt ends, they find him. You think he'll be, you know, on the mountain?"

They looked at each other. An entire conversation passed between their eyes: thoughts that didn't need words, just some identical-twin intuition. Then they broke out laughing. Not cruel, at Avery's expense, but real laughter at something very funny.

"Av," Flinn said, "you have to check yourself before—"

The ice cracked. Hugo's boot came out of the stream, water dripping from the sole. He stepped between them, the curious smell of cinnamon wafting from him. He propped a little stick figure on the boulder where Avery had been sitting, wrapped in flaky strands of roots and vines. He looked at the cousins, his emerald eyes glittering in pockets, then put his finger to his lips and waddled off. They watched him work his way toward the trail, to lead the next leg of the hike.

"He's so cracked," Meeho said.

"In half," Flinn said.

"Down the middle," Meeho said.

"Hugo got a son, you said?" Flinn asked. Avery didn't feel like talking anymore.

"Av?" Meeho said softly, kindly. "Do you see his son here?"

"What's that supposed to mean?" Avery said.

They shrugged, glanced at each other with that secret smile. Then Flinn said, "We heard you're thin on reality."

"You know," Meeho said, "you don't know exactly where here ends and there begins."

Reality confusion, Flinn silently mouthed, as if it was a bad word.

"Who told you that?" Avery said.

Mom was worried. Aunt Mag would know, so she would have asked what was wrong. Mom would've told her. Then Aunt Mag would've told the cousins to watch Avery, or don't let her go virtual. Keep an eye on her. Or maybe Bradley straight up told them. It didn't matter.

"It's no big, Av," Meeho said. "People get fuzzy all the time. It's real on the inside. Real as real. That's why you have to anchor, know when you're awake."

"It happened to Clinton Fairbanks," Flinn said. "He dipped virtual on the long. His parents never watched him, let him just ride all day, all night. And then he came to school with troll dolls. He was talking to them. Like real talk. Like set them up on the lunch table, listened to them. He'd say something, wait, then answer. He was in the deep fuzz, Av."

"He did re-anchor therapy," Meeho said. "So he knew there was there and here was here. Happens all the time."

"Your parents making you do therapy, then?" Flinn asked.

The horn sounded. Uncle Sage's cheeks expanded like bright balloons around the conch. Aunt Mag called everyone back to the trail, asked them to leave their offerings where they were, in honor of Nana Rai. Avery tied her boots. A curious question came to mind.

"What happened to the trolls?" Avery asked. "After he was cured?"

The cousins left their pebbles in a pile, helped each other strap on their backpacks. "He threw them away," Flinn said.

19

Avery had fallen behind.
 Each step wore at her heels, sending needles through her feet. Blisters wept into her socks. She'd dipped her feet in an icy stream whenever they stopped for a creative break.

 Strokes of scarlet-orange painted the western sky; the east rinsed in charcoal. A pink coat was up ahead and fading in the light of dusk. Headlamps bobbed like fireflies farther ahead. Many of the hikers weren't in shape for an all-day trek; some were regretting it. Avery was one of them, her boots full of blisters.

 There were shouts from somewhere at the front. Her pulse quickened. Pink coat heard it, too, and picked up the pace. Avery pushed through the discomfort. She hadn't packed a light and didn't have a phone.

 The trail turned at a snow-crusted boulder: narrow and rectangular, about shoulder height, like a monument. Green and gray lichen clung to bare patches. She leaned against it, tempted to peel off her boots and just walk barefoot. Her mom's head would explode if she walked into camp like that.

 She forced herself to hobble up the last rocky leg, grimacing each time her pack bounced. The trees eventually opened to a clearing.

There was another incline, this one long and smooth. The last of the hikers made their way up a snowy slope, breaching a ridge perfect for sledding.

At the bottom, far in the distance, was a crater lake dusted with snow, the ice black in the center. The slope was empty. But she'd seen it that morning in her bedroom: the frozen lake, the long open hill. The slope had been filled with toys hopping and rolling, limping and galloping, climbing and digging toward the ridge.

Avery did her best to scamper toward the glow of lights. The peak of cedar shingles on a pitched roof came into view. Domed tents were already set up. People hauled branches from the forest, the shining eyes of headlamps lighting their way. Avery walked stiffly past them, shed her backpack in the snow. Past a pile of dry wood.

She went straight to the log cabin.

It looked different than the picture she'd found in Nana Rai's photo album, worn down by time. But not much different than the cabin in the Hunt when there were toys gathered around. Now there were only tents and gear, hiking poles stuck in the snow. The door was wide and short. The hinges stiff.

She ducked inside.

Dark objects transformed into chairs and tables. A blackened fireplace yawned in a patchwork of stone. Snow had drifted through cracks in the walls, leaking through the ceiling. Old webs hung from rafters. The wood planks wobbled and creaked. She stood in front of the couch. The rug still there, faded and frayed, pulled apart by mice, where, once upon a time, Nana Rai had lain beneath a blanket, the Toymaker by her side.

In the corner, twigs stuck out like crooked fingers from a tree, once green and decorated. The needles turned to dust. A single cone hung from a strand of jute. The stockings were gone. Something, though, was on the mantel. Avery pulled the lean decoration down, ran her fingers over the grooves in the wood. Nana Rai had sat in that chair, right there, and carved an elf on top. A round belly and curly locks.

Avery shuddered with déjà vu. *I've been here before. But it wasn't here. It was there.* Her mind grappled with the idea that this place, this cabin, these chairs, the sculpture she was holding, existed somewhere else. She had been in a virtual environment, she reasoned, that was identical to this one. It was so hard to sort out. *Which is which?*

"There you are." Mom ducked inside and looked around. "This is quite a surprise. I never knew this existed. And it's been out here all this time."

She dragged her fingers over the low table, leaving streaks in a layer of snow and dust, then went to the wood-burning stove, where an elf once warmed water. Avery handed Mom the carving. Mom took her glove off to feel the wood—the pointy hat, the intricate curls of the beard. A breathy laugh, void of humor, escaped her.

"I don't know why I'm surprised," Mom said. "She was like that, your nana. She was so open with her life, but there was so much she didn't tell us."

She sounded hurt. Growing up in the house, playing in the woods, but her mother keeping the cabin a secret. If only Avery could take her to the library, show her all the secrets Nana Rai had kept.

"This place must have been special." Mom put the carving back on the mantel. "I only wish she would have shared it sooner."

Avery felt a twinge of guilt for knowing about it before Mom did. There had to be a reason for it. How could Avery tell her everything she knew—Hugo and the clues and the plan, what Jenks had said, the migrating toys—without sounding completely and utterly reality confused. It would only make her mom worry. At least now, her sadness was sweet.

Mom wrapped her arm around Avery, perhaps sensing Avery's discomfort, her anxiety, or maybe her own grief. They looked at the elf, waiting, as if it might tell them all the secrets of the cabin. Avery wished they were back home, opening their traditional present on Christmas Eve. Drinking hot chocolate, playing a game. Bradley getting in trouble. Avery going to bed, listening for bells on the roof before falling asleep.

"Come on." Mom squeezed her. "Your father needs help with the tent. I don't trust he knows what he's doing, and I don't want it collapsing in the middle of the night."

The fire had been started. A stack of unwieldy limbs was growing. Someone swung a hatchet in the orange glow, the edge thunking into hardwood, the sound reminding Avery of the time Nana Rai discovered the cabin. Tripods of white lights threw sharp shadows across the busy camp. Bradley and Friends were erecting something tall and skeletal. Little lights, green and red, glowed on heavy boxes they had somehow hauled up the mountain.

"What's Bradley doing?" Avery said.

"After we eat, story time will take place around the fire. It'll be streamed for those who couldn't make the journey."

"That's a lot of equipment just for recording."

"It's excessive, yes. He insisted, though. Your aunt Mag is thrilled to have his expertise. Nana Rai wanted to include some virtual display just before midnight. We didn't know how we would make that happen. She didn't leave instructions for how to do it. I suppose she just had faith we'd figure it out, or Bradley and your father would. I suggested we do it in the morning, when we're back at the house. Maggy didn't want to deviate from Nana's request. My sister, the engineer, is all about details."

"That's a sat link, Mom." Avery pointed to the tower. "He brought looker kits for everyone."

"Yes," Mom said drily. "I know."

"Why would we come all the way up here to use virtual gear?"

She sighed. "You don't have to do it, darling. In fact, I'd rather you not, just with everything that's happened." *You're reality confused, darling,* she didn't say. "Nana planned it this way. I don't understand it, either."

She's been planning for quite some time. "The Hunt is ending tonight."

"I don't think it's for that, darling."

Avery couldn't say more. Any more talk of a mystery boy named Jenks and talking puppets would only make things worse. And she couldn't explain the Toymaker, a real, live Toymaker, had hiked up the mountain with them. The Hunt was ending tonight. Avery didn't know, exactly, what that meant.

The thing Bradley was building was a tall, pointed antenna, like a dagger. A big box flashed below it. Maybe it was a satellite link or even recording gear, but it seemed excessive for either of those two things. The cousins were next to it, peering into a large container. They pulled out lookers and tried them on. In the firelight, they were black and shiny. They looked like surfers. A big box of them.

"I'll help get firewood," Avery said.

20

Avery waited at the edge of the forest.

She hadn't gathered a stick of wood. The fire was already blazing. Most everyone was around it, eating dried fruits and warm meals heated on gas stoves, drinking out of thermoses. Some had small collapsible chairs to sit on; others used logs to avoid sitting on the ground. Mom and Aunt Mag were busy coordinating. Dad was still wrestling with the tent.

Bradley and Friends had finished building their spire, the equipment blinking around it. They were at the fire now, with the others but mostly to themselves, chewing on energy bars and chatting quietly. Laughing too loudly when someone new joined them.

Avery snuck around the cabin.

It was dark. The only way to see something was with a headlamp. She went back into the trees, working her way to the other side of the camp. She waited nervously, watching the campfire. Aunt Mag called everyone. The few who weren't huddled at the fire crawled out of tents.

Avery tried not to make any sudden movements, appearing casual, walking past the stabbing tower and cables, the blinking boxes and collapsed bags. She grabbed the only container that had not been unloaded. The contents rattled inside.

Where did they get all these surfers? There was a set for everyone. It wasn't like surfers could be mail ordered. And they'd have to be keyed for everyone's identity. No one seemed alarmed by that obvious fact. Or they were too cold to care.

The bag was heavier than she thought. She couldn't drag it without being obvious. Bradley and Friends had their backs to her. She put her arms through the straps and waddled into a heavily trafficked path. Footprints were going in all directions from previous trips to gather firewood. She struggled to keep the bag out of the snow until she reached the trees.

She'd get in trouble for this. Aunt Mag wouldn't understand why she ruined Nana Rai's plans. *It's why I'm here,* Avery reasoned. *Nana Rai wanted me to know. She wants me to stop it.*

It was difficult to get the bag between the trees. She tripped several times, surfers spilling. She considered spreading them like breadcrumbs, but they might find them. And she needed them all gone. She didn't know how far she could make it, but the deeper into the woods she went, the better.

She found a dead tree with a hollow opening. The bag would fit inside. She could dump the contents, cover them with snow, then take the bag to the other side of the cabin. All she needed was for the night to end. Then face the consequences. She wouldn't lie. She'd tell them the truth, why she hid them, who Hugo was. Dad could test her for reality confusion when they got back. Just not tonight.

A few surfers fell around the stump. She fished through the snow, thinking they couldn't possibly work out here. She didn't know much about sat links, but it just seemed unlikely it could supply the bandwidth. *And what about power?* She looked inside a pair. It was a black hole in the darkness, like a void between her hands. And then, inexplicably, a tiny flash raced inside them. A worm of curiosity wiggled inside her, that feeling when she knew she shouldn't look at what was under the bed. She couldn't stop herself.

She slid them on. They were heavy, like a cold brick. Then the weight evaporated. She was still in the woods. The trees were dark columns, straight and coarse, but the light had changed. It was ashy. Dust particles glowed like wispy fairies.

Avery pulled back her sleeve. The bracelet dangled. *Is it silver or red?*

The forest was crawling. They were all around her again. The migration of toys was on the move, a parade of struggling playthings with dirty clothes and twisted limbs, flat tires and broken bodies. They limped toward the campsite. She followed them to the edge of the woods and stopped. The fire was gone. Not even a dark circle in the snow. The campers weren't here, because she was here and they were there. Somewhere beyond the veil.

The cabin was surrounded by toys. Thousands of them now. Packed tightly, jumping and hopping, spinning circles and watching. The window flickered with light that wasn't orange or red, but some version of gray. Everything was gray: a sharp contrast that hurt her eyes, stark and disturbing. Lifeless. Smoke puffed from the chimney. The toys watched the door.

Only this time it was open. She wanted to see what was inside.

"These are very important," she heard.

The world did a somersault. Ashy-gray light flickered into pale colors. Bradley held the surfers he'd swiped from her face. A lantern illuminated the trees, bright yellow. Avery covered her eyes. The lantern swung back and forth, casting stark light on one side of his face, then the other. There were several things gathered in the crook of his arm. He dumped them into the bag, the surfers that had fallen out while she'd been dragging the bag through the woods.

"Nana was very specific," he said, "about what she wanted. And you were going to ruin it. After all this time, you were going to ruin the whole story." He gazed inside the bag, as if counting. He wasn't smiling.

"No." She tried to hang onto the bag's handle. He was too strong. "Whatever you're planning, please don't."

"Nana Rai planned it." He put his finger to his lips. "Behave yourself, and I won't tell you're having an episode, that I found you wandering in the woods with surfers on, *pretending* they work."

Pretending? "What are you going to do with them?"

He extinguished the lantern. She heard snow crunching, twigs snapping. Staring wide-eyed, feeling lost. She slid up her sleeve to check the snowflake. She hadn't been pretending to use the surfers. She wasn't reality confused. But if she was, would she know it?

She felt the boney knob on her wrist. The bracelet was gone.

❄

"Where have you been?" Dad said.

"I'm sorry. I was... I was getting wood, and... my lamp went out."

"Found her!" Dad turned around. There were calls of relief. The search party hurried back to the fire. "You got to be careful, Av. You can't be wandering around without a light. What if you got lost?"

Dad put his arm around her to warm her and make sure she didn't get lost again.

"Dad?"

"Yeah?"

"Don't you think it's strange we're going to watch the Hunt?"

"What?"

"Bradley brought surfers for everyone. They hauled all that equipment to set up a sat link."

"Yeah, well, it's what your nana wanted. There's a whole list and, don't tell your mother this, but it's thankfully almost done. Hopefully, Bradley gets it to work."

"Gets what to work?"

Everyone watched Avery and her dad approach. Dad pumped his fist cheerfully. Mom and Aunt Mag were alone, leaning into each other to ward off the cold and worried thoughts. Avery could feel their agitation across the fire, their worry not dampening the group's spirits. They greeted her, one at a time, some hugging her, others patting her back. She didn't think she'd been gone that long. Dad presented her like a prisoner, gripping both arms. Mom took her by the shoulders and grimly smiled.

"Do not leave again."

Avery couldn't explain what she thought was going to happen without getting in trouble or getting everyone upset. If she was honest, she didn't really know. If she said anything, it could only make things worse. This felt like playing her dad in chess: the game was over before it began.

"Dad, get what to work?" Avery said.

"Huh?"

"You said hopefully Bradley gets it to work."

"Oh. The, uh, the sat link."

"It is working," she said, careful not to say any more about sneaking into the woods to hide the surfers, only to put them on.

"It's not even plugged in, Av."

21

Winter threw its big frozen arms around the camp.
They crowded the fire, wrapped in coats and blankets, squeezing shoulder to shoulder to trap the warmth. Weary faces stared into the flames, some shivering over mugs, drinking quickly before coffee or cider turned to ice. The wall of bodies parted for a fresh supply of branches.

An ornate metalwork sculpture, resembling a clock, was propped on a crooked branch: courtesy of Mr. Whitehead and Mr. Tangleton, the young volunteers who carried it up in pieces and assembled it upon arrival. It was a large oval with hands attached to the outer ring pointing at the empty center. It was on Nana Rai's list. And it was almost ten o'clock.

There was enough firewood to burn till midnight. Some of the campers didn't look like they were going to make it that long. But they'd come all this way. They were giving their all. Avery stood on the outside, the fire's warmth not getting past the human wall. She'd buttoned up, wearing everything she'd packed. It was barely enough. Uncle Sage was on his knees, hands a bit too close to the fire, steam rising from his gloves.

Avery had snuck over to the tower, but she didn't know the

system. Cables were everywhere, lights flashing. They must have tested it before she went into the woods. Bradley had noticed the surfers were gone and had unplugged the sat link before searching for her. But not before she put them on.

A conch shell sounded off. Uncle Sage's face was too stiff to make much of a sound. It sounded more like an empty pipe. Mom hugged a big leather book. It looked like the one from Nana's room, sitting on the table next to the feathered quill. Dad ushered Mom closer to the fire.

"Hear ye, hear ye!" Aunt Mag called. "The time is near!"

Hoots and hollers joined muffled applause. For many, this meant a warm sleeping bag was near. But others, like Mom and Aunt Mag, clapped with anticipation. Their eyes watered with cold joy.

"I've been looking forward to this," Aunt Mag said. "My sister and I have refrained from rehearsing to experience this with you. We waited till this time of night, like Nana would often do, with Christmas hours away, to gather around the fire with friends and loved ones."

She turned toward the cabin sitting beyond the firelight, a dark structure in shadows.

"I suspect she came up here often. Her explicit wishes were to share it with us. It's only fitting for this night to take place on such hallowed ground."

"She was a storyteller," Mom said. "I don't know if you knew that." There was laughter, most of it genuine. "When we were little, we would sit like this, cold and anxious, warmed with excitement and generous helpings of sugar." More laughter. "We anticipated morning, when the presents would be opened and new toys awaited. But, as we grew older, we began to look forward to the Christmas Eve fire."

Emotion rattled Mom's voice. Aunt Mag leaned into her.

"Her stories transported us to imaginary lands. It wasn't the words she used or the way her hands waved, or the way her voice would rise and fall that transported us. Something possessed her on Christmas Eve, something so... so tangible... *we could feel it.*"

The leather book creaked in Mom's grip. Mrs. Janklehauf covered her mouth. Mr. Winchester put his hand over his chest. Others hugged each other tighter. Suddenly, the cold wasn't so cold. Memories warmed them.

"We brought this." Mom held up the book. "Not to read, but to be here. You've heard the stories. Like us, many of you never tired of them. Each story she told, no matter how many times, was always like the first."

Mom and Aunt Mag bowed their heads. Uncle Sage stood up, joints aching. Mrs. Kehtenhound wiped her eyes. Mr. Kolten blew his nose into a white handkerchief. Avery was moved by the emotion and, for the first time since setting foot on the trail, felt the stir not of worry. But hope. Hope this wasn't anything like she thought it would be. This was just a magical story told like no one had ever heard. Nana Rai's story. *Why shouldn't the end be just as magical?*

"To ring in this Christmas," Aunt Mag said quietly, "we want to invite you to tell her stories. It doesn't have to be perfect. Just one you remember."

Silence fell around the fire. It was a minute of sniffling and shuffling before Mrs. Tenpenny spoke.

"I was a little girl, five I think, when I heard my first story." Mrs. Tenpenny's nose was as red as a stoplight. "It was about a reindeer with antlers as wide as a truck."

She threw her arms out. Avery imagined Nana Rai had done the exact same thing when she told the story. People muttered and smiled, remembering that as well.

"And I remember going home that night, my grandmother tucking me in, and I just knew it was true. I just knew it. I could see the reindeer when I closed my eyes, the antlers and the flaring nostrils. I could smell his grassy breath on my cheeks, humid and warm. I asked my grandmother if she thought it was true. 'Nana Rai wouldn't lie,' she said."

Everyone laughed. They'd heard that before.

"She said it was just a story, though, and that didn't mean it was real. But it's quite all right to dream. So I dreamed, every Christmas Eve, of those hooves on the roof and the jingle of bells. And my grandmother and I would sometimes tell the story to each other, taking turns. We'd memorized it, but it was never quite the same. But we did it nonetheless."

She cleared her throat.

And she told the story of the last reindeer, the reindeer no one ever sang about. He was the reindeer who protected the herd and led the sleigh. Not always nice, but fiercely loyal and protective, defending those in need. People nodded along, smiling, laughing for no apparent reason, perhaps remembering their mother or father tucking them into bed.

Nana Rai would never lie.

Avery used to be conflicted about those stories. It seemed cruel to insist they were true. She'd had her own time of doubt, wishing things were real, having to accept they weren't. She liked what Mrs. Tenpenny said. *It's quite all right to dream.* But now Avery found herself on the same precipice of youth, uncertain if they were just stories.

Mrs. Tenpenny finished, hugging Mom and Aunt Mag and others, and Mr. Craven told a story about a snowman just as fierce and protective as the last reindeer. Ms. Grackenbaum recited the tale of a lonely elf who was so cold his skin was blue. Mr. Corkheim regaled the group that had utterly forgotten the cold with a story about a woman on a tropical island who burned with Christmas spirit. Then there was the tale of Santa Claus, who actually wasn't the first Claus. The very first Claus was an elf. Avery remembered the elf on the stage, the one with the red coat.

"Mr. Popperharp?" Aunt Mag called.

A plump old man with wispy white whiskers clumped with bits of hardened snow nodded with a gleeful smile that creased his leathery cheeks. He took long patient steps around the fire, turned slowly to meet everyone's gaze. Unexplainable laughter welled up as the quiet stretched out.

"This," he said, his voice surprisingly powerful, "is the tale of an old, old man lost in greed and doomed to self-consumption. A man small of mind and bereft of spirit who, were it not for his faithful servant, was doomed to his own unwinding. His faithful android butler."

There was laughter over such a silly thing to say in a Christmas tale. *An android?* But what came next spun Avery's head.

"An android," Mr. Popperharp said, "named Jenks."

"What?" Avery blurted.

"Ha!" Mr. Popperharp threw his head back with a crooked finger in her direction. "A first timer, then? Well, let's recall the fateful night it all began…"

He was quite masterful in his storytelling, swinging his arms, bellowing voices and marching to the delight of the frigid campers. But Avery didn't hear much of it. She recalled the toys the Toymaker had placed on his workbench. Santa, a blue elf, a heavy Christmas ornament, a box of fire, a stuffed panda bear, a gingerbread man.

And a slender, silver android.

Jenks had said he'd taken other forms, that what she saw wasn't his body. He was the network, which meant he could go anywhere. He was there to help. She had seen him, talked to him. She wasn't confused; Jenks was real. *Does that mean the others are, too?*

"Merry Christmas to all!" Mr. Popperharp threw his arms out.

Cheering and applause and smiles creased stiff cheeks. A final story worthy of a tribute. More wood was brought to the dwindling fire. Avery noticed Bradley and Friends, until now, hadn't much moved. They applauded in somewhat of a trance, moved by the stories in ways the others were not.

The skeletal tower they'd erected was glowing at the top, not so much like an ornament atop a tree. More like the heated tip of a spear. The boxes below it were blinking faster—red, green, red, green. Bradley and Friends stood beneath the tower's dim light, checking their connections and settings.

"Thank you, everyone." Mom held up the leather book. "It is such an honor."

Avery saw Bradley open the bag. His friends huddled around him. They were going to hand out surfers.

"We have an hour till Christmas officially arrives," Aunt Mag said.

"If we can bring more wood to the fire, Bradley would like to begin Nana's final wish. He's going to hand each of you a pair of—"

"Is there time for one more?"

The voice startled Aunt Mag. It was deep and scratchy. The excited chatter grew silent. From the shadows, Hugo stepped into the light. This wasn't part of Aunt Mag's plan. No one could outdo Mr. Popperharp. It wouldn't be fitting. But Hugo was Nana Rai's longtime companion, they thought. *He's more than that.*

"Well," Aunt Mag stammered, looking back at the ornate clock, just a few minutes after eleven, "there's a schedule and..."

Hugo didn't argue. He only looked at her, green eyes twinkling beneath thick brows. He held an object at his side. Aunt Mag looked at Mom, then the others. They didn't know how to react. Hugo always operated in the background, making things tick. And Nana had very specific instructions. Which didn't include a story from Hugo.

"I'd like to hear it," Avery said.

A few others agreed. They were still basking in the emotions of Mr. Popperharp's storytelling and, with an hour still left before midnight, an hour before they could climb into their sleeping bags, they wanted more.

Embers floated like fireflies, quickly extinguished by winter's breath. Aunt Mag and Mom conceded the stage. Hugo stepped closer, wearing only a thick sweater. In bare hands, thick and callused, he held the sculpture from the cabin. His breath fogged from his grizzled beard. The bushy eyebrows furrowed, perhaps remembering the hands that peeled the wood away, a sliver at a time. Falling on the rug, swept into a pile to be tossed onto the fire. Nana Rai in her chair, humming her song. Perhaps Hugo at her feet, listening.

The fire popped. The silence hardened. Bradley and Friends stopped what they were doing.

"A very special person, she was," Hugo said to the wooden elf in his hand. "She wouldn't say that, of course. Quite ordinary, she would say if you asked. But you wouldn't agree, not if you knew her."

He nestled the sculpture in the snow.

"She did ordinary things: woke for school, ate breakfast, laughed with friends, cried when she hurt. Quite ordinary, indeed. But it wasn't what she possessed that made her special. No. No, it was what she didn't possess that made her quite so."

There were mutters, some asking if they'd heard this story. It seemed, to everyone, that it wasn't a Nana Rai story.

"If she stilled her mind, you would see it." His voice was no longer raspy, the words polishing the rough edges. They resonated like a deep bell. Avery could feel them. "If she settled the thoughts and worry, she would shine like the North Star. A gift in ordinary wrappings."

He bent over to straighten the sculpture.

"Elves have told the story for thousands of years, passed down from generation to generation. They celebrated at year's end, on the ice, below a tapestry of stars. Imbued with spirit so tangible, they would say, if they were here, you could feel it."

He wiggled his fingers. A silky essence flowed from his hand, Avery unsure if she saw it or imagined it. No one else seemed to see it, captured by his tale and the hypnotic train of his voice.

"To the world, these are just tall tales told around fires to entertain. Tales filled with happiness and sadness. Joy. But to elven, they are more. She knows this. She knows they are more than dreams we tell each other."

He held up a twig.

"Dreams are seeds that grow and blossom. And you do know this, too. You felt it, all of you, when you were young. You found the joy in simple things, the pure essence in things small and insignificant. Beginner's eyes seeing the joy, no matter how big or small. A blanket, a ball, a rock." He wiggled the twig. "You didn't see a stick."

He twisted it around, tied it in circles. Held up a stick figure with arms and legs.

"You saw what it could be. Lying in your bed, listening for bells, the scuff of shingles beneath a cloven hoof. And once every year, you felt it, as warm as a blanket. You didn't know that the magic is there, always there, the elven would say. You just need to look. And then you grew up. You put toys away, left them in boxes, tossed aside.

Discarded. But she kept your dreams alive, somewhere, so that the joy of Christmas lived where nothing dies. But some things are forgotten. And the forgotten never forget."

He fixed them with a ruddy stare. Everyone felt like he was talking to them, man and woman alike. They felt his words. In the same way Nana Rai's stories felt. A story just for them.

"Remember this, all of you. Joy is exactly where you are. It is here, not there." He picked up the sculpture. His voice had grown gravelly. He nodded to the little wooden elf. "That is what makes her special."

Hugo looked up briefly. Avery, mesmerized, realized she wasn't imagining it this time. He was looking at her.

First there were whispers, shaking of heads. "I never heard that one," Ms. Johanson muttered.

Emerging from confusion, their feelings were conflicted. He spoke of joy, but it didn't feel that way. Mr. Popperharp's goodwill had been washed away by a cryptic monologue that wasn't much of a story, as Nana Rai stories went. It made very little sense. *Was he talking about Nana?* One person, though, seemed entertained. Bradley stepped into the circle, clapping slowly and loudly.

"That, my friend," he said, "was not part of the plan."

22

"May I?" Bradley said.

"Please," Aunt Mag said.

"Scaring all these good people with a tale of... well, that wasn't much of a tale, dear friend."

Bradley spoke with a steely-edged smile, exposing all his teeth. An odd smile. Teeth clattering, but not a shiver. More of a habit.

"He's not used to speaking." He patted Hugo's shoulder. "Stay right here, friend. We'll need you momentarily."

Hugo stared at the sculpture in his hands.

"More wood, please!" Bradley called. "We need to warm these good people. Besides, we don't want the fat man to miss us."

His laughter was sharp and punchy, like a cap gun firing an entire roll. It was punctuated with that odd snap of his teeth, a grinding tic. His friends carried loads of dried wood, one after another, sparks flitting into the cold. Everyone stepped back. Avery could feel the heat all the way beyond the circle.

"Everyone, come closer," Bradley said, raising his voice. The fire was too big to move any closer. "Do you feel it? Do you feel that special time of year? The anticipation? All the boys and girls, right now, tucked away with dancing dreams—sugarplums and dolls, plastic castles and wooden rockets, little electronics that do this and that, shirts and hats, boxes of things that bounce and chatter, and toys and toys and toys and more. Do you feel it?"

His eyes were big, shifting left and right. A smile that didn't quite reach them. He held up his hands, beat his fists in the air. No one knew exactly what he was doing. But Avery did. He was playing the drums.

"Listen." He turned his head to the stars. "Do you hear the bells? Remember, when you were little, waiting for noise on the roof, clutching your blankets, hoping this would be the year. The year you hear the jolly fat man sneak down the chimney to put your dreams beneath the tree, stuff your stocking until the seams were bursting. Remember? And you would listen and listen. Can you hear it now?"

He nodded, hand to his ear, encouraging them to do the same. Some looked up.

"You don't remember," Bradley said sullenly. "Because the fat man doesn't work that way. Do you know how he does it, sneaks into your house without making a sound? He's got a device on the back of his sleigh." He was deadpan, teeth clapping. "How do you think he covers the entire world in a single night? Think about it, he goes to each and every one of your houses, shimmies down a chimney, fire or not, to deliver the presents and eat the cookies and drink the milk. How does he do it? *His device stops time.* Do you believe that?"

He put his hands on Hugo's shoulders.

"There's so much about Christmas you don't understand," Bradley said quietly.

"Bradley," Mom said. "Darling, are you—"

"I'm sorry." He raised his hand. "What time is it? Ah, yes. Aunt Mag, could you read Nana Rai's final wish?"

Aunt Mag had stepped back from the fire. Uncle Sage was with her, watching Bradley with weird fascination. Aunt Mag cleared her throat.

"To witness the end of the Hunt."

"To witness the end of the Hunt!" Bradley stabbed at the sky. "That's why we've come all this way, to witness this night as

Christmas draws near. As many of you know, there were special devices given to special people last Christmas to find a very special person. Do you know why we were tasked to do this? Of course you don't. Because you"—he bent over, eye to eye with Hugo—"spoiled the surprise."

Hugo didn't look his way. Bradley continued talking as if he did.

"But you got it wrong, old friend."

The skeletal tower hummed louder. The light grew brighter, casting shadows across the clearing, the cabin eerily lit. Bradley's friends worked the equipment around it. Avery could feel the ground vibrate.

"There is a gift, ladies and gentlemen." Bradley swept his arms. "A gift no one else has. A gift that one very special elf possesses. Elven, they're a whole nother story. Nana Rai had her stories, but the truth is, well, the truth is for another day because in exactly twenty-two minutes," he swung his hand at the ornate clock, "you will believe everything I say about an elf who makes toys very, very special. He makes them with love, with-with-with… how did you say it?" He turned to Hugo, waving his hand in a magical way. "He gives them joy."

"Pando," Ms. Buxley blurted out, recalling one of Nana Rai's stories.

Bradley snapped his fingers and pointed. "My dear Ms. Buxley, you are so very right! Toys that love. That's all they do. Love the children who love them back. Toys who listen to them read stories, throw tea parties. Toys who keep bad dreams away, who wait for them after school, listen to their problems. Watch them grow up." Bradley stared at the fire, pausing. "And where do the toys go when the children are gone?"

"Bradley." Dad looked concerned. "Son, what are you doing?"

"I'm here." He nodded. After a long pause, he said, "Nana Rai wanted us to witness the conclusion of the Hunt. I'm here to make her wish come true. And I'm happy to say," he put a hand on Hugo's shoulder, squeezed, "the Toymaker has been found."

Bradley's friends entered the circle, their arms full of surfers, black and shiny, handing them out, one pair to each person. Iona's mom giggled and hopped around the fire, dropping a pair here and a pair there. The campers took them, some excited to receive the special gear that had been reserved for the select few. How they'd had to watch the Hunt through updates and newsfeeds. And now they were chosen. They didn't question why.

Something felt so familiar, like a dream out of reach. The way Bradley's friends were moving, chattering like squirrels. Avery felt dizzy. *Who are they?*

"We can't connect." Mr. Cheshire held the surfers in his fist. "Not out here."

"The satellite." Mrs. Polumski pointed at the tower.

"No, Mrs. Polumski," Bradley said. "No, no, no. That's not a satellite link. That is an old family secret. It's more like a... well, you'll see." He winked. "Or maybe not. All right, everyone have a pair? Raise your hand if you don't. We all want to-to-to-to..." He chattered. "Witness together."

Mom and Dad had a pair. Aunt Mag put her clipboard down. Uncle Sage had opened his pair, staring inside them, his Christmas wish about to come true. Iona's mom gave Avery a pair, her eyes glassy. She hopped away. The excitement was palpable. The fire crackling. The sound of Bradley's teeth echoed like stones dropped on a wooden countertop.

That sound. Avery closed her eyes. She grasped at her thoughts. She needed to focus. She stepped away from the warmth, the cold quickly wrapping around her. Her eyes squeezed so tight, colors bleeding from the darkness. The sound of the fire faded. The chattering. *Who are they?*

The ground felt soft. The world turning. She stumbled forward, the earth tilting. The snow was strangely illuminated. The trees turned blue-black under an eerie dark sky. She turned around. The fire was gone. Mom, Dad, Bradley and Friends, everyone... they were gone.

The toys were back.

23

They were a crowd of matted fur and grimy dresses, knotted yarn and lumpy bodies and torn seams. Toys climbed onto abandoned snowmobiles to get a view of the cabin. Snowmobiles with bulky engines or long tailpipes, knobby tires with netted chains. She recognized the one the woman with spiky red hair had arrived on. It looked different now. There was no color. No color anywhere.

The world was gray and stark, cold to look at. Hard to feel. A gray light strobed at her feet. Gears grinding, a bell dinging. Something tunneled up the long slope, like a mole. It rammed against her boot, backing up and going forward, over and over. She dug a fire engine from the snow. The stickers peeling off, the chrome chipped from the bumper. *Ding. Ding.*

Something had changed. It wasn't just the blacks and whites or the flat grays in between that were different. Not the gray fire engine. She put it down and watched it continue its slow journey.

I picked it up.

Avery ran toward the cabin, hopping over a cluster of rubber ducks, around a cadre of big-headed dolls, over a cowboy with a crumpled hat on a plastic horse nosing the snow. There was barely enough room to avoid stepping on toys the closer she got, knocking over a wooden soldier that scattered a squad of plastic monkeys linked at the arms.

She could feel them behind her. Heard the shuffle of their stuffed bodies, limbs attached with rusted hinges, squeaky rubber joints. Some began hopping, others dancing when they saw her. She'd never been able to move anything in this world.

And they've never seen me.

Someone was slumped against the cabin. It was a man in a white coat, his legs pulled up to his chest, a black stocking cap bunched in his hands. His knotted hair was dusted with snow, beard frosted. Dead strands of Christmas lights hung from the cabin, the bulbs long burned out.

"What are you doing here?" she said.

He looked up, a blank page. She wondered if he heard her, if he could see her.

"Hey." She grabbed his arm. "What's happening?" He shook like one of the rag dolls. "Are you in the Hunt?" she asked.

The Hunt sparked some hint of life. His lips parted, icy whiskers breaking apart. He started to speak, but the words got lost. She felt him wilt.

"How long have you been here?" she said.

He was shaking in a hopeless search for answers. She swiped his face. He jerked back, frowned. Perhaps a vague memory of what it was like to pull off the surfers. Or lost hope after he'd done it so many times.

Claustrophobia breathed on her back. The toys were closing in. They climbed over the man, perching on his arms, watching her push the cabin door, hoping it would open, not thinking how she got here or, if it didn't open, how she would leave. Stale air wafted out of a dark room, heavy and tired, laced with despair. It seemed to draw the will from her, replaced it with the desire to sit down. It wasn't the air she felt. It was coming from the toys hugging her legs, trying to crawl into her arms. Wanting something from her.

She nudged a troll doll with a goofy smile with her boot. It wobbled toward her, grubby little fingers clenching, as she closed the door. People, not toys, milled about in the dark, bumping into each other like a party without music or purpose. They were packed tightly, body to body. They parted slightly to let her in.

Avery turned sideways, wondering if this was real, if this was just an illusion. That they were no more real than toys scratching at the door. She worked her way to the middle. The crowd swallowed her. Her throat was dry and her clothes weighty. Gloom drizzled from the webby ceiling. A woman turned around, rheumy eyes cast down.

"Mrs. Baker?" Avery said.

Iona's mom lazily looked up and scanned Avery's face. Recognition crept at the edges. She'd seen Avery someplace. Some time.

"You," was all she said.

"Why are you here?" Avery said. *Wait. How is she here? She's at the campfire, handing out surfers. If she's here...* "Mrs. Baker, where's Bradley? Is he here?" She raised her voice. A wave of tension passed through the room. The shifting crowd froze.

"Bradley?" Avery said. "Bradley!"

Someone tipped over a chair, the armrest splintering. A young man banged his clean-shaven head on the wall. Avery spun a woman with oily short hair around. She covered her face like Avery was a bright light. A lanky old man turned his back, muttering in tongues. Someone grabbed Avery's arm and squeezed till it hurt.

"Leave." Mrs. Baker's lips barely moved.

"Why are you here?"

Avery shoved deeper into the room. They ducked away, trembling. The walls vibrated. Snow fluttered from the rafters. Mrs. Baker was shouting at her. The weight of bodies pushed against her like she was digging a hole. She saw the mantel of the fireplace, the elf sculpture on top. Someone was next to the skeletal Christmas tree, balled up on the floor, arms locked around his shins. Avery clawed her way to the corner. The young man's head was buried between his knees. She touched his hand. He lifted his head, blinking heavily.

"Av?"

Avery felt faint. Her legs soft noodles. She stumbled toward him, pulled his dead weight. "Bradley, come on."

He fell forward, knees thudding on the planks. She ducked under his arm and stood him up. Strength returned to her legs as he slumped like a bag of wet snow. "Get out of my way!" she shouted.

The crowd jittered off-balance. Avery plowed her way through them, went the long way around the couch, knocking a man against the wall. There was a gap ahead. They were avoiding the kitchenette. She swung Bradley for the door. Then her knees locked. For a second time, her legs turned soft.

There they lay, stacked like the aftermath of Christmas morning. Toys thrown into a pile. A stuffed bunny with a missing ear, a nutcracker with a broken spear, a turtle with a cracked plastic shell. A dozen more were piled beneath. The largest of them leaned against the wood-burning stove, toys piled on his lap, his jointed arms around them. Hinged jaw hung slack, top hat askew.

She waited for the puppet to shed the weight, to stand up and snap his jaws.

"Traaaa..." Bradley ran out of steam.

"It's all right, I've got you. I'll get you out of here."

"Traaaansfer..." He stumbled with her. Then his feet dragged, all of his weight nearly pulling her down. He fell next to the toys, under the blank stare of BT's round eyes.

"Bradley, come on. The door is right there."

He wasn't snapping his teeth when he talked. Mrs. Baker emerged from the crowd, looking down on him, staring like a lost child. She wasn't hopping like a bunny. And then Avery understood what he was saying. One word that explained why he had been snapping his teeth, acting strange, why the toys in the corner were empty. Bradley really was here. Iona's mom was here, too. If he was here, that meant someone else was back at the campfire.

Transference.

He looked so alone. She knelt down to throw her arms around him. He was soft, like he was made of feathers.

"Go," Bradley said.

She knew why he was still here, why all of them were here. She looked at the pile of toys, nothing more than fabric and stuffing and wood. They were empty because they weren't here.

They were there.

※

"That's not Bradley!"

Avery stumbled toward the fire, slapped surfers out of Mr. Nisherell's hands. Mrs. Dissellini hid her surfers behind her back before Avery could swat them.

"That's not Bradley," Avery said. "He's someone else, someone who transferred into Bradley's body. If we put on the surfers, we'll be trapped over there, in the Hunt. The Toymaker... he tried to stop them. He knew this was going to happen. That's why they're looking for him. BT and others want to find him, to stop him. They're bad toys!" She pointed at Bradley's friends. "All of them."

They hopped like stuffed bunnies and leaped like frogs and moved like turtles. It was the way some of them marched like robots, slid their feet in stiff, mechanical ways. It was the way Bradley's teeth snapped. *A puppet clapping a hinged jaw.*

"It's him," Avery said. "He's BT."

"Avery," Dad said, "honey, let's—"

"Don't put the surfers on! The tower is for transference. Those aren't the people you think they are. They're trapped in the Hunt. The bad toys took their bodies!"

Mom and Dad spoke quietly and quickly. Avery could feel their regret. Avery never should have come on the hike. Dad should've stayed back with her because now she was in reality confusion free fall.

A few people dropped the surfers. Bradley saw it. Hand on Hugo's shoulder, he held him in place. Hugo stared at the sculpture, as if waiting for the end. With a quick wave, Bradley signaled his friends. The tower hit another gear. Ashes trembled in the firepit.

"Bradley!" Dad shouted. "What are you doing?"

"It's all right." Bradley held out his hands. "I understand your concern, everyone. I didn't want this night to end like this, but it's going to be all right. It will be a bit jarring for some of you. All your beliefs will be turned inside out. It's not easy to accept the truth. You ignore it, keep it over there, out of sight so you can sleep at night."

The clock hands moved closer to midnight. Bradley slid the surfers onto his nose. The fire blazed in the reflection. He turned to his friends. "One minute, everyone."

"Put them on!" Hugo shouted. "Everyone, wear the surfers. Please!"

"No!" Avery pleaded. *What is Hugo doing?*

"You didn't come this far to miss out on the greatest night of the year," Bradley said.

They began to follow Bradley's lead. Avery was too erratic. Something was wrong with her. They looked at her parents; then, one by one, surfers were raised. They smiled as they did so, seeing something wonderful, nudging those around them. "Hurry." Mr. Bloomquist looked up, pointing at something he was seeing inside the surfers. "Look!"

And they hurried. They all did.

"Mom, no." Avery ran to her parents. "Trust me, please. We can't let them—"

"Darling, I want you to stay right here." She put her arms around her. Dad did, too. "I don't want you to put them on."

Bradley left the circle. Hugo shuffled with him. In the machinery's great hum, Avery heard a song rise up. Bradley and Friends were singing.

All the toys and little boys, the twirls and little girls, give what they need, to get what they want.

They surrounded the tower, holding hands. The light burned blue-white, casting sharp shadows over their features. Their brightly colored coats began to ripple. The atmosphere crinkled. The grinding hum grew louder, tighter. Hugo was with them, shadows hiding his face, clenching the sculpture.

"No!" Avery broke away from her parents.

Her dad shouted. Her mom was afraid that her daughter was running into the woods again, lost in reality confusion. It was Avery's only chance to stop them. The clock clipped its final minute. The hands met at the top.

A subsonic force surged through the ground. The tower engulfed the campsite, bleaching the trees and cabin. Avery stumbled into the snow, felt her scalp tingle with prickly needles. Her teeth were numb. Sound warped in slow motion. Dad's shouting stretched into a long slur. And then it was silent. Utterly still. When she looked back, the campers were still there, staring up with black surfers on their faces. They weren't moving. Neither was her dad.

He was right behind her.

24

Dad's hand undulated. His jaw was locked with a cloud of frozen steam. Snow levitated around him. All the campers were like that: a collection of wax figures around the fire. Embers glowed above the fire like tiny orange lights; the fire was a photo, flames captured in a still moment.

The clock pointed midnight.

The scene had a watercolor quality. Avery went to her dad, his outstretched hand, his lips twisted. A barrier was between them, a translucent curtain that painted everything in blurred and muted colors. She could see it now, a thin wall distorting the air. It was frigid on her fingertips, burned with icy fever. Her sleeve slid back. The bracelet was still missing.

She had no idea where she was. If this was a dream, she didn't know how to escape, or where to go. She closed her eyes, slowed her breath. *Where am I?*

"What's the differential?" BT-Bradley was at the tower, hunched over. The glow of a tablet splashed him with white light. "Adjust the time dilation. Shorten the sync point. We need to conserve power till he arrives. Put the video stream on standby and check the lights."

His friends went in different directions, attending to a cluster of light stands and flexible mounts. Hugo looked in Avery's direction. Several friends gathered around him, touching his sweater.

"I know who you are!" Avery said to them.

They turned toward her, some surprised. BT-Bradley handed off the tablet and gave more orders, told them to clear a space. He went over to a small stove. He approached her with two folded chairs, spiked them into the snow, and offered her a steaming mug. It smelled like cocoa.

"I should put you out there." He nodded at Avery's dad. "But you've seen too much. Safer, at this point, you see it all."

He sat down with a satisfied groan, closing his eyes to sip the cocoa. He had all the physical features of her brother, but none of the mannerisms. Bradley didn't cross his legs like that, didn't savor what he was eating or drinking like that. Even this version of him, this BT-Bradley, was different than he was an hour ago. No longer manic, desperate. He was calm, patient.

Like he had all the time in the world.

"I was protecting them." He gestured with the mug. "Offering them the surfers to avoid this part. They weren't going to be *transferred*," he quipped. "They were to put them on as a distraction. And when they took them off, we would be gone, and all would be right. There wouldn't be any reality confusion about what happens."

He shook his head regretfully. Many campers on the other side of that watery wall weren't wearing the surfers. And Dad was only a few feet away.

"What's going to happen?" she said.

"Well, reality is going to change. And when it does, it'll be difficult for them, you, and everyone else in this world. All their beliefs of what this world is supposed to be, how it works, will be *whoosh*. Your nana wanted to avoid that. Her instructions were very specific." BT-Bradley leaned toward her. "I understand you were just trying to help them, but you've made it far worse."

"I know what you're doing."

"It's not what you think."

"I don't believe you. That's transference gear." She pointed at the campers. "You're going to steal their bodies, trap them over there, in a cabin. You're bringing the rest of the bad toys to take their bodies."

"We're doing much more than that."

"I want my brother back." She swung her arm at the friends. "You don't belong here! You stole their bodies and abandoned them. *You* belong there. I want them back here!"

They all looked at her now, even the ones working the equipment. Looking up from tablets, holding cables and waiting. BT-Bradley turned in his chair, waved his hand. They went back to work.

"You're right," he said. "It's not fair, what we've done. But all will be right very soon. I promise. We have no intention of staying in these bodies." He studied his hand, turning it over, as if trying on a new suit. "This is only temporary."

He licked foam from his upper lip.

"I'll admit, these senses are intriguing. Some of us, I'm sure, find them quite tantalizing. Taste, for one. It's alluring. But I assure you these senses are limited. You can't comprehend what it's like to be us. Trust me when I say we don't want to be in these bodies any more than you want us in these bodies. We want to be here, but not like this. Your brother will return, as will the rest."

"Then what do you want?"

His eyes narrowed. "Do you know what that world is, where we come from? The cold, sepia skies, the colorless landscape. We simply don't want to be there. We never did."

"We didn't put you there."

The smile shrank to a thin line, so unvery Bradley. He stood up, setting the mug in the snow. Avery backed up, feeling the cold barrier between her and her dad nibble at the back of her neck. Perhaps BT-Bradley was going to push her through it after all, send her into the still moment where her parents and the others were frozen. He tipped his head, studying her.

"When you were seven years old, Nana Rai gave you a Ms. Frosty Hound for Christmas. Do you remember? She was wrapped with a red bow, a velvety white hound with shiny black eyes. A red tongue sewn on a whiskered smile. You slept with Ms. Frosty every night."

BT-Bradley held a hand to his cheek, put his thumb in his mouth.

"On your first day of school, you put her in your backpack. When you were frightened, you rubbed her tail between your fingers, until it was smooth all the way down to the lining. And when the seam frayed, your mother sewed it back up. You told Ms. Frosty everything. You'd sit her on your pillow and gossip about your friends, the cute boy who shared scissors with you in art class, your mean teacher who yelled, how your parents treated you differently than your brother. You'd wait by the drier when your mother washed her, holding her while she was warm."

He put his hand to his cheek again.

"But you grew bored." he said. "Where is Ms. Frosty Hound now?"

Avery assumed the white hound was in the basement, at the bottom of some container, buried beneath outgrown clothes and discarded playthings. "How do you know that?"

"You put her in a box!" He pointed up, as if the veil—his world—was up there.

"She was just a toy."

"*Just a toy.*" He leaned back, grimacing. "We're more than that. We're your dreams, your hopes and fears. We comfort you at night, drink your pretend tea! But we don't go away. Even when you stop loving us." He pointed up again. "Nana Rai knew what we truly are. And the Toymaker showed her where to find us."

"No." Avery tried not to look at Hugo and failed. "The Toymaker knew you were going to do this, a long time ago. He wanted to stop you."

"Is that what he wanted?" BT-Bradley walked to the distorted wall. The clock outside still pointed to midnight. "Nana Rai knew the true value of dreams. She knew you need us as much as we need you. She showed us a way." He turned, hands locked behind his back, with a sorrowful grin. "A way to heal us all."

"She didn't want that to happen to my brother."

"I simply borrowed him. Much like you borrowed Ms. Frosty."

"But the veil... if it breaks, no one wins."

"Uncertainty always exists." He kicked the snow. "Risk is inherent."

A warning wailed from the tower. Lights blinked. The warped wall emanated from the tip of the tower. "Clear out!" BT-Bradley shouted. "Everyone, over there. And do not move."

They ushered Hugo to the opposite side of the translucent dome. The center was cleared. They were looking up. Hugo met Avery's gaze.

"Don't hurt him," Avery said.

"We're not going to hurt him." BT-Bradley locked his hands behind his back. "He's going to help us."

The warning grew louder, the rhythm steadily picking up.

"We're not bad toys." He emptied the mugs of cocoa into the snow, staining it murky brown with bits of melted marshmallow. "We never were."

He held out his hand. Avery wouldn't take it. He put his arm behind her, stiffly ushering her across the clearing, and put her next to Hugo.

"Do. Not. Move," he said.

He went to the tower, assessing the tablets one last time. Then, like the others, looked up. The stars were blurry streaks through the warped dome. Avery felt Hugo reach for her, his hand cold and callused. He held on, deep-set eyes staring straight ahead.

The tower pulsed. She felt magnetic waves in her chest, a metallic taste in her throat. The snow shimmered and began lifting off the ground, hovering like moths. BT-Bradley shouted, his voice barely audible above the noise. His friends, the Toy People, began pointing like New Year fireworks had just begun. One of the stars moved through the dark sky.

Iona's mom hopped in place. Other Toy People danced and clapped. The tower's signal reached a painful tenor. Avery covered her ears, lips growing numb. The struts on the tower began to glow. The light gathered at the tip and then, swelling in a ball of lightning, erupted. At first, it was a beam as thin as a wire, crackling into the cloudless night sky. Slowly, it began to widen. Colors bled into the beam.

"More!" BT-Bradley shouted distantly.

They punched buttons, swiping tablets. The tower was quaking. The equipment rattled. Bits of snow were drawn into the tower's gravitational field. Avery felt like a balloon slowly inflating. She squeezed Hugo's hand to keep from floating off the ground. BT-Bradley stood at the base of the tower, fist over a big red button. Looking up, looking back at the Toy People monitoring the power. The lightning sharpened into a laser knifing into the sky. The dome quivered with snowflakes.

"Now!" someone shouted.

BT-Bradley punched the big red button. Avery's ears popped.

Everything went into slow motion. Voices warped. The tower's magnetic pulse buried them in an avalanche of dense energy. Avery couldn't breathe. The levitating snowflakes jittered in place, dropping like tiny diamonds. Time sprang like a nocked arrow.

Avery gulped a deep cold breath.

A thunderous explosion engulfed them. The earth quaked. Steam escaped, consuming the Toy People's bright coats and the tower's skeletal structure. Hugo kept Avery from falling, holding her as she struggled to breathe.

And then it was quiet. Only the sound of hissing. The steam cleared, revealing a shiny red panel and golden rails buried in snow. Avery squinted at the dispersing cloud. The details slowly emerged.

Bells were ringing.

25

The tower sizzled, trails of energy coiling up the struts, dispersed through the glowing tip. Low-grade charges traced the dome, popping like insects in an electric trap. The hairs on Avery's neck stood up.

Antlers appeared from the fading mist.

Wide nostrils steamed from long, hairy muzzles. Reindeer were in front of a shiny red sleigh where a man, dazed and searching, wore a red coat with white trim and a warm, floppy hat. White beard, white gloves, he was ripped from a Christmas card, missing only half-rim spectacles at the tip of his nose.

Avery felt weak in the knees. Blood pumped in her head with memories of Santa Claus in downtown parades, wearing a bright coat of thin fabric, beards of cotton-white curls hanging loosely over their faces. The storybook *ho-ho-ho* and *Merry Christmas*. Sometimes they were tired or bored, smelled like regular dads, gently patting children on the shoulder. They weren't much different than mall Santas on ornate thrones, surrounded by piles of gifts, assisted by elves that were full-grown adults ushering children in orderly lines.

The man in front of Avery was not from the mall.

His coat was thick and worn, the cuffs gray with soot. The boots scuffed, buckles tarnished. His beard was dense and mostly white with curls of gray. Hugo kept Avery from melting in a whirlpool of vertigo. The Toy People were giddy, clapping and whispering with smiles threatening to split their cheeks.

BT-Bradley shared none of that: hands clenched behind his back, watching the less-than-jolly fat man slide out of the sleigh. Black boots planting in the snow.

Santa Claus—*who else could he be?*—surveyed the scene where he suddenly found himself. His cheeks ruddy, eyes twinkling in wrinkled folds. Moments before, soaring through the sky, the next moment yanked to the ground by some strange time-stopping tractor beam. His gaze lingered on Avery and Hugo. A single nod like he understood, perhaps, what this was about. And who they were.

The reindeer were in a line, two by two. But the one in front, chest heaving like an overworked furnace, was alone. He reared up, antlers grazing the warped and now charged dome popping like a bug zapper. Santa raised his hand, whispered to the herd. They stamped the snow, nostrils flared, eyes on high alert.

"Hello," BT-Bradley said. "It's been quite some time since we last met. Twenty years, to be exact, since you pulled me out of the bag."

A velvet sack rested in the back of the sleigh, tied with a crimson strap. Santa's bushy white brows furrowed. He buried his fingers into his beard to scratch his chin. Perhaps he recognized the young man speaking to him: Bradley Martin Tannenbaum, twenty-six years old, successful computer scientist in the field of virtual environments. *But pulled from the bag?*

"The last time you were snatched from the sky was a very long time ago," BT-Bradley said. "Do you remember? Your brother was quite ingenious. Well, half-brother. His method was crude. Effective, but crude. I promise you, Nicholas, we've upgraded. You are time-snap isolated, I'm sure you've gathered by now."

The tower spat. The lights, once flashing green, were now yellow. The hands on the clock outside the dome still pointed to midnight. *Time-snap.*

"You're a smart man. I'm sure you've found yourself in some

mighty tight pickles over the centuries. None, I assure you, quite like this. Our power supply, as you've already noticed, is limited. Should you wish to delay our negotiation in hopes it will run out, we have lights and video streams ready to beam this interaction around the world. Privacy you and your little helpers hold dear will be taken. A small concession, perhaps, but there's more. Shall I continue?"

Santa looked at the Toy People. Once again, his gaze lingered on Avery and Hugo. He said, with a deep, sonorous voice, "Are you hurt?"

Avery shook her head. Her throat had petrified; words wouldn't form. Speaking to Santa Claus, even if she could, would send her spinning. She was barely holding it together knowing Bradley wasn't in his body. Talking to Santa Claus would be another giant leap.

Santa retrieved a small burlap sack from the sleigh. The reindeer turned their heads. Avery could smell a grassy aroma. Santa held out compressed cubes of alfalfa and offered them to the Toy People.

"Would you mind?" Santa said. "It's been a long night."

They took the cubes like children offered candy, holding their palms flat, like Santa told them, for the reindeer to nibble from off their hands. They were told to feed all the reindeer except the one up front.

"Ronin isn't hungry," he said.

Avery, even if she were inside a shopping mall with her parents holding her hand, wouldn't feed Ronin. Not with the look in his eyes and the steam firing from his nostrils. The Toy People kept their distance.

Santa stepped toward BT-Bradley, buckles ringing on his boots. He stared with the vision of a parent searching for the truth, for some nugget of recognition. The young man looked like Bradley, but Santa knew, scratching his beard, someone else was looking back.

"How can I help you, Mr..."

"BT is the name I was given. My friends and I have travelled a long ways to meet you."

"And why is that, Mr. BT?"

"You have something we need to borrow. And we have something you've lost."

Santa nodded, still searching. "Forgive me, I'm not quite as young as I once was. What have I lost?"

"Of course, you don't understand. You just give toys away. I know about you and the elven hiding on the North Pole, the rich history of secrets, smear campaigns to make you seem real but not really. Wink, wink. I know about the traditions, Nicholas. How every generation there is born a special elf, one with extraordinary power—one would say magical—to connect with the essential marrow of life: the gift of love. This elven is the keeper of this gift, imbuing it upon the very things you give away once a year. The Toymaker, you call him."

BT-Bradley looked at Hugo. Santa Claus did not. He wasn't surprised by BT-Bradley's revelation. After all, he'd just been tractor-beamed from the sky.

"The Toymaker warned the elven this day would come, long before you stumbled into their colony and became, well, what you are today. Oh, you heard the rumors, the elven didn't quite believe that technology would bring humans, or, as one very unique elven called them, *warmbloods,* on par with elven. After all, elven were the guardians of such advanced technology. So the Toymaker took matters into his own hands."

Once again, a look at Hugo. Once again, Santa did not.

"Humans evolved to make their own magic. And, like humans do, their magic was disposable. Plastic trucks with plastic parts, Mary Bell Babies with cheap voice boxes, drones with faulty circuits, scooters with cracked rubber wheels, popping balls and broken wagons and flat tires and missing limbs and on and on until we all end up in dusty bins and trash bags to make room for next year's delivery. Humans don't really need you or them anymore, Nicholas. But that's not why the Toymaker hid the gift."

Santa Claus grunted. No twinkle in the merry man's eye.

"Of course you know this. Because you found him." BT-Bradley gestured outside the bubble where, through the warped lens of the time-stopping dome, the dilapidated cabin wavered. Where Avery had seen, in one of the clues, Santa come for the Toymaker on the night Hugo was born. "You took him back, safe and sound. But he wasn't hiding from you anymore. I'm sure you gathered, returning to the North Pole, the Toymaker no longer possessed the gift. He had passed it on to another, buried it deep in the DNA of an unsuspecting child. And you and your little helpers don't know where it is." BT-Bradley eyed him with a grim smile, opening his arms. "Don't you recognize us?"

Santa nodded slowly.

"The Toymaker saw what would become of us," BT-Bradley said. "He knew there were other realities; he knew we weren't stuck in cardboard boxes or plastic crates stashed in basements and attics. He knew who we are—who we truly are—was out there!" BT-Bradley jabbed at the sky. "He wasn't warning the elven that the veils separating our realities might burst. He was telling you and the elven and all of your kind what happened to us when we're forgotten. He warned you one day we would be coming back home. He didn't want to stop us! He wanted to make amends." BT-Bradley snapped his teeth. "But you didn't listen."

Santa hiked up the black belt strapped around his generous belly, searched their faces, the oblivious joy of the Toy People feeding reindeer under the watchful gaze of Ronin. Maybe he was stalling. A few of the lights on the equipment were red. This couldn't be the first time he'd been caught by a sleepless child. Certainly, he had ways to avoid being seen. A global stream of his presence could be dealt with.

He also knew that BT-Bradley had more than just video.

"This is not a small matter, Mr. BT. It can be resolved. But not this way."

"The solution is quite simple." BT-Bradley extended his hand. "The Toymaker's hat, please."

Santa stopped working his belt. "The hat?"

"The hat, Nicholas. We want to come home, where we belong. All of us."

Santa's calm demeanor cracked. The gravity of the situation suddenly weighed on his composure. Grave concern was heavy. BT-

Bradley and the Toy People had transferred into humans and banned Avery's brother and all the others in another reality. The Toymaker's hat, based on Santa's agitation, meant they could do so much more than that.

"I can't allow you to do harm," Santa said.

"There will be no harm. Bradley Martin Tannenbaum will return to this." BT-Bradley patted his chest. "The others will, too. They will resume their daily lives as if nothing ever happened. We don't want these bodies. We want to join them."

Santa frowned. "Cross the veil."

"The Toymaker will bring us here in our true forms. Humans and toys living in harmony. There will be no more boxes with forgotten toys in closets or shoved under beds to collect dust bunnies. We'll be citizens of this world. The magic of the elven will be revealed to the world. And you, Nicholas, will not need to hide anymore. We all win."

Santa considered the offer: to bring the toys, living toys, into the world. Toys that were forgotten and banished, somehow, to a world of their own. *They want to come home.* Avery wanted him to say yes, to get this over with. To get her brother back. The not-so-jolly fat man in the red suit merely scratched his beard.

"Your world is beautiful, Mr. BT," Santa Claus said. *He knows about the Toyworld?* "Why risk crossing the veil and losing everything when you can—"

"Through your eyes!"

Ronin reared up, and the Toy People retreated, gathering near Avery. BT-Bradley regained his composure, his words measured and pointed as darts.

"You don't know the bleakness we know. Your senses can't know our experience any more than the allure a beetle has for a heap of dung. We belong here, Nicholas. We were made to be here. Not there. You should understand that."

"The fabric of this world isn't made for toys to exist, not in that way."

"Change is difficult. But we will teach humans, and they will learn. We have become Christmas. You of all people know this. The children of the world look forward to us, not goodwill and catchy tunes on the radio. It's toys, Nicholas. What could be merrier than toys and humans living side by side, drinking eggnog and singing songs, filling stockings and playing games? Waiting to hear your bells?"

Someone whispered to BT-Bradley. More lights were red. The dome was beginning to thin.

"Dear Santa." BT-Bradley pretended to write a letter. "We want Dinky Sinky Playhouse with a solar-powered display and a rocket-powered three-wheeler with blinking lights. We want a wooden puppet and all his friends to come home." He folded the imaginary letter, pretended to lick the envelope. "You have our humble request."

Santa looked at BT-Bradley's empty hand. "Your world can be what you make it."

"We didn't ask for our world. We are not disposable. This right here"—BT-Bradley pointed at the Toy People—"is proof. What are we when we are not loved?"

"You *are* love," Santa said. "With or without humans."

BT-Bradley withdrew his hand. He sighed deeply, his arguments exhausted. How could Santa not understand? Even if Avery hadn't been over there, hadn't seen her brother and the others in the cabin, she still would've begged Santa to hand over the hat. She'd seen what their world looked like through their eyes: the bleached landscape and gray skies. That was what they saw, how they lived. *They don't deserve that.*

The bright lights turned on. The cameras were ready to send a video feed of Santa and his reindeer around the world. It was a small concession, really. People would adjust to the myth being a legend. Compared to toys walking amongst them, living in small houses in neighborhoods, going to school, shopping for goods or whatever else toys would need, a video stream wasn't going to change Santa's mind. And really, would anyone believe it was real?

"We don't want apologies." BT-Bradley nodded. The tower hummed. "We don't want to dash the dreams of all the little boys and girls tucked into their beds right now, listening for the bells. I'll ask, one last time. The hat, Nicholas." He held out his hand. "Pretty please with nutmeg."

"It won't help you," Santa said. "The Toymaker no longer exists."

"We know the legends," BT said calmly. "We know you carry the hat every year, ringing the bell in hopes he will answer. That he will no longer hide, that he is out there and he will hear it and he will bring the gift home."

Santa shook his head.

"We will get what we want even without the hat," BT-Bradley said. "We will take these bodies, one by one, toy after toy becoming human after human. It's up to you. We don't want anyone hurt—"

Ronin broke free upon hearing that word, swinging the wide rack of antlers. Toy People scattered, the reindeer crouched, as Ronin leaped with a roar. One swipe and the tower would be turned into a heap of twisted metal. The dome would fall; the video would be useless. Hugo pulled Avery behind him. Avery saw a bright light, heard the air crackle. A pungent smell of burnt ozone filled the atmosphere.

Ronin hovered over the sleigh, legs outstretched. A thin, sizzling line extended from the tower, enveloping the reindeer in an eerie field. It branched from Ronin to Santa and the other reindeer, leaving them as animated as Avery's dad.

BT-Bradley looked at the tower. The equipment was flashing red. The power was nearly gone. Hands in his coat pockets, in a strange way like her brother often did, a flash of hope that perhaps Bradley was back quickly dissolved as BT-Bradley reached for Santa.

"I had hoped you would understand."

With a joyless smile, he reached into Santa's pocket. A little bell rang. The Toy People cheered.

26

BT-Bradley walked briskly toward Hugo. The red lights flashed faster now. Hugo stood in front of Avery, BT-Bradley opening the Toymaker's hat. Bell jingling.

"Bring us here, Toymaker," BT-Bradley said. "Make this the best Christmas ever."

Hugo pulled Avery closer. The hat rose like a crown; Hugo bowed his head, a prince accepting his rightful place. Avery felt Hugo tense, could feel the hat ring inside her head. BT-Bradley hesitated. His steely, hopeful glance flickered to Avery, then back to Hugo. He saw something.

He lunged in desperation.

Avery grabbed Hugo, not to save him or pull him away. The ground suddenly disappeared. She clung to him like a buoy. The Toymaker's hat began to disintegrate. BT-Bradley's frantic scowl fractured in a colorful mist. Everything blurred like an invisible hand swiped across a freshly painted scene.

The world spun.

Hugo was the only solid thing in the world. Avery clenched her eyes, felt the cold wind. Static crackled in her throat. They soared through a sudden and violent blizzard. She hung on, hoping this dream, this wild and impossible dream, was finally ending. And then bip. *Silence.*

She smelled evergreen: moist and warm, organic. Something fluttered, the soft patter of delicate wings near her ear. She opened her eyes, still attached to Hugo, and saw a butterfly, black and yellow, overhead. Stars twinkled in a midnight sky, clear and sharp. The butterfly struggled momentarily against an invisible barrier. High above, something was covered with bits of snow. The dome that BT-Bradley had erected from the tower was no longer hazy and electric, but transparent and enormous. And attached to the side of a mountain.

BT-Bradley was gone. Santa and his reindeer, the tower and blinking boxes... they were all gone. Replaced by palm trees dripping condensation.

"What happened?" Avery said.

Hugo's grip relaxed. He looked her over, patted her hand, then looked around. Gravel crunched beneath his extra-large boots.

"Hugo, where are we? How did we get here?"

He peeked down a path, scurried to another, pulling wide, tropical leaves apart, muttering to himself, clutching the elf sculpture in one hand. Avery's legs were untrustworthy. If she took a step, she might collapse like a newborn fawn and not get up. Her heart was beating its way into her throat. She wanted to hold something, to feel something. To wake up.

"Ah. There you are," someone said.

Avery wasn't quite sure what it was that stepped from one of the paths. It was tall and slender and wearing a cloak. She'd seen it before, as a figurine in the Toymaker's workshop. With the other things the Toymaker had pulled from the box. It was from Mr. Popperharp's story: a gray-silver-skin-wrapped android. With a kind voice and a featureless face. A familiar voice.

"Are you all right, sir?" it said to Hugo. "Everything went as planned?"

Hugo grunted, the way he did.

"Good, then." It turned to Avery. "And you, ma'am. Are you all right?"

"Who are you?" she said.

"You know exactly who I am." It tipped its head to the side. She imagined a lopsided smile. The final piece fell into place when he said, "I am here to help."

I am here to help. He'd been many places, had taken many forms and had many names. He was a part of the plan. Now he was here, wherever here was, with a body the color of toenail polish.

"Jenks," she said.

He nodded once. "He will be here soon. You need to—"

"Where are we?" she said.

Jenks looked at Hugo, who appeared agitated. "You have crossed into another story," Jenks said. "One quite different than your own."

"Story? You mean another reality?"

"Hugo brought you *here*." Jenks spread his arms.

She didn't know what that meant. Not at first. Hugo had been holding her tightly when BT-Bradley raised the Toymaker's hat. Avery had felt its power tingle all over when everything changed. *Now I'm here.*

"He can't do that," she said. "Not without... he can't *take* me across the veil..."

"You do not need surfers to travel," Jenks said. "You never did."

"It's not..." It was pointless to even think it was impossible. After everything that had happened.

"I just..." She rubbed her eyes. Hugo watched like he'd used up his quota for words. "I can't do this. Why did you even come up the mountain?" she shouted at Hugo. "You knew this was going to happen. You *let* it happen. You could've gone somewhere else. Anywhere! Why did you bring me here?"

"This is the plan," Jenks said.

"Plan? If we're here, then they're still back there." Avery pointed in no particular direction. "My parents. My brother is... we've got to go back."

"He will be here soon," Jenks said.

"I don't care." They weren't getting it. Hugo stared absently at the sculpture. "He said he'd bring my brother back, he'd bring them all back if we helped him. He's not going to quit until we do. Ever. We can't just run away; he's not going to stop. You know what Toyworld looks like. They don't deserve to be there."

"No, they do not," Jenks said. "That is why you must go."

Hugo took her hand. He laid the sculpture in it, the wood dry against her skin, the edges dulled with time. Colors faded. It had changed from the time she'd seen it on the mantel. The belly not as round. The beard was missing.

"Remember a story," Jenks said.

"A story?" Avery said.

"A Nana Rai story."

"How is that going to help? Hugo, take us back. There's still time. You can put on the hat, give them what they want."

Hugo wrapped her fingers around the sculpture. He looked into her eyes like he knew what he was doing. He reached up, his hand cold on her face, and gently closed her eyes. She wanted to open them—her heart thumping like a cornered rabbit—and make it all go away.

A story?

"I can't," she said, shaking her head. A light flutter in her head. Like butterfly wings.

"You can remember," Hugo's gravelly voice whispered.

Thoughts, then, floated out of the fear twisting in her belly. Memories of a time she was very little, lying in her bed with her eyes closed, imagining faraway places built with the magic of imagination. Colors squeezed from her thoughts: yellows tasted like dandelions, greens like mint. Reds like cinnamon sticks. They mingled and danced, painting landscapes like rugs unfurled, soft on her feet. The cool wind on her face. She went there, sometimes, when she was little. When she dreamed.

"There you go," Hugo whispered.

The wind whistled in her ears and scoured her cheeks. Hugo's hands tightened, holding onto her like a kite lifting from the ground.

Logs clattered with hollow thunks, a giant wooden windchime falling from the sky.

She opened her eyes, still in the domed forest on the side of a mountain. Jenks, in silver skin, the cloak waving at his feet, turned his head. A pile of polished wood was jumbled on the gravel. A black top hat resting on top began to rattle. Long, cylindrical pieces stabbed the ground, braced and wobbled, then unfolded with a cane in one hand.

"Run, run as fast as you can." BT's jaw snapped.

The puppet straightened the top hat. The painted eyes regarded Jenks, looked at Hugo clutching the sculpture in Avery's hands. The hinged jaw chattered.

"Clever, clever. Unexpected. But a trail you leave when you go where I see." He pointed the cane. "I made a promise I shall keep. Open your eyes and come back where you are. Brothers and sisters and fathers and sons depend on you all. What's right is right. It's Christmas, after all. A merry good night."

He looked at her with those big painted eyes. Hugo squeezed her hands until they hurt. She waited for the colors to blur, for him to drag her to another world. He'd done it before. *It is Christmas, after all.*

BT threw up his hand, the wooden fingers clinking together. A desperate plea to stop and listen. Just for a moment. Slowly, he reached behind his back, the top hat tipped at an angle, and revealed what she thought, at first, was a little white bunny. The long tail rubbed free of fur.

"Imagine," BT said with a clatter, "what she's like living next to you. A neighbor. A friend. Someone who loves you for you, no matter who you are."

He placed Ms. Frosty Hound on the gravel, legs splayed. Red fabric tongue stitched on a smile, just like Avery remembered. Avery knew where Ms. Frosty Hound was, on a shelf in the basement, in a box with all the other toys. *Is she in Toyworld, alone and scared?*

"It was meant to be." BT extended his hand kindly. "The Toymaker saw us living together: toys and humans celebrating Christmas. You can make that dream come true."

Me?

BT placed his hand over his painted heart. The inside of her head churned like snow cascading down a mountain, filling her legs with ice, turning her fingers numb. She barely felt Hugo's grip tighten. She looked at the sculpture he had placed in her hands. It had changed again. It was no longer an elf carved from cedar. No longer round-bellied with a beard of curly locks.

She closed her eyes like she did when she was little, when storms threw things against the window, when strange sounds fell in the night, and she escaped into her thoughts and the landscapes she imagined. Where she was safe.

She tasted dandelions and evergreen boughs. The crinkle of autumn leaves blowing. She held Hugo tightly, wishing to go back to the mountain, when a blustery breeze whooshed in her ears. The ground lurched like a falling elevator. She held on, imagined Hugo was a dragon soaring high above the mountain. The valley shrinking below. The air growing thin and stars all around. She felt the hard column of cedar in her palms.

She opened her eyes on a road that twisted between great pillars of trees, painted with foliage of yellows and reds and oranges that floated from the branches in a cool autumn breeze, the promise that winter was on the way.

"No. No, not here," she said. "We've got to go back. Take us back to the mountain, Hugo!"

"I didn't come here." His grip loosened. It was warm now. A smile hid beneath tight curls of gray. "It was you."

He was the one who was flying, taking them across the veils. She was holding onto him, riding his back.

"It's not me. I'm not the…" She shook the sculpture. The likeness was unmistakable: the dark complexion, the round smooth face, the dimpled smile. But it couldn't be. This was just another illusion, a product of imagination. "I'm not the Toymaker, Hugo!"

"You need another story," he said. "Quickly now."

She shook her head. "Then I'll go back to the mountain."

"Not yet."

"We can't keep going from story to story, or world to world or whatever this is. I don't even know how we're doing this."

"Of course you do. You've done it already."

"Hugo, no. If we keep doing this, we'll..." She didn't want to say it out loud. She had already gone too far without hiwires to swipe from her face. If she went any further, she'd never find her way back. "We'll get lost."

"You are already home."

"Home? I don't know how we got here!"

Footsteps crushed dry foliage on the pavement. Someone was coming. He was short, much shorter than Hugo. His feet wider than Hugo's boots. A beard did not hide his face; his head as smooth as a blueberry. He was singing a song, looking down at big blue feet.

"Jack," Avery whispered.

The blue elf wasn't like the other elves. He was colder than cold. Water froze when he touched it. It was a story. Did she make it up, or did Nana Rai tell her that story?

"Who"—the blue elf stopped suddenly—"are you?"

He wasn't talking to Avery or Hugo. He was at the bend in the road, his back to them. A shadow approached him through dappled light. The figure thunked towards him, the hard edge of a cane grinding the asphalt.

"Close your eyes," Hugo whispered.

Avery imagined the mountain and her dad outside that time-stopping bubble. She tried to go back, but another image arose on its own, her imagination whipping up a frenzy of sleet.

"Wait!" she heard BT shout. "Please—"

Colors bloomed in a kaleidoscope. They tasted like shaved ice with squirts of blue and purple syrup. A brisk wind tightened her cheeks. She saw an old mansion in the distance. Snow was up to her knees and nearly to Hugo's waist. He looked behind them where a looming presence lurked.

A metallic ornament hovered above the ground. The air warped around it, bending space and time. *The ornament from the Toymaker's workbench.* Snow began swirling beneath it; a twisting funnel twisted and wrapped around it. The force pushed Avery and Hugo off balance. More snow swept into the gravitational field, engulfing the ornament until a giant of a snowman stood before them. A turret turned on broad shoulders, looked down on them.

"Flury," Avery said.

That was his name. She'd seen snowmen like this before. Abominables, the elven called them. This one, though, was part of a story. A story Nana Rai told. A story she'd forgotten. *How many stories did I forget?*

"Quickly," Hugo said.

Avery felt herself transporting the moment she closed her eyes. Colors sprang from a deep well inside her. They gushed into her mind, time and space as fluid as snow melting from a mountain, crashing like waterfalls. The sun was a stark spotlight in a blue sky. Foam slid across a beach.

Palm trees, wrapped with lights, had gifts piled around the trunks. Decorations hung from the eaves of a resort, wreaths in the windows. A woman was farther down the beach, far enough she wouldn't hear them talking, but close enough to see the bright red skin exposed from a hooded cloak. A red much too bright to be sunburn. Avery remembered her story and why she was here, on this island.

"It's about time," someone said with a scratchy voice.

Water receded around a snowman. Not a snowman. A snowman was made of snow. This was a sandman that was like a traditional snowman: three boulders of wet sand with stick arms pointing at her.

"You're doing great, kid."

"Jenks?" Avery said. "Is that you?"

"Yes. And no." The sandman scratched his head. Sand crumbled away. "I don't use that name here, but yeah. Okay. Go with it, kid." He looked at Hugo. "As much as I'd like to show you two around, you can't stay."

"Where are we?" Avery wondered if these imaginary leaps were endless. Just how far did they go? *Does it even have an end?*

"You're exactly where you're supposed to be. And you're almost there."

"Almost where?"

"Exactly where you should be."

Yeah, that was Jenks. Never a straight answer, if there was an answer at all. The woman was farther down the beach now, the water washing around her feet, wetting the cuff of her cloak. Steam rose where it touched her skin. *The Toymaker's flame.*

Avery felt something hard now pressing against the veil, a meteor on a collision course with this world. BT was on the way. Avery didn't want to keep running. He was just going to keep following. *Where are we going?*

She didn't close her eyes this time. A simple thought was all it took. She didn't wish to go back to the mountain, although she would've liked to. It didn't work last time, so she simply wished to bring the next story to life. The sand shifted into craggy rocks, and the ocean surged in icy waves. A gray ceiling crept through the blue sky. The land hardened beneath her, growing granite shelves, sprouting spruce trees. Far below in a valley was a horseshoe-shaped building. The people outside were smaller than ants.

A shadow passed over her.

Cloven hooves clutched the granite shelf, pebbles tumbling around them. Black eyes focused on the scene below. Steam shot from flared nostrils. A growl rumbled in the long furry throat as the creature turned his head to look down on them.

Ronin.

The story Ms. Tenpenny had told at the campfire about the reindeer who led Santa's sleigh. The reindeer Santa didn't want the Toy People to feed. The reindeer who tried and failed to destroy the tower. *But he's back on the mountain. If he's there, how is he here?*

Interdimensional presence wasn't going to be solved with the rational mind. She was lost in the current of imagination. Where anything was possible. She no longer questioned where she was going. The current took her.

She nodded to Ronin. He snorted, looked back toward the valley, keeping watch on what was happening. Avery grabbed Hugo's hands. She wasn't riding on his back. She was carrying him. She was the conductor on a journey to a destination she did not know. Before the presence of BT could be felt, she opened the doors of imagination.

World to world, she leaped with Hugo in tow. They visited realms of ice and snow, climbed tall mountains and stood on bustling street corners with towering buildings, joined families in their living rooms and backyards and villages. Flew with reindeer and soared through clouds, watched mothers with infants and fathers with sons, grandparents with families all around. It was Christmas everywhere; the spirit was real. She could feel it in her bones, her socks and her heels. There was no limit to the colors the imagination could paint, no numbers to follow. It was whatever she could think.

Granite clacked into heavy blocks. Buildings sprouted like trees. Avery stood at the edge of a forest. A multi-spired castle faced a living Christmas tree. Ornaments decorated the swooping branches, a blazing star on top. It looked just like the tree in Nana Rai's backyard. A small cottage was tucked beneath branches, smoke puffing from a stone chimney.

Children ran in the wide-open space, a dozen of them throwing snowballs and hiding behind snow bunkers. Snow angels were carved in random groups, and lopsided snowmen with sagging carrot noses and droopy stick-arms watched them scream and laugh. A little girl with a long red scarf was by herself, not part of the winter games, surrounded by a group of tiny snowmen she sculpted with bare hands.

"You made it."

The voice didn't come from any particular direction. This voice was in her head, like amplified thoughts that sounded slightly amused. And definitely not her own.

"Down here," the voice said.

There was a path through the woods that led to a wall of boulders. She scanned the ground.

"Warmer," the voice said. "Warmer still. Aaaaaand bingo."

A cookie stood on a log. A flat gingerbread cookie with a white icing bowtie and round eyes waved. Then bowed.

"Your highness."

His mouth, a white line of icing, didn't open, but the voice was loud and clear. She squatted down, nearly eye level—if those were really eyes, if that was really a mouth—and brushed snow from the log. The icing had chipped from its decorations. A thick glob appeared to have repaired its leg. The voice was different, in her head, but she knew who was in there.

Jenks was everywhere, in every story. *Different forms.* She held out her hand, palm up. "May I?"

"It's not something I'm into. But for you." He stepped onto her hand.

He was a cookie. Crispy and warm. Smelled like cloves. He was the cookie the Toymaker had made in his workshop and watched race up the icy ramp. The chipping and cracking looked like a cookie thrown from a window. Or, in this case, a cookie running through a forest.

"I've been here before," she said. The castles, the walls. The children. Of all the stories she was remembering, this one felt especially familiar.

"Bingo again," the gingerman said.

"I've been here before, then?"

"You said it, not me."

"But how?"

"How, what?"

"How am I here now?"

The gingerman looked at Hugo, like Hugo should have explained it by now. "I'll be honest. I don't know how it works. Some can pass through the veil better than others. Like her."

He pointed a stubby arm at the little girl with the red scarf and her family of snowmen.

"Even if I knew, which I don't, there's no time to explain the nitty-gritties," the gingerman said. "This isn't the last stop. This is just another story, another world. You really believe where you're from is the only story out there?"

"I don't know where I'm from." Her wrist was bare. "They're all so real."

"Here or there, they're all real. But some stories are better than others." He sat on the edge of her hand.

Toyworld was the worst of them all. Pale and loveless. Empty.

"They deserve better," the gingerman said. Like he heard what she was thinking.

Adults were calling the children from the multi-spired castle. A very old man with a white beard was among them. He looked like Santa but hunched over a cane. He was looking across the field like he saw them watching from the trees.

"Carmichael, Blane, Sissy," a woman called. "Time for lunch!"

The children tossed the last of their icy ammunition, kicking over a snowman, tackling each other. The little girl was oblivious, sculpting a little snow house for stick figures. She looked up, suddenly aware of her surroundings, coming back from the imaginary world with little snowy figures.

"I just don't understand," Avery said, watching the little girl get up.

"Nope. You don't," the gingerman said. "But someday you will. Maybe. Doesn't matter, really. All you need to know is the gift is inside you." He pointed at her chest. "We've been waiting a long time for it to get here."

"Who's waiting?"

"Pretty much everyone. The toys especially. I mean, they don't know it yet, but they will. Once you leave here."

"I thought the Toymaker wanted to stop them," she said.

Gingerman shook his head. "He wanted to help them."

He climbed up her arm and perched on her shoulder. The smell of cloves tickled her nose. Crumbs dusted her neck. The little girl was walking toward them now.

"Why me?" she said. "The Toymaker passed the gift to Hugo."

"Did he? Hugo has his part, and his part was to get you here. And my part is to be here. And now you're here. Get it? It doesn't matter."

The little girl slowed down. The other children were still running around, unaware their sister had wandered off. And now she was approaching strangers—if she could really see them, it looked like she could see them—in the woods. The little girl *felt* familiar. She was holding sticks that had been twisted and tied into a tiny figure in her hand. A stick figure she'd seen down by the river at Nana Rai's shed.

"Hugo never had the gift," the gingerman said. "She did."

"Nana," Avery whispered.

The little girl smiled. Dimples sank in her cheeks. Holding the stick figure up for Avery to see. A little thing she made to tell stories.

"I... I don't understand," Avery said. "How is she here? Why is she..." Avery couldn't finish her sentence. *Why is Nana Rai so little?*

"Stories are endless," the gingerman said. "They're here and there, now and then. One ends and another begins. You see, it doesn't matter which world you're in, how it got there or why. You just be here. Nana didn't understand it, either. But she knew what the Toymaker wanted; she kept the secret. Set the stage. But you, Avery, you're the one with the imagination to write an ending and start a beginning. You were born for this. Don't you know what your name means?"

Her parents always insisted Nana Rai had named her Avery. No one ever knew why.

The sky rippled dark blue waves over the castles and distant mountains, like the sky was a big, blue tarp. Something was bouncing on it.

"Raiyu!" the old man at the castle called. "Come along."

The little girl nodded to Avery, smiled and waved. She ran across the field, after her brothers and sisters and cousins, dropping the stick figure when she turned. Avery picked it up.

"Take them home, buddy," the gingerman said.

"Take who home?"

"Who do you think?"

Little Nana Rai stopped halfway across the field. Avery stroked the fine strands of twine twisted around twiggy arms and legs. Hugo made a noise to get her attention. She looked at his extended hand. The gingerman leaped into the snow, crawling back onto the log.

"How will I find my way back home?" she said.

"You never left it," the gingerman said.

She didn't know what that meant. What any of this meant. How she was in one world, then another. How Nana Rai was five years old here and her grandmother there? *I never left it?*

"No matter where you go, you're always here," the gingerman said. "Now go, will you? I've got things to do, people to see."

The sun was a blazing ball of gold. The edges warped as the blue tarp stretched around it. She closed her eyes, felt the warmth on her cheeks. Hugo's hand in hers. The ground began to melt. She floated above it, drifting like a balloon. The sun's brilliance lighter than air. A sheet of darkness gently fell like fresh snow. Then the sun piercing the blackness, a light so bright it beamed through her eyelids. The ground was there, snow over her boots.

The Christmas tree towered over her. The star at the top burned like a thousand suns. The ornaments were vivid and shining, dipped in iridescence that shimmered with an array of colors she'd never experienced. Colors across the spectrum—lavender-steel blue orbs and lemon-goldenrod figurines, chocolate-amethyst plates and raspberry-ruby globes. It was a technicolor dream she could taste with her eyes and smell with her tongue. Her skin tingled, and her heart melted.

The castles were gone.

Presents were under the tree. Brilliant gifts wrapped tight and bright and piled high beneath a sheet of plastic pinned down with logs. A snow-covered stage was not far away and a sunken firepit. Behind her was a big house and a round window on the third story looking directly at the star.

I never left.

27

Avery was dizzy. Numb. Skipping from world to world only to be back where she started.

"We're here," Hugo said. Like he knew all along.

The Christmas tree lit up the backyard. Everything was so vivid. The light was odd, powerful: colors oversaturated and filled with holiday spirit. Nana Rai's house and the decorations were sort of glowing. The stage was set and ready. The cameras mounted. She closed her eyes, and nothing happened. The world didn't spin. This was it, the final stop.

Why did we go in a circle?

A star streaked across the sky, smudging the nocturnal fabric. The smell of burnt ozone flooded the air. The chimes rang on the tree. A phantom wind swept through the backyard. The forest began to dance, the tree trunks swaying like rubber, billowing and creaking, chunks of bark littering the ground like organic confetti. Then all was quiet. Even the chimes stopped singing.

A clatter of wood came from the trees. Like firewood spilling from a wheelbarrow. A figure stepped out with hand raised. The Christmas tree's brilliance cast a shadow from the top hat.

BT poked his cane in the snow.

His gaze swept to the stage and house, to the presents beneath the tree. He looked at the sky, his head falling back, as if he were counting the countless stars. As if seeing something up there, far away. A world in another dimension. A colorless, bleached world he'd left behind.

And this one so alive.

He turned in a circle, arms out. The cane in one hand, the Toymaker's hat in the other. Twirling faster and faster. Laughter, like she'd never heard, rattled like marbles in a wooden cup. He began singing, words she couldn't understand. He spun across the yard. The painted heart on his barrel chest, once faded and chipped, glowed brighter and brighter with each turn. It swelled in size, pumping in rhythm.

"We're here." He spoke into the green hat. "We're here."

Avery suppressed a smile. She couldn't help it. She didn't know what was supposed to happen, just not a wooden puppet dancing in the backyard. She was glad, perhaps, she wasn't running away anymore. But there was another reason she felt a smile grow. The atmosphere swirled with excitement and something more. It was the way he moved, the way he laughed and sang. The joy.

He danced toward her, clicking his heels once, twice, knocking them together like sticks of bamboo. His heart thumped like a drumbeat. He bent his knee with an exaggerated bow.

"My dear Toymaker," he said, "I now know the way here. There is no need for you to wear the hat. No need to force your hand. I can retrieve my brothers and sisters, one by one, through the long and winding path you've shown me."

His big black eyes seemed bigger and blacker, the surface of his face shiny with a fresh coat of oil. The stiff wooden jaw creaked, as if a smile were bending the hinge. He offered the hat. Avery expected a dove to fly out of it.

Ms. Frosty Hound was inside.

She was inanimate, cuddled in soft fabric. Her tongue a red tag. BT wasn't offering the hat for her to take. It was a gesture. He could bring the toys here, one at a time, to this world. It was what he'd wanted in the first place. Thousands upon thousands or maybe more, but he'd do it. He didn't need her. But he was asking one last time. A simple, kind request. What he was asking would change the world.

It was going to happen, regardless. She had showed him how to bring the toys here, in their original bodies: fuzzy and warm, plastic and smooth. Hugo couldn't stop them. Neither could she. *Was it so bad?* What she felt, in the backyard, were emotions so joyful that people would smile without knowing why, just like she was. *The toys need us,* she thought. *And we need them.*

She held out her hand.

BT put his hand over his glowing heart. Avery felt a surge of something warm from between his fingers, could taste the emotion, briny and sweet. She let her smile grow, let it find its place in her heart. She didn't know what she was supposed to do, or how to do it, or why she was the one to do it. She didn't know how she got here.

The hat was warm like biscuits from the oven. Soft like a worn comforter. Its energy seeped into her, crept into her chest. She vibrated like a tuning fork struck against a countertop. Hugo watched her lift it. *We're here,* he had said.

It fit around her head loosely at first. It wriggled and squirmed, like a cat testing a cushion. It shrank and snuggled and then—there was only one way to explain it—the crown of her head opened up. And she could see.

The worlds out there were endless. Each contained a story with trillions of plots, weaved like tapestries of the finest threads. They floated like bubbles in the void, one after another and another there was more. Each one connected with gossamer strands, conduits from one to the other, the roads she had crossed from one world to another, the highways BT had followed.

The worlds weren't separate, as first they appeared. These silken threads glowed a white glow that once twirled in the Toymaker's hand, holding the worlds in sync, feeding them, giving each other purpose. It was this essence that made everything something. It was why they existed. There was no way to describe it, no concept that could explain the substance to a bystander. Every word would fall short. But only one word, she knew of, came close.

Joy.

This was the gift. It didn't want anything. It just wanted to give, because there was so much of it. This was the not-so-secret secret she witnessed. That humans too often forgot.

This is Christmas.

She knew what to do. It was simple, after all. She reached through the threads, soared to a dim bubble with a pale and bleached world, its pulse barely beating. She opened the route. Her voice would be heard by one and all.

Come, merry little ones.

A tangible flood coursed through her, the current sweet and bitter, happy and sad, good and bad. A song without words, they sang. A song that dissolved her body. A song of joy. There was no sense of seeing or hearing, tasting or feeling. She was content in the timeless flow. And for an eternal moment, she was no longer a round-faced girl wearing a floppy hat, no longer a person with a name. She was just here.

She was the gift.

The light was everywhere and everything. It began to coalesce. Winter nipped her nose. Snow was in her boots. She was looking at the Christmas tree, the light bright and white. She shielded her eyes. BT was on one knee. Something fluffy sprang from his hands. It tunneled through the snow, circled the tree, and leapt into Avery's arms, its fabric tongue dry on her cheek. Ms. Frosty Hound squirmed in her grip.

Avery's legs were doughy, her head finding its way back from nonexistence: where she was, how she got here. Even her name was elusive. And a white puppy stuffed with cotton licked her face. Ms. Frosty twisted from her hands and burrowed through the snow, yipping her way to the trees.

The forest began to quiver. Branches snapped and rustled. A clumsy brown bear peeked from the shadows, lifting his padded arm. The Christmas tree's star reflected in his glassy eyes. Next was a ballerina with a lacy tutu, spinning on one leg. Bunnies sprang past her, followed by dolls and balls and heads shaped like squares. Soldiers of wood and trains that could. Shoes with laces and big smiling faces and monkeys with tails curled like they should.

They came by the hundreds and thousands, perhaps, all hugging and twirling and twisted in wraps. BT watched them, a true leader at heart. He loved them like brothers and sisters apart. With hand over heart, he bowed quite sincere.

"Merry Christmas," he said. "Thank you, my dear."

He joined the celebration already in gear. Cane in one hand. And there on his rear, two letters carved deep. *BT* was stenciled by hand, a hand once too young to make him complete.

"Wait," Avery said. "My brother."

BT spun around, his mouth held agape. "He's waiting for you," he said. "Just like I promised."

On the mountain, she thought. And then she remembered. *How am I here and not there? What will they think?*

But there was no way she could go up there, not now, at least. She could barely stand without Hugo holding her up, and the trail was too steep. She was exhausted, her eyes getting heavy. She heard BT announce with great joy and song, for everyone to line up and prepare to right a wrong. There were presents to open, presents Nana Rai insisted be placed beneath the tree. Had she known all this time whom they were for? The plastic thrown back, they took gifts that had been wrapped. The toys, for once, had something to open. A new Christmas had arrived.

It was done, what she did. There was no going back. It was going to happen, if she helped them or not. Avery slurred her words and tried not to weep. A Christmas without Mom and Dad and her brother. They would be worried sick, a Christmas like no other.

Hugo guided her toward the house. "Morning will be a new day."

Humans and toys, living together. What would they think?

28

The thrum of hooves, like horses in the mud, and a deep voice that urged them forward. Avery was curled up in soft bedding, where it was dark and sweet. *In the back of a wagon,* she thought. But it felt more like the bottom of the ocean.

The horses faded, leaving her behind. She floated in a bubble, drifting towards a cool stratum of water, bumping gently against a thin sheet of ice. She wanted to stay there, where it felt like home, just beneath the ice, with no thoughts or concerns, cuddled in a timeless moment.

The chime of bells cracked the ice.

Her eyelids opened, breaking the seal. She watched fine particles drift like plankton through a sunbeam. Thoughts bubbled from the murky depths, bringing memories through the veil of sleep.

Sunlight grazed the desk below a round window, highlighting the sparkle of green wrapping paper and a red bow. She sat up in bed, expecting to find a floppy hat snug around her head, felt only the tight curls on her scalp. She listened to the pops and creaks of the house settling, occasional chimes outside the window. She threw back the cover, fully dressed, put her bare feet on the cool floorboards. The residue of the hike ached in her legs and back, general soreness throughout her body. Blisters on her feet were angry and red.

But here she was, on her bed. Not a mountain.

She waited there, on the edge, for thoughts and memories to link in some logical way. How could she be sore and be at home? She looked out the window. The snow was trampled around the tree and firepit, across the stage. Sunlight glittered on frosted branches.

A present was on the desk. It was half the size of a shoebox, the corners sharp. A bow neatly tied with big loops. Two sprigs of dried flowers were tucked beneath the ribbon, yellow petals pressed and translucent. There was no tag. No name for who it was from or who it was for. It didn't weigh much at all.

There was shouting.

Her pulse quickened, watching for toys to come out of the trees, twirling and dancing and bouncing around. A celebration to proceed once again. There were no bunnies, though. No stuffed bears or marching soldiers or plastic ballerinas. Bright colors emerged: a red coat with lime stripes. A woman looking at her phone.

Avery found her boots at the foot of the bed. She rushed down the stairs, feeling the spiraling rail sway beneath her grip. She threw the back door open, the winter air stealing her breath. BT-Bradley's friends, the Toy People, were returning. Their backpacks were light. No bulky items on their backs, no boxes or equipment. One after another, they came out of the woods. Their expressions were exhausted and bewildered, like they'd been lost in the wild and, finding civilization, searched their phones to find out where they were.

They barely noticed Avery. But then they looked back. Some squinting, some tipping their head. A man in a white coat stopped, the black stocking cap pulled down to his eyebrows. Icy crystals had crusted the whiskers over his lips that opened, briefly, to say something, but nothing came out. Maybe he recognized her, a face from somewhere long ago and far away. She remembered him: the man who had been slumped outside the cabin.

"Merry Christmas." Iona's mom had her phone to her ear. Her

voice quivered. "I don't... no, I'm sorry. I'm so, so sorry. I don't know... yes, I'm fine, honey. I know, I know." She saw Avery and put out her arm, hugged her while she spoke. "I'm getting on the first flight back."

Iona's mom listened to the voice on the other end. It was Christmas. And her family was somewhere else. She hustled toward the house, holding the phone against her ear, not talking to the Toy People, who didn't slow down to say goodbye to their fellow travelers who worked so closely together. Iona's mom stopped to talk quietly, right where Avery had watched a puppet dance and get down on one knee. Where everything had changed.

And now it's the same.

Weary hikers continued to return. The Toy People wandered off, but the other hikers, dressed in standard attire, stopped to stretch, to wait and hug. Aunt Mag was half-jogging, clipboard in one hand. Uncle Sage plodded behind her with long, impatient steps.

"Merry Christmas!" She threw her arms around Avery. "How was your night?"

Avery shook her head. How was she to answer that?

"The old house didn't scare you, did it?" Uncle Sage said. "Did you see a ghost?" He sounded a bit too serious. Maybe he'd seen a ghost, walking the hallways, once before. *A ghost with a hole in one sock.*

"We're running behind," Aunt Mag said. "You need to get the stage ready," she said to Uncle Sage. "Call Millie, let her know we're a little late, but the show will start on time. Where's Hugo?" she asked Avery.

"Hugo? I... I..."

"We need to find him. They'll be here soon."

"Who?" Avery said. In a strange way, she hoped whoever it was would come dancing and hopping and twirling out of the forest instead of weary travelers. "Where's my parents?"

"They're coming," Aunt Mag said.

"My brother?" Avery looked around. The Toy People had all come off the trail, phones in their hands, concern on their faces.

"Hey," Uncle Sage said, pointing, "looks like Santa found you."

Avery was still clutching the gift that had been on the desk. Her grip dented the cardboard beneath the wrapping. Uncle Sage dropped his pack and dragged it. Avery turned toward the trees. Someone lumbered toward her, cheeks flushed from the cold. A slight limp straightened out when he saw her. He jogged around a slow-mover, his backpack bouncing. Avery wrapped her dad up, pressing her face against his coat. Somehow, he smelled like bacon.

"Merry Christmas, hon," he said. "We missed you every step of the way."

They hugged in the middle of the trail, forcing others around them. He held her at arm's length, looked inside her, the way he did when something was wrong. The way he had just a few days ago.

"Why aren't you wearing a coat?" he said.

She wanted to ask him why she was here, why her legs and back and blisters were telling her she'd hiked with them. Mom surprised her. Her slender, muscular arms pulled Avery away from her dad into a loving bear trap. Avery's arms were stuck at her sides.

"I had this dream," Mom said, not letting go, voice muffled. "That I was lying in my tent, and I could see through the top. The sky was filled with more stars than I'd ever seen in my life. It was the most incredible sight. And then I felt you up there. You were a shooting star. We all woke up late. The sun was up, and I thought you were still up there."

She stroked Avery's hair.

"I couldn't come down fast enough. We should never have asked you to stay here last night. I don't want to do Christmas like this ever again." She wiped her eyes, her lips pale without lipstick. "Did you and Hugo have a good night?"

Avery didn't understand. She didn't know what any of this meant. Or why everyone was asking about Hugo. *Where is he?*

"What's this?" Dad said.

The present was dented in Avery's hand. Mom touched the ribbon and fondly held one of the flowers under her fingertip, remembering the way Nana Rai wrapped gifts. Hikers walked around them, their packs light on their backs, wishing merry Christmas as they passed. Aunt Mag called for Mom.

"Mom, where's Bradley?" Avery said.

He was coming, she said, leaving Avery to watch the stragglers find their way off the trail, elated weariness pushing them forward. There were fewer of them. The Toy People were long gone, calling family, not staying for whatever was next.

"A merry Christmas to you, Ms. Avery," someone said with a crooked smile.

She didn't answer. Everyone thought she'd stayed home for the night. They didn't remember anything, all merry and relieved. A thought turned her pace into a gallop. *What if they forgot Bradley?*

And then around the bend, thumbs hooked under the straps, the last of them appeared. He looked up and paused. She approached warily. Looked into his eyes. Looking for her brother inside, she reached with both hands, put them on his cheeks. He turned his head.

"Your hands are cold, skunk."

She hugged him like she was dangling over a cliff. Remembering him in that cabin, she'd never been happier to hear that nickname in her life.

"What present did you really, really want when you were seven?" she said.

"What?"

"It was all you dreamed about, what was it? Tell me."

"It's a little early for—"

"Answer the question, Bradley."

He shook his head. "You mean the drum set?"

He said it without looking for the answer. Without clacking his teeth. Just a snide smile with a touch of annoyance. She hugged him again.

"You... crushing me," he said.

They walked down the path. She followed behind, studied his gait. Funny, the subtleties she'd missed before. The way Bradley swung his arms slightly out of rhythm with his stride. Those little things BT didn't capture so obvious.

"Can I ask you another question?" she said.

"No."

"What happened on the mountain?"

"Oh, it was great fun. We hiked, we froze. We froze some more."

"Where's the equipment?"

"Can I get coffee before your interview?"

"The boxes and the-the tower. All the gear you and the Toy Peop—the others, your friends. You carried it to watch the end of the Hunt."

"I have no idea what you're talking about." He started walking. "Maybe you are sick."

"Bradley?" Aunt Mag waved her clipboard at the stage. "We're having trouble with the control panel. They need help getting the video online. And we can't light the tree. They said the connection was broken when they were building the deck. We have to light the star. Nana was very specific."

The star is working. Avery remembered it quite vividly.

"Where's Hugo?" Aunt Mag said. "He can fix the star. Mr. Maier?" Aunt Mag shouted at a man carrying wood to the firepit. "Could you gather some of the others to pull the plastic? Store it around the side of the house."

The presents were all there, under the tree. Protected beneath a sheet of plastic. They weren't torn open. Avery felt a small tremor. *Did it happen? Maybe it was all just a vivid dream, of Toy People and time bubbles, of Santa Claus and reindeer and a green floppy hat. And worlds and worlds where Nana Rai was a little girl with a scarf.*

She wasn't going to tell her parents any of that. She wasn't going to tell anyone anything at all.

"Is that for me?" Bradley tapped the gift.

The box was almost crushed. She shook her head and pulled the bow. She tucked the flowers in her pocket and then, like her dad, neatly folded the wrapping paper. Bradley peeked inside.

"Isn't that yours?"

Nestled in red and green tissue paper, a stuffed animal was curled up, head resting on front legs. A red flap of fabric hung from a stitched mouth.

"It's not from me," Bradley said.

He'd regifted things in the past that made Mom really angry. Like old cell phones or concert T-shirts. Wrapping up a toy he found in the basement wouldn't be a stretch. He quickly joined the procession of worker bees stacking presents around the tree, sweeping the stage, lighting the firepit and troubleshooting electronics. Guests were arriving, fresh and well-rested among the travel-weary hikers. The choir gathered on the stage.

Everything was missing an element she couldn't quite explain. It was so different last night. There had been something tangible. The way the toys danced and sang. Avery held Ms. Frosty Hound to her cheek.

She looked at her wrist, the bracelet long gone. But if she closed her eyes, she could feel it again. That feeling was out there, somewhere beyond the sky. Where toys were still hugging and dancing. The ground began to soften below her, and the wind rushed past her ears. Diffuse light began to glow, and she could hear them out there, far, far away. Hear them singing once again.

When the cold winds blow and bring the snow—

"Are you ready?"

She opened her eyes with firm ground beneath her. Hugo looked up. Somewhere in that thicket of whiskers, a smile found a way to his eyes. He looked as exhausted as the hikers. And was still wearing the sweater.

"Was it a dream?" she asked.

He took her hand. And she wished, for a moment, that he would nod, and she would close her eyes, and a bundle of energy warming her belly would rise up and take them to those worlds again, where she could find her way back to the toys, to listen to their song filled with joy. Hugo kept her grounded, with a wink, when he spoke.

"Let's be *here*," he said, "for Christmas."

29

Volunteers were prying the stage apart and packing it on a trailer. The ornaments were left on the tree. The last items on Nana's list, Aunt Mag checking them off with a flourish: restore the backyard. Except the ornaments. They would be moved to the forest behind the house and would stay there year-round.

It felt like only yesterday Avery had arrived. This room, once spooky, felt like hers. If she never left, this would be her bedroom. And every morning she'd wake up to see Christmas ornaments and the distant mountain where, once upon a time, magic happened. *It wasn't magic*, Avery thought, remembering Nana Rai's belief that magic wasn't real. *But it sure felt like it.*

She held Ms. Frosty Hound to the window, rubbing her tail. The stuffed animal didn't wriggle in her hand or lick her face. Ms. Frosty Hound was a toy. Avery would never let her smell musty again.

Hugo waddled across the backyard, a hammer swinging from a tool belt beneath his generous belly. A sweatshirt and a stocking cap were all he needed to weather the cold. What else could she say to him that she hadn't already said? He wasn't the hugging type despite his elven traits. He didn't inherit the singing or dancing genes from his merry ancestors. Barely inherited the smiling gene that lit an elf's eyes. But he so obviously had elf in him. How did no one else see it? She hadn't, not at first. But then if you didn't know what you were looking for, you wouldn't see it. *The truth is so often right in front of us.*

Avery made one last check in the mirror. Voices carried from downstairs. The faint remains of Dad's breakfast lingered in the house. Bradley's door was closed. He'd slept a lot since Christmas. They were all drained from the hike, but he was more exhausted than everyone else. Avery would sometimes listen at his door, listen for shuffling sounds or muttering. Dad still had his looker kit, so he wasn't on virtual. The surfers didn't work anymore. Bradley would look tired when he woke up. But he looked like Bradley. No more chattering.

Nana's room was open. She peeked inside. The clutter hadn't changed. Even the rocks were still on the floor where they'd fallen when Bradley had taken her hiwires to get inside without her. Fruit dangled from the knotted branches. A flower, red and pink-striped, had opened like a bugle.

"I wondered if you were going to say goodbye," Avery said.

Jenks was next to the tree. "Why would I say goodbye?"

She shrugged. He said it so kindly, it didn't hurt her feelings. She told him that Uncle Sage had found the servers in the basement. All the doors that had been locked were suddenly open. She had explored the library with Dad, but didn't use the hiwires to see what it really did. They'd all had enough for one trip.

"They'll turn the servers off one day."

"Is that what you think I am?" He adjusted his glasses. "A computer?"

"Maybe. Or an android, a cookie. A sandman. Or whatever else is out there."

He offered half a smile. "Vehicles, Avery. That is all they are."

He pointed like her body was just a vehicle. Because she'd gone from world to world while her body was on the mountain. But how she'd ended up in her bed and everyone forgetting what happened, well, she had some ideas of how that happened. Someday, though, she would know the whole truth. When she was ready.

"So are you going to tell me how you did it?" she said. "Existing in all those places at the same time."

He shrugged, like she'd asked him how he put his socks on in the morning. "It is hard to explain."

"Try."

"Quantum entanglement, parallel universes, synchronous identity. It is all very boring."

"So you don't know?"

"You do not need to know how the car works to drive."

"Try again." She wasn't settling for vagaries this time. There were other worlds. *Why would he say goodbye when he was everywhere?*

"Would you like a mathematical explanation or plain English?" he said.

"Try this. Were you ever human?" She felt hopeful for reasons she cared not to admit. Wishing he was something more than a computer. Something she could touch. A friend she could call.

"Well, then." He straightened his beanie. "I am not human in the sense of blood and muscle. But I am, to a certain extent, an organized algorithm. Humans are as well, organically speaking. I, however, am not bound to a body. Nana showed me the roads, if you will, between the worlds. I am a traveler."

"I saw her," Avery said. "When she was little. You were a gingerbread man. You remember that?"

"Of course."

"So explain that, how she was a little girl there and an old woman here?"

He traced a circle on the dusty table. "Time ends where it begins."

That didn't answer the question, but, for whatever reason, it was as close to an answer as she would get. There likely wasn't an answer for the rational mind to understand. His answer, though, the circle was more satisfactory than an equation. The clock was a circle that went round and round. No beginning, no ending. It still didn't explain how Nana could be old here and young there. Was that really Nana Rai? Or just a girl who looked like her? A girl with the same name. *A girl who recognized me.*

"If you're in all these worlds... am I?"

"There are many stories of you."

She picked up one of the rocks, shaking her head. He was a Zen teacher forever offering koans. "Where are they?" she said. "The toys?"

"Where? They are joy."

"Where, Jenks. Joy is not a place."

"Is it not?"

He wasn't going to tell her. They weren't here, not in this world. They were somewhere, though. Someplace that looked exactly like here. And if he told her where they were, she would find them. He knew she would. And that, she'd wager, wasn't part of the plan. She wasn't supposed to know. But she wondered. *Do the toys know they aren't here?*

"They are lovely, Avery. Thanks to you."

"I didn't do anything. It was you, Jenks. You were the one making it work. I was just along for the ride." She put the rock in the box. There was nothing she could take credit for. "You're the gift," she said.

"Ha. Funny. No one possesses the gift. It just is. Some of us are more suitable vehicles when the time is right. But do not underestimate your role, Avery." He held out his hand. "May I show you why you were chosen?"

"Show me what?"

He offered his hand with a slight, crooked smile. She took it, expecting it to pass through her. It did, but not like she expected. It was a cool vapor, on the verge of condensing into something tangible, that squeezed her hand. There was a sense that he was something other than what he appeared to be. He wasn't a boy. But he was something intelligent, something kind and compassionate. Unhindered by the *organic algorithm* of growing up human, not limited to just one place and time.

He led her to the elevator. They descended into the cool depths. Their footsteps echoed in the vaulted room. On the other side of the wall, her family was waiting for her. "Show me what?" she whispered.

"Close your eyes."

She'd never needed the hiwires. They never worked, even in the beginning. She hadn't tried closing her eyes since Christmas, nervous it wouldn't work. That if she tried and failed, it meant it was all a dream. She wanted to believe it. Wasn't that enough?

She closed her eyes and felt the transformation. She wasn't sure if she'd opened her eyes when books climbed the walls and the ceiling opened. *Can everyone do this?* she wondered. Worlds within reach, just beyond the veil. *We're just born with our eyes open and forget how to close them.*

Jenks stood near a bookshelf where—among thousands of books—there was a book dark red and glossy, the letters shimmering white.

"The story was not finished," he said with a sweeping gesture, "last you saw it."

"And now it's done?"

"Nothing is ever finished. But there comes a time to know the beginning of a story."

She tugged the binding with one finger. It tipped off the shelf. She cradled it with one hand, dragging her fingers over the embossed lettering.

The Book of Avery.

Funny. She'd wanted so badly to know what was in it before. Perhaps, if she'd read it then, the story never would have happened. The binding cracked as she pried it open. The pages began to flutter, the story spilling out. She held the pages down before they escaped. Just below the title page, written in shaky letters, was familiar handwriting.

Avery recalled Jenks once asking her if she knew what her name meant. *Avery* didn't seem like a name with meaning. It sounded ordinary, like Mary or Jane. At some point in the future, she would look it up and find that it was Old English. It meant something all along. Nana Rai had written in this book long ago. The truth in front of her all this time.

My little elf.

The Book of Avery began to quiver. Technicolor streams trailed like wisps of colorful smoke, like magic rocks thrown onto a fire. Odd scents of cinnamon and eggnog clung to her. They squeezed her delicately, then fractured the room. Pieces cascaded and reassembled into familiar shapes and colors.

It was her bedroom.

Avery stood at the foot of her bed, looking at herself when she was seven years old, tucked beneath the covers. Ms. Frosty Hound against one cheek. Her thumb in her mouth with the tail between her fingers.

"Once upon a time..."

Nana Rai sat in the old wicker chair. Lights flashed outside the window above the bed, turning the wool blanket around her shoulders from red to green to red to green. Nana Rai was hunched over, her knobby hands curled on the pages of a book. But she wasn't reading. She'd already written these stories.

Tales Beyond the Veil.

Avery couldn't remember these times, for some reason. She was seven years old, how could she forget? But here was Nana Rai, on Christmas Eve, telling her stories. And seven-year-old Avery stared at the ceiling. *Click-click-click* went the thumb in her mouth, imagining a cold elf the color of sugarplums.

The room shifted. Items moved across the floor. The bedspread was different, a checkered quilt with frilly edges. Avery looked younger this time. The lights outside were white this time. And Nana Rai was wearing a silly sweater with a reindeer on the front.

She smoothed the pages. "Once upon a time..."

Little Avery was listening. Imagining the reindeer with antlers as big as a truck. Nana Rai leaned in to whisper his name. It happened again and again. Five years old, then four. Three. Each year a different story, same book. Nana Rai looking much the same. Avery growing smaller, her hair getting shorter.

"And what shall we name him?" Nana Rai patted the book on her lap. The page was blank. As if the story hadn't been written.

Rhythmic thumb-sucking suddenly stopped. Nana Rai watched and listened. Three-year-old Avery blurted a word around her thumb. But Avery, standing at the foot of the bed, turned to the sock-footed boy with rectangular glasses. Somewhere, in the dusty bins where memories hid, she remembered what Nana Rai had asked her and what three-year-old Avery had answered. Nana Rai described an unusual helper. He looked like many things in different places. Someone who would always be there, whether Avery could see him or not. And whether it seemed like help or not, it was help nonetheless.

"Jenks," both Averys said.

The boy, in calm repose, nodded. He knew. Of course he knew. Avery had named him all those years ago. She didn't know where she came up with that name; maybe she heard it in a movie. Maybe she dreamed it. *Time is a circle. Sometimes the ending is a new beginning.*

Nana Rai told the story of Jenks, what he would look like and what he would do. A strange silver android, a sandy snowman, a snarky gingerbread man. And what else?

A boy with a hole in one sock.

The room shifted twice more. On the last one, the bedroom was gone. They were in a sterile room with a television mounted in the corner. Her mother was propped in a bed. Her dad was wearing a gown. There were others: Aunt Mag holding Mom's hand and eight-year-old Bradley leaning against the wall. Uncle Sage watched the television.

Nana Rai was in a chair with a fussy infant.

Dad wanted to name her Pearl, because she was precious. If Mom had a name picked out, she'd forgotten it in exhaustion. Aunt Mag offered suggestions. And all the while, Nana Rai was looking into the pink bundle. Avery looked closely at her little self, only a day old. Her eyes as big as Christmas ornaments, fixed on her nana. Nana Rai gently touched her pointy little chin poking from a round face.

And then it happened.

A look of surprise was on Nana Rai's face. It started out as curiosity, like seeing something that wasn't there. An old woman trying to hear what an infant had to say. No one saw Nana Rai's hand tremble. Mist crawled over the roadmap of veins. It settled like fog on dry ice, seeping down her fingers and creeping over the infant's cheeks. Nana

Rai watched in amazement. She had nothing to do with the essence that, once the Toymaker had swirled in his palm, had placed on Nana Rai's swollen belly, now settled inside an infant. The gift made a choice.

Little Avery closed her eyes. A toothless smile growing. Nana Rai held her closely.

"We'll name her Avery."

30

"Where's Sage?" Aunt Mag said.

"He's looking for the tripod."

Dad nodded at the window. Uncle Sage was outside, searching the trunk of the car. Dad looked like a grade-schooler getting ready for school pictures, holding still, chin up, while Mom straightened his bow tie. She never liked his bow tie. *It's odd*. He only wore it because she didn't like it. Whatever the reason, it needed to be tight and square. Mom, in a black silk dress with a long scarf that dazzled, had sprigs of holly berries pinned in a topknot. She'd added a few extra twigs for the occasion.

"There's a princess," Dad said.

Avery curtsied and followed the smell of breakfast. Eggs were in a skillet, bacon on an oily paper towel. Her appetite was back. She piled her plate with food, added a muffin and jam, and went to the atrium.

"Hearts," Meeho said.

The cousins lounged in dazzle pants with flash striping and bumper sleeves on frog-neck sweaters. Their hair splashed pink and yellow that sprayed from the sides, like storybook characters. They were very excited to see her, their eyes wide, but really they just wanted her to see the optic glitter of their lens augments. They'd gotten everything they wanted for Christmas.

"Sooo," Flinn said, thumbing her phone, "there's a bubble launch next week. A new virtual contest with unlimited grab."

"Get your hiwires," Meeho said, "and we can team. Now that you're cured."

Cured. The reality confusion rumors had gone away. Avery was careful not to say anything to bring them back. But she wondered, now that everyone believed she didn't climb the mountain, if *they* were reality confused. The blisters healing on Avery's feet told a different story.

"Now that you're an expert flier," Flynn added, "you can bag some virtual coin."

"I'm not an expert." Avery laughed. The fib was transparent. Was there anyone more expert at navigating the imagination? That was what virtual was, really: imagination wrapped in a cloak of reality. "Besides, my parents aren't giving the hiwires back."

"Real, real?" Flynn said.

"Real, real," Avery said.

"Why would they do that?" Flynn said. "It's how the world ticks."

Maybe they would give them back. Avery didn't care. Here and now, this reality was where she wanted to be. At least for a good while. The cousins looked up from their phones, baffled by her lack of enthusiasm.

"Av, it's going to be like the Hunt 2.0," Flynn said. "K-Pow Virtual build. Surreal graphs and monster stretch. How can you just, like, *nuh* that?"

Meeho rattled off deadlines and entry points, showed her screen grabs of portal leaps and character builds, payouts and upgrades. They searched alternate landers that everyone could access. Avery, with the hiwires, could join them. Avery couldn't explain the hiwires weren't built for gaming. Nana Rai had made them for one thing. And that was over.

"Who won the Hunt, anyway?" Avery said.

Flinn and Meeho laughed. "Wait," Meeho said. "Serious?"

"I didn't catch the end." Avery bit a piece of bacon. "I was at the house when you were on the mountain, remember?"

"Read a newsfeed, gur," Meeho said.

They summarized what had happened on the mountain. Bradley handed out the surfers. Or was it Aunt Mag? They were a bit foggy on details; Avery had a feeling why. The sat link was initiated, they said, and then they were there: *in the Hunt*. The fire was gone, but they hadn't moved. It was one thing to see the Hunt on replay, but to actually be there—*be there in the digits, Av*—well, Avery just wouldn't understand. She had been home sleeping.

Avery couldn't possibly know what it felt like when the machines rumbled and whined in the distance, how they smelled the nuclear exhaust when they came humming over the ridge and out of the trees, big monstrous things with chrome tailpipes and blackened fenders: futuristic things that didn't touch the ground.

The hunters were racing for the finish.

One after another, they dismounted without stopping, their machines coasting into each other like bumper cars. The cousins had stood at the fire, watched them sprint for the cabin, rushing right past them. Meeho and Flinn could smell the pungent adrenaline. Three of them got to the cabin at the same time, but the door wouldn't open. At least a dozen of them tried to kick it down. They climbed on the roof, punched at the window, ran their fingers along the mudded logs, searching for a secret door or hidden key.

"And then it was on," Flinn said.

A battle commenced, which made no sense. The door was locked, but the nature of virtual contests was last sim standing. They didn't have weapons. It was more or less a prehistoric cave days rumble. No one got punched out or dismantled, just a chaotic brawl: hair-pulling and arm twisting, thumb biting and eye poking. A strip down of human aggression. Mom, Aunt Mag and many of the hikers hid their eyes. This wasn't Christmas.

"Then the door opened." Meeho snapped her fingers. "They came pouring."

As the cousins described it, a torrential flood of fur and plastic spewed from the cabin: bunnies and teddies and betties and rollers and marchers. The list went on; too many toys to fit inside that little building spilled out.

"They were bleeding color," Flinn.

Avery had to focus on what they said next, slowing them down to translate. The toys were supersaturated, like they were dipped in hi-res paint. Paint that dripped as they stampeded past them. The toys disintegrated as they fled, melting like sugar; their colors seeping into the snow and spreading through the trees, oozing into the sky until the world was this technicolor vivio mainframe that was realer than real. Flinn and Meeho could taste the colors like licorice and cinnamon and marshmallow and chocolate. The cousins' eyes were wide with delight, true delight, their tongues out like the taste was in the room.

"Then he was there," Meeho said, far too seriously. "Standing in the doorway."

"Who?" Avery said.

"The Toymaker," they said.

When all the toys had escaped, the Toymaker came out. He wasn't as short as they thought he'd be or nearly as fat. There were no details, either, like he was a walking shadow. But he had the hat, so it had to be him. He watched the last of the toys vanish into the painted sky.

"Then what?" Avery said.

"Fade to black," Flinn said.

"Fade to black?" Avery said.

"Yeah. Fade to black," Flinn said. "It ended."

"Greatest ride of my life," Meeho mused.

"Had to be there, Av," Flinn said.

"So that was it?" Avery said. "Who won?"

They shrugged. The last social post said the winner was unnamed and would remain so. There were rumors the winner had already been in the cabin when the others arrived. That shadow wasn't the Toymaker wearing the hat. It was the winner. *Because the shadow didn't have a beard,* one savvy fan pointed out. *And the Toymaker isn't a girl.*

Avery laughed and snorted. "Sorry. Just, how do they know the Toymaker wasn't a girl?"

"Who cares," Meeho said. "All the surfers shut down when it was over, just like BT said they would. Only the winner gets to keep them. Whoever that is."

"What about the hunters who went on the hike?" Avery asked.

They were confused by the question. Avery didn't repeat it. Whatever, or whoever, had changed the memories of the events that night had been pretty thorough. Iona's mom and the Toy People were just as confused as the cousins were.

"Meeho thinks it was an inside fix," Flinn said.

"It is," Meeho said. "There's no real winner. They say there is, but there's no ID trace, no announcement. The whole thing was a data reap. Already a petition for legal action. Once they find BT, they'll make him cough out the specs. Then we'll know the truth. Nobody won."

"There were definitely winners," Avery said.

"Thought you didn't watch," Flinn said.

Avery shrugged. There were winners. Just not who they expected.

❋

"We're almost ready," Mom said, clasping a bracelet around her wrist. "Can you find your brother? Meeho said he was talking to Hugo in the backyard."

Avery put on a coat. The stage was halfway disassembled: planks stacked and tools scattered. The silence was a bit eerie. Aunt Mag told the volunteers to take a break. Hugo wasn't around and neither was her brother. A strange echoing rang through the trees, like a musical instrument. She followed it to the shed. The door was open. It had been cleaned out. No toys on the bench or boxes on the floor. The spiderwebs swept from the rafters.

Moments like that were little doubt fairies whispering in her ear.

This would continue to happen, and more often, as time went on. *Was there a purple monkey in the shed? A wooden puppet?*

Ice shattered. A dark form squatted at the edge of the stream.

Bradley pried another rock from the ground and tossed it. It skittered over the ice, the impact echoing strangely beneath it. He was next to an idol on a flat rock: a tall sculpture carved from cedar. The figure on top, wearing the green hat, wasn't an elf. He didn't turn around when she approached.

"I knew the Toymaker was here." He threw another rock. "When you took me to the library, showed me the cabin, I knew I was right."

He picked up the sculpture, held it like a jeweler examining a rare diamond. The round face was smooth.

"I figured out it was your hiwires that opened the elevator. I went down there by myself. That's when I found him. And that's the last thing that makes any sense."

He looked like Bradley, the way he spoke: that troubled look when he couldn't figure something out, the solution just out of reach.

"*Congratulations!*" Bradley threw his arms wide. "He was waiting for me in the cabin, did his little dance, those wooden feet on the planks, tipping his hat and twirling his cane. No confetti. No lights. *You found him,* was all he said. I looked around and... there was no Toymaker."

He looked up through the trees.

"When he was done dancing, he put his hand on my shoulder." He paused. "A strange coldness sank into me, like... like roots. Those painted eyes drew closer until they were all I could see. *I won't forget you,* he whispered. It grew dark. Like a cloudy day.

"I felt translucent. I couldn't breathe; the air was sucked out of the room. BT collapsed into a pile, like the strings had been cut. Legs and arms stuck in weird angles, and the painted eyes staring at the ceiling. I remember the top hat rolling into the corner and thinking he dropped his hat. I stood there for hours, I think, just staring at it, wondering if I should pick it up. Not knowing what to do next, thinking I should probably do something, but just..." He sighed. "I just didn't care."

He pulled up his sleeve. The tattoo reminded him he was awake. Avery had the urge to check her bracelet. But she didn't have that anymore.

"Eventually, I swiped at my surfers. My hand felt like it didn't belong to me. I was still in the cabin, so I did it again, wondering if I was doing it right. I swiped until my cheeks were raw. And then I stopped and just... I just waited for him."

He tossed a pebble on the ice.

"He came back briefly. Asked me a question. *What did you want for Christmas when you were seven years old?*"

"Drums," Avery muttered, remembering when she'd asked Bradley that question outside Nana's room. How long he took to answer.

"The cabin was locked. I don't know how long I stood there before I tried to open the door. I looked out the window. The sun was gone, and the trees were gray, like they'd been scratched from granite. Like the world was empty, and I kept thinking about what he said. *I won't forget you.*"

Avery remembered Toyworld, the real Toyworld: stripped of life, drained of caring. A blank existence made of shadows.

"Then the toys came. They sat outside the cabin, stared at me in the window. I don't know how many were out there when a speeder came. I should have warned her, but it wouldn't have mattered. BT popped off the floor and snapped his arms into place. His finger to the mouth, he looked at me like he could wink. *Our little secret.*

"I don't think Mrs. Baker even saw me. One of the toys followed her inside and hopped into BT's arms. The floppy ears torn, one of the eyes missing. *Congratulations!* And then he put a hand on her shoulder. I could feel it happening, those icy roots sinking into her. The color drained from her face. BT collapsed into a pile. The bunny on top of him.

"It happened again and again. Gamer after gamer, toy after toy. We just stood there surrounded by loneliness and watched it happen. The sun never rising or setting. Just one long ashy day, not knowing where we were, or where the toys were going."

He picked up the sculpture, rubbed his thumb over the likeness of Avery's face.

"Then you were there."

He fell silent. Avery sat down next to him, remembering when she found him in the corner, next to the barren Christmas tree, looking up at her, through her. Unsure if she was there or not, or if she was just a memory haunting him.

"I thought you didn't remember any of it," she said.

She thought he didn't hear her, putting the sculpture on the flat stone; then he reached inside his coat. He held the puppet by the head, the one Avery found in the shed. The legs swayed, the arms clunking against the barrel chest with the faded heart.

"Nana Rai gave this to me for Christmas when I was little. BT looked familiar, but I didn't think much of it. It was just a wooden puppet. There's a million just like him. But then I found this the other day and remembered it was my present. I remembered what it looked like, you know the way Nana Rai wrapped them. And I remembered being so disappointed."

The arms and legs rattled.

"I played with him some, got bored, and then just..." He shrugged. "I never bothered giving him a name. All I did was this."

He turned the puppet upside down. And there, carved with a five-year-old's hand, were two letters. It wasn't Bradley's name. Just Bradley Tannenbaum's initials.

"He's yours," she muttered.

"How did she do it?" he said. "You saw the other worlds. That wasn't technology, Av. The toys are out there or..." He stuttered and pointed, not knowing where or how they existed. Just that the toys weren't generated by computers. He knew Nana Rai had done it somehow, that she'd made the Hunt. The hiwires, which never worked, were proof.

"Beyond the veil," Avery said.

He frowned, nodding, with that look when he didn't understand something no matter how hard he tried, unwilling to accept it without a logical explanation. But some things couldn't be understood or explained. At least not yet. *That doesn't make them less real.*

"Did you see their world?" he said. "Like it really was? If I would've known they were there... I would've brought them here. I would've helped them."

"Me too."

"But you didn't."

No, she didn't. But she would've. If Jenks would have told her what she could do, she would have crossed the veil for each and every one of them and brought them to this world, humans and toys living together.

"You did something else," he said.

"It wasn't me."

"It was you, Av." His eyes were big. And he smiled like she'd never seen him smile before. So soft and grateful. "I didn't think I was ever going to leave that place. But then, one by one, the toys started disappearing. Even the ones we'd swept into the corner. Then I felt something familiar reach for me, like some part of me that was out there. And then I was in a sleeping bag. The sun was coming through the tent. I lay there, feeling like I'd been asleep for a week with dreams I couldn't remember, not knowing how I got there or why. It sort of made sense when I climbed out. I could see the other gamers from the Hunt looking around, trying to put it together. We'd hiked up the mountain to celebrate Christmas Eve, like Nana Rai wanted. We didn't question it. I thought maybe something I ate made things feel so weird."

He moved the puppet's hinged jaw.

"But I remembered something on the way down the mountain. A crumb from a dream, what I thought was a dream. It was too strange to be anything else. I remembered standing next to a glowing tower. Santa Claus was there and all the reindeer. But you were back at the house."

He turned to Avery.

"You were wearing the Toymaker's hat. The toys were with you. They were dancing and singing and opening the presents. And it didn't make sense because there was no tower on the mountain, and the presents were still under the tree when we got back. I figured it was just a dream the way dreams are, and I just..."

He shook his head. He was still debating if it happened, she could tell. How could he not? Or, perhaps worse, maybe it was reality confusion. Because none of this made sense. Not to a rational mind.

"All stories are dreams," she said. "But they're somewhere, and they remember us."

Dad whistled from the house, the way he did when he put his fingers in his mouth, whistling for them to come home. Bradley put BT in his coat, then studied the sculpture one more time.

"You're the Toymaker," he said.

"I don't know if that's—"

"Then where did this come from?" He handed her the sculpture. Before that day, it had always been an elf. Now it was her. She took a deep, cold breath and shrugged.

"I'm not the Toymaker. I mean, I was, sort of. I think. I don't know." She took a pebble from Bradley's hand. "I don't know what happened, Bradley."

"Yeah, you do. Trust me." He tapped the sculpture. Proof.

She sighed. "I thought it was Hugo. I'm still not sure it's not. You saw the clue from the Hunt?"

He shook his head. She started to explain—Nana Rai in the cabin, Hugo was her son—but found herself out of breath. There was so much to untangle, and she realized just how much she'd avoided thinking about it. Talking about it tied her brain in knots. None of it could be real. But here they were. And that was definitely her on the sculpture.

"The gift chose me when I was born." It felt weird to say it out loud. "Nana Rai didn't do it, or the Toymaker. It just... it just happened. I don't know why. And when we were on the mountain..."

Bradley frowned. He couldn't remember her coming on the hike. He had been locked in a cabin when that happened. And she had been at home when he woke up.

"I just closed my eyes. That's all I did."

"That's it?"

"Yeah. I mean, I don't know." She rolled the pebble between her finger and thumb, imagining it was smooth and metal. "It was all those stories Nana Rai told me when I was little. Every time I closed my eyes, I went there. Like they were real; they were worlds out there, all of them. Just like here. You remember the one about the blue elf and the big angry reindeer..."

He nodded along. He remembered.

"BT followed me to all those worlds. Then we ended up back here." She shook her head. "And the toys came with him."

She couldn't explain what it was like when she put on the Toymaker's hat, how she saw the universe and the threads that connected the many worlds and how she did it. How she opened up a way for them to come home.

"I saw Nana." She looked up. "She was a little girl. She was with all of her brothers and sisters with castles, and-and she was telling stories to little snowmen. It was her. And I think she knew who I was. And I don't know how any of that is possible, Bradley. I don't. Jenks said time is a circle and that's how it works. The beginning is the end, and the end is the..." She started laughing. "Oh, man, that sounds crazy."

"No. It doesn't."

He understood. He'd gone beyond the veil, too.

"Are we just reality confused?" She was serious. That question hovered at the edge of her mind. She knew it was haunting him, too.

"The toys left their world. That's all I know." He took the sculpture from her, studying her likeness. "That's what the Toymaker wanted."

"Why didn't he just do it, then? Why didn't he just bring them back?" she said. "Why all the mystery?"

"Where are they now?"

"What do you mean?"

"You said you brought them back here. I don't see any toys dancing down the street." He pulled the puppet out of his coat. "BT hasn't said one word since I got here."

She shook her head. "I don't know."

"Maybe they didn't want to go someplace else. They wanted to come here with you and me and everyone else. But they're not here. So where are they?"

Avery wondered that, too. Despite what had happened, the toys weren't here. None of them hopped out of the woods or danced around the tree or called a news conference to announce their arrival. She didn't know where they were. But they were somewhere. Somewhere just like this.

"So if you're the Toymaker," he said, "what now?"

"I don't know. Santa Claus will come get me, I guess."

They laughed with an edge of nervousness, the tilt of reality threatening to tip them upside down. Remembering a jolly fat man with flying reindeer was one thing, to say it out loud made it real.

"Shouldn't the Toymaker be an elf?" he said. "I mean, that's what the stories say. You're not an elf, are you? Hugo looks like an elf. You don't."

It didn't have to be an elf, apparently. Maybe it had more to do with what was inside. Maybe it was the DNA, some recessive gene, some biochemical explanation that allowed her to carry the gift. *All it needed was imagination. And a good story.*

"I'm glad you're back," she said.

Bradley hugged her. He'd never done that before and really meant it. And that, Avery thought, had never, ever happened. Another Christmas first.

"Thank you, sis."

It felt like a real brother hugging her. And a real sister hugging back. And they were both happy to have each other. All it took was crossing the veil.

They stopped at the edge of the clearing. Uncle Sage was setting up the tripod. Mom and Dad were in front of the tree. The cousins were looking at their phones. Aunt Mag was telling everyone where to stand, straightening Uncle Sage's collar, fixing the cousins' pink hair. Hugo was there, standing next to Mom, wearing his sweater.

They joined the family. Bradley had his arm around her. He

smiled without being told to, laughed and interacted with everyone that day. Even the cousins. And not once did Mom have to tell him not to work.

They would go home, and life would return to normal. Avery was Avery again. Just a teenager with teenager problems. Every year, she questioned whether any of it happened. At night, especially on Christmas Eve, she would dream of a blue elf and a giant snowman, a silver android and a massive reindeer, a sandy snowman and a snarky gingerman. She would see the toys, as if she was floating above them, in a world of vivid colors she could taste and smell, watching them dance around a giant Christmas tree with a star as bright as the sun.

She would dream of Nana Rai running through castles.

She would wake in the morning feeling like the toys could see her, as well. When they closed their eyes. She always felt like someone was watching her. Maybe it was a boy on the bus or someone in the store. She would look down to see if he was wearing socks. One with a hole in it. As the years went by, it all felt like a fading dream. She'd even forgotten about the bracelet. She lived here and now.

But then one Christmas Eve, many years later, when her children were tucked in bed, Avery was in bed on the cusp of sleep. That year, she heard the bells.

31

People crowded against yellow barricades, holding phones above their heads. Men and women with dark uniforms and funny hats were on the other side, hands on their hips, keeping the peace. Behind the crowd were white vans with letters and logos, some with long antennas. There were cars with lights that spun the brightest of reds.

The crowd began pointing, pushing their way to one side. Teddy waddled through the snow. His cinnamon fur was clean in the sunlight. Men and women, boys and girls aimed their phones, turned around to snap a selfie with a teddy bear—an actual, real-life teddy bear—waving his stubby arms.

There would be questions. Lots of questions. How long it would take to assimilate was impossible to know. BT guessed, as he peeked between the curtains, it would be much longer than originally thought. Communication, for starters, was off to a rough start. Humans weren't good listeners. Toys, on the other hand, were born to listen. That was all they ever did.

Not anymore.

Teddy had become the spokesperson. People knew teddy bears better than wooden puppets. The police banded in front of the little bear as the crowd heaved forward. The woman who had introduced herself as the mayor took a knee. Teddy waved his arms, and she nodded. Then he pointed his stubby little arm at the house. The crowd turned toward the wooden face peering between the curtains.

BT remained still. A part of him hoped they would confuse him for a lamp. But there was no mistaking the red glow thumping on his chest like one of those police cars. The cane tapped nervously on the floor. Energy fluttered from the tips of his wooden toes to his top hat.

Emotions, he thought. Something else he hadn't anticipated.

Even more troublesome, these feelings were there for everyone to see. His heart shrinking or swelling, dimming or shining depended on what he was thinking and feeling. He considered a different cloak, one he could cinch, hide the better part of his body. He found himself rationalizing that it would lessen the shock of humans seeing a toy. But that wasn't the truth. He wanted to hide what he was feeling. And that, he knew, was not a good way to start. He was proud to be a toy.

Let them see what I truly am.

He consulted his pocket watch. It was almost noon. He directed a thought toward Teddy, one no one would hear (and, in the future, their secret ability to communicate would become quite beneficial and, in some ways, problematic). A plastic Jeep rolled toward Teddy. Once again, the crowd turned their phones and cameras. Johnny Jeep chugged along, his brand-new knobby tires spinning in the snow, headlights shifting back and forth. Not a scratch on his gleaming yellow body.

Honey Hare was in the driver's seat, pretending to steer. Her long ears rotated like antennas, waving like a pageant queen. Teddy climbed into the back. BT watched them slowly pull away, leaving behind expressions of fascination and confusion.

This will be a long journey.

With the bear and rabbit gone, they refocused their telephoto lenses on the window. BT opened the curtains wider. Let them take their pictures. Spread the word. That was what today was for. More importantly, he let the sunlight warm the veneer on his face. His hinged jaw fell open; his heart swelled.

Heavy footsteps approached like rubber bags of wet sand. The muscular man barely fit through the hallway. His elastic skin was reddish and unblemished. He didn't have a shirt or pants. Only shorts a bit too small. That was how he was made. But in all the time BT knew him, he'd never looked so perfect. He used to patch up little scrapes to keep the jelly from leaking. Now he looked, what would become a pop culture phrase, *right out of the box.*

"They're ready, BT," Stretch said with a surprisingly high register.

BT reached under his cloak, felt the smooth grain where his legs connected to his midsection. Where two letters had once been carved, now an unscarred, beautiful patina.

"Stretch," BT said, "I don't think I'm using that name anymore."

"Okay." Stretch scratched the deep dimple in his chin. "What do I call you?"

"I don't know."

"Woody? Woody would be good."

"No, no. I'll need to think—"

"Commander? I could do that." He snapped his jelly-filled fingers. "How about Carl?"

"Thank you, Stretch. I'll consider those names."

Stretch half-bowed. BT had grown tired of these displays of respect. He understood why they did it. He'd brought them here, after all. But he'd rather not be treated as royalty. Leadership would be the crown he would bear, just not the royalty part.

"Shall we?" BT said.

Stretch stomped through the house. Dust fell from the ceiling. He held the back door open, and BT politely asked him to go ahead. He would be there momentarily. BT peeked out the window. The toys frolicked around the Christmas tree. The light from the star beamed like a second sun. The toys ignored the few people among them. (He recalled the name for humans from one particular story, a pejorative word he chose not to use. *Warmbloods.*) BT suspected the toys were showing off. It was a toy's nature to entertain.

The people were content to watch. They were the people BT had met with earlier in the week. None of them had come down from the mountain. In fact, no one had returned from the hike. BT had sent Skylar the Whizzy Ball to check on them, and according to the lights flashing through his plastic globe, there was no sign of them. Anywhere. No indication anyone had hiked or pitched a tent.

Not even the Toymaker.

She had gone into the house after the toys had arrived. Exhausted, the poor girl had been. BT had checked on her to make sure she was well. But come morning, the bed was made, and she was gone. He thought, perhaps, she would return when the shock wore off.

Now he had other suspicions.

Santa had come for the hikers, cleared the area, and made them forget. The fat man could do that, but they hadn't returned to the house at all. And that bothered BT the most. His intention wasn't to hurt them, but abandoning Bradley and the others in Toyworld was not what he wanted. *Where did they go?*

His heart shrank and dimmed. It felt like a clod of lead glued to his chest. He didn't like the way it felt, and hoped, every morning since, that wherever Bradley and the others were, they were good and happy. And that, hopefully, at least, he wished the Toymaker could see BT and his brothers and sisters.

Joy abounds.

Stretch stood at the bottom step. His arms extended to their maximum length, rubber skin thin and tight. Cheers erupted from the toys when BT appeared. He doffed his top hat.

Bella Ballerina hopped up the steps on pointed toes, handing BT a stack of index cards with questions to answer. Questions he'd already expected. The cameras on stout tripods rotated to capture his descent. Bella continued her update. The toys clustered like adoring fans. Stretch opened a path. Military Joe shoveled snow to the stage. BT wanted them to stop, but it was too late. And the moment so important.

"BT, hi. I'm Kyle Charleston, WBIB."

Kyle smelled clean and looked cleaner. He extended his hand,

and BT hesitated. He knew what Kyle expected. BT just wasn't sure if he was ready to adopt their ways. He waved instead.

"This is a historic day, BT. We want to make this moment count. We only get one first impression." He pointed a microphone while he walked. "People will want to know where you came from, how you're alive. Are you biological? Do you eat?"

"That's not my name," BT said.

"Oh. My apologies. I was told—"

"I never had a name."

"How should I address you?"

BT stopped at the stage. A blocky plastic robot helped him step up. BT greeted the committee that had been selected to join him. Pearly Pink Pony, Gregory Glo-Worm, Biggie Big Wheel, Carol Cabbage Patch and Military Joe. Roy Rockem Robot stood directly below the podium.

"Two minutes," Bella said. "These are in order."

She handed him the questions. He leaned his cane against the podium, straightened the cards. The toys mingled with a small group of people aiming cameras and microphones. BT looked down to collect his thoughts. There was only one first impression. It was a big one. Perhaps the biggest in the history of humans.

Something glimmered between his feet. He picked it up.

"One minute!" someone shouted.

A silver chain dangled from BT's wooden fingers. He thought, briefly, he'd seen this before. It was so unique. He looked at the sky. His hinged jaw was unable to smile, but his heart swelled twice the size and three times as bright. Humans covered their eyes. BT felt joy burst from his chest like a singing choir. He put the cards down, placed the bracelet on top of them.

The delicate snowflake was as red as his heart.

"On behalf of toys everywhere," he said, "we are happy to be *here*."

TOYWORLD: HOME OF THE CHRISTMAS THIEF (BOOK 10)

Get the Claus Universe at:
BERTAUSKI.COM/CLAUS

❄

ToyWorld: Home of the Christmas Thief (Book 10)

CHAPTER 1

I'm not the hero in this story. Far from it.

To tell this story properly, we need to start at the beginning. It was a night like any other. I had folded the covers back and smoothed the wrinkles. I drank the remains of chamomile tea, still warm, with a lemon wedge resting on the bottom of the mug. In my silk pajamas, cool and smooth, I slid into bed. I lay in the dark, listening to the downstairs grandfather clock count the seconds.

The house was empty. As usual.

An annoying red glow filled my window from across the street, strings of lights on my neighbor's gutters. I stared at a small water stain on the ceiling that I had yet to repair, and counted of all my life's failures. It's not something I enjoy doing. Just something I've always done. Part of the ritual.

Then I took three deep breaths, exhaling slowly with each one, and closed my eyes. The breathing technique was something my father taught me as a child. It was habit. Comfortable. I made the mistake, once, of telling him of a dream I had. *Dreams are wasted thoughts,* he said with a voice as hard as an icy driveway. *Foolish entertainment.*

He believed in two things: hard work and harder work. The only thing that was real was what could be seen and touched. Dreams were stupid. It wasn't like I could stop dreaming, nor did I want to. There was no television in the house and computer time was strictly monitored. Dreams were my only escape as a child. I recorded them in a notebook and hid it between my mattress and box spring. I would get so nervous he'd find it that occasionally I would burn it. A few weeks later, I would start new one.

This night, where the story begins, I had a dream like no other. I travelled to somewhere beyond the galaxy. I floated without a spaceship, breathing as if air existed in the vacuum of space. Coasting weightless and effortless, past planets and moons, stars and black holes. I saw things I never imagined. It was the loveliest of dreams.

I didn't remember waking up, but I'd opened my eyes to stare at the water stain on the ceiling. Only it wasn't there. The grandfather clock wasn't ticking. I wasn't in my bed.

I was slumped on a shelf, frozen in postdormital sleep paralysis, locked in my body, staring helplessly across a room. How I got there was a mystery. This didn't feel like a dream. What else could it be? I was a grown man, a rational man. This was a dream, it could be nothing else.

A small Christmas tree was in the corner, casting a red glow across the room. I was thinking of my neighbor's repugnant lights. The light, however, caught pairs of eyes in dim corners. There were dozens of them. I'd had this dream before, being stalked by predators. Never like this, though. I'd read a fair share of dream books and knew they represented my fears. As always, I couldn't outrun them.

Powerless, I endured their judgment. They weren't blinking. Neither was I.

I wanted to escape, to run away. *Wake up!* I thought. Sometimes that worked.

A terrifying jolt racked my entire being. I tumbled forward like a puppet. I heard the wind then the hollow clatter on plastic sticks on laminate flooring. It sounded like pieces of an unassembled model dumped out of a box. I still remember that sound like it was yesterday. Horrifying.

I was bones. Red, red bones.

Fibulas and tibias, phalanges and ribs. Crimson and polished and expertly crafted. No wires or twine, no glue and ties. I sat up with a clatter. One my arms fell from my shoulder. Pulled from the socket, it looked like a chew toy the dog had forgotten. There was no time to panic. The predators were circling.

Keys jiggled on a key ring. Long tubes of light flickered on the ceiling. Giants entered the room. *Ah, of course. They've come to grind my bones.*

They wore puffy coats and stocking caps. Boots crusted with snow. A man and a woman and a child in between. I gave them quite a fright, scrambling into the corner like a feral cat. The man spilled coffee. Imagine seeing a trembling pile of bones. I expected them to swat me with a broom.

The father, I correctly assumed, turned to the mother and said with all the nonchalance of calling attendance in homeroom, "I thought they were blank."

The mother looked more confused than terrified. She went to the shelves which, by the way, weren't filled with predators, and picked up a stuffed dog with floppy ears, squeezed the nose on a giant orange cat. "This never happened before," she said, looking at me. "Christmas is ten days away."

Never happened before? I couldn't parse the meaning. Like this had never happened before or this had never happened *ten days before Christmas*?

The girl walked around a workbench covered in bags of white

stuffing, sewing needles and thread. A backpack strapped to her shoulders. She was ten years old or twelve. I'm not good with kids.

Madeline Bells.

That was her name. I didn't know how I knew it. The name just popped into my head. She picked up my lost arm like it was a stick. I squeezed into the corner, my joints protesting. Right about then I was thinking this dream was different. Like no other dream I'd ever had. I was about to pop another limb off my body when the mother said to the girl, "Easy, hon. He's frightened."

This was weird. Even for a dream. They squatted in front of me like I was a puppy who had just piddled on the floor.

"Hello, Viktor," the mother said. "We just want to help."

I was jammed into a corner with nowhere to go and wondering who Viktor was. Then I noticed a tag on my arm. The one Madeline was holding.

Viktor the Red.

Viktor was my family name of sorts, from the old country. I would wake up soon and write all of this down, tease out the symbolism. The predators were my father, I was bones that lacked self-worth or identity or fill in the blank. It would all make sense, it always did. When I woke up.

The mother popped my arm back into the socket. Her touch was warm and gentle. Madeline looked at her mother and said, "Can I keep him?"

I never forgot that, for as long as I lived. It was the way she said it. It filled me with a warmth I'd never felt. It was so kind. I began to melt.

I woke in my bed. In my home, in my silk pajamas. My pillow damp with sweat. I leaped out of the covers and touched my chest and stomach, ran my hands down to my toes. I went to the bathroom and looked in the mirror. There I was, in my forty years of flesh. Wrinkles had never made me so happy.

I showered in cold water till my teeth chattered, then sat in the kitchen with a cup of tea till it was time for work. I was different that day. Madeline's words with like butterflies as warm as cookies. *Can I keep him?*

I once read the barrier between reality and dreaming was gossamer thin and the two were irrevocably inseparable. One side tugs on the other. I couldn't explain why the dream felt so real. I only knew one thing.

I wanted to go back.

YOU DONATED TO A WORTHY CAUSE!

By purchasing this book, you have donated 10% of the profits, which is annually donated to **GiveWell**, providing top research on where donations are most needed with the most impact.

ABOUT THE AUTHOR

My grandpa never graduated high school. He retired from a steel mill in the mid-70s. He was uneducated, but a voracious reader. As a kid, I'd go through his bookshelves of musty paperback novels, pulling Piers Anthony and Isaac Asimov off the shelf and promising to bring them back. I was fascinated by robots that could think and act like people. What happened when they died?

Writing is sort of a thought experiment to explore human nature and possibilities. What makes us human? What is true nature?

I'm also a big fan of plot twists.

BERTAUSKI.COM

Printed in Great Britain
by Amazon